THE COLOR DEAD

A DICKIE FLOYD DETECTIVE NOVEL

DANNY R. SMITH

❀ Created with Vellum

ACKNOWLEDGMENTS

I would like to offer a special thanks to my beta readers, whose eyes for detail have helped me polish this novel: Scott Anderson, Michele Carey, Teresa Collins, Andrea Hill-Self, Steve Jenkins, Henry "Bud" Johnson, Phil Jonas, Ann Litts, Dennis "Deac" Slocumb, and Heather Wamboldt. Also my wonderful wife, Lesli, and daughters Jami and Randi Jo.

A special thanks to Steve Jenkins who also shared his knowledge and expertise of the operations of Gorman Station, a unique and challenging outpost of the Los Angeles County Sheriff's Department. Others who have held assignments there and took the time to assist me in my research include: John Grisbach, Jim Jeffra, Steve Newman, Wayne Stickle, and John Sylvies. Any inaccuracies about Gorman Station, its operation, history, or region, are my mistakes—not theirs—or have been altered for the purpose of the story.

Narcotics Bureau legend Ernie Banuelos provided his expertise and knowledge of marijuana grows, and the procedures, tactics, and efforts of the Marijuana Eradication Team (MET). I am grateful to him for the education.

I have flown the skies, sailed the seas, and patrolled the dark allies of South Los Angeles and beyond with my good friend and former training officer, Sgt. Mike Griffin. I am grateful for his friendship, and I thank him for his technical advice on the operations and equipment of the Los Angeles County Sheriff's Department Aero Bureau.

And last—but never least—my good friend and long-suffering editor, Patricia Brennan. Without her guidance, I would never know if something should lay or lie, or if it had laid or lain, and I would literally lose my ever-loving literary mind.

For the partners and loved ones of

Deputy Arthur E. Pelino
End of Watch: Sunday, March 19, 1978

Los Angeles County Sheriff's Department
Gorman Station

In the blood business, finality was compassionate. The dead no longer suffered pain, and the terrors of their final moments were behind them. For the survivors, a sense of peace could accompany the scenes of unspeakable violence, in the way gentle winds persisted against the black-green skies over the ruins of a tornado. The destruction, the pain, the death that was left behind, those were manageable things that required sensible and logical responses, plans, and actions. Perhaps the tasks to recover and rebuild were only distractions from the terror that had struck when the winds roared like trains and giant hailstones crashed through the darkening skies and earthly possessions were mercilessly uprooted and hurled from one place to the other. Those were moments that seemed like lifetimes, as the battle had yet to be measured and survival was uncertain. Death, though, is finality. Certainty.

———

1

I sat anxiously with Josie's mother, Esmeralda, an awkward silence between us as I fussed with my hat. Josie's mother sat picking at the fabric of the oversized chair that swallowed her frail body. A clock ticked slowly against the wall. The pool filter hummed outside the open patio door. I glanced quickly through the living room window at the sound of a passing vehicle, and so did she. The car passed, and each of us returned to waiting in silence. I drew a deep breath and let it out slowly, easing some of the tension. Esmeralda sighed, seemingly her way of expressing similar disappointment. Her thoughts were likely no different than mine, only in Spanish. My bilingual skills were limited to the few basics: *alto*—stop, or more accurately, halt; *manos arriba*—hands up; *muerte*—death. Those weren't the words I needed in my communications with Josie's mother—I hoped. When I first arrived, I had smiled at the small woman with graying hair, and asked where Josie was: "*¿Dónde está Josie?*" Esmeralda, her small dark eyes showing fear and concern, had shaken her head and shrugged. "*No sé.*" She didn't know.

Like many cops, I was quick to assume the worst. Josie was missing, so something terrible had happened to her. My experiences had conditioned me to think that way. But I had also been trained and conditioned to never give up, so I forced myself to see my partner alive and well. There had to be a reasonable explanation of her absence.

Josefina Sanchez had been a deputy sheriff for twelve years. She had survived three shootings and dozens of altercations. She knew the streets, and she knew the hustlers, gangsters, and junkies who roamed them. She had put countless bad men away, and she had even put some down. Josie was a cop any other would be proud to have as a partner. It wasn't as if she was the vulnerable type, and her personal lifestyle wasn't the type to put her at risk. As far as I knew.

Though two things did bother me: Josie and I had picked up a new murder case three days ago, one that had *bizarre* written on it from the start. It was a case of a gunshot victim found in the mountains near rural Gorman, the last stop headed north through Los Angeles County. Gorman felt more like an outpost in Wyoming than a sheriff's substation in southern California. When we were given the assignment, I had frowned at Rich Farris who was manning the desk and had dispatched the callout. "Gorman?" I questioned. "Are you shitting me, Rich?" After Farris explained the basics of what he knew—a man was found in the woods with a single gunshot wound to the chest and a rifle at his side—I had said, "Rich, this sounds like a suicide to me, or an accidental death. Maybe a hunting accident?"

Farris said he had thought so too, at first. He had been at Homicide a long time—several more years than I had—and he had handled scores of suicide cases in which men had taken their pistols or rifles out to their favorite hunting or camping grounds and sat down beneath the shade of a large oak or pine for last moments of reflection before taking their own lives. He said, "When's the last time you saw a dude off himself standing up?" I hadn't. For whatever reason, people didn't want to fall, once dead. They'd sit beneath a tree, behind the wheel of a car, or on their favorite sofa or chair, or maybe they'd lie down in bed. But rare was the case of the man or woman who put a bullet through their own power plant while standing upright, thus allowing their dead bodies to fall to the floor or ground. Even the soon-to-be departed were hesitant to take a fall.

What bothered me most about the latest case and Josie's absence was a comment she had made after we had wrapped up Thursday evening and driven back into civilization. Josie had asked if we would be going back up to the mountain over the weekend, and she seemed puzzled that I had suggested we take the weekend off and start back up on Monday. It hadn't sounded good in my head when I said it, and it tasted sour coming out of my mouth. But we were scheduled to be off for a three-day weekend, and there was no immediate workable information that needed to be pursued right away. The captain had been complaining about overtime again, and I didn't care to give him more to gripe about. So, I had thought, why not take a weekend off? I suggested to Josie that we let the case sit for three days, handle the detail we had been asked to deal with Sunday evening for another detective on an unrelated case, and then we'd get back to the new murder Monday. The murder on the mountain. Josie had frowned and questioned, "On a fresh case? We're going to just park it?"

The question I had now was would she have taken it upon herself to work the case over the weekend without me? I didn't think so, yet there was a possibility she had. I had told her to enjoy a few days off and I'd pick her up from her home at five on Sunday.

I glanced at my watch, looked through the front window toward the quiet street, and then my eyes slowly drifted back to the anxious mother.

The second thing that bothered me was how little I actually knew of Josie's personal life. She was private, even after six months of partnership, careful to guard against revealing much of her life outside of the job. Was she seeing someone? If so, had she been having trouble with him? Or her? Jesus, I didn't even know whether she was straight or gay. Not that it mattered, but it accentuated the point that was troubling me: I knew almost nothing of my partner's personal life. Floyd and I had had no secrets when we were partners, and probably still didn't.

I forced myself out of my naturally pessimistic thought pattern and considered the fact that she may have just gone away for the weekend without telling anyone. It was a question I'd have to ask Esmeralda. But how?

I glanced at my watch again, and only five minutes had passed. I had been waiting for more than an hour now, and I needed to do something other than sit here and worry. I stood up from the couch and paused, searching my brain for the Spanish translation of "Excuse me." Esmeralda waited, watching, seemingly knowing my thoughts. I nodded, smiled, held up my index finger and said, "*Momento,*" and walked outside.

Under the bright sunlight, I put my ball cap on, thumbed my phone to life and called Floyd. I waited impatiently as the call went unanswered and was eventually picked up by voicemail. I disconnected and called again. Same result. I shoved the phone in my pocket, removed my hat with one hand and wiped dampness from my forehead with the other. An airplane passed overhead, inbound to LAX, I assumed, as I caught a glimpse of it against the late afternoon sun to the west. I shifted my weight from one leg to the other, antsy, my mind racing as I fought to control my emotions. Not being able to get ahold of either of my partners—my new one, Josie, or my old one, Pretty Boy Floyd—threatened to send me over the edge. For a brief moment, I pictured them somewhere together, living it up, a dark barroom or maybe a Jacuzzi.

Through the open front door I could see that Esmeralda had left her chair. She was probably in the kitchen making something to eat. That's what Mexican women of her generation did at times of peril; they fed you. They fed everyone. The more people they could feed, the more content were their lives. You'd never see them partaking, only providing. Nurturing. Mothering. God bless them all.

I sent another call to Floyd's phone and was startled when it was answered. "Hold on," a woman snapped. It was Cindy, Floyd's wife, but she wasn't her usual friendly self. I waited and listened to the sound of a slider being opened and the faint sound of a boy's voice. I then heard Floyd. His voice was distant at first but seemed to draw nearer. I pictured Cindy walking the phone to him, my old partner standing at the barbecue, a meat hook in one hand and a can of beer in the other. The uniform of the day would likely include board shorts, flip-flops, and a cowboy hat, no shirt. Never a shirt. He'd have wire-rimmed mirrored circles covering his eyes, something Elton John or John Lennon might wear on stage, something he had grabbed at the market when he picked up a box of beer and two bags of ice. He'd be content in his haven, his private retreat from the world, all the peace and quiet a man could want right in his own backyard.

"What's up, Dickie?"

2

Floyd hovered a meat hook over a sizzling tri-tip while sipping his beer at the barbecue. His son ran toward him, then jumped into the pool not far from where Floyd stood, tucking himself into a cannonball mid-flight. He landed with a whoosh, and water sprayed across Floyd's back, cooling his shoulders. He jolted and thrust his beer toward the sky, cat-like instincts saving it from a wave of water.

"Cody, not in the shallow end, bud," he said flatly.

Cody went under and headed to the other end, a skinny porpoise gliding effortlessly through the crystal-blue water. Like his father, he had taken to the water early in life and spent hours every week swimming laps for exercise.

"Little shit," Floyd mumbled, smiling as he swigged his beer and watched the boy turn at the far end of the pool, still not coming up for air.

Cindy appeared at the slider, her blonde head and tanned shoulders squeezing through the small opening. She swatted at a fly and spoke as if it was urgent. "How much longer on the meat?" she asked.

Floyd regarded the slab of beef smoking on the grill. He dropped the curved part of his meat hook from a couple inches above the center of the four-pound tri-tip. It had no bounce, which indicated it was far from finished. He glanced at his watch and turned back to his bride. "Fifteen, maybe twenty minutes. I don't know."

She waved her hand at another flying intruder and disappeared, the glass door hitting hard in its frame.

"The hell is your problem," Floyd said at the closed door. He took another drink of his cold beer, and it felt good going down. He cherished his days off, though few they were nowadays. That was the life of a homicide detective.

"Dad, watch this!"

He looked in time to see Cody launch himself from the top of the slide and into the water, foregoing the slow ride down.

"For fuck's sake," Floyd said, before the boy surfaced.

The sound of the slider drew his attention again, and he turned to see his wife approaching with his cell phone held out toward him.

"What's up?"

She didn't answer. She handed him the phone and turned to walk away. Floyd let his eyes settle on her ass as she did, and he smiled and took another swig of beer. If there was one thing he loved, it was a nice ass. If there were two things he loved, it was a nice ass and cold beer. If he had to list three things, he'd add a medium-rare steak. It was a perfect day, he thought, until his attention turned to the screen displaying "Dickie Cell."

"What's up, Dickie?"

He listened while watching Cody climb out of the pool, the young man's eyes upon him. Nearly a teenager now, the kid watched him closely at all times. Cody emulated him in many ways and cherished the time they had together. Floyd knew this, and he could see the look of concern in the boy's eyes each time he took a business call at home. Many times, those conversations would result in a change of demeanor, and then attire, followed by a hasty departure in the county car. Floyd always felt guilty when it happened.

Dickie said, "I need your help, partner."

"What's up?"

"Josie."

Floyd waited a moment, his eyes on Cody who now stood nearby toweling off. He knew the boy would be taking in every word, wanting to know the details. He turned back to the barbecue and dropped the hook on the slab of meat again.

"What about her?"

"We were supposed to meet at five. I have no idea where she is."

Floyd set the hook down at the side of the barbecue, picked up his beer, and took a swig before speaking. "Well, it's not my turn to watch her, Dickie. Cindy won't allow it. Not that I wouldn't mind—"

"I'm at her house. Her mother is worried."

"Whose house?"

"Josie's. Her mother lives with her, and from the best I can get— because wouldn't you know it, she only *pinky panty*—Josie didn't come home last night."

Floyd mumbled, "Jesus, dude. So you want me to come *pinky panty*; that's where this is going?"

"You speak it better than me."

"Dickie, you can't order tacos in Spanish. Why don't you call Miguel, or Joe the Mo, one of them assholes who gets paid to *habla*? I'm fu—" he glanced at his son "—I'm in the middle of cooking a tri-tip."

Dickie said, "Dude, I've got a bad feeling on this."

"You always do," he said, though he could hear the concern in Dickie's voice.

"But I also don't want to blow this up just yet, get others involved, just in case I'm wrong."

Floyd considered it a moment. "You think she's gone missing? What, like she's been kidnapped?"

"Yeah, something like that."

Floyd took in a deep breath and let it out slowly, thinking about the situation. The situation with Dickie and the situation at home, his son watching, hoping no doubt that he wouldn't leave, and his wife already pissy about God knows what.

"Dude, she's single. Come on, man, she probably spent the night somewhere, know what I mean?"

"Yeah, maybe."

"I mean, maybe give it some more time, a few more hours?"

"Yeah, fine. I'll just sit here with her mom and hope she comes home."

Floyd noted the tone: disappointment, irritation.

"Jesus, man."

"Plus I need to get down to Orange County," Dickie said, "take care of Lopes's informant. That's why I was picking up Josie."

"Okay, okay," he said, motioning for his son to step closer. Floyd picked up the meat hook and handed it to Cody. "Watch the meat, little man."

He could hear Dickie still talking on the phone, ". . . get more information from the mom, and maybe toss her room, see what I can figure out about her personal life. The woman's a complete mystery to me."

"Settle down, Dickie, I'm on my way. Text me her address."

Floyd disconnected and held his son's gaze for a moment. He glanced at his watch and made a mental note of the *time of notification,* grabbed his beer and polished it off as he headed for the house. He set the empty can on a poolside table before pulling the sliding glass door open and pushing through the drape on the other side.

Cody said, "Are you leaving?"

He paused in the doorway and looked at the kid once more. "I won't be long, buddy."

Floyd started for his room, ignoring his wife's admonishment about leaving the door wide open behind him.

Within minutes Floyd had changed out of his board shorts and into a pair of jeans and a buttoned short-sleeved shirt. It was his day off; he wasn't putting on a suit. He detoured to the back door, flung it open again and called out to his son: "See ya later, meatball. I promise I won't be long." The boy's shoulders sagged in apparent disappointment, and his mouth turned down in a pout.

Leaving the door open, Floyd turned to find Cindy waiting behind him, her hands on her hips and eyes narrowed. He leaned in to kiss her goodbye, and she turned to offer a cheek.

"What's up your ass?"

"Nothing."

Floyd didn't have the time nor inclination to play the game she might have expected as a result of her terse response. The game where he would ask again what was wrong, and she would continue to deny that anything bothered her, and they would go back and forth in that manner until she gave him both barrels, providing a list of all that was "up her ass." He grabbed his gun and badge from the top of the refrigerator and without looking back, said, "See ya tonight." He left the front door standing open.

Shades on, Floyd wheeled his county car from the driveway and took off down the street, smiling broadly at the brunette across the way who stood in shorts and a t-shirt, watching him leave. Her husband hadn't been home for a few weeks, and Floyd wondered if they were separated. The thought occurred to him he should find out someday, just in case she needed anything. It would be the neighborly thing to do.

As he merged onto the freeway, Floyd kept one eye on the road and the other on his phone. He had put Josie's address into a mapping program that would tell him the fastest route, the shortest route, and where to watch out for hazards and the highway patrol—one and the same in Floyd's mind. Once the address was programmed, he thumbed his ETA into a text message to Dickie, and watched impatiently, waiting for a response. *Delivered*, showed on the screen. After a moment, *Read*. "Attaboy, Dickie. Come on." There, the three dots danced on his screen, showing him Dickie was typing something. But then they stopped. And started. Stopped. "What the hell? Come on, Dickie." He hoped for more information, an update, anything.

He placed the phone in its cradle on the dash. The screen darkened. Floyd reached over and touched it to bring it back to life. The cycle continued: Dots. No dots. Dots. Finally, a thumbs up emoji. "Jesus Christ," Floyd said.

He turned on the radio, unable to contend with the silence that came with being alone. Floyd pictured his old partner, Dickie, sitting at Josie's house. It was probably quaint, and her mother likely wore a dress and tennis shoes, frail hands clutching a handkerchief. He had never met her, but he had met many like her. The mothers of wondrous Latinas. Dickie probably sat with his hat in his hands, turning it while massaging its brim into shape, anxiously awaiting his partner.

He glanced at the phone again. Nothing.

Floyd replayed the conversation they had had while he was out back cooking, and the more he considered it, the more he felt an urgency taking hold. Or maybe it was that he had shifted gears and was now in work mode. Game time. Helmets and shoulder pads, time to light something on fire and cause a wreck. He cracked a grin at the thought, remembering those words spoken by his high school football coach.

As he sailed along, his mind drifted back to Cindy and the look she had given him, and the avoidance of a goodbye kiss. Floyd again wondered what it was that had been up her ass, and dismissed it as most likely having something to do with a hormonal imbalance.

Floyd touched his phone again to bring it to life. Still no messages. Restless, he thumbed over to emails and began scanning through the numerous unread messages that appeared, while sailing along the I-5 doing seventy. But dodging lousy drivers didn't provide enough activity to keep Floyd entertained, and the emails soon bored him as well, so he returned to wondering what might have happened to Josie, if anything. He smiled at some of the ideas that followed, picturing Josie at various undis-closed locations enjoying herself in the way that a smoking-hot single woman might. Dickie was just wound too damn tight, he reasoned, settling into his seat and wondering if this would be all for naught, a dry run. He didn't care; it was an excuse to get out of the house for the night. He'd miss Cody, but Cindy he could do without until she managed to unfuck herself.

3

E smeralda hovered near the doorway as I looked around her daughter's bedroom, hoping for a hint or a clue as to Josie's whereabouts. There were many questions swirling around in my head: What plans had she had for last night? Was she seeing someone? Had she forgotten that I would be picking her up this evening at her home? Could she have confused our plans and thought we were meeting at the office? I had checked with the bureau, and Jimmy Wells on the desk had said no, he hadn't seen her. When I called back and asked him to go around the corner and check her desk, he grudgingly did so, and returned to report she was not there. There was no sign that she had been in the office at all, he had said. Her desktop was orderly and uncluttered, her chair tucked beneath it the way one might do when they leave for the day as opposed to leaving for a few minutes or an hour. He didn't think she'd been in.

I couldn't shake the idea that I might be overreacting. This was why I had not yet reported anything to my lieutenant, and it was why I had asked Jimmy Wells to keep a lid on my checking up on her.

Standing in Josie's room, I couldn't help but picture the scene of our latest murder and remember the time we spent together on the long drive home from Gorman. I could hear her voice and smell her flowery scent and I wondered if she saw me there in her room at that moment. No, I insisted, Josie was alive and well and there would be a good explanation for her absence; she wasn't looking down from the heavens. I was certain of it. Nearly.

I wished her mother would leave me alone in the room. I didn't know what she thought about my being there at all, but I knew she wouldn't be comfortable with me going through drawers and closets and searching beneath pillows and mattresses as I would be doing if she weren't standing at the door. I wanted to know every detail of Josie's life at this moment. It occurred to me that I could take her computer to our tech guy at the office who could hack his way beyond the password. That would allow me to see all of her online history: websites, chats, and messages. I wondered if she used the dating sites, as so many singles now did. Some married people too, I supposed. I could always have her computer searched later if Josie didn't surface or if answers didn't emerge in the near future. Don't jump the gun, I told myself, while making a mental note to take the computer.

The thought of the office gave me another idea: I needed to search her desk and her locker at work. But when and how, without drawing unwanted attention? Her absence felt surreal to me, and at times I was convinced that all of it would be nothing but silliness when she walked through the door to find me and Floyd entertaining her mother.

Where the hell *was* Floyd, anyway? He would be here soon, I reasoned, glancing at my watch again. It had been thirty minutes since he sent a text to confirm he was on his way. He'd be here any minute, ready to *habla. Pinky panty,* as we called it in the ghetto, the way it often sounded when someone tried to ask you in terrible English if you spoke Spanish. It really sounded more like *peeky panny,* but *pinky panty* was how it had evolved among the troops. Not that Floyd was an accomplished Spanish speaker—he didn't get paid the five percent that *true* bilingual deputies were paid—but he was better than I was. Mainly because he had liked talking to the Mexican girls when we were young and working patrol in South Los Angeles. He had found there were benefits to being at least conversationally bilingual. All of us could tell someone to stop and put their hands in the air, but it required substantially more linguistic prowess to find out if there was a *Sancho* in a girl's life and whether or not that would prevent her from meeting for beers after work.

All I currently needed to find out from Esmeralda was where her daughter had gone and with whom she went. Floyd could get us that far.

But I didn't need to know Spanish to see the worry in a mother's eyes. She seemed to instinctively know that something was wrong. I needed Floyd here to *habla* with mama and also to provide balance and keep me grounded. My needle tended to redline as I assumed the worst in all scenarios. Floyd would likely start with the view that everything would be okay, no big deal. He'd suggest that it was something personal that she didn't want anyone to know about, and then he'd come up with a made-for-Penthouse fantasy story that involved several other beautiful women, an island or remote mountaintop cabin, and plenty of alcohol. I hoped that would be the case, that she was just away with friends, but I knew it wasn't. She wouldn't have left her mother worrying; she wasn't that type of person. My gut told me something bad had happened to my partner.

The idea of a mountaintop cabin stopped all other thoughts in my head.

Liebre Mountain was the home of my latest victim and all of his clan. Which included brothers, uncles, aunts, and cousins, as well as an array of other men, some of them bearded, all with guns. And most either on meth or selling it, maybe both. Josie and I had planned to head back up the mountain tomorrow morning to work on the case. But tonight, the evening before our three-day weekend came to an end, we had planned to drive to Orange County together to check on Davey Lopes's informant, Maria Lopez. Lopes had flown to Texas for an extradition and wouldn't be back for two days. He didn't like the idea of leaving Maria unattended for long periods of time, as the Mexican mafia had put a green light on her—an order for her to be killed by any gangsters who might have the opportunity to do so. Josie had told Lopes she would check on her, and I had told Josie I would go with her. In fact, I told her I would drive her there and even buy her dinner. The offer had come from guilt about how I proposed we handled the case.

Had she missed that part about me going with her? Maybe she went to check on Maria Lopez by herself. But why would her phone be turned off? Maybe it was just dead and she didn't have a charger with her.

It was an unlikely scenario, but I had to consider it a possibility none-theless. Lopes, a veteran detective who worked Unsolved Homicides, had become accustomed to utilizing my partner for some of the necessary interactions he faced with the female informant. Lopes had a case going against the Mexican mafia. The informant, Maria Lopez, a former corrections officer and associate of the mob, was now testifying against some of the gang's most notorious players. But before she was his informant, and before Lopes knew that she was involved with the mafia, and before two pee-wee gangsters who were loyal to the most notorious of all prison gangs, *La Eme*, had gunned her down as she sat on the steps of her grandmother's home, the informant and Lopes had had relations. In fact, Lopes had been on his way to pick her up for a date the night she was shot and left for dead.

There was also a history between Lopes and my partner, Josefina Sanchez. They had worked together briefly, and during a chow run, they found themselves fighting with a rapist in a public restroom. That case had resulted in a civil suit against them, and the impending trial had been the premise of several after-hours rendezvous that involved alcohol and God only knows what else. Lopes had more going on with assorted women than half of the playboys in Hollywood.

Josie, a life-long bachelorette, lived here in Downey in this modest home with a swimming pool and Jacuzzi. I glanced over at her aging and widowed mother who lived with her, who still stood in the doorway, silently waiting and watching.

I held her eyes for a moment while remembering Lopes telling me about the night he had gone drinking with Josie, and the next day, he awoke at the side of her pool. I could hear the pool motor running out back, and I pictured Lopes sleeping outside on a lounge chair. He told me he awoke near the pool semi-clothed and confused. He had checked the back door to her home and found it locked, so he left through a side gate. He claimed he couldn't recall the events of the night, but was pretty sure "nothing had happened." Lopes had been concerned about what had happened because he had never blacked out before.

I glanced at my watch and wondered how much longer it would be before Floyd arrived, and then continued looking around the room. Neat, clean, very little on the walls. A black and white photo showing two little girls, one of whom I presumed to be Josie. Who was the other? A boombox sat on crocheted doilies that covered a chest of drawers. There were knickknacks, figurines, and a jewelry box sitting on a vanity.

Josie's mother hovered in the doorway, clutching her sweater as if it was a shield. Against what?

I thought again about Josie and Lopes and the Mexican mafia angle to the situation. I remembered that after she and I had bonded as partners, the topic came up one night over drinks. She had smiled and her eyes had sparkled as she recounted the evening that Lopes ended up at her house. "At the bar, the dumbass was drinking craft beers like they were Coors Light, and he started getting drunk. For some reason, he began ordering shots of tequila. I had one, he had two or three—at least. Then, he switched to Jack and cokes. I told him, 'Dude, you don't mix like that; you'll get sick.' He waved me off and said, 'Don't worry, I'm a Marine; we drink the blood of our enemy and chase it with turpentine. I'll eat a box of nails and spit out a barbed wire fence.' All sorts of other macho bullshit. Next thing you know, I'm helping him out. I put Lopes in my car and gave his keys to another deputy who was there and asked him to get Davey's car to my house. When we get to my place, he pukes in the front yard. I have a spare room, but honestly, if Marine boy is going to be puking, he can do it outside. I don't need blood and turpentine all over the carpet, a fucking barbed wire fence in the spare room. Right? So, I put him to bed on the patio with him begging me to join him. Of course, for the last hour, he's all over me like a monkey humping a football, a goddamn dog in heat. So I locked the patio door and went inside. Because honestly, if I had to have any more interaction with homeboy that night, it was going to involve duct tape and a sap."

She had gone on to say that nothing had ever happened between the two of them, and I knew she would get mad if I asked too many questions about it. I wasn't her mother, she would say.

A car door clunked outside, pulling me from my thoughts. Esmeralda must have heard it also because she turned to look toward the front of the house, though she wouldn't be able to see anything from where she stood at the threshold of the master bedroom.

"Excuse me," I said—in English—and walked past her. I figured she would know what it meant. I had heard the Spanish version and it wasn't much different. *Perdóneme,* or something similar. If I could figure out that *perdõneme* meant *excuse me—or pardon me*, shouldn't she be able to figure out that *excuse me* meant *perdõneme*? I would think about that sometimes when driving through East L.A. or Huntington Park, noticing the various signs in Spanish. *Dentista. Farmacia.* Why not let them figure out that "dentist" means *dentista* and "pharmacy" means *farmacia*?

When I entered the living room, I saw Floyd coming up the walkway to the open front door. I met him on the porch. "Thanks for coming, partner."

He lifted his chin and squinted at me. "What the hell's going on here, Dickie? And where's your hat?"

I ignored both questions for the time being and gestured for him to step inside. "I need you to *habla* with Josie's mom, find out everything you can about what her plans had been for the weekend. We picked up a murder on Thursday, our kickoff for a three-day weekend, up in Gorman—"

"Gorman? For fuck's sake."

"—and we rolled in late that night, early Friday morning. We agreed to take the weekend off—since your captain cut our overtime again—and decided we'd pick the case back up tomorrow. Give it a few days to simmer. It's a body found in the woods and it's probably a relative who did it, so not likely a killer on the run scenario. Besides, nobody would even know the body has been discovered, most likely. The point is, there was no rush to get back up to the mountain, as much as I love stepping on rattlers while processing crime scenes. Tonight, we were supposed to go check on Lopes's informant down at the safe house in Huntington Beach. I told Josie I'd pick her up about five. From the best I can understand mama, Josie left yesterday afternoon or night and she hasn't been back. She obviously hadn't planned anything, or mama wouldn't be so concerned. You can see she's rattled, but I just can't get much more out of her."

Floyd nodded. "Okay, let's do this. I have a steak on the grill and a cooler full of cold beer at home."

"My hope is she's going to come bouncing through the door—"

"Hungover and walking funny."

"—before we start going through her panty drawer."

"I'll handle that for us, just to keep the embarrassment down to a minimum," Floyd offered, grinning.

I didn't grin back. "But actually, my gut tells me something is seriously wrong."

Floyd glanced past me. I followed his gaze and saw Esmeralda standing in the hallway, listening. She, like many Spanish-speaking residents, probably understood more English than she ever let on. I looked back at Floyd. "Know what I mean?"

He nodded. "Yeah, I do. We usually aren't wrong on our guts, Dickie. You sure you don't want to call it in, get Metro and their surveillance teams out here?"

I pondered it a moment. "Let's talk to mama before we make any decisions, and then we probably better get down to Huntington Beach and check on Lopes's girl. I just pray she's alive and well. Jesus."

Floyd acknowledged with a nearly imperceptible nod, and brushed past me. "*Hola, Señora, como esta?*"

Esmeralda replied, "*Se llevaron a mi hija*," and began crying.

Floyd turned his head to me. "She said they took her daughter."

4

"Why does she say that?"

Floyd frowned at me and then looked Esmeralda in the eyes and softly asked, *"Por qué dices eso?"*

"What did you say?"

Esmeralda began speaking in Spanish, rapidly. Floyd said to me, "I asked her why she said that. That's what you told me to ask."

I nodded at Esmeralda who was now waving her hands and shaking her head, continuing with a steady flow of words, most of which I couldn't understand interspersed with a few I recognized: *no, pero, por qué, si, and muerte.* "Wait! Did she just say, '*muerte*'—death?"

Floyd nodded.

"What else is she saying?"

He held his hand out at me. "Hold on, Dickie."

Esmeralda trailed off to a mumble as if she had run out of energy. Her gaze dropped to the floor.

"What did she say?!" I demanded.

Floyd frowned. "Jesus, I don't know. She was going off, something about curses and spirits and evil shit."

"What did she say about death?"

We both watched as she continued mumbling to herself in her native tongue and turned to walk away.

"She's saying something about lighting candles to ward off the evil spirits."

"But what did she say about death?" I asked again.

Floyd frowned at me. "She probably said she's going to kill the two assholes in her home if they don't figure out what happened to her daughter. I don't know, dickhead; she's gone off in a fit of Hispanic panic. It's what they do. Before you know it, she'll be out back chopping the heads off chickens or building an altar."

I turned to the view of the street where Floyd's blue Taurus sat behind my charcoal gray Crown Vic. In my peripheral vision I saw Floyd take a seat on the adjacent couch and cross one leg over the other. He was wearing jeans and a buttoned dress shirt that was untucked, likely to conceal a weapon. I too was in casual attire today: a pair of Dockers and a golf shirt with the Homicide Bureau logo, a bulldog smoking a cigar and wearing a fedora. But my shirt was tucked in and my gun visible along with my sheriff's star that was clipped onto my belt above my hip pocket. A Dodgers ball cap in traditional blue with "L.A." embossed on the front—a stark contrast to the black caps of similar design worn by the local gangsters—replaced the fedora I would wear with my suits.

Floyd said, "Well, what's next? She doesn't know shit, other than that Josie left yesterday and hasn't come home and now there is evilness in the air."

I took a seat across from him in the oversized chair, removed my cap, and propped it on my knee. Esmeralda was talking into a cell phone from the kitchen behind us. Her urgent and worried tone broke through the language barrier; she was telling friends and relatives about our situation.

"I wish she wouldn't broadcast this to the world just yet," I said, nodding my head toward the kitchen behind me.

Floyd glanced her direction and waited a moment. "She's talking to her sister, from what I can gather. We need to come up with a plan and get the hell out of here. In an hour they'll be showing up with food."

"Who?"

"Sisters, cousins. It'll be like a viewing before the funeral around here until we find her. This place is going to fill up with Mexican women dressed for church and armed with candles and rosaries and pots of food. You watch, they'll build an altar somewhere in the house and start burning incense and the sisters and cousins will be praying around the clock and eating and drinking wine."

"No shit?"

"Just women, too; no men. They'll bring the plastic Jesus out and pictures of the Virgin Mary and someone will be sure to sprinkle holy water all over the house."

"For what?"

"Rid the mojo, the evil spirits. Something has happened to Josefina and anything that happens is always related to a life force and must be addressed through prayer. Lose your keys? Light a candle and pray. Don't bother looking for the fucking keys, just wait until Jesus returns them."

"I'm not waiting on Jesus to return Josie. We need a plan."

"Damn right we need—"

Floyd stopped as Esmeralda hurried through the living room, opening every window. The front door—which had been left cracked open—was pushed to stand wide open, and she fanned the air with open palms as if swooshing bugs outside.

"The hell's she doing now?"

Floyd shrugged, and then spoke to her in Spanish. After she replied, he looked at me and smiled. "She said the house feels heavy, that there are unwelcome spirits that need to leave. She's trying to get them out. What's our plan?"

"You think Lopes would have any ideas about this?" I asked.

Floyd shook his head. "Didn't you say he's out of state?"

I nodded.

"Wait, could she have gone with him and not mentioned it?"

It was a possibility. "Maybe. Should I call him?"

Floyd considered it for a moment. "Send him a text and ask who he took with him on the extradition. That might resolve this whole deal."

Esmeralda reappeared with a jug of water and went from corner to corner sprinkling its contents along the baseboards.

I raised my chin and pointed it in her direction. "Holy water?"

Floyd nodded. "Text Lopes and let's think about Plan B, just in case we don't hear back from him right away, or we do, and it doesn't resolve this. We have to get out of here before the family starts showing up with food."

"I'm at a loss, partner. Checking with Maria Lopez is the only thing I can come up with right now. Unless . . ."

"What?"

"Nah, she's not that stupid."

"What, Dickie?!"

I scooted to the front of my chair and put my cap back on my head. I glanced over my shoulder to see Esmeralda now walking the inside perimeter of the home with a smoking object in her hands. It looked like a giant doobie, like the joint Cheech and Chong had smoked in one of their movies. But the pungent odor was nothing like the sweet smell of burning marijuana; this smelled like a sagebrush fire. Her eyes were glued on the smoke that wafted from the giant burning joint and she spoke in a low but ferocious tone and I recognized some of the words as cursing. I looked back at Floyd, who sat grinning.

"Did I tell you about the case we picked up last week?"

He shook his head.

"It's one of those strange deals that has weirdness written all over it—"

"We love weirdness, Dickie."

"Our victim had just been released from the joint after doing three years for raping his niece. He lived in a trailer up in the mountains by Gorman. He—the rapist—was found by hunters. He had a single gunshot through the chest and a matching hole in his right hand, likely a through-and-through that ripped through his heart. The point is, we were supposed to go back up there tomorrow, and, well . . ."

"You think she'd go up there alone? Over the weekend? Why would she do that?"

"I doubt it. I don't know, nothing makes sense. The only reason I even mention it is that when we found out the guy had raped his niece, you could see it got to Josie. Like it had angered her more than you'd expect from a seasoned cop, man or woman. You know what I mean?"

He nodded.

"Let's get out of here. We're not doing any good here and mama is about to send me over the edge with this voodoo shit." I stood from my seat and glanced at my phone. "No word yet from Lopes."

"Your call, Dickie. I'm just here for the beer."

We started for the door and I heard Floyd behind me telling Esmeralda something in Spanish that I assumed would be about us leaving and being back later or calling. I stopped, turned back, and retrieved a business card from my wallet as I approached her. She waited while I wrote Floyd's cell number on the back. I held her gaze while instructing Floyd to tell her to call the number with any news, no matter what time of day or night, and we will be back to check with her later. I waited. When he finished, I said, "Let's get her cell number, partner, and then we're out of here." Floyd wrote in his notebook as Esmeralda provided her number carefully, one digit at a time, some of the numbers pronounced in Spanish, others in English.

5

W e stopped by Lakewood Sheriff's Station and dropped Floyd's car in the parking lot, made a quick pit stop inside, and left with fresh coffee for the road. Neither of us ventured to the front desk, nor did we drop in on the sergeant or watch commander to let them know who we were and that we were leaving a car there. We were flying low, staying beneath the radar, and the fewer contacts we had, the fewer questions we'd have to answer. Though we didn't handle a lot of cases at Lakewood, we were familiar enough with the station to find fresh coffee and the men's room without any assistance.

On the way to Orange County, Floyd wanted the details about our Gorman case. I filled him in, describing the scene, the circumstances of the discovery, and the victim's history. I said, "I'm pretty sure we'll figure this one out."

"Ya think? I mean, you're not real bright, Dickie; don't shit yourself about that."

"We haven't talked to anyone on the mountain yet—family wise—and we had planned to go back up tomorrow. There were no press releases or next of kin notifications, so as far as we know, the family shouldn't know he's been discovered."

Floyd grinned. "You're assuming they know he's dead."

I nodded. "It makes the best sense so far. I mean, who knows, right? But that's where we're starting."

"What's the background on your victim, other than diddling little girls?"

"Meth and burglary."

Floyd huffed. "No shit, huh? Who would've guessed?"

"He has two brothers, the father of the little girl, and another dipshit who's done time for murder. They reduced it to a manslaughter, but he was booked for murder. I don't know the circs on that case yet 'cause it happened up in Kern County. We'll look into it though, I can guarantee it. But the father of the girl, he's got nothing. Clean as a whistle. The copper up there knew him, but only because he knows everyone on the mountain. Did you know those guys live up there?"

"The cops?"

I glanced over and then back to the road. "Yeah, the cops. Deputies, just like you and me. Only thing is they live in houses, one of which doubles as the station. Used to be, there was a jail cell in there they'd hold arrestees until they could ship them off to Santa Clarita, or County. But they don't hold arrestees there anymore after one of them was killed back when."

"I remember."

"You were in third grade."

"No, I remember hearing about it. Didn't they talk about that in the academy?"

I shrugged. "I don't remember, but I heard the story when I was in high school. Growing up in Newhall, that was a big story. That and when the four chippies were killed in a shootout right up there off of the Five, by that coffee shop. Remember that?"

"I heard about it."

"I was in elementary school when that happened. One of the guys ended up barricaded in a house right up the road from our school. I'll never forget it. They locked us in for the day, no recess. They talked about it a lot during the academy, too. I remember one of the chippies had put spent cartridges in his pocket while reloading, just the way they'd practiced shooting at the range. *Police your brass*. That was important back before it cost someone their life. That's why now we dump our brass on the ground, let the trustees pick it up when we're done shooting."

Floyd nodded.

"But anyway, the Gorman thing, the deputy had arrested some crazy dude and had taken him into the substation to book him. At some point during the process, the guy takes the deputy's gun away and shoots him with it. The deputy's wife comes out of the other room, talks the guy into the booking cage and locks him up. She calls Santa Clarita and waits the thirty or forty minutes it takes to get help up there, her husband dead on the floor and his killer locked in the cage a few feet away. Can you believe it?"

"Wild west."

I slowed and glanced over my shoulder, realizing the San Diego Freeway was coming up fast and I needed to move over and transition onto it. At least, that's what the directions on my phone had indicated. When I settled back behind the wheel, I said, "Oh boy. You wouldn't believe it. You've never been up there?"

Floyd shook his head.

"The guys that work there have dogs, something they started after the deputy was killed. That was back in the late seventies, I think. They're also all EMT trained, because it's a hell of a roll to the nearest hospital. I think most of them are trained in search and rescue also, and they're certified in off-road vehicle driving. They even have motorcycles they can use when they need them. Their vehicles have radios that allow them to talk directly to the chippies, the fire department, the forestry department—you name it."

"What the hell would they say? I mean, why would anyone need to talk to a fireman?"

"They border Kern County to the north, and Ventura County to the west, if you can believe it."

"Ventura?" Floyd questioned.

"Uh-huh. Also, they have Pyramid Lake to deal with, and I think some of those guys are trained in boat operations too. I know we have deputies that patrol that lake on a boat, but I'm not sure if they're part of Gorman or something else."

"Anyone can drive a boat, Dickie. The only thing different from driving a car is you sit on the wrong side, like you're in Europe, and you have a throttle rather than a gas pedal. Easy stuff. I've driven 'em out at the river. You want to talk about a party . . ."

"The Gorman deputy that handled our case said their area covers more than three-hundred square miles. What'd we have in Firestone, four-and-a-half square miles?"

"Plus all of LAPD's area."

"That's true."

Floyd reached for the radio in the brief period of silence. I stopped him. "Hang on, I wasn't finished."

"Jesus, dude, how much do I need to know about that place?"

"No, we were talking about the case. The father of the girl has no criminal history, but the other brother does. What do you think about that? I mean, there's always a first, right? Or do you think this asshole child molester got himself killed another way?"

"Well, you know how that goes; she probably wasn't the first girl he diddled. Coulda been anyone, I'd suppose. Plus, if they're all on the meth up there, anything's possible."

I thought about it while Floyd turned the radio back up on an eighties rock station. If there was one thing I'd learned over the years, it was that you never wanted to set your mind on a theory and work a case from that direction; you'd be sure to miss something if you did. He was right, there were probably plenty of others who had been victimized by our latest victim, William Brown. But his teenage niece and her daddy would be the first couple of people we'd talk to once we got back to the mountain case.

As soon as silence settled in, the thoughts of Josie rushed back into my head. The conversation had been designed to take her off my mind for the time being. I knew Floyd didn't much care about my latest case, he mostly wanted to keep me occupied. He knew me better than anyone else did, and he knew that my level of concern was bordering on panic and worsening with each passing moment.

He must have seen the seriousness wash over me. "Dickie, we're going to find her."

"I know," I lied.

6

The safe house was situated in the northeast part of Huntington Beach, five miles inland near the city of Westminster. It was a far cry from points south where the city's ten miles of sandy beaches were populated by sun-worshiping, bikini-clad girls, surfers, skaters, and beach volleyballers. We were a long way from Compton—in Southern California terms—and more importantly, in the matter of the protected informant Maria Lopez, we were a long way from the Avenues in northeast Los Angeles and the Alps of East L.A. and Whittier Boulevard and the other barrios around the Southland where gangsters were quick to act at the direction of the Mexican mafia. Hispanic street gang members throughout would learn of Lopez's status on *la lista,* and many of them would take the opportunity to ingratiate themselves to the mob by spilling the blood of a "rat." Gangsters almost always end up in jail or prison, and when they did, they hoped to be in good graces with the Mexican mafia, *La Eme.*

We picked Maria Lopez up from the safe house and drove to the nearby Westminster mall. She wore shorts and a white polo shirt to blend in with the crowd. I wondered if Lopes had told her how to dress, or if she was smart enough to know. You wouldn't see a girl in East L.A. dressed the way she was dressed today in her shorts and polo, and when boys and girls from the barrios came to the beach, they stood out from the rest. They looked like clowns in their oversized shorts cinched tight by black military-style web belts, and everyone knew they were trouble waiting to happen. I had put an oversized button-up over my homicide polo to conceal it, along with my gun and badge. We were just three civilians chilling on a warm, west coast evening, as far as anyone else would know.

I drove around the giant perimeter of the mall that was congested with cars and people walking to and from the various shops and restaurants within it. I hoped to find a place where we could pick up coffee or sodas and sit on an outdoor patio away from the crowds of shoppers and those just hanging out, which, I was surprised to see, included a few gangster-looking assholes.

Floyd noticed them too. "You suppose these punks are the real deal, or just Orange County wannabes?"

I glanced into my rearview mirror to see Maria in the back seat solemnly staring through oversized sunglasses. Her hair hung carelessly, concealing much of her impassive expression.

"They look like little bitches to me. What do you think, Maria?"

"Little poo-butts," she said. "I'm not worried about them. Come on, park your ride and let's do this. I'm dying to be outside."

I held her gaze in the rearview mirror as I turned up a row, looking for a parking spot. "You stay in most of the time, Maria?"

"Lopes don't want me going out unless he's with me. That's about once every six or five days. Him and the *hoochie* mama he brings with him."

She was referring to Josie. That I knew, because Lopes had been using Josie frequently to accompany him on his visits with Maria in order to avoid any false allegations or the appearance of impropriety. Lopes and Maria Lopez had had a brief but intimate relationship prior to the attempt on her life. She had been shot multiple times by two gangsters carrying out a mob-ordered hit. Miraculously surviving, Maria had disassociated herself from the mafia and became an informant for Lopes, the man with whom she had been directed to develop a relationship so she could glean information and pass it along to *La Eme*. It had been a solid plan, as Lopes was single and had an eye for younger ladies. A former Marine and thirty-year veteran of the sheriff's department, he had quickly fallen for her beauty and charm when he met her at Pelican Bay state prison where she had worked as a corrections officer.

Now she passed the time at a safe house with a GPS device attached to her ankle. Her two children, who were otherwise in the care and custody of the state farther south in San Diego County, saw her on the weekends. She had gained twenty pounds, her eyes had dulled, and her alluring smile had yet to return since that shocking night on her grandmother's steps.

I ignored the grating comment, knowing that it stemmed from regret and jealousy. Maria Lopez had hoped to break away from the life into which she had been born, and to start fresh. Lopes had been part of that hope, she had later revealed to him. But it would never be; that was the grim truth of it. Life had dealt her a bad hand, one that would forever impede the dreams of an otherwise beautiful soul.

I also knew she would have no way to know that Josie was missing, or she wouldn't have said it. From the many conversations I had had with Lopes about Maria Lopez, and from the few times I had spoken with her, I knew she was a good person at heart, doing the best she could in a difficult situation. I also knew that she had strong feelings for Davey Lopes, and those feelings would likely grow stronger as time went on. He was her "handler," and a cop/informant relationship had its own especially difficult dynamics.

"We're going to talk about her today," I said, wheeling the Crown Vic into a spot.

Floyd popped out of the passenger's seat before I had turned off the car and was intently scanning our surroundings when I joined him. He nodded as if to say it was clear, so I opened the back door and motioned for Maria to come along. The three of us walked through the lot, Maria's head down and mine and Floyd's on swivels, carefully taking in our surroundings as we approached a bistro. It had a roped-off area on the patio outside where plastic tables and chairs sat beneath umbrellas. Floyd removed a section of the rope and replaced it once the three of us were inside the cordoned area and seated in a corner with our backs to a wall. I imagined the rope as crime scene tape and forced the thought from my head.

A waitress appeared, took our order, and repeated it back: "French dip with fries and a Dr. Pepper for the lady, two black coffees for the gentlemen." *Gentlemen.*

It was late, beyond the dinner hour, so we sat unhindered by the presence of others and spoke openly while awaiting our order. "Maria," I started, "how are things going for you?"

She looked away through her round sunglasses. "What can I say?"

What could I say to that? She had been left for dead and now was alone and in hiding. The life of a beautiful young lady shattered by violence in the dark of night.

"When's the last time you've heard from anyone?"

"Anyone, like who?" she asked.

"Lopes . . . Josie. Either one."

She shook her head. "I don't hear from *her.* Lopes is who I talk to and last I heard he was out of town. He said he'd check with me next week."

I nodded. Floyd continued to scan our surroundings though I knew he would also be paying close attention to the conversation.

"You saw them before Lopes left though, right?"

"A few days ago, yeah."

"What day?"

She seemed to think about it for a moment. "I guess it was the night before last."

I frowned. I didn't know that Josie had come down with Lopes on Friday night, if Maria had her days right. We had picked up the new case Thursday afternoon, worked into the early morning hours of Friday, but then were to be off until Monday. Lopes must have wanted to check on Maria once more before leaving town, and had asked Josie to accompany him. Probably last minute, since I didn't know about it.

"Tell us about that," I said.

She locked the shades on me. "Is something wrong? Has something happened?"

Floyd looked at her, but looked away when she met his gaze. In the moment that passed, I decided against revealing anything to her. "No, there's nothing wrong. Lopes asked me to check in with you while he was gone. I was just wondering how the last meeting went. Did everything seem okay with them?"

"Like, between them? He said there's nothing between them."

30

Maria Lopez obviously still had strong feelings for Davey Lopes, and she might have also been jealous of Josie. She was at least jealous of Josie's freedom and ability to be with Lopes, in my opinion. The thought of it caused me to reconsider my plans.

"Something may have happened to Josie, Maria. You are one of the last people who spoke with the two of them and I'm just wondering if there was anything different about your meeting. Primarily I am interested to know if Josie acted any differently than she had in the past."

It was difficult to read her through the shades, but she was staring straight at me, her face expressionless. It was the first time I noticed the scar on her throat, and I assumed it was left from a tracheotomy she had received as a result of her being in a coma after being shot. I imagined the numerous scars that covered her body as a result of the multiple gunshot wounds she had suffered, and I thought about the scars on my own body as I looked back at her, likely with a similarly blank stare.

She still hadn't answered. "Maria, can you tell me about that last meeting? Did Josie talk about any plans she might have had? Did she seem anxious?"

Maria shook her head. "I don't remember anything. They came by and she had brought me some ice cream. It was nice of her. I think she gets the feeling I don't like her."

"Why do you say that?"

"Just girl shit, you know? Two fillies and a stud, there's going to be some tail swishing."

"You like horses?"

"Why do you ask?"

"The analogy. Not many city girls would use country analogies to explain things."

She waited as her food was placed before her and our coffees were delivered. When the waitress walked away, Maria's eyes followed the waitress until the patio door closed behind her. "When I lived up near Pelican, I wasn't far from the country. The hills are full of cattle and you'd see cowboys riding through the herds at times. For a while, I dated a cowboy. A *vaquero*. I mean, he was a guard at the prison, but he was a cowboy too. I'd never ridden before and he taught me how. He knew a lot about animals and shared his passion with me."

Maria looked off to the north, likely searching for the memories, seeing the beautiful land that represented a freedom she would never enjoy in the same ways that she otherwise might have been able to.

"He would use animals to relate to human behavior. He'd say about a colt that wanted to buck that it had too much energy, like a kid. They both behaved better when you helped them spend some of that energy in positive ways. 'Decrease his energy and increase his confidence,' he would say. 'Do that before you get on him.' He told me once that a single mare could ruin a whole string of horses, and two mares were guaranteed to fight if a stud was in the pen. One would pin her ears at the other, maybe turn her ass and get ready to kick. They swish their tails when they're angry, so that's all I meant by it. Josie and I would probably get along fine if Lopes wasn't in the same barn as both of us. Know what I mean?"

I nodded and glanced to see Floyd revealing a slight grin. "Yeah, I think we both know what you mean."

"I think also that Josie wants kids. She asks about my children a lot and she seems sad that they are mostly apart from me. It is sad, but it's nice that Josie feels that way too. Like I said, if we both didn't have feelings for Lopes . . ."

She trailed off and a moment of silence followed.

"Josie is missing," I blurted out. I regretted it the moment I said it, and I could feel Floyd's eyes on me. Maria had shown me a side of herself that I had suspected was there, and as with others throughout my career, I trusted my instinct about her.

The revelation visibly startled Maria, and she stared at me. She removed her glasses and carelessly set them on the table next to her untouched sandwich and fries. I took a long sip of my coffee and waited.

"What do you mean?" she finally asked. "Like she's been taken?"

I shook my head. "We don't know, but she's missing, and I feel that it's something serious. You and Lopes were two of the last to see her, as far as we know. I was wondering if you had a feel for anything that was different from the other times you've been with her."

"The mafia?"

"God, I hope not. Why do you say that?"

She stared at her plate a long moment before picking up a fry and dipping it into a blob of ketchup. She dropped it and retreated from her plate. "I put nothing past the mob. They will do anything to keep me from testifying."

"How would taking Josie help them?"

"To let me know they're close. Very close. If they know she's part of this, they know more than any of us would have realized."

The thought had briefly crossed my mind, and I didn't like hearing the words. I looked at Floyd who just stared back at me.

Maria continued, "But she was the same as always that night. As I said, she even brought me ice cream. If something was on her mind, she sure didn't let it show."

"And Lopes?"

She sucked at her teeth. "Shit, Lopes is always cool."

WE DROVE OUT OF ORANGE COUNTY IN SILENCE AFTER WE DROPPED Maria Lopez back at the safe house. Floyd had pushed his sunglasses into his hair as the sun cast its last rays of orange light across the clear coastal sky, and he propped a foot on my dash as he slouched in his seat.

"What now, Dickie?"

I didn't know. *What now?* It wasn't often I found myself clueless and without direction, but I found this time that I was both of those things. *Mexican mafia.* That wasn't something I even wanted to entertain. But what else could it be? Where was my partner, Josie? I checked my phone for missed calls but there weren't any.

"You want to call Esmeralda, or just go back to the house and check in with her?"

"Your call, Dickie." He glanced at his watch. "You ruined my barbecue hours ago so now you're stuck with me, and don't think for a minute that I'm not putting in for overtime."

"I just don't know where else to go. What else could we do? I'm clueless, partner."

"I'm still hoping it's just some bizarre, weird, single broad shit. She's off sailing to Catalina with a Navy SEAL or sitting by a fire in a cabin up in Big Bear with a lumberjack. I'm betting on it, to be honest. How's a badass like Josie Sanchez going to get taken?"

"I hope you're right," I said.

"I'm always right, dickhead. Now let's go by Lakewood and grab my car. I'll follow you back to the house so we can see what kind of voodoo shit mama has going on. If nothing else, I'm hungry now, and I'm always up for being in a house full of Mexican women and food when I'm hungry. Hopefully some of her cousins are young and cute."

"You're always thinking—I'll give you that."

He smiled. "And after dining and dancing with the cha-cha girls, you can buy me a beer."

7

E smeralda was surrounded by women who appeared similar to her in age; there were no young, cute women to be found at Josie's house. Not even Josie. Candles burned and a breeze blew through all of the opened doors and windows, allowing or encouraging the evil spirits to leave. An hour after we arrived, Floyd and I stood on the street in front of her home, our bellies full of quesadillas, rice, and beans, but with no more direction in our search for Josie.

"You need to call it in, Dickie."

I leaned up against my car and sighed.

Floyd glanced at his watch. "It's nearly midnight now and she's still not back. Nobody's heard from her. Even I'm starting to get nervous."

"It won't do any good tonight. I say we go back in there and go through her room, properly. I couldn't do it earlier with mama hovering about. I want to go through everything. Steal her computer for Lonnie to have a look at, see if we can find any credit card statements or receipts so we can start tracking transactions. Phone is off and unaccounted for. I would think since it's a county phone we can get that pinged without writing paper on it. Other than that, I'm fresh out of ideas. You have any?"

"Yeah, we need to get ahold of Lopes and have him start checking with other mob informants. Get that goon back here and he and I can start beating balls while you run the paper end of things."

"Why do I have to run the paper end of things? Maybe I want in on the action."

Floyd began walking back toward the house. "Because that's how it works, Dickie. Come on."

I followed him inside, past the gathering of ladies in the living room and toward the back of the house to the master bedroom. I waved my hand nonchalantly to signify to the women that we would be fine without their assistance or oversight. There had been bottles of wine opened and Esmeralda, though still worried, had begun to relax. When we walked into Josie's room, I closed the door behind us. "I don't want her hovering again," I said to Floyd when he glanced back.

We didn't need to divvy up assigned search areas; Floyd and I had searched hundreds of rooms together over the years and there would be no stone left unturned nor any effort duplicated. The two of us worked in silence, Floyd beginning at the dresser while I started on the opposite side of the room at a desk. When we finished, we had a small pile of papers, a cell phone we believed to be a personal one that was no longer in use, and a laptop computer gathered at the end of the bed. I stood staring at the pile, disappointed at the lack of potential.

Floyd was at the side of the bed on his hands and knees shining a flashlight beneath it.

"Anything of interest?" I asked, still hopeful.

He grunted. "Shoes. That's about it."

I waited while he finished. He stood up and arched his back, jerked his head violently—first to the left, and then to the right—popping his neck. He glanced at his watch. "What now, Dickie?"

"I'm going to head in to the office with this stuff. I'll go through her desk and see what else I can come up with. Then I'll start writing paper on these cards—" I nodded toward the stack of paperwork on the bed that included credit card statements "—so we can get a warrant signed first thing in the morning."

Floyd nodded. "I'm going to head home then, get a couple of hours sleep and a change of clothes. I'll be in tomorrow. After all, what better way to start my vacation than spending time with you at the office?"

He grinned, but I didn't grin back. I was thinking about Josie and wondering what could have possibly happened. The mafia thing was all I could come up with at the time. What else could it be? I thought about the new case she and I had caught up in Gorman, but as far as that went, the only possibility was that she had gone up there by herself and got stranded on the mountain. It was unlikely, but it could happen. The cell phone coverage up there was spotty at best, so that could explain her phone being off.

"Hey, don't come in dressed up tomorrow," I said, the two of us now making our way back toward the front of the house. "We may take a ride up to Gorman after things settle down at the office."

Floyd frowned, but we were now stopped at the edge of the living room and all eyes were upon us. Silence had befallen the gathering of ladies.

"Tell them we're going back to the office with this stuff," I said, slightly lifting the laptop and small stack of papers I held in my left hand, "and we'll keep them posted. Remind her to call with any information."

He nodded and addressed the room in Floyd's version of Spanish, which caused some of the ladies to tilt their heads and frown, likely trying to decipher his words. When he finished, one of the women said in perfect English, "I'll be here with her until Josie comes home. Keep us posted."

I nodded and we stepped outside, leaving the door open behind us just in case the evil spirits dared to follow us out.

8

B y the time I arrived at the office it was nearly two in the morning. All of the lights were shut off other than those scant lights used by the personnel at the front desk—which stayed on 24/7—and the flickering glow of a muted television. I had come in through a rear door, keying it open quietly and holding it as it closed behind me, only allowing the soft click of the locking mechanism. At this time of night, there were only two possible scenarios for the desk crew: they would either be busy with the phones, dispatching teams of investigators to various locations throughout the county, or they would be settling in for a rest on a quiet night. The occasional assignment to graveyard on the desk was one of the most diffi-cult parts of the job. Every investigator had their turn in the barrel, but such an assignment was only a distraction from his regular workload and routine. Many times, an investigator would be in the middle of a new case when his turn in the barrel came up. There had been more than a few times when investigators worked a case all day and evening, came in to work the barrel on the graveyard shift, and then continued working the fresh case the next morning. If the phones were quiet, there was no shame in dimming the lights and leaning back against the wall in a chair to get some restless sleep. It was the life of a homicide dick.

I turned on the section of lights that hung above the two rows of desks that were home to investigators assigned to Teams Five and Six. I set the laptop and stack of papers from Josie's on my desk while focusing on the desk next to mine. Josie's. As Wells had described on the phone yesterday afternoon, there was nothing about her desk to indicate she had been in the office since we left for our weekend off. Everything appeared orderly and tidy, just as mine had before I piled potential evidence of a missing person on it just moments ago. I pulled her chair away from the desk and lowered myself into it slowly, studying my partner's work area as if it was a crime scene and evidence might be found there. The drawers were all tightly closed, but I knew they would be unlocked. Almost no one locked their desks at Homicide even though many contained weapons and personal valuables. Case files were stored in expandable folders called poor-boys, and every desk held a dozen or more of these, in which resided the contents of the cases currently being worked. Although these files were considered classified, they were not secured within the building. I pulled the center drawer open first, slowly and reverently.

Josie's desk contained case files, office supplies, personal care products, knickknacks, and a few edged weapons—a four-inch, fixed-blade knife with an ivory grip that was stored in a handmade, custom tooled sheath with her initials, and several folding knives of various makes and sizes. But I found no information about her personal life or future plans and activities.

I leaned back in Josie's chair, deep in thought, and my eyes suddenly felt heavy. I allowed my eyelids to rest closed for a moment and it felt good.

"Dickie, what are you doing here in the middle of the night? I didn't know you were here."

His voice jolted me awake but my head was clouded and it took a moment to clear the cobwebs. I was staring at a familiar detective who was speaking to me, but my mind wasn't processing his words. As if tuning in a radio, I suddenly focused on the pale blue eyes that were locked on mine and began hearing his words.

"—last night and transferred it to her voicemail."

It was Patrick Capini. Most just called him *Cap* or *Cappy*, or The Godfather. Cap had been at Homicide for more than thirty years and had investigated thousands of death cases. Some self-styled experts or television personalities made similar claims only because they had supervised a bureau of detectives and considered all of their subordinates' cases their own. Cappy, however, had actually stood at every single death scene he said he had, and there were literally thousands of them. He was considered the godfather for a damn good reason.

"Wait, what, Cap? I'm sorry, my brain had slipped into neutral."

"You're beat. When's the last time you slept?"

"Just now."

He chuckled and walked around the cluster of desks, pulled the chair from my desk and had a seat. His gaze drifted across the desk where I sat and seemed to settle for a moment on the placard that read: *Detective Josefina Sanchez – Homicide Bureau*. He looked back at me. "Routine integrity check?"

I was almost embarrassed that he caught me at my partner's desk but wouldn't know what I was up to and probably think it was on a personal level. "Something like that," I responded, buying time to consider what needed to be revealed at this time.

There had been many occasions during my years at Homicide when I had sought Cappy's advice on cases, drawing from the wisdom that came with his unmatched experience. He was not only smart and experienced, but he was respected by all because he always had time for his peers. Cappy was a class act and I was proud to call him a friend. He waited as if he knew there was more, his steely eyes watching me as if I were across the table from him in an interrogation room. The eyes of a man who had faced hundreds of killers in just that type of environment. I couldn't bullshit him.

"I have a problem, Cap."

Patrick Capini leaned back in his chair, crossed one leg over the other, and listened attentively while I laid out what few facts I had. Josie and I had picked up a case in Gorman and spent the bulk of Thursday on the mountain. Since there had been no media or press or spectators, we decided to wait a couple of days to notify the next of kin. We wanted to see who, if anyone, would report him missing, and when. Besides, we had been buried with cases and there hadn't been a weekend in our six months together where one or both of us hadn't worked. This was a rare opportunity to take some time off, and the strategy might work in our favor. "So we planned to take the weekend off and head back up the mountain tomorrow morning—" I glanced at my watch "—this morning."

I told Cappy we had intended to check in with Lopes's informant last evening, as Lopes was currently out of state. I was going to pick Josie up around five, and when I went to her home, she wasn't there. Her mother, who only speaks Spanish, was upset, and the best I could get from her was that Josie had left the afternoon before and hadn't returned. I told Cappy that Floyd came out to give me a hand, talked to her in Spanish, and she told him that someone had taken Josie. Floyd reasoned that she was assuming someone had taken her daughter. From what we could gather, Josie had left the house of her own free will, alone. I told him how we had gone through her bedroom and office but didn't come up with anything of interest. I directed his attention to the laptop computer and a small stack of papers on my desk. "That's about all we've got."

Cappy looked at the gathered *intel* and nodded, then locked his eyes back on mine. He must have known there was more, and he was the type of man who could look a confession out of a killer. Just watch and wait in silence until the poor bastard screamed he couldn't take it anymore and confessed all of his sins.

"We met with Maria Lopez—that's Lopes's informant—and she hadn't seen or heard from Josie either. The last time Maria saw Josie there was nothing unusual about her demeanor. I don't think there's anything there. It's really all I've got, Cap."

Now it was my turn to wait. After a long moment, Cappy said, "Give me your top three ideas on what might have happened."

I considered it briefly. "She was grabbed by the Mexican mafia because of the case with Lopes, she got bored over the weekend and went back up to Gorman to work on our case, or she was abducted by a serial killer as a random victim, caught off-guard somehow."

Cappy had pulled at his neatly groomed gray mustache while he listened, his eyes drilling into mine. He adjusted in his chair, uncrossing one leg and then crossing the other before he spoke. "All three of your scenarios involve crime. You don't think there could be any other explanation? She went to the mountains with a boyfriend and is out of cell phone range? Or sailed to Catalina and turned the phone off? You don't think there could have been an accident that we have yet to learn about, or one that maybe hasn't been discovered?"

I shrugged.

After a moment, he continued: "Okay, so tell me why none of your three scenarios is likely the case."

As I put the answer together in my head, I could see where Cappy was leading me, and I found myself again in awe of his talent as an investigator. The way he was working through this, absent any emotion, was no doubt the way he approached every case.

"I can't see the end game to the mob grabbing her. What good would it do them? Also, Josie is barely involved in that case, so it doesn't make sense."

"Unless they want to get at Lopes and would do so by grabbing his attractive and more vulnerable partner."

I considered it a moment.

Cappy said, "Next."

"What?"

"What about your Gorman theory, that maybe she went back up there? Show me the holes in that theory. Talk me out of it."

"She wouldn't go by herself," I said. "I mean, she's off training now, and she's a good investigator who is self-motivated, but I don't think she'd go up there on a fresh case without us talking it through. And if we did that, I would tell her not to go."

"Bingo. You'd tell her not to go. She knows that, so maybe she was bored, had some ideas about the case and wanted to check some things out that might help. You guys would meet up later to go up there and she'd be able to shine some light on a few things, showing you she is a self-starter and that she has good instincts."

"But that wouldn't be good instinct, Cap. That would be stupid on a case like this one."

He nodded.

I continued, "And if that's what she did, she shouldn't have been gone overnight."

"Unless there was an accident, or she had car trouble or something. That's the problem with being in those mountains; one thing goes wrong and it becomes a survival situation."

A long moment passed as I thought about that. *A survival situation.*

"And the serial killer abduction is just a far-fetched, made-for-television drama," I continued. "Josie is too smart and too tough to be abducted by a sexual deviant. That's the least of my worries."

Cappy didn't reply. His expression was blank, and for a moment I wondered where he went. Suddenly, he seemed to focus, and we were connected again. I said, "Well?"

"Throw out the impossible, brush aside the improbable, and usually what you have left—right there in front of you—is your answer. I'd agree on the stranger abduction being nearly impossible, so throw it out—for now. The Mexican mafia is your next most unlikely of the scenarios, but still a possibility. If it were me, I'd get back up on the mountain ASAP, and before you waste another minute thinking about it, you need to notify Gorman Station and have them start searching for any trace of her or her vehicle up there. Maybe get Lopes or someone from Prison Gangs to start working the mafia angle, just in case. That's my suggestion, but what do I know?"

I chuckled at the absurdity of that last part of his statement. Cappy smiled in return.

He rose from his chair and paused. "I'd also suggest you get ahold of your lieutenant ASAP and get him on board. You don't want to surprise the brass with something like this if things goes sideways."

"How do you know I haven't?"

He grinned. "Wells told us something was up when we made the relief last night. He said you were trying track her down but told him to keep a lid on it. He told us not to say anything."

"Of course he did," I said. "This place is worse than a hair salon."

Cappy nodded and began to walk away.

"Wait, what were you saying when you came over and I was still half asleep? Something about a voicemail."

He paused in thought. "Oh, that someone had called for her last night, right when we were making the relief. I transferred the call to her voicemail. It was before Wells told us about what was going on. In fact, that might have been why he said something, now that I think about it. He was standing there when I grabbed the phone, right at shift change."

"Who was it?"

"I don't know," Cappy said, "a woman with a Spanish accent."

He waited while I considered the information. It could have been her mother. It could have been anyone, and there was no sense in overthinking a call coming in. We got calls all the time, day and night. The daytime calls were usually other professionals; the middle-of-the-night calls were usually informants, witnesses, or the family members of victims, all of whom seemed to have very different schedules than the bulk of society.

"Okay, Cap, thank you. I appreciate your thoughts and insight on this."

He waved a hand as if to say it was nothing, then turned and walked away. My eyes drifted back to the screensaver displayed on Josie's computer to see her smiling face, Josie and another young, attractive woman. The photo showed their upper torsos in bikini tops, the two of them with their arms wrapped around each other at the beach.

9

When my lieutenant answered his cell phone I could hear the sounds of traffic and pictured him on the freeway, headed to the office in the darkness. Though I had no idea which freeway, because I didn't even know what city he lived in. I also had no idea what time he usually arrived at the office, because he was always there before me. Now I guessed that he was an early riser, a man who liked to beat the morning traffic into L.A.

"Sorry to bother you, Joe, but I have to bring you up to speed on a situation."

I spent five minutes briefing Lt. Joe Black on the details regarding Josie potentially being missing, just as I had done first with Floyd and then with Cappy. The more I told the story, the more Cappy's thoughts and ideas resonated. There was no guarantee that Gorman would be the right path, but for now it made sense. Cappy had broken it down and constructed a methodical way to address a situation that was a complete mystery with no clues and no obvious starting point. There was still a chance that nothing had happened to her at all, and if that was the case, we would find out soon enough. In the meantime, I had to play it as if one of the three nightmares would come true. After my talk with Cappy, I set my sights on Gorman but kept the mafia at the front of my mind.

When I finished briefing Lieutenant Black, he asked what course of action I had planned.

"Floyd is helping me on this, and I'm sure he'll be coming through the door any time now. My plan is for the two of us to be up on the mountain at first light, searching for her car. When I hang up with you, I'm calling Santa Clarita to see about getting a Gorman deputy up and heading into the woods ahead of us."

"Richard, I want you to also notify Major Crimes. They are the experts on kidnappings, and they have the resources with surveillance teams and the high-tech crew to do things that we just don't have time to deal with. Anyway, you know what I mean, you came from there. Get them involved and tell them I've authorized any overtime they might incur on it. I'll handle Captain Stover when he comes in; there's no sense in waking him up and starting his Monday off like that."

It was nearly five in the morning by the time I finished talking to Joe and notifying Lieutenant Michaels of Major Crimes. I then called Santa Clarita Station and asked how I could get in touch with a Gorman deputy. At first, I was told they would be in at seven, but after identifying myself and telling them I had a homicide case up on the mountain, I was told they would have one of the two resident deputies return my call. I provided my cell and waited in the dim light of the quiet office, staring at my partner's vacant desk.

Deputy Steve Kennedy called ten minutes later and at first seemed less than pleased with being awakened at this time of the morning. He told me he was the other resident deputy at Gorman, the partner of Charles Kramer who had called us out on our latest murder case. I told him a very short version of the situation with Josie, and he said he and Charlie would head up the mountain at first light, along with Bumper.

"Bumper Morgan?" I asked, citing the famous character in Wambaugh's best-selling novel, *The Blue Knight*.

"Bumper the Belgian Malinois. He's my four-legged partner who can track a tweaker across ten miles of mountainous terrain, find him, and chew the crotch out of his jeans, all without breaking a sweat or stopping to shit."

"I look forward to meeting you both," I said. "Oh, and Kennedy?"

"Yes sir."

"This stays on the mountain. Nothing official yet in your log, on the radio, or even to the brass at Santa Clarita. Got it?"

"No problem."

"Thank you very much."

"You're welcome, sir."

I glanced at my watch again. 5:15. In a couple of hours, the early birds would start filing in. The sea of desks—home to eighty investigators and their six lieutenants—would be bathed in fluorescent lighting. Computers would be switched on and the various tones of ringing phones would be interspersed with greetings and chatter, and the Los Angeles County Sheriff's Homicide Bureau would come to life investigating death.

Before I had called my lieutenant, I had sent a text to Floyd telling him to throw a suit in the car but show up in jeans and boots, that we were headed to the mountains. I wanted to get out of the office before the masses arrived.

Floyd arrived just as the coffee finished brewing, marching into the kitchen with purpose. "I was hoping you'd have a fresh pot ready."

I poured us each a cup. "You ready?"

"I was born ready, Dickie."

I looked past him toward a wall of windows that showed the first signs of light outside. "I want to get out of here before anyone shows up."

"What about search warrants? I thought you were going to write paper on the credit cards."

"Lieutenant Black said he'd see to it the search warrant was handled, agreeing we needed to get up to Gorman. He'd ask someone on the team to write it or let Metro deal with it. I told him I'd leave her laptop and the credit card statements on my desk for whoever he assigns it to. He'll brief the captain when he gets in and liaise with Metro."

"No shit, bringing our old team in to give us a hand, huh?"

"It was Joe's idea, and it makes sense. They've got all the cool shit."

Floyd sipped his coffee and started for the hallway with me on his heels. "Did I tell you I ran into Michaels a couple of weeks ago?"

"No, where?"

"I was at the tech crew to pick up a video they enhanced for me, so I stopped in at Metro to say hello. He asked if I was there to try to get my job back."

I chuckled. "We should do it. We never knew how good we had it there, especially working for him."

"Yes, we did know how good we had it, but your dumb ass just had to go to Homicide."

"You didn't have to follow me."

"What am I going to do, leave you unsupervised? Jesus, Dickie, that'd be a disaster."

I didn't respond. The truth of the matter was we'd been partners for a lot of years in several different assignments, and both of us had wanted to make it to Homicide. In our department, Homicide Bureau was an elite unit. Hundreds of solid cops apply to go there every year and only a few are selected. Some deputies apply year after year but never make the list. I liked to equate it to making the big leagues in baseball. It was something to be proud of, and it's where Floyd and I had been determined to work.

But it was also a daunting assignment and after a few years of doing it, the wear and tear would begin to show, with few exceptions. Cappy was an exception. He was one of the few who was blessed with the coolness of an island dweller. Most of us at Homicide were A-types who were wound too tightly to begin with, and the stresses of investigating murder would wear us down over the years. But here was Cappy, more than thirty in and not a hair out of place. Whatever it was about that man, they needed to figure it out and look for similar traits in future applicants. Or clone him.

We drifted across the empty parking lot under the yellow glow of high lamps that would soon flick off and rest quietly until nighttime came again, and headed toward the two sedans that sat backed into adjacent spots. I didn't know if other partners were that way, but Floyd and I took the partnership thing far beyond a working relationship; even our cars insisted on staying together. Which is why he was at the office in the predawn hours on his first day of vacation. I needed his help and didn't have to ask for it. We loaded up into my car and headed out.

My headlights washed across the wall of dark glass that was the back side of the bureau, and moments later I was accelerating up an onramp and heading north.

Floyd said, "Should we stop and grab breakfast to go?"

I glanced at him in the passenger seat and shrugged. "I'll stop if you want. My guts are a mess, to be honest about it. I'm not sure I could eat. Do you want me to stop?"

"It's okay. Let's just get up there and get to work."

We rode in silence against the flow of headlights heading south toward the city. I was doing eighty and there were few cars on our side of the freeway heading north. Usually I pitied the poor bastards stuck in that rut, the ones who day in and day out would spend an hour or more commuting each way to the routine of their predictable jobs. Today, I envied them. Surprises could be overrated.

LONG SHADOWS STREAKED ACROSS THE WEST SIDE OF INTERSTATE 5 against the mountains of sage and scrub brush. A few months ago, these hillsides would have been painted orange, yellow, and violet from the sprawl of California poppies, goldfields, and lupine. In another month they might be covered in snow. And yet we had not left Los Angeles County. Tall pines capped the mountaintops, reaching into the soft glow of the morning sky. As I glanced back and forth from there to the road, I kept thinking about Josie.

Had she run off the side of the mountain and spent the night braced against the cold? That would be a blessing compared to what I feared may have happened. If she were alive and on the mountaintop at all, that would prove that God watched over his children. But deep inside I felt a cold-ness, a certainty that told me we were headed in the wrong direction, that she wasn't up in the wilderness waiting to be rescued following a minor mishap. My gut told me Josie had encountered grave danger.

Pyramid Lake, a 180,000-acre reservoir fed by Piru Creek and supple-mented by the California Aqueduct, sits surrounded by the Angeles National and Los Padres National Forests. After passing it, we started through the stretch of highway known as the Tejon Pass, or *Portezuela de Cortes,* as it was known by the Spaniards. The mountain pass links Southern California with the San Joaquin Valley to the north. Whereas most travelers continued north through the snaky pass, we would veer off on the 138 before reaching Gorman and proceed to Three Points. From there we would leave the pavement and travel into the mountains on gravel roads that connected remote properties tucked in among the forest, some hidden from view and others chained off with posted warnings to keep out.

When we hit the gravel, Floyd said, "This place has *Tweakerville* written all over it."

He was looking out his window, taking in the sights.

"Right up here," I said, "me and Josie had a big rattler cross the road in front of us."

"Jesus, did you shoot it?"

I chuckled. "No. I didn't even run over it. Josie made me stop and wait while it crossed, glaring at us while it took its time about it."

"I would've run over that sonofabitch, and then I would've got out and shot it a few times too. I hate those bastards."

"Well, you better watch where you step then when we get out."

"I'm not getting out, Dickie. Not until you clear the area of all snakes."

As we climbed, we came to a hairpin corner with ruts and blots of mud caused by the runoff of a natural spring that trickled along the rocky draw of the canyon. We continued on, the gravel crunching beneath our tires as we continued to climb, the big V-8 under the hood groaning as it worked. "We need one of those broncos."

"Like O.J.'s?"

I glanced over. "No, dummy, like the cop cars they drive up here. Broncos or Blazers, whatever they are. Four-wheel drive cop cars. I'm going to tell Stover we need one."

"Good luck with that. How much farther?"

"Just a little way, I think. When we get to the top here, we should be able to see back down into these draws. Her red Taurus should be easy to spot, even if it went off the edge. I've been looking for fresh tracks and haven't seen anything."

"There were plenty of tracks across that muddy spot back there. We should've stopped and checked."

I shook my head. "I didn't see anything that looked like a car had gone through recently. There were truck tire tracks and some type of off-road deal, from what I saw. Probably the Gorman deputies in their Bronco; they were going to be up here at first light. Might have also been one of those side-by-side jobs; you see them all the time up in the hills now."

The Crown Vic had begun ticking under the hood during the final push to the top of the mountain, so when we leveled off, I shut it off and allowed it to rest while we took advantage of the view into the canyons below and south to where the vast land seemed to stretch as far as you could see. I had assured Floyd there were no snakes, so we walked from one spot to another and glassed our surroundings, sharing the one pair of binoculars that remained in my trunk with other gear.

"Lookit," Floyd said, passing the glasses back to me and pointing his finger to direct my gaze.

As I raised the binoculars to my face, I said, "What am I looking at?"

Floyd leaned into me and I could smell his cologne and his Copenhagen breath as he reinforced the direction with his finger. "There, that house."

I saw it, a cabin or log home tucked into the trees a mile or so from where we stood. I focused the glasses, zooming in and out until the view was as clear as it could be, and I saw movement outside of the structure and a small plume of smoke rising from the chimney. But there were several homes scattered throughout the mountains and we had seen the smoke from other chimneys on this cold mountain morning. "What is it I'm supposed to be seeing? Other than the house, that is."

Floyd pulled the binoculars away from me and put them up to his face again. "The red car beneath that carport, Dickie."

1 0

The mountain road took us away from the view of the cabin Floyd had spotted, and for a while, it felt as if we were getting farther away from it rather than closer to it. I had started to second-guess the direction we traveled, but Floyd argued there would be no other way to get there. "Stay the course, Dickie."

As is often the case on these mountain roads, soon we were driving north again and the sun was no longer in our eyes, but to the side and behind us, and it felt like we were headed in the right direction. Clouds of dust rose from beneath the car as we slowly crept along the rutted road. We seemed to still be gaining in elevation and I wondered if we would soon drop down on the other side. The cabin was below us, though it appeared to be farther into the mountain range than from where Floyd had first spotted it. I knew that we had been climbing steadily since we left that location and we would be far above it by now. I pictured a rough road going down and wondered if we would be able to drive in. Then I thought about the red car Floyd had spotted, and decided if it could make it in, so could we. From where we had seen it, we had been unable to identify its make or model, only that it was a red sedan. Front-wheel drive would allow a car to go places my Crown Vic, with its rear-wheel drive and heavy chassis, could not. It also occurred to me that we had no idea how long the car had been there. If it was Josie's car, it hadn't been there long. But if it wasn't Josie's car, it could be that the car had sat there for years, unable to drive out.

Finally, we leveled off at the top of the mountain and our road started to the left and began to drop in elevation. A quarter-mile farther and we came to a stop. The road was chained off and several signs were posted: KEEP OUT, TRESPASSERS WILL BE SHOT, TURN AROUND OR GET SHOT.

"Neighborly sort," I jested.

"Probably tweakers, dude. I bet they're running a meth lab down there and they've got it boobytrapped all the way down. That and cameras. These assholes take this shit seriously."

I wouldn't be deterred. "Ya think?"

"I'm telling you. That or growers. There's all kind of pot grows in these mountains, and those places are guarded by Columbian hitmen, cartel-hired killers," Floyd said, staring at me through his Ray-Bans.

I shut off the motor and popped my door open. "Let's have a look around."

"There's snakes."

"Come on, you pussy, let's go."

He grinned and stepped out of the car. "Pop the trunk."

I did and he reached in and retrieved my AR-15.

"For the snakes?"

"The *asesinos*."

I frowned.

"The hitmen, Dickie, Columbian drug dealers. *Los pinches asesinos, narcos*."

"Watch, they'll be Irish."

We both grinned and Floyd racked a round into the chamber of the rifle. "Let's go, Dickie. I'm Scottish, so I've got us covered either way with translation."

He was ready to go. We were both dressed in jeans and boots. He had worn his when he came back early this morning, and I had changed into mine at the office. I always kept spare clothes and boots in the trunk of my car because you never knew when your next case would be a body in a canyon or human remains found at a dump. With boots I knew we would be able to make the walk from the gate to the cabin below with no problem, even if the terrain worsened as we dropped into the clearing where it sat. We couldn't see it from where we stood at the gate, but there was no doubt that this road took us down there. The problem was not knowing what awaited us.

"Maybe we should get the Gorman deputies up here to assist us."

Floyd looked around, but there was nothing to see. "Where are they, anyway? I thought they were supposed to be up here this morning."

"The fork a couple miles back? They would have taken the turn to the right where we went left."

"Well why'd you take us the wrong way, Dickie?"

"Because you spotted the goddamn car, that's why. I knew we had to keep to the left to get back over this direction. I figured we'd drive up to that cabin and have a look around, see if it's Josie's car, and be done. Plain and simple. But nothing's ever that simple for us."

He seemed to consider it for a moment before responding. The quail were talking in the distance and the wings of a mourning dove whistled as she passed over our heads. When she did, a small bevy of dove flushed from nearby brush to join her, their wings clapping together as they gathered speed and pursued her. The noise had drawn us both to watch, but when they vanished in the sky, we faced one another again.

"Well," Floyd started, "We could go back to your murder scene and see if we cross paths with the resident deputies, and then come back. We could go for a little hike and see how it looks down there, and then decide about what to do. Or, we can say the hell with it, ram the gate, and head down the mountain, guns a-blazing. I vote the latter."

The quail seemed closer and I pictured them walking through the brush toward us. I wondered if they were California quail or Mountain quail. I didn't know if you could find both up here or not. The California quail were more common than the larger Mountain variety, and though I had hunted the latter a few times in life, I had never seen one. It would be just my luck that a covey of Mountain quail would walk out of the brush and over the top of our car as we stood here armed for *banditos* and *narcos,* but not quail.

"I like your second option, work down a little way on foot and see what we can learn before committing to anything. We can always hike back out and call for help, or go back and find those deputies, as long as you don't get us in over our heads with your cowboy shit."

"*My* cowboy shit?"

"Let's go," I said, and started down the road in front of him. I stepped over the chain with its warning signs hanging to deter the less determined.

Floyd said, "And watch out for snakes, Dickie."

We walked for nearly a mile winding east and west and gradually north as we gave up elevation and descended into the shadows of the mountaintop behind us. Neither of us spoke, even when we would stop briefly to assess what lay ahead and to catch our breath. Though it was mostly downhill and level, we had walked briskly against the coolness of the morning, both of us eager to have a closer look at the cabin in question and the red car Floyd had spotted. The road had turned, and we were walking to the east when the sun peeked over the mountaintop and shone in our eyes. I pulled my ball cap lower in an effort to block its glare, but it seemed to be on an even plane with my vision and there was nothing I could do about it.

Floyd started, "Goddam sun—" just as a rifle shot pierced the stillness.

Floyd un-shouldered the AR and squatted as I grabbed my Glock from its holster and stepped off of the road into some brush. It had come from the east where we were blinded by the sun, though it didn't seem to be directed at us. We both had been shot at before and we knew the difference between someone shooting and someone shooting at us. Following the barrel of his rifle, Floyd inched closer to the side of the road until he too was in the brush, but on the other side of the road from me. I was along the side of the mountain that had been cut through many years before to build the road we traveled; Floyd was on the downward side where one slip could send him sliding down the mountain. I watched as he continued and thought to warn him about snakes in the brush but decided not to. I moved forward as well, staying on my side of the road but keeping pace with Floyd. It was slow moving, and the morning was once again silent. After moving about twenty feet, he stopped and dropped even lower, and then turned to make eye contact with me. I nodded, and he motioned me to his location.

I looked into the sun once again and realized it was no use, there was no way to see in that direction. So I squatted as low as I could and hurried alongside Floyd. When I stopped, I was out of breath. Floyd pointed toward the woods below.

"What?" I said, panting quietly.

"Use your glasses," he whispered, nodding toward the binoculars that hung around my neck, "and tell me what you see through there." He again pointed with his finger.

The enhanced view bounced around as I continued trying to catch my breath. As I settled, I saw movement below in the area where Floyd had pointed. I took a deep breath and held it in order to steady my sight, as if I were looking through a scope and preparing to take a long shot. That was when I saw the man with the rifle walking casually through a clearing below us. I could just make out part of the cabin we had seen before where the red car sat parked beneath a shelter.

I lowered the glasses and removed the strap from around my neck, handing the binoculars to Floyd. "Dude with a rifle but he's walking pretty casually. Doesn't look too excited."

Gazing through the glasses, Floyd sat focused and still.

At a whisper, I continued, "Maybe he shot a coyote, or a bobcat, some other creature he spotted from his kitchen window."

Floyd continued glassing silently.

"Or maybe he sent a warning shot after hearing our car," I added.

Floyd seemed to be leaning into the glasses. I could see the wrinkles at the corner of his eye and knew he was squinting into the lenses, trying to get closer to whatever it was he saw.

"Maybe," I said, after thinking it through for a moment, "it wasn't even that guy who fired the shot. These people probably carry guns everywhere they go up here. All of them."

He finally spoke, still looking through the glass. "It wasn't him. There's someone else with a rifle out there."

I grimaced. "How do you know?"

He lowered the glasses and turned to look at me. "Because that guy's carrying a shotgun, not a rifle."

"You're sure?"

"I'm sure, Dickie." He handed me the glasses. "Have a look."

I put the binoculars to my eyes and looked for the man with the rifle— or shotgun, if Floyd was right—but I couldn't find him. "Where'd he go?"

"He was headed for the cabin the last I saw him. He was probably out for a morning quail hunt."

"Dove. It's not quail season yet. September is dove season."

"I know that, asshole. But do you think these tweakers up here care about seasons?"

"Wait a minute!"

"What?"

I handed the glasses back to him. "There's our man with the rifle. Two-hundred yards to the east, dude on a four-wheeler with a rifle slung over his shoulder."

Just then I could hear the four-wheeler's engine and it occurred to me I hadn't heard it before. "Where'd he come from? How come we didn't hear it until just now?"

I could see Floyd raise the glasses above the line of sight to the man on the four-wheeler, and then he panned farther east. "I think he came over that hill, Dickie. That's why."

"It's a rifle though, right?"

"Yeah, this time it's a rifle. I can see the scope from here." Floyd lowered the glasses. "We need to move farther down. The four-wheeler's gone now too. Everything is concealed behind that tree line, and we're not going to see anything from this angle."

He was right about not being able to see much from where we were, but I didn't know that I agreed we should go farther in. We had now seen a man with a shotgun and another man with a rifle on a four-wheeler. But this was the time to do one or the other, go in or retreat. I hated to retreat, not having had the chance to see that red car better. But I hated going in, picturing the chain and warning signs stretched across the road, the ones we had stepped over and disregarded.

"Okay, let's go," I said.

But as we stood up, a voice from close behind us bellowed, "Hold it right there!"

We were on private property and a man had a right to defend his land. Floyd and I were likely on the same page, because neither of us spun and engaged the owner of the voice, assuming by his command he would be armed. It would be best to talk our way through this. After all, he had had the jump on us, yet we had not been shot. I didn't look back as I raised my arms slightly from my sides, the gun still in my hand. "We're cops," I said. "Los Angeles County Sheriff's Homicide."

"Sorry, detective, I didn't recognize you in your jeans and ball cap."

The voice was calm now, almost quiet. I turned to see Deputy Charles Kramer holstering his pistol. Another deputy stood next to him holding an AR-15, watching us through mirrored, wire-rimmed sunglasses, a blank expression on his face. I holstered my pistol and Floyd turned slowly, careful to keep the barrel of his AR pointed down.

"No problem, guys," I said while stepping toward the two of them. Both were dressed in Class B uniforms, green pants beneath tan uniform shirts with soft badges and name tags sewn into place replacing the metal ones. These were the uniforms worn by deputies assigned to custody facilities, many training bureaus, and outposts like Gorman or Catalina where the daily demands of their duties were very different than those of the inner-city uniformed deputies. It was the same reason Floyd and I were dressed in jeans and boots today. I stepped forward and shook Kramer's hand, and then offered my outstretched hand to his partner while introducing myself.

Kramer said, "This is my partner, Steve Kennedy."

"Ah, I spoke with you on the phone in the middle of the night. Nice to meet you."

Greetings and introductions were made and then I got to the part that had been nagging me since the moment I turned around. "Didn't you guys recognize that Crown Vic back there as a cop car?"

Kennedy said, "Yeah, as a matter of fact, we did. That's why we started down the road on foot, to save your asses."

I frowned and looked to Kramer. "This property is owned by a kook named Johnny Watkins. He's a survivalist with a military background and he has a following. There's probably a dozen families—or whatever you'd call them—living here, spread around the property in cabins and trailers," Kramer said, waving his arm from west to east to indicate a wide swath of land. "They are all armed and they train for the day they have to fight the government."

"How big's the property?" Floyd asked.

"About two-hundred acres or so," Kramer continued. "We call it the dickwad compound. 'Cause Johnny Watkins is about a dickwad. Johnny Wad." He grinned after he said it.

"So that's why you thought you'd have to save us, huh, 'cause Johnny Wad and his commandos don't like visitors?" I said.

Kennedy nodded. "These guys are assholes, sir; I can tell you that. If they spot you on their property, they'll take a shot at you. I guarantee it."

Floyd said, "Well I say we go introduce ourselves; I'm dying to meet these assholes."

"Plus, there's a red sedan parked down there under some type of shelter. We couldn't get a good look at it, but as I mentioned on the phone this morning, my partner, Josie, drives a red Ford Taurus."

Kramer shook his head. "I know the car you're talking about. It's right next to the main cabin under a makeshift carport deal. It's Johnny's old lady's Buick, been parked there for years. I don't think it runs, not even sure it has a motor in it. Besides, I can't imagine your partner would end up down there for any reason, even if she made the wrong turn and found that gate," he said, nodding up the road, the direction from which each of us had walked. "I'd say you might be stirring a hornet's nest that doesn't need to be stirred."

Floyd grunted. "Sounds to me like it does need to be stirred."

"The problem with this place is these guys will die for their cause, and they are also very vocal and aggressive in the local political and legal arenas. They've got an attorney who shows up every time something goes down out here, must have him on retainer and speed dial."

The mention of speed dial gave me a thought, and I pulled my phone out of my pocket and checked for a signal. There was none.

Kramer said, "You won't get a signal here. Try up there on the top of that peak." He had turned and looked at the highest peak that was southwest of where we stood.

"So, you don't think we should check this place." It was a statement, not a question.

Kramer shook his head and Kennedy said, "Not unless we have damn good cause or a warrant. Maybe a SWAT team."

Floyd said, "I am a SWAT team."

The two uniformed deputies turned and began moving up the road we had come down, a gesture for us to follow. We did. Both Kramer and Kennedy were lean and fit, and it occurred to me they probably walked these mountains often, searching for lost hunters or hikers, or sneaking in on meth labs or pot grows. The mountains were full of loonies and it would be a dangerous place to be a cop. I, personally, felt much more comfortable in Compton.

Kennedy glanced over his shoulder to make sure we were behind him before he began with a story. "Johnny Wad has a son, a little shithead named after his father but goes by 'Junior'. We call him Junior Wad or Little Wad. It's not often you find these assholes off of the wad pound."

He said, "Anyway, Junior was out poaching deer and a neighbor had called it in. I catch him, and because he's an asshole, I take him in rather than citing him. He didn't have any identification with him, so that means I can *take him before a magistrate* rather than issuing a citation. So, I hook him up and he's pissed. I tell him, 'Unlucky day to be caught off of the wad pound.' He doesn't know what the hell I'm talking about, but I have a good laugh about it."

We all stopped to catch our wind at a hairpin corner with a view of the two-hundred plus acres of compound below us. Kramer started smiling as Kennedy grinned and continued with his story. "You guys might not know this, but we cover Pyramid Lake also. In the summertime, there's boat deputies assigned there full time, but we end up going there fairly regular to back them up or transport arrestees to the station for them. You can imagine the shit they deal with in the summer at the lake, and on the infamous Vaquero Beach."

"Cowboy beach, huh?" Floyd said, making sure I knew the translation.

Kennedy nodded. "Well I'm coming off the mountain here with Junior Wad in my back seat, and I'm driving my Bronco—you'll see it when we get up the hill here. There's no cage in it, and I usually have my dog, Bumper, with me, but I didn't have him that day for some reason."

"Do you have him today?"

"Yeah, he's waiting in the truck. The window's down and if I call him —" Kennedy tapped at a whistle that hung around his neck by a lanyard "—he'll dive out the window and come to save the day. The dog is badass. Ever since we had a deputy killed in the station, Gorman has been a canine assignment. We all have dogs."

"That's the deputy who was killed by the ding, and his wife locked the guy up?"

"Yeah, that's the one. Schaeffer. Back then we'd book prisoners at the substation which is also where we lived, for free. That was one of the perks. But since that happened, we don't take prisoners there; they go to Santa Clarita."

"That's crazy," Floyd said.

Kennedy turned to continue hiking back toward the gate where our vehicles awaited us, and we followed, waiting for the rest of the story.

"So anyway, I'm coming off the mountain when I hear a call about someone drowning at Pyramid. I haul ass down there, code three. Junior's in the back seat having the time of his life like he's in a *Dukes of Hazard* episode. I get there and it was a Forest Service guy who had called it in, just a regular dude who goes around and checks forest properties and stuff, not a cop. They drive those green pickup trucks but there's no lights or sirens or any other police equipment on them. Maybe a spotlight. I pull up next to the ugly green truck and see a hundred feet offshore there's a couple people splashing around. I figure one of them is the forestry guy who had probably swam out to save someone, not knowing that will usually get you killed. Well, he's not far from the dock, so I grab a hundred-foot climbing rope out of the back of my Bronco and run out to the end of the dock, throw some rope out there and help drag the two of them in. I get them up on the dock and start CPR on the drowning victim, a teenage boy. The forestry guy is on his back, ready to die from exhaustion. The boy starts breathing again and the forestry guy has mostly recovered and is sitting up, and suddenly he points back to where I had parked and said, 'Who's driving away in your rig?' I look over, and sure enough, it's going down the road. I'm like, 'Oh shit!'

"I run to where I had parked my Bronco and see it fading away. I'm in full panic mode now. I jump into the Forest Service truck, fire it up—thankfully the guy had left his keys in it—and haul ass. Obviously, I had left my keys in the Bronco too. We're used to doing that, especially with the dogs. We leave the trucks running and the air conditioner going, and at least one window halfway down so the dog can get out if we need him. Anyway, this skinny little asshole Junior Wad had slipped his cuffed hands from behind his back to his front. Since there's no cage in the rig, he just climbed in to the driver's seat and took off.

"Now I'm in pursuit of my sheriff's patrol vehicle, driving a stolen green forestry truck. I'm hauling ass down the Five thinking, is this really happening? I put it out on the dude's radio what's going on and tell them to patch me in with Santa Clarita. Now Junior is about to Castaic and he's headed south. All I can think about is that this asshole is headed into the city with a police vehicle. My AR-15 rifle is in there, his rifle that he had been hunting with is in the rig, and who knows how this is going to end, right? Plus, I know these assholes are all anti-government survivalist types, so he's a ticking time bomb to begin with."

Our vehicles were in sight, but we stopped again to catch our breaths and hear the end of the story.

"I drove alongside him and rammed him with the green beast I had stolen from the forestry guy. Here I am, ramming my own police vehicle that this handcuffed asshole is driving. Every time he looks over, he's smiling, and I get more pissed off. So, I think, well, he is a fleeing felon

62

now, having stolen my cop car, and he is clearly a danger to society, so I better not let him keep going into the city. I've got to stop him."

I looked over to see Floyd grinning. We both knew where this was going, though I had never heard about the incident.

"You shot him," I said.

"I tried like hell. See, he sped up and was ahead of me after I rammed him. I'm left-handed, so I stuck my revolver out the window and began shooting across the hood of the truck I'm driving, and into the back of my Bronco. It was the weirdest thing I have ever done or experienced. In fact, I wasn't even sure it was all real. But I empty my gun into the truck, and I see that I hit it a couple of times. One of the bullets went through the rear window.

"Now we're doing about ninety miles an hour and we're almost to Santa Clarita. I'm reloading my gun with one hand while steering with the other. The traffic is getting heavy and I'm thinking I've got to put an end to this. I floor it, and this piece of shit pickup I'm driving is rattling and shaking and I think it's going to blow up or fall apart on me. I get up next to my Bronco and Little Wad is still looking at me, but he ain't smiling anymore now that I've thrown lead at him. I raise my gun and start shooting through the passenger window and into the driver's door and window of my Bronco. I can see bullets hitting the door. The dipshit ducks down, and I'm not sure if he's hit or not. But suddenly, he pulls over and stops."

"Did you get him?" I asked.

"Not even once. But apparently, he didn't like me shooting at him and decided it was time to quit. By now there were several cars that had joined the pursuit, sheriffs and CHP. We get him out, put his hands back behind his back where they belonged, and tie a hobble around his feet and attach it to the handcuffs for the ride to town."

"Damn good shooting," Floyd said.

"My captain didn't think so."

"Yeah, well, fuck him. That took balls to do what you did."

Kennedy smiled and nodded. "I had trained down in South Los Angeles, Lennox Station, and I hadn't ever been in a shooting. Nearly twenty years on the job when this deal with Junior happened, and I was like, this is crazy. Want to know what's even crazier?"

"Let's hear it," I said.

"Six months later I get into another shooting and kill a guy. Walked in on a grow and two or three Mexicans start runnin' and gunnin'. I dropped one of the dudes and we ended up catching the rest. The Grow Team came in and recovered about five-hundred marijuana plants and a hundred-thousand dollars' worth of equipment. How they get all that shit back into the mountains, I have no idea. But there's more of that up here than you'd care to know about."

Suddenly we were all silent. My mind immediately had gone back to Josie. The idea that maybe she had come into a pot grow somewhere in these woods rattled around for a moment and stirred a level of distress inside me.

The four of us trudged back to our vehicles, my gray Crown Vic sitting at the gate, covered in dust, and a black and white Ford Bronco with a light bar on the top parked behind it. I could see the head of a dog moving around inside, peering through the windshield, and I could hear his high-pitched whine.

"Looks like they fixed your truck up for you," I said, looking the Bronco over but not seeing any bullet holes or broken glass.

"Oh, that deal happened several years ago. This isn't even the same rig I had back then."

"Whatever became of Junior?"

"That's why we were sneaking down the road behind you. He's out. He did eighteen months at Tehachapi and rejoined the movement, invigorated. Word came back that he'd joined up with the white pride crowd in the joint, tattooed some swastikas and bolts and shit on his body, and now he thinks he's a real badass and a soldier in the fight against a repressive government. He has adapted the ideology of the 'freemen'."

"The freemen?"

"Yeah, it's a movement, militant types who believe no laws apply to them, that there is no governing authority over them. They believe in something they call 'common law', whatever that might be. The bottom line is these assholes in the Wad Pound are a lawless bunch looking for a fight with the Man."

I thought about that for a moment. "Well, they might get one. I won't be deterred by any hillbillies up here while I'm investigating a murder and looking for my partner. Right, Floyd?"

"Damn straight," Floyd said. He had a foot propped on the bumper of my car and the AR resting on his knee. "Now, what's the plan? I say we go down there and stir up some shit."

I looked at Kramer. "Did you guys go back to the crime scene?"

"We drove down the road where you'd stop and walk out to that tree where your guy was killed, but no, we didn't walk out there. We've just been trying to cover all of the roads up here, looking for your partner's red Taurus."

"Let's go back up there. I'd like to see the crime scene again, have Floyd see it, and then maybe expand our perimeter search of that area. Make sure there are no pot grows or meth labs nearby. The more I'm up here, the more I realize that murder could be about a number of things, not just the fact that my victim was a child molester."

There were nods of agreement and we filed to our respective vehicles. The Bronco backed twenty yards and flipped a U. I followed in the dust and did the same. We would trail them to my latest crime scene and have another look with fresh eyes. I wanted Floyd's perspective and thoughts. He tended to think outside the box because his mind worked differently than most others'.

Floyd and I were scanning the landscape as we crept along the bumpy road, trailing the Bronco by a considerable distance to avoid being smoked out by the truck in front of us. After a few minutes of riding in silence, Floyd said, "I'm starting to get a bad feeling about all of this."

"Yeah, right? Like she's not out on an island or up in a cabin with a lumberjack?"

He nodded. "Yeah, that and also your murder. This place is full of assholes, and you need to be careful coming back up here to work your case. If it was me, I'd add a nice rifle to the trunk, something with a scope and long-range capabilities. I'd also never come up here alone, and I'd make sure these boys from Gorman knew where you planned to be every time you came up the hill. They seem like some solid dudes."

When we reached the fork in the road, we took the left that would lead us to the area where the murder had occurred. It was a sharp turn from the direction we traveled, and the Bronco was nowhere in sight.

Floyd asked, "Are you sure that's the right direction? Where'd the cops go?"

"This is it. They're quite a way ahead of us, I think."

The road began to curve to the right and drop in elevation, and then it straightened. The Bronco stood parked in the roadway, an eighth of a mile ahead of us, its occupants nowhere in sight.

Floyd said, "Is that where the murder scene is?"

"No," I said, puzzled at what I was seeing. I accelerated and came up behind it, a cloud of dust rolling over us as we stopped. I looked left and right. "Where the hell did they go?"

1 2

Bumper the Malinois had his head out the driver's window, looking into the woods and whining. I noticed he wore a bark collar, and I realized that was the reason he would whine but not bark. He had a worried expression on his handsome face, golden brown and black with pointed ears. Bumper glanced in our direction and then refocused toward the woods that were perpendicular to the Bronco. Floyd and I quickly exited our vehicle, guns drawn, and started in the direction Bumper watched.

We had moved fifty feet from our position behind the Bronco and had just penetrated the tree line when we spotted Kennedy and Kramer. The two mountain deputies were standing to the side of a worn path, a game trail of sorts, and both were looking down at the earth. I called out to announce our approach, and both glanced our direction in response. Kennedy nodded and motioned for us to come on down the trail. When we arrived at their location, he pointed to an obvious blood trail along the path. "We had a wounded deer run across the road in front of us and into these woods. Looked to us like he'd been shot."

"The rifle shot," Floyd said, turning and looking back up the trail we had come down. He pointed in that direction. "Is that the direction of the dickwad compound? I'm all turned around."

Kramer stepped a few feet farther down the trail and squatted to study the ground.

"If you followed this trail back, past our vehicles and up and over that mountain, it would put you back in the general area of where you had parked at that gate, the Watkins's place," Kennedy answered.

Kramer said, "Lung shot."

The three of us went to him and crowded around the spot he studied on the trail. He was pointing at a larger volume of blood than the previous spots he had shown us as he said, "One lung, not two."

Every homicide detective knew that bubbles in the blood were indicative of a lung shot, but how Kramer was so certain that only one lung had been hit on the deer intrigued me. "Why do you think?"

"See how this blood is almost pink?"

"Yeah—"

"That color, and the bubbling, indicates he was hit in the lung."

"Right, but how do you know it wasn't both lungs?"

Kramer stood and looked past me, back up the trail behind us. "To hit both lungs you've got to make a ten-ring shot, and lots of times, that means you're taking out the heart too. Right through the entire boiler room. The deer don't go far after taking a hit like that. So my guess is, the deer was quartered to the shooter, and the shot hit just one lung and was probably a through-and-through. Either way," he said, now stooping back down to study the blood, "take out a lung, you can color him dead. It's just a matter of time and distance before he drops."

Floyd squatted next to Kramer to study the small volume of pinkish, bubbly blood. "Neither pink nor red, the color dead."

Kramer stood up and looked farther down the trail. "My guess is he's probably not far. Another hundred yards at the most."

"Was it a buck?" Floyd asked.

Kennedy said, "Yeah, a little forked horn buck. He was young."

I shook my head. "Poaching. Killing out of season and obviously without a license or tag."

"No doubt," Kramer said. He looked back the direction we had come again. "You'd think Junior would have learned his lesson about that."

"Think it was him?" I asked.

"Good chance of it. Him or someone else down there."

"Either way," I said, "it gets us on the property, right?"

"That's what I was thinking," Kramer said. "Come on, let's go find that deer for our evidence."

Kramer turned and walked slowly down the trail, studying the ground with every step. We followed, allowing distance between us, careful to walk slowly on the uneven mountain trail that had been built by the hooves of cattle and deer over many years of traveling the same routes between their food sources and water holes and bedding sites. The silence of the woods allowed every footfall to be heard, so we stepped carefully to avoid branches, twigs, and dry vegetation. A chipmunk scurried from a nearby tree, causing me to grab the grip of my gun. Floyd grinned, and we paused to watch the little rodent, a gray squirrel-looking creature with small black and white stripes and attentive, buggy eyes. He jumped onto a log and stopped, sat up on his haunches and watched us while he nervously munched on something he had gathered.

I whispered, "Little bastard scared me."

"That's how you get shot," Floyd said, addressing the small creature.

Kramer said, "Right here."

I turned to see Kramer and Kennedy both moving briskly and care-lessly away from the trail into a thick stand of chaparral.

"I think they found our deer."

Floyd brushed past me and started in their direction. "Well, come on, Dickie."

A young buck with small antlers that forked on each side—giving him a total of four points, not including the brow tines—lay amongst the shrubs. His eyes were fixed toward the treetops above us, and his tongue hung from his open mouth, thick, pink, frothy blood oozing from it.

Kramer, carrying an AR-15, approached the downed animal from its backside, and poked at its hindquarters with the tip of his rifle barrel. The deer had no reaction. "He's dead."

He was a beautiful creature, I thought, gazing at the young buck before us. I had no issue with legal hunting by those who chose wild game as part of their sustenance. But needless killing bothered me greatly, and I found myself looking forward to a confrontation with the Wad family. Watkins. Big Johnny Wad and his little offspring shithead, one of whom had prob-ably killed the deer. It was unlikely this clan had anything to do with—or any knowledge of—my missing partner, but at that moment, I didn't care. The backwoods, anti-government, lawless clan of misfits had suddenly become my enemy.

Maybe I was just wanting to pick a fight with anyone in order to distract myself from the reality of the task at hand. I had to consider that, though I argued to myself that regardless of the situation with Josie, I also had a murder investigation on this mountain, and it seemed to me I was already becoming acquainted with the dynamics of this off-the-grid community of which our victim had been a part. Someone on this mountain had killed him; of that I was fairly certain. Now we had a reason to go onto the Watkins compound with legal authority, which meant that if we ended up having to kill a bunch of dickwads, we'd be justified in doing so. They could put a chain across the road and threaten violence, but if they were to act on those threats against lawmen, they had a battle coming. I was in just the right frame of mind for a good old-fashioned shooting feud, and I knew that Floyd would be with me on that.

"These bastards."

Floyd looked me in the eyes. "I know what you're thinking."

"What?"

"Same as me."

I nodded.

Kramer said, "You boys ever gut a deer?"

"I have," I spoke out.

"I've seen it done," Floyd added.

"Well, we're gonna gut this one and then drag it back to our rig. It'll be a lot lighter without the guts and it won't rot as fast. We'll head up to that mountaintop over there," he said, pointing toward a peak we couldn't see, "Liebre Mountain, and I'll radio for Fish and Game to come out. We don't need a warrant to go onto private property when investigating game violations. We'll bring Fish and Game out though just to make it official, plus they can deal with Bucky."

"What will they do with him?" I asked.

"Used to be," Kramer started, "they could have the meat processed and provide it to shelters that help the needy. But like everything else, the bureaucrats fucked that up, saying it wasn't safe. I'd guess the hungry would have another opinion about that, but you know these elected officials are smarter than the rest of us."

"Yeah, they're doing a great job up in Sacramento running our lives," I said.

"It almost makes you understand how these people up here go off the grid," Kennedy said. "I mean, I don't agree with the lawlessness of it—obviously—but the idea that we are over-governed, and that we don't need politicians controlling all aspects of our lives, resonates with me. I'll be honest, that idea resonates with a lot of people up here on the mountain, even the most law-abiding among them. It's why they're here."

"There's a line though," I said, "and it's there to keep our society civil. I'm just not sure some of these people get that."

Kennedy started his work on the deer by inserting a knife beneath the skin at the bottom of its belly and carefully running it up toward the sternum, opening him up. It made me think of autopsies, and it spurred a thought. "Hey, in the event you are wrong, and it's not a through-and-through wound, let's try to recover that round. Maybe it came from the same gun that killed the rapist."

Kennedy looked up from his work, a fixed blade knife covered in blood held in a bloody hand. "You bet. Hey, Charlie, come grab that hindquarter and hold his legs open for me."

Kramer stepped over and grabbed a hoof and pulled it perpendicular to the deer. The back half of the deer was now twisted ninety degrees from the front half, and its blood-smeared white belly was exposed, opened by the cut of a knife. Kennedy held the bloody knife with his teeth and used both hands to reach into the cavity and remove the buck's innards. Kramer stepped out of the way as the guts spilled out of the deer, though he held onto the leg as instructed. Kennedy pulled the gut pile away from the deer, took the knife from his mouth and wiped it on his pants. "This is why we only wear Class B's on the mountain."

He flopped the deer open and stuck his finger in a hole that had torn through the rib cage and hide of the deer. "There's your exit wound, Detective. I don't think you're going to recover a projectile."

"Through and through and probably still going," I said. Kramer frowned at me, unsure if I was serious.

The two lean mountain deputies each grabbed an antler without any discussion about it and took off toward the truck, dragging the deer behind them. Floyd and I followed.

"I guess you boys don't need any help?" Floyd jested.

Kennedy called back over his shoulder. "We've got this one, Detective. You guys can drag out the next dead body we come across."

"Jesus," I said, "let's hope not."

At the top of the mountain Kramer radioed for a game warden and was given an ETA of two hours. Kennedy washed up at the back of the Bronco using water from a large orange water cooler and drying his hands and arms with a towel. The back of his rig was packed with tools of the trade that only deputies at faraway outposts would think to carry: hundreds of feet of rope, carabiners, and harnesses for climbing and rappelling. There were shovels, axes, and a chainsaw. When asked about the latter, Kennedy explained that when you're on mountain roads, it's not uncommon to come across a road blockage from a fallen tree. It's easier to move it in pieces. There were several water containers, blankets, ammunition containers, green parkas with sheriff's department insignia, extra boots, and several duffle bags that Kennedy said contained everything from extra clothing to fire-starting materials and survival gear. There was a large box with the word MEDIC boldly written in red.

"That's a hell of a first-aid kit," I said.

Kennedy smiled as he finished repacking the back of his vehicle. "That's because it's a paramedic's kit, not a first-aid kit."

"What's the difference?" Floyd asked, stepping closer. "Can I have a look?"

I moved closer as Kennedy opened his kit to show him. Nearly every-thing was contained in sterile packaging, the type of containers we would often have to account for in our crime scene documentation, generally referred to as paramedic debris: gloves, forceps, IV tubes, suture kits, chest tubes, and an intubation kit. There were bottles of iodine and alco-hol, a tourniquet, a blood pressure cuff, a stethoscope, and a clear bag marked NaCl 0.9%. I pointed to the bag. "Morphine?"

He chuckled. "I wish. Nope, sodium chloride. Saline. It's used for hydration, fluid maintenance. Keeping the veins opened up."

"Damn," I said, "this is serious shit. You guys are trained to use all of it?"

Kennedy nodded. "We're all EMT trained up here on the mountain. I'm also a paramedic."

"No shit, huh?"

"Yep. I put myself through paramedic school after seeing how long it can take to get help up here. We see a lot of death, believe it or not. Mostly accidental or recreational death, and some suicides. Not too many murders, but a lot of death nonetheless. Sometimes death happens even while we're trying our best to prevent it. We can only do so much though, trying to keep people alive long enough to be life-flighted off the mountain. You never get used to watching them die. I know you guys see death every day, but I'd rather see them dead than watch them die."

I nodded, somberly. Floyd said, "You guys might've been able to save Bucky, if you'd brought this kit down the trail."

It was cop humor exacted with purpose, a mechanism we all adapted to keep sane. Relatively speaking, that is. Kennedy grinned. "I'm not that good, partner."

A helicopter crested the peak and we all looked up, using our hands to shield our eyes from the mid-morning sun. "That's interesting," I said.

Kennedy said, "Not really. That's sixty-nine adam, our airship out of Santa Clarita."

"Ah, yes," Floyd said, "I've had a ride in that bird. Scary shit the way it takes off and lands on the station's roof."

"Those are sweet little birds," Kramer chimed in, "AStar 350. That bird replaced the old Hughes 500, a loud, uncomfortable rattletrap. It was like a jeep and these AStars are like Porsches. They'll do a hundred and twenty with all the cop shit weighing it down, a buck-thirty stripped. Those spotlights weigh a ton. Those there are air-conditioned, they can carry seven people, and you can get a good three hours of flight time off a tank of fuel. That's pretty handy for these parts."

"Anyway," Kennedy continued, "they cover our asses out here a lot. I'm sure, but they might be out here in response to my request for a game warden. I put out our location, Liebre Mountain, so they would have known we were on the peak and they could come by and spot us."

"Hare Mountain," Floyd said. "Rabbits everywhere, apparently. At least at some point in history."

I shrugged. "Yeah, haven't seen one. That's what it means though, huh?"

Floyd nodded.

Kennedy said, "I never knew that. Never would have guessed. Don't see a lot of bunnies up here."

Kramer moved closer to the truck and gestured toward the bird with his hand. "I better grab a handheld in case they have something to say."

The bird whooshed over our heads and then banked hard to come back by, its rotors straining to chop through the sky. After it completed its turn, the nose of the bird dipped, and a whirling noise replaced the sounds of chopping. It slowed as it came overhead, sat for a moment, and then dipped hard to the left and raced away.

"What the hell are they doing?" Floyd asked.

"Showing off, mostly," Kennedy said. "Kramer probably picked them up on the radio and told them we had a couple of hours before the game warden would be here. They'll go somewhere and come back then, if they're able."

Kramer was back at our sides, a radio in his hand. "They'll be back," he said.

The mid-morning sun warmed my back and shoulders and I turned to glance at the bird again as it shrank against the horizon. "Well, I don't know about you guys, but I can't stand here under the sun for two hours."

"We can move down a bit and find a shady spot to park," Kennedy suggested.

I glanced at Floyd. "I say we go look at that crime scene while we wait. That's what we had planned to do before the deer hunting adventure diverted us."

Floyd shrugged. "Why not."

"Well, we probably shouldn't drive around too much with the goddam deer tied to the hood of our truck, cooking," Kennedy said. "I think we'll shade up and meet you guys back here in two hours."

"Sounds like a plan," I said, and started for the driver's door of the dusty Crown Vic.

Kramer called out, "You need to trade in that Crown Vic for a four-wheel drive, Detective."

I smiled and waved, and Floyd and I loaded up and started back down the hill.

L ittle evidence showing that a murder had occurred at this location. Four days earlier, we had collected the victim's remains and a rifle that leaned against the same tree where he had stood at the time of his death. It was a Winchester Model 70, and it did not appear to have been fired; its chamber was empty and appeared to have been recently cleaned. The only odor I had detected was that of lubricants. We had found the attached magazine to be loaded with four .30-06 cartridges, a common caliber used for deer hunting, causing us to wonder if the victim had been poaching—hunting deer out of season. All that remained was the hole I had carved in the tree to recover the projectile that had passed through the child molester's chest, and a few stains of red along the bark and in the dirt at the base of the tree.

After taking it all in, I turned to Floyd. "Well, here it is."

He looked around with an expression that told me he was likely thinking there wasn't much to see. He turned his attention to the tree and seemed to study the bullet hole, the bark below it, and the stains at the bottom. "Execution."

"Why do you say that?"

"He was up against the tree, no?"

"He was against it or damn close, I'd say."

"Yeah," Floyd agreed, "I don't see any pattern of blood spatter that would indicate otherwise. Looks to me he had set his rifle down, maybe to rest."

"Or surrender."

Floyd shot a look my way. "That's an interesting thought."

I shrugged and began walking a circle around the tree, looking at the ground. As I continued to do so, I enlarged the circle of my path, expanding the search for evidence. Floyd stood at the tree, squatting slightly to be eye level with the site of the bullet's impact, and looking in the direction from where the bullet would have traveled. After a few minutes of each of us being in our own thoughts, analyzing the scene and doing our best to reconstruct the killing, Floyd spoke first.

"Your killer was either very close or very far away."

"Oh? Tell me why."

"The slope of the ground. If the killer is farther than a couple of feet away, he's going to be much lower than your victim. So unless that shot had an upward trajectory, I'd say it was damn near point blank."

It occurred to me that we hadn't yet been called for the autopsy, and I wondered if it had taken place today while Floyd and I were on the mountain. The coroner's office would call our bureau to notify us when an autopsy was scheduled, and they were supposed to give us a two-hour notice, but they seldom did. Either way, I wouldn't have been able to make it today. If I had missed it, I would call the examining doctor and ask about the trajectory of the gunshot wound, and see if there was anything else of interest. Sometimes the results of an autopsy could surprise an investigator and raise more questions that would need to be answered, or issues that would need to be addressed. Generally, we attended all autopsies of murder victims, for just those reasons.

During our scene investigation we had determined and documented the height of the bullet strike to the tree. We would need to have that correlated with the entrance and exit wounds of the decedent, measured from the bottom of his feet, which the medical examiner would document in his protocol. These measurements would help us determine the trajectory of the bullet. I would also want to know the doctor's opinion as to the distance from which it had been fired. If a person is shot at close range, there will be physical evidence left on his body, such as soot, stippling, or tattooing, which allows one to determine the approximate distance between the muzzle of a firearm and the victim.

More importantly, I needed to get the expended projectile that had been recovered from the tree over to the crime lab; it was evidence I had yet to deal with over the weekend and hadn't even thought about since this nightmare with Josie had begun. I would need to have Serology examine the bullet first, and hopefully there would be DNA that could determine with certainty that the projectile recovered from the tree had passed through my victim's body. If not, someday an attorney would argue that the bullet was in the tree coincidental to the murder, and that his client, with the matching gun, had shot that tree on another occasion. He'd probably say it happened while the client was out deer hunting.

Once Serology had completed the examination, the bullet would go to the Firearms section of our crime lab where its rifling characteristics would be examined. If the expended projectile was not badly deformed, an examiner would determine the number of lands and grooves, and the twist —the direction in which a bullet spins—of the particular barrel through which it had been fired. These general characteristics can help identify the manufacturer of the weapon. Most importantly, those markings left on the expended projectile would allow firearms experts to match the bullet to the gun from which it had been fired. If nothing else, we would be able to determine with certainty that the projectile recovered from the tree had or had not been fired by the rifle left at the scene. I was confident it had not.

I stood near the tree, looking out across the terrain to where the shot might have originated if it had not been fired at close range. It would take some work to discern where the shooter had stood or knelt or lain, and that was something that would be done by our crime lab with the use of lasers and GPS devices and computer programs, should it become necessary. I doubted it would.

With a rifle, the shot could have been made at fifty yards, or at hundreds of yards. These factors might help determine motive and allow us to piece together the events that occurred that day. It was easy to imagine the man with his back against the tree and a killer facing him down. That was more than likely the scenario, given the wound to the hand. But could it have been something other than a defensive wound? Could that have been coincidental? I didn't believe in coincidences, but I knew better than to dismiss any possibility before all of the evidence was in. If it was determined that the projectile had been fired from a pistol, then we would know for certain the shot was made at close range.

I walked twenty yards down the sloping, needle-covered forest floor, stopped, and turned to look at the tree once again.

"It's steeper than it looks. Walk down here and look back."

Floyd joined me. "I'll be damned."

After a moment of gazing at the tree where the body had been found, Floyd turned and looked in the direction of the nearby ridges and the faraway mountains, then up as if studying the tops of the trees that surrounded us. After a moment, he said, "I hope it was point blank. Otherwise, this is going to be a bitch to figure out."

I left him there and returned to the tree where William Brown had drawn his last breath, and I began looking on the ground in the immediate vicinity for an expended cartridge casing. I could bring up the "prospectors," a group of retirees who, under the direction of Master Chief Petty Officer William "Bill" Grady, volunteer their services to our bureau and to other law enforcement entities. This group had assisted homicide detectives on numerous cases with their metal detectors, recovering expended shell casings at locations where small metal objects would be otherwise impossible to locate. However, I felt the likelihood of a casing having been left behind was minimal. There was no evidence that more than one shot had been fired, and if it came from a rifle, it would likely have been a bolt-action weapon that doesn't automatically eject the expended cartridge. Of course, if the bullet was fired from an AR-15-style weapon, or an autoloader pistol, I would give serious consideration to having that search done as the casings from those types of weapons were ejected automatically—and energetically—making them difficult to locate in the best of terrains.

Floyd was still thirty yards from the tree in the direction from which the bullet had been fired. He was scanning the terrain, looking left and right, up and down. Seeing Floyd at that distance, he appeared small and low compared to where I stood. He put his hands on his hips and began studying one particular tree, glancing from it to me, and back to it again.

"What's up?"

He waited a minute and looked back and forth a couple more times. "Think your killer could have been in a tree stand?"

"I have no idea. What do you have? Is that tree marked up?"

He was studying the base of the tree as he answered, "Sort of."

I walked down the grade to meet him. He pointed at the base of the tree, about three feet off of the ground where the bark had been rubbed, leaving noticeable scars.

"What do you suppose that is?"

I thought about it a moment as I surveyed the tree above and below where the bark had been peeled away. There were no other marks. "I think it's a rub."

"Like a deer rub?"

I nodded. "That's what it looks like to me." I then turned and looked back to the place where my victim had died, noting again that it did appear to be substantially higher in elevation than where we stood. "I think we're wasting our time with this. I think it was a close-range shot. The victim knew his killer and he saw his death as it was delivered, and he likely knew why he was going to die. I can't get beyond the defensive wound to the hand. That indicates to me he was looking into the eyes of his killer during his final moments. Maybe he was pleading for his life. He might have been listening to the killer as he was being sentenced to death."

Floyd said, "The girl's dad."

"That or an uncle. Let's get out of here. I want to go up to the peak and make a few calls, see what's going on with Josie." I glanced at my watch. "Maybe somebody knows something by now."

I turned to hike back to our car but first walked directly to where William Lance Brown had met his demise, visualizing the murder as I did. When I was ten feet from the tree, staring at the victim in my mind, I stopped, raised a make-believe rifle to my shoulder, and aimed it at the child molester. He backed against the tree with his hand held out in front of him, begging for his life. The rifle was in arm's reach but he was too afraid to go for it. "*Blam!*"

"Did you get him?" Floyd asked.

I lowered my invisible weapon and looked behind me and to my right. I didn't see my expended cartridge, but it gave me an idea of where it might have gone. I slowly stepped to that area and looked around again. After a moment, I said, "That's how it went down, just like that."

"Probably."

"With a rifle, that's a sure ten-ring shot."

"If we don't find a casing, you might not ever know for sure."

I turned to him and smiled. "Unless someone tells me."

As we drove slowly to the peak of the mountain, we scanned the area looking for clues of anything and signs of life or death. Floyd said, "Too bad that bullet went through the deer."

"I'm sure he would agree."

"It would be interesting if the same gun killed both that deer and your child molester."

I looked over at him just as the Crown Vic found a rut. Floyd's head rocked back and forth, and so did mine. "Yeah, that's what I was thinking earlier, down at the deer."

"Where does the clan live? The girl who was raped, and her family?"

"That I don't yet know. I was just told they were up here on the mountain, but I haven't had a chance to get back to the case. Josie and I—"

My mind went to my partner and I could picture her smile and hear her voice. Suddenly I was pissed that we had taken the weekend off. As I had started to explain to Floyd, Josie and I hadn't run with the case through the weekend like we otherwise might have. They had cut overtime again and I had been warned about working on my days off. In the past, it wouldn't have mattered; I would have worked the case without being paid to do so. Floyd and I would have been back up on the mountain all weekend working for free, chasing a killer. Josie and I should have been as well. If we had, she wouldn't have gone missing. Why had I altered my approach to the job? Was I trying to be easy on Josie, thinking she wouldn't want to work for free the way Floyd and I and many others in the bureau did? Why had I thought this way? Overwhelmed with guilt, I couldn't recall what I had started to say, so I said nothing at all.

After a long moment, Floyd said, "Don't beat yourself up, Dickie. It's not your fault. Whatever has happened, it's just the way it is. You know that. Every single death shows us that: when it's your time to go, it's your time to go. Nothing you can do to stop it. I'm not saying that something terrible has happened to Josie, but whatever it is, it's not on you. It's all a part of destiny."

We rode along in silence, the Crown Vic covered in a thick layer of dust. Occasionally I would turn on the wipers to clear the windshield, but I didn't use the wiper fluid lest it become a muddy mess. As we climbed toward the peak, I finally finished my earlier thoughts. "We were going to research the family of the girl before notifying the next of kin. I wanted to see the reactions when we told them about their loved one's death. We also wanted to see if anyone would call the station to say he was missing, before we made notification."

Not that that had been a leading factor in taking the weekend off, but since we were going to let the case rest a few days, we figured it could be telling whether or not anyone made a report of it. It would be like a gangster getting killed and there were no car washes to raise money for the funeral, and no graffiti memorializing his death. That's when you knew he was killed by his own gang. By family. Then you just had to find out why. I think the *why* in this case was the easy part. Unless we had it all wrong.

I parked the car on top of the mountain and let the dust settle before opening the door. Floyd and I met at the hood of the car and faced south toward Los Angeles as I searched my phone for a signal and my mind for answers.

14

After I hung up with Joe Black, I shook my head to answer the question I saw in Floyd's eyes. "No word on Josie yet. They're running with it as if it's a worst-case scenario. They've put together a task force with Metro taking the lead. Major Crimes has a surveillance team sitting on her house, keeping an eye on it and mama. Joe says there's nothing we can do down there right now, so we might as well keep working the murder case up here in the event there's some type of overlap between it and Josie being gone. I don't see how there could be, but . . ."

I trailed off at the distant sound of a vehicle. Its growling motor provided me an image of a truck moving slowly up the mountain road.

"I think our boys are back," Floyd said.

"That or the game warden," I said.

"What were you saying about working your murder case?"

"Oh, I don't know. Just that there's not much we can do down south, so we might as well hit it hard up here, see if there's any overlap between Josie and the case we caught. Besides, I need a distraction before I lose my mind."

Kennedy and Kramer pulled up in their rig, followed by a white pickup. It was the game warden, a peace officer employed by the State of California Department of Fish and Wildlife, formerly called the Department of Fish and Game. The man who stepped out of the truck wore green jeans and a khaki uniform shirt. He answered to "Spence" but was introduced to me and Floyd as Jacob Spencer.

"Jake or Spence, either one," he said, as he released his firm handshake. He was tall and thin, mid-thirties, short-haired and clean-shaven. Beneath his Fish and Wildlife ball cap were friendly brown eyes and a boyish grin. He had a prominent Adam's apple under a noticeably narrow chin.

With the introductions behind us, we all gravitated to a semi-circle at the front of the sheriff's Bronco where the dead deer remained tethered to the hood.

"He must be about cooked by now," I said.

Kennedy grinned. "Depends on how you like your meat. This one's still a tad rare for my liking."

"We were just down the road a bit, parked in the shade until Spence rolled up. I don't imagine he's cooking too much yet," Kramer added.

Spence suggested we load the deer into the back of his truck where it would be concealed from public view when we went off of the mountain. It was surprisingly light to lift with two of us on each end. Spence left the tailgate down and leaned on it as Kennedy provided the details to the game warden. He told him about the single shot that Floyd and I had heard, and that we thought it had come from the Watkins property. Spence said, "No surprise there." Kennedy went on to explain that there had been a murder last week, and that I was the investigator on that case. He pointed to the south and told Spencer that the crime scene was on the other side of the mountain. Kennedy told the warden that the deer had passed in front of them as they were leading us back to the crime scene, and that he and Kramer could see it was injured, probably shot. He told him we had tracked the wounded deer a short distance and found it dead in the brush.

"I'd say we have more than enough probable cause to go onto the property and ask some questions," Kramer said, "maybe see about a blood trail." He then went on to explain that we were interested in poking our noses around the property just in case someone from the compound had something to do with our murder case.

For a long moment I considered mentioning Josie. I had nearly talked myself out of it when it occurred to me that this was a man who spent all of his time in the mountains. Even the Gorman deputies didn't come up here without a specific reason. It would be wise to have him aware of that situation on the outside chance that something had in fact happened to her up here. So, I gave him the brief story about Josie being considered a missing person, and I described her and her vehicle to him. I told him the chances of her being on the mountain were very slim, but that we had little else to work with and were covering all bases. The game warden made some notes in a small notepad he had drawn from his breast pocket.

"Either way, Spence," Kramer said, "this dead deer and the gunshot gets us on the property as long as you are part of the equation. We don't want to take a chance of being challenged by any of the Watkins clan and have this goddam thing turn into Ruby Ridge." Kramer then looked from Spencer to me and added, "These assholes will protest us being there anyway, but they know damn well they can't keep a warden off of their property. Well, we're there assisting him, so they won't have an argument about us being on private property without a warrant. They won't like it, but they'll know we're on solid ground and that should keep things from escalating. They're not as stupid as they look."

"So, we go there to investigate the deer," I said, reiterating the plan, "and snoop around for anything else of interest. Check out the red sedan— just to be certain it's not Josie's—and maybe collect the names and horse-power of people who are living there."

Floyd said, "The survivalists."

Kramer nodded. "Bingo."

"Who got killed?" Jacob Spencer asked.

I pulled my notebook from my hip pocket as my mind went blank when he asked. "William Lance Brown."

Spencer smiled. "What a shame."

"You obviously knew him."

"I know the whole clan, him, his daddy, his brothers . . . You'd be surprised how small it can be up here on the mountain."

"He did time for raping his niece," I said.

Spence stepped over to close the tailgate, and we all took a step back to give him room. He said, "That's what they say, anyway."

"Well, they convinced a jury of it. Do you know something they didn't?"

The tailgate closed with a solid thwack and a plume of dust rose from the truck. The thin warden turned, facing us now with his smile still in place. "Let's just say that the girl wasn't exactly a daisy."

Floyd said, "Well neither is Dickie, but that doesn't mean he should be raped."

I frowned at Floyd before turning to Spencer. "Tell me what you know about it. I don't have anywhere to start other than that my dead guy did time for rape. That seemed like a pretty good starting point, to be honest. But I don't know anything else about him yet, this Mr. William Lance Brown, much less his family or the hillbilly dynamics of it all."

Spencer folded his arms across his chest. "Well, I know that before he went to the joint, Billy, like everyone else in his family, was using and selling meth. Up here it's a little bit like the old bootlegging days where they soup up their cars or trucks and use mountain roads to avoid the cops. There are all sorts of places they manufacture up here. They move their camps around and then they sneak to town or go out to the Antelope Valley or head down to the city using backroads until they're clear of local law enforcement, those of us who know who they are and what they're up to. I've chased the little shit a few times myself and lost him. They use motorcycles, four-wheelers, four-wheel drive pickups—whatever. The point is, Billy was running drugs for his family—I'm sure of it—so maybe the drugs got him killed. As far as his niece, Joanna Harding, she's a wild child and always has been. When she was fourteen, I caught her out here in the woods with a dude who was four or five years older than her. They had been getting high and making out. I'm sure they would have had sex if I hadn't come along."

"What happened on that deal?"

"What do you mean?"

"Did anyone go to jail?"

Spencer shook his head. "I called one of the Gorman deputies out and they cited the boy for possession of less than an ounce of marijuana, and sent them on their way. What else can we do?"

"Do you remember the boy?" I asked.

Spencer shook his head. Deputy Kennedy asked him if he remembered which Gorman deputy came out on it. Spencer took a moment to consider it. "This was quite a while back, five years maybe? I just can't recall."

"Do you keep a log or a notebook, something you might be able to research?" I asked.

"Yeah, I do both. They require the daily activity logs and I keep notebooks too. I can go back through them, see if I can find it."

"I'd appreciate it," I said. "I'm thinking that maybe the boy she was with is someone we want to talk to also. You never know. If they were an item, maybe he's the one who exacted revenge."

"If you're going to talk to every boy that girl got high and probably naked with the Harding girl, you're going to be up here a while. Honestly, I'd bet it had more to do with drugs than anything else."

After jotting down a few notes about what Spencer had told us, I asked what he could tell me about the victim's family.

"Just what I told you. They're a bunch of anti-government tweaker assholes. That about sums up the whole clan." He nodded in the general direction of Kennedy and Kramer. "They can tell you."

Kennedy and Kramer were both nodding in agreement.

"Let's do it," Floyd said, more than ready for some type of action.

"Just one thing," I said as the group began to disperse, "not a word about us—" I wagged my thumb toward Floyd who stood next to me "— being Homicide. We haven't even notified the next of kin on this case yet."

There were affirmations of various forms and to varying degrees, but we were all on the same page: nobody was going to reveal that Floyd and I were there investigating a murder. Not yet, anyway.

We caravanned to the entrance of the Watkins compound and Spencer opened the gate with one of about a hundred keys that were held on a large metal ring a softball would easily pass through. I knew that cops in these rural areas, along with the fire departments, had locks for every gate. By law, they had to have access to or through all properties.

He led the way down the winding mountain road into the valley below. We came upon a clearing that was divided by a creek. As we came to it, I could see that water trickled along the bottom, scarcely filling the deep and wide crevice that had been carved by the runoff of lashing downpours. The canyon walls sloped gradually on the other side of the creek where cabins, trailers, and makeshift buildings and shelters were tucked into a stand of tall pines. We crossed a handmade wooden bridge, one vehicle at a time. I could feel it shimmy and hear it creak beneath the weight of our vehicle.

Several men emerged from various buildings, all of them clad in jeans and boots under flannel or wool shirts. Some of the men wore sidearms, and all of them had varying amounts of facial hair. Most wore hats. None of them appeared welcoming or friendly or the type you'd choose for a neighbor.

Spencer stopped thirty feet from where the men stood, the front of his truck pointed in their direction. Kennedy and Kramer, who were second in line, pulled along Spencer's left side and stopped. I went to the right side, and the three of our vehicles were now lined up as if prepared for battle. I wondered if it would come to that. You didn't encounter openly armed men very often in the city while investigating homicide cases.

As Floyd and I popped our doors, he said, "Watch your ass, Dickie."

"That's what I've got you along for," I replied.

"Good morning," Spencer bellowed as a general greeting. None of them replied.

"Any of you boys been shootin' this mornin'?" he asked, seeming to adapt a mountain man way of speaking.

The eldest of the group, a man with a long gray beard and hair pulled into a ponytail, took two steps forward. "What's your cause for bein' on private property, Officer?"

"We're investigating a poaching complaint, and there was a shot heard from somewhere in this canyon."

"What's your evidence," he challenged.

"I got a dead buck in the back of my pickup, you want to take a look."

"We didn't hear no shots. Musta come from over on the other side of the mountain. What are they doin' here?" he said, jutting his chin toward Kennedy and Kramer and then looking in the direction of me and Floyd.

"They're up here on another matter," Spencer explained, "and I asked them to come along and give me a hand. Blood trails are a bitch to find, so I figured the more the merrier."

The man was tugging at his beard with his left hand; his right remained free, a thumb tucked into his belt just in front of the pancake holster he wore on his right hip. From where I stood, his weapon appeared to be a government-style .45 auto.

He said, "Them county cops ain't got no authority to be on my property, Mr. Spencer."

I found it interesting that he knew the warden's name.

"But *I* do, Mr. Watkins, and I have the authority to bring in assistance from any other law enforcement officer in the state as I deem necessary. They are my guests, sir."

The solemn face of Johnny "Wad" Watkins showed no emotion. He held his gaze toward Spencer for a long moment before turning away. He made a motion with his hand and the other men followed, retreating toward the buildings.

"Hold on a second there, gentlemen," I said, "we need to get some names from you all."

None of them looked back. Floyd and I started for them. I said, "Hey!" as we began jogging after them. I had pulled my gun. "Hold it there, assholes." I could see Floyd had his out too. In an instant I realized Kennedy and Kramer were alongside me, each of them pointing guns at the crowd of men who came to a halt and began, one by one, slowly turning back to us.

"You got no right—"

"We're the fucking sheriff, asshole, and we've got all the right. You boys want to come out armed, trying to intimidate a man in uniform, well you best save that shit for when the mailman comes by."

Watkins smiled, raising his hands as if he surrendered. The others slowly followed suit. He said, "Well, okay, fucking sheriff, have it your way. We are peaceful, law-abiding citizens, and we don't want any trouble with the law."

I lowered my weapon but didn't holster it. "We'll be happy to holster our weapons if you all want to place yours on the ground there and step away from them. It'd make us feel a lot better, you understand."

"No sir," he said, "we don't intend to do that."

"Okay, well, Mr. Watkins, you have it your way. We'll stay ready then and conduct our business that way. We'll need all of your names."

"And we'll need all of yours, too," he said.

WE GATHERED THE NAMES AND BIRTHDATES THAT WERE PROVIDED TO US and trusted that they were legitimate. Nobody had identification with them, because, as Mr. Watkins had pointed out, there is no law that said they needed it. But as seasoned street cops, we knew to mix things up, move from one to another obtaining information, and then circling back to have each clarify the names and birthdates they had provided. Only one of the men stumbled when asked to restate his birthdate, but he was the oldest of the group—probably pushing seventy—and his bloodshot eyes and bumpy red nose provided an unstated testament to his inability to recollect.

Floyd and I stayed with the men in order to ask a few questions and make sure that their weapons remained idle. I asked about the others who lived there but weren't present. I asked about their neighbors: did they have any, how far away were they, did they know them? I asked how often they heard shooting in the mountains during the off-season.

None of my questions were answered, and then Watkins said, "You two are homicide detectives, aren't you?"

I glanced at Floyd who stood in his fighter's stance, silently watching through dark shades. Ready, as usual. Ready to work, ready to dance, ready to fight. Born ready.

"Why would you think that?"

He nodded toward the Crown Vic. "Pretty obvious y'all are detectives."

"Yeah, I'll give you that. But why would you think we work Homicide?"

Watkins smirked. "I hear things up here on the mountain. I see things sometimes too."

"Why don't you tell me about that."

He shook his head slowly. "No sir, I think I'm 'bout done talkin' to you." He looked down behind him and carefully lowered himself to a seat on the dirt. The others did the same.

Floyd said, "Well, one thing about it, we know who the leader is."

Watkins, who was clearly finished speaking to us, dropped his head into his arms that were folded and resting on his knees. Though he had tried to be clever and coy, I learned a lot from our brief conversation. As Floyd had pointed out, there was no question of who was the leader. I also now knew that *he knew* there had been a murder on the mountain. There was a chance he knew who did it. Maybe he had been there and watched it happen. Maybe he had ordered it done. Maybe it was he who pulled the trigger.

I looked around and saw four buildings that appeared inhabitable: the main cabin, a smaller cabin, and two single-wide trailers. I knew there could be more tucked into the trees. There were three pickup trucks and two sedans, including the dust-covered red car beneath the shelter. There were tools and debris stacked on the hood and fenders, and it certainly wasn't Josie's car. A four-wheeler was parked near the cabin and another was outside one of the trailer houses. A pair of motorcycles leaned on their kickstands near another trailer. All in all, I estimated four families. The sizes of those families was anyone's guess.

Where were the women? I scanned the windows of the structures but saw no movement, no signs of life. The idea that there was something more significant beyond our view tugged at me. A camp. A main house. A circle of tents with a large cleared area in the center where they held meetings and briefings over bonfires, sipped moonshine and caressed their guns. Maybe cooked their meth and traded their women or girls. The place made me think of Waco, Texas, and the Branch Davidians. What I didn't want was a similar standoff and firestorm with this armed and contentious group of anti-government types.

A chopping sound from the distance grew louder and more profound until a sheriff's helicopter suddenly appeared on the eastern horizon. Each of our guests glanced up—though Floyd and I never took our eyes off the men in front of us—and their leader chuckled. "Bringin' in the reinforcements, uh?"

I shook my head. "Nope, they're probably just cruising by since they know we're here. It doesn't make you nervous, does it, having them around? I mean, there's nothing hidden back in those woods that we should know about, is there?"

Watkins snarled. "There's nothing on my property at all that you should know about, Detective. In fact, y'all need to finish up what you've got to do and get the hell out of here."

The bird made three circles and peeled away, likely seeing that everything was going smoothly down below. Jacob Spencer drifted back to where Floyd and I stood babysitting the group of mountain men. He shook his head as he approached. "Nothing. We're going to have to go back to that road and see if we can pick up a blood trail."

I turned to face him and lowered my voice. "I've accomplished my main goal. I wanted to be certain about that red sedan and get some names for future reference. I'd like to find a reason to take Watkins in, but I don't think that's going to happen today. Not without a warrant, and we've got no probable cause for one."

Kennedy and Kramer came up and joined us, and we exchanged shrugs and looks of disappointment. The Watkins clan watched, waiting patiently. I walked over to Watkins and asked him to stand up. He did. We stood face to face for a moment, our eyes locked. It occurred to me this could last a lifetime, that he was as stubborn as me.

"Mr. Watkins," I finally said, "I have this feeling you and I are going to get to know each other."

"You might regret it," he said.

I took it as a threat, or at least posturing, two dogs pissing on the same fence. My mind rushed with similarly tough-guy responses, but all I said was, "I already do."

When we topped the mountain, all three vehicles stopped clear of the gate. Spencer, who had led the caravan out of the compound, jumped out of his pickup and jogged past the row of vehicles with his ring of keys in hand. He secured the gate behind us and began walking back toward his truck. As he passed my window, I stopped him with a word. "Spence."

"Yes sir."

"Watkins said something interesting back there when he and I were having a friendly chat, hinting that he hears and even sees a lot that goes on up here on the mountain."

Spencer waited, his brows crowding together as he listened.

"Do you ever run across cameras up here? Trail cams, or any type of security cameras? I know they have wireless jobs you can put about anywhere now."

"I mean, once in a great while. That's sort of a needle in a haystack deal, not something I would necessarily notice. Most of those trail cams are camouflaged so they'd be hard to spot, even if you were looking for them."

Floyd said, "Maybe we should look around that crime scene once more before we head down off of the mountain."

It was a good idea. I checked my cell phone. No signal. "First I want to hit the top of the mountain and check in again."

He nodded. "Whatever, Dickie. You're going to have to feed me here pretty soon."

I glanced at my watch and then looked out my window to see Spencer was waiting, lingering at my door to see if there was anything else.

"Thanks, buddy," I said. "I've got your card and I might be reaching out to you again if we come back up. Be sure to keep us posted if you hear or see anything of interest up here."

"I will," he said, and started back toward his truck.

As Spencer passed the Bronco that sat between my vehicle and his, he tapped the side of it twice. Kennedy, the deputy behind the wheel of it, gave him a thumbs up, and soon we were leaving a trail of dust and the dickwad compound behind us.

We peeled off from the others and parked facing south on the top of Liebre Mountain. When the dust settled, I lowered our windows and shut off the ignition. I was about to make a call when I heard the sound of a vehicle coming up behind us. I watched the sideview mirror until the four-wheeler carrying Watkins popped into view. "What the hell is he up to?" I asked, rhetorically.

Floyd popped his door and was out as he said, "We're going to find out."

By the time I came around the back of the car, Floyd had squared off with the bearded man who had cut the engine and stepped off of his four-wheeler.

"What are you doing, following us out?" Floyd asked. He jutted his chin toward a rifle that was secured on the front of the four-wheeler in a rack. "You plan on chicken-shitting us on our way down the hill?"

Watkins smirked. "You come around here messing with my family, and don't expect me to keep an eye on you? You boys started this."

"Nobody's messing with your family, pal," Floyd replied.

"How'd you like it if I were to mess with your family? Maybe follow you home and come up on you on your property. How would you like it?"

He had crossed a line with Floyd that shouldn't be crossed. I prepared for whatever was to come and had an idea what it would be. But there was only silence for a long moment as the two stared at each other, both of them postured for a fight. I figured Floyd would have hit him by now, and I was surprised that he hadn't.

Floyd turned his head and tilted it the way a dog might react to seeing a tennis ball as he looked beyond Watkins. "That's an odd place for a piano," he said, quizically.

Watkins turned to look behind him, following Floyd's gaze. Floyd twisted violently to his right as he threw a soul-crippling left hook and landed it squarely in Watkins's midsection, doubling him over. He crumpled to the ground, bent over, gasping for air.

I knew from my own experiences sparring with Floyd how a blow like that felt. A shot landed over the liver could knock you out. I had been dropped to the canvas a time or two as a result of just such punches, and I would never forget the resulting internal pain. The blows I had received while sparring were the result of punches held to about half- to three-quarter speed and impact. I couldn't imagine taking the full monty.

Watkins's face glowed red as he fought to catch his breath, curled in a fetal position on the ground.

Floyd said, "Don't ever fuck with my family, old man. Don't ever even think about it."

Floyd turned and walked away. I kept my eyes on Watkins, mindful of the rifle that sat secured on the front rack of his four-wheeler. I wondered if Watkins was thinking about it as well.

I stepped past Watkins, keeping my eyes on his hands as he held his midsection, knowing he wore a pistol on his hip. I pulled the rifle out of the rack, unloaded it, and returned it. I started to throw the bullets into the brush but suddenly thought better of it, thinking they might be good for a comparison at some point. Watkins watched as I put the four shells from his rifle into my pocket. His eyes were squinted, anger beginning to replace the pain that had shown moments before. I pointed at the pistol on his side. "I'll leave you with that just in case you come across a bear. I trust you wouldn't be foolish enough to yank it out before we're gone. That would be a fatal mistake."

I backed away, keeping my eyes on him.

Watkins said, "You two sons of bitches, you boys just fucked up big-time."

"It isn't the first time," I said.

As I reached the car, I could see Floyd ready to go but watching Watkins closely in his sideview mirror. I stepped inside, fired the motor, and we left with a rear wheel spinning, throwing dirt and rocks at the man who sat licking his wounds. Both of us watched our mirrors closely until we had rounded several corners and put a couple of miles between us and the top of the mountain. I finally settled back in my seat and began cruising slowly. Floyd's jaw was still locked tight and the veins in his neck were bulging as he drew deep breaths to calm himself.

"Nice left hook," I said.

He looked over and held his Ray-Bans on me without speaking.

"I never did see that piano you were looking at," I continued.

Floyd grinned. His expression suddenly softened, and his neck and shoulders relaxed. "You're an asshole."

I laughed. "How am I the asshole? You're the one out there starting fights."

"Get me off of this mountain, Dickie, before I kill someone."

15

Halfway down the hill, I realized we had forgotten to return to my murder scene, and I had also failed to call in for an update. I checked my phone but there was no signal. I hadn't expected to find one. We rode in silence, slowly winding down the dirt and gravel road. Checking out the mountains had given me something to do, but now Josie was on my mind. Now that we had finished the task of checking the area, my thoughts turned to other possibilities.

I couldn't help thinking of the Mexican mafia. Though Josie's role in Lopes's investigation was minimal, she was more vulnerable than Lopes, and her disappearance would evoke tremendous emotion and have a greater impact on the law enforcement community. The mob had committed far more egregious crimes and I wouldn't put it past them to kidnap a cop. And then what? That was the question. What would they do with her and how would they play it? If it was the mob who took Josie, I hoped that she was to be used as a bargaining chip so that we had more time to figure this out. It was only a glimmer of hope, but something to hold onto.

It was early afternoon, and we would be back in civilization and headed downtown before traffic thickened during the afternoon rush. Soon I would be able to call the office and get an update on the case. But as we reached the bottom of the mountain, doubt about the mafia crept into my soul and I worried that she was stranded somewhere in the woods. Or being held at a compound. That we had missed something up there and now we had departed.

It also occurred to me that if Watkins had anything to do with Josie's disappearance, we had just placed her at greater risk with the confrontation and Floyd's outstanding left hook. Shit.

Floyd said, "You almost need a helicopter ride over this place to get a better perspective. I'm all turned around."

I envisioned Santa Clarita's bird circling above the compound. "Yeah, maybe we should do that. Let's see how everything else is going back at the office and maybe set something up for later today or tomorrow."

"Or a small plane."

"We don't have access to a small plane, as far as I know."

"Dickie, we can commandeer whatever the hell we need for something like this. I guarantee you someone over at Aero has access to a small plane and knows how to fly the damn thing."

We were now on pavement, so I got on the gas and pulled my belt across my body to hook it up. Floyd followed suit. "You're probably right."

"Something to think about, Dickie. Where are we going?"

"Heading back to the office, unless you have a better idea."

"Food, Dickie. That's my better idea. You're killing me."

"We'll grab something in Santa Clarita and take it to go. I want to get back to the office and make sure this thing is going in the right direction."

I continually checked my cell for a signal, and as we dropped into the basin known as Castaic, it showed three bars. I hurriedly brought up the front desk number saved in my phone simply as *187*. Easy to remember and first on the list, it was easy to find.

The call was answered by Veronica, the amazingly cool and collected civilian who manned the phones Monday through Friday during the day. "Homicide Bureau, how may I help you?"

"Veronica, it's Dickie. How's everything going there?"

A pregnant pause followed. I could hear the concern in her voice when she spoke again. "Hi Richard," she said, "they've been waiting for you to call. Lieutenant Black has had me calling every half-hour or so, trying to get ahold of you."

I glanced at Floyd and frowned while replying to her, "What's up? I just now got back in cell range."

"What's going on?" Floyd asked.

I shrugged, keeping my eyes on the road as I steered with one hand and held the phone to my ear with the other. This was in violation of the California Vehicle Code, a document Floyd and I considered to be a rather lengthy and overly wordy list of suggestions that didn't apply to working cops. To hell with the chippies. I glanced at my speedometer to reinforce my position on the matter; we were doing eighty-five.

Veronica said, "I'm sorry to hear about Josie, Richard."

"Thank you. What's up?"

"They've moved the task force to Whittier. Lieutenant Black wants you to call him on his cell. I can text you the landline to the command post also, if you need it."

I glanced at Floyd as I responded to Veronica to gage his reaction. "Why the hell would they move it to Whittier?"

"Whittier? Jesus," Floyd said.

In my ear Veronica was saying something about Metro and the Tech Crew, but between Floyd's comment and my attempts to listen to him and to Veronica and keep the car racing straight ahead, I missed the details. I could read between the lines though, and the gist of it was that Metro was running the missing cop case and that they would do so from their home base where they had the home field advantage, all of their equipment and resources, the Tech Crew next door, and fewer homicide dicks popping in every five minutes to see if there was news. I thanked her and disconnected while gliding to the right, aiming for the Magic Mountain Parkway offramp.

"Where the hell are you going and why are those assholes working this case out of Whittier?"

Whittier was in the eastern part of the county. The old Monte Vista High School, which had been purchased by the county and converted into the Sheriff's Training and Regional Services center, or STARS, was one of the most inconvenient places to drive at any time of the day. The training bureau had since returned to Biscailuz Center in East Los Angeles, named after the 27th sheriff of Los Angeles County, and STARS was now home to various units including Major Crimes, Commercial Crimes, Arson Explosives, Special Victims, and Narcotics Bureau. The Costco-sized warehouse across the parking lot from the main campus held the central collection of property and evidence that had been seized by deputies throughout the department's twenty-three patrol stations, four major jail facilities, and assorted detective assignments around the county.

Metro Detail was part of Major Crimes Bureau, and their offices filled the C building of STARS Center.

"They're working it on the home turf for obvious reasons, the main one being to keep homicide guys from trying to take over the investigation. It's what you and I would have done too, had a case like this landed in our laps when we worked Metro. And I'm going to feed you and head over to Santa Clarita Station."

"What are we doing at Santa Clarita?" he asked.

"Well, Veronica is texting me the number for a landline to the command post. If they wanted me to have that, they might have concerns about talking on the cells. We're right here, we might as well go by and use a phone, maybe check in with the flight crew about that helicopter ride."

I glanced at Floyd to see him nod his approval. He pointed his finger through the windshield. "Wendy's."

I veered in that direction and pulled into the drive-thru. We picked up a couple of chicken sandwiches and were back on the road in five minutes, headed east on Magic Mountain Parkway. We would be at the station in ten minutes. It was almost two, and by the time we would hit the East L.A. interchange—whether or not we stopped by Santa Clarita Station—the traffic would be building up. I hoped that whatever business needed to be discussed between us and Metro could be said on a landline and they wouldn't ask us to drive there. But you never knew. Major Crimes was the department's secret squirrel unit, the place where undercover cops identified themselves in documents by their assigned bureau numbers rather than names. The list that identified who belonged to which number was closely guarded. While assigned there, your name was taken out of the department's database of personnel so that if someone made an inquiry to verify employment, there would be no record of your existence. This was to protect the cover of those involved in clandestine operations. On a case like a missing cop, they would take no chances with keeping tight seals on all communications. This was the unit that had the capability of tapping into cellular activity, and the personnel there were well aware that others could do the same.

We arrived at Santa Clarita Station and I drove into the back lot that was crowded with patrol and detective vehicles. We parked on the back side, furthest from the station and hopefully out of the way. When we got out, I shielded my eyes from the sun and peered up to the roof where the AStar-350 helicopter sat on its pad. Floyd came alongside me.

"Did you ever hear about the time that bird was blown off the roof?"

He chuckled. "No, you're shittin' me."

"It was in the nineties. You remember Marty Long, the pilot called Psycho?"

Floyd was shaking his head.

"Well, he flew a SWAT team up here one day in the big Sikorsky, and when he got here, the little Hughes they used to have was sitting on the pad. It had rained all night and the helipad was slick, and for whatever reason, it hadn't been tied down like it's supposed to be. Anyway, Psycho decides he can set down just enough on the apron of the helipad to offload the team, being the hot-shit pilot he was. Well, it worked great except the rotor wash from the Sikorsky blew the Hughes 500 clean off the roof and into the parking lot."

"Jesus."

"Uh-huh. That was his third or fourth ah-shit that cost the county a couple hundred-thou, and they finally had to bench him. Rumor was he had honed his skills while dodging rocket-propelled grenades in Vietnam. He was good, but a dinosaur in every way. He wasn't part of the evolving, more politically correct and friendly sheriff's department."

We began walking toward the back door of the station. Floyd said, "Isn't he the one who got into a shooting, as a pilot?"

"That would be him. Psycho. Yeah, he had set the bird down on Alameda once when a couple Firestone deputies were knee-deep in the shit outside the projects on ninety-seventh. He parked his helicopter in the middle of the road and ran across the street and into the action. Someone got ahold of a deputy's gun or was trying to grab it or something, and Marty capped the dude in the head."

"Damn."

"Then he loads back up and lifts off, him and his observer. Everyone about lost their minds over that. But like he had said in his own defense, what was he going to do, leave his bird parked on Alameda for the next four hours waiting for Homicide?"

Floyd laughed. "That's a classic."

We stopped at the door. Not having the code, we'd wait a minute for someone to exit. There was always traffic in and out of the back doors of stations that provided direct connection from the patrol parking areas to the jails. I turned and looked over the crowded lot as two patrol units rolled in bumper-to-bumper and swerved into tandem spots reserved for patrol cars arriving with prisoners. There were two men in the backseat of one car, a woman in the backseat of the other. All three appeared drunk or loaded and certainly white trash. I said to Floyd, "Times have changed since I grew up in this valley."

A total of three deputies accompanied the two men and one lady prisoner, and one of the deputies keyed open the back door while looking skeptically at me and Floyd.

"We're from Homicide," Floyd said. The deputy nodded and opened the door, and I grabbed it and held it open while the deputies filed in with their prisoners. We followed, and the door closed behind us. I started through the hall toward the watch sergeant's office where I would check in and ask about the best place to make a call. Floyd veered to the left, saying he needed to use the restroom and he'd catch up in a minute.

The radio crackled with activity in the background while phones rang nonstop. I stood waiting for the sergeant who had acknowledged my presence with a nod as he switched from one line to another, stabbing at blinking lights with a meaty index finger. Soon, Floyd had caught up and waited with me.

Finally, the sergeant slammed the phone onto its receiver and looked up, forcing a smile across his frowning face. "Gentlemen, how may I help you?"

I introduced us to the sergeant and told him we were from Homicide. His name was Castorina and I knew he had come from Narco and had a good reputation. He looked us up and down, silently noting our jeans and boots. I glanced down at my attire. "We're doing warrants later," I said, offering an unnecessary explanation. "Are you the watch commander today?"

"I am," he said, somewhat exasperated. "And of course, with the lieutenant off today, all the complaints would have to come in. '*Your deputy swore in front of my kid.' 'I got pulled over and the deputy made me sit on the curb while he searched my car. He didn't have a warrant.'* Then, a man from Gorman calls and says one of our detectives slugged him in the stomach. I sent that one back to Detectives, let them deal with it."

"Wow," I said, "that doesn't sound right. It was probably a Kern County detective. You know how those guys are."

The sergeant nodded. "Anyway, how can I help you guys?"

I told him we needed to find a quiet place to use a landline that wasn't recorded. All of the main lines to the stations were automatically recorded and a constant beeping in the background reminded you of it. The phones in the secretariat and the detective bureau were not. Typically, I navigated toward the detective bureau when popping in at one of our stations, but I wanted to speak freely without anyone overhearing me. Besides, now that I knew someone back there was getting a call about a detective slugging someone up in Gorman, the last thing I wanted to do was to let the detective sergeant know we were around and give him the crazy notion it might have been us.

"I noticed the lieutenant's office was empty and the lights were out," I said, "and thought maybe we could use his office."

Sergeant Castorina waved a hand as to indicate it was no big deal. "Yeah, I don't care. Have at it. Shut the lights off when you come out."

I shook his hand and we went back down the hall and into the quiet office. I flipped the lights on and helped myself to the lieutenant's chair. Floyd plopped down in one of the two guest chairs across the desk from where I sat. I punched at the digits on the phone, entering the number that had been texted to my phone.

Floyd said, "Can you believe that punk beefed me?"

The line was ringing. I tucked the mouthpiece beneath my chin and said, "He has no idea who we are. We never gave him our names."

In the earpiece a familiar and friendly voice said, "What the hell are you two up to now?" It was Lieutenant Michaels.

"Hey, L-T, what's going on? Me and Floyd are up here in Santa Clarita."

"Yeah, I heard you guys went up to Gorman today. How'd that pan out? Any leads?"

"Nothing. A few assholes on the mountain, the survivalist types, but nothing on this deal with Josie and nothing new with my latest murder case. What have you guys got going?"

"You're on a clean line?" he asked.

"Yeah, I'm on the private line in the watch commander's office. The first two I tried were beeping. This one is clean."

He paused a moment, and Floyd and I looked at each other in anticipation. Floyd frowned and nodded toward the phone as if to say he wanted to listen. I stood up from my seat and leaned across the desk. Floyd did the same from the other side, and we stood with our heads a few inches apart and the phone receiver between them.

Michaels said, "I've got you on speaker now and Lopes from your bureau is here along with a few guys from my team, Sergeant Jack Smith and Deputies Gil Trujillo and Eddy Warren. You know everyone, right?"

"Right, boss. I have Floyd here with me and he's listening in as well."

"Okay, well," he started, "we're going to keep this tight, buddy boy, because Lopes has an idea and I'm giving him the nod. But it's the type of deal that could get us all fired and prosecuted if it goes south, got it?"

I pulled my head away from the phone to look at Floyd. He smiled.

"Got it, boss," I said.

"Okay, Lopes has offered up his girl as bait, the cute little informant he has stashed away down south. If this is mob related, we want to know that sooner rather than later. Follow me?"

"So far," I said, "but hey, Lopes, are you sure about this, brother?"

His voice was distant but unmistakable. "Yeah, Dickie, I'm sure. We have to find Josie."

"Okay," I said, "thanks, Lopes. Go ahead, L-T."

"Well, actually, I'll have Lopes brief you. It's his deal really and we're just supporting him."

Lopes's voice came across louder now as if he had moved closer to the phone. "So my thought on this is that if the mafia has anything to do with Josie, they did it with the intent of negotiating for Maria. They want her accessible so they can finish the job because they know she can take down all the big players with her information. I'm going to offer her up, but they will want to see us put her out there; they're not going to take our word for it."

"They have to know we wouldn't negotiate, don't you think?"

Lopes said, "You'd be surprised. They negotiate shit all the time with corrections officials, feds, and some of the other agencies too. You don't even want to know some of the stupid shit some of our so-called colleagues have done in the past to appease those assholes."

"Really? Cops negotiate with the mafia?"

"It's happened, Dickie, trust me. But it has to be believable. The way we make it believable is to go to the top and tell them some bullshit about our informant—*their girl*—is pissing backward anyway, and not much value to us, and that we would rather negotiate under the table than to have word get out to the public that a cop has been kidnapped. Make them think that is our greatest fear, the absolute worst thing we could imagine happening, while minimizing the value of Maria Lopez."

Floyd whispered, "Jesus."

"How do you want to play it," I asked. It only took a second for me to consider it. I trusted Lopes and I trusted the Metro team. If nobody got killed, it would be a win-win. If only Josie survived, it'd still be a win. In that brief moment of consideration, I saw the pretty face of Maria Lopez with her smiles and dimples and her cool demeanor, and I thought about the night her own people gunned her down on the steps of her grandmother's house. But I forced all of those thoughts from my mind and put Josie foremost in the picture. This was about Josie, and she had made no bad choices. I left it there with my conscience.

"Here's the plan," Lopes started.

WHEN LOPES FINISHED, LIEUTENANT MICHAELS CAME BACK ON THE phone and said, "It will take some time to get everything in place. I'd say tomorrow night could be a go. Why don't we plan to meet here at about four and we'll see where we're at."

"Okay, boss, four at STARS. We'll be there."

I placed the phone gently on its cradle and Floyd and I took our seats. We were quiet for a moment, contemplative. Floyd was looking away, but I could tell he was deep in thought.

"Well?"

His eyes came back to me. "It's a gamble, but what do we have to lose?"

"An informant."

He nodded and ran his fingers through his hair, let out a breath and said, "Let's go."

"Wait, what about Aero?"

"Oh yeah. How do we find them?"

I shrugged. "Their bird is on the roof, so they can't be far unless they're gone for the day." I glanced at my watch. "I can't imagine they leave before three. I'll page them."

Floyd leaned back in his chair and stared up at the ceiling. He appeared fatigued. I knew I was. I picked up the phone and held it while running my index finger along the printed instructions on the base of the phone. I found what I was looking for, hit the star key and then punched in eighty-three to connect to the intercom. I tapped the mouthpiece on the handset and heard the thump come over the station speakers. "Anyone from Aero please call the watch commander's office. Aero bureau, watch commander, please." I placed the phone back on its cradle and leaned back, watching deputies and professional staff alike passing through the hallways.

"I think they need a bigger station," I said.

Floyd glanced toward the glass partition behind him and then settled back in his chair.

I continued, "I don't think this place has changed since I was a kid, but they have about a hundred more deputies here now."

Floyd closed his eyes, uninterested. The phone rang and I picked it up. "Watch commander's office, this is Jones from Homicide."

"Did you call for Aero?" the caller asked.

"I did. Who am I speaking with?"

"Deputy Banks. I fly sixty-nine adam."

"Perfect, thank you. My partner and I are working a murder case up on the mountain—"

"You guys are the ones that were up on Liebre this morning?"

"Yep, that would be us. Anyway, it's difficult to get the lay of the land from the ground, and we were wondering—"

"You boys want a helicopter ride, right?"

"I don't know that either of us *wants* a ride, but we think it might be useful. We've both spent plenty of time in birds and neither of us is too crazy about them. In fact, I'm still puzzled about how they stay in the air," I said.

"They don't always."

"Great, thanks. That makes me feel a lot better."

"When do you want to go up? We've set down for the day, but we'll be back in the friendly skies of Santa Clarita tomorrow from eight to four."

"Tomorrow," I said, looking at Floyd. He shrugged. Back into the phone I said, "Let's plan it. We'll be here at eight."

"Make it nine. Our shift starts at eight, but it takes us a bit to get up in the air."

I told him nine sounded perfect and hung up. Floyd nodded, his way to ask for the details.

"Nine tomorrow, they'll fly us out there and give us a tour."

"Great."

"Then we have the operation with Lopes and Metro in the afternoon down in Whittier. It'll be a busy day."

Floyd pushed out of his chair. "Well then, we better get crackin', Dickie."

16

When we arrived at the office, I dropped Floyd at his car and both of us left without entering the building. We had discussed it during the drive back and agreed that by now everyone would know about the situation with Josie and we would be bombarded with questions and conversation. We were exhausted, mentally and physically. We had worked most of the weekend. We had worked all night. Floyd was supposed to be on vacation. Also, we were still dressed in jeans and boots which would bring even more questions and conversation if we went inside.

We parted company and I headed home, thinking about Josie and then the murder on the mountain and all of its dynamics. As I exited the freeway and started through the congested roads of Burbank, I was reminded of the chores that needed to be handled before I collapsed for the night. As a bachelor, laundry and grocery shopping were minimal but necessary tasks, and I had a feeling this would be the last free evening I would have for a while. I stopped by the cleaners and dropped off a bag of suits and shirts to be laundered, and left with half a dozen hangers of crisp, clean ones. I stopped by the market and bought coffee, yogurt, pastries, cereal, and milk for breakfasts. It was a rare occasion that I cooked dinner at home since Katherine and I split up. Since Katherine dumped me, to be more accurate. But just in case, I picked up a few cans of soup, chili, refried beans, a pound of hamburger, grated cheese, and a package of tortillas. Bachelor life could be as simple or complicated as one wanted it to be. I kept it simple. Which meant I only housed the bare necessities and I didn't flirt with the new neighbor, a redhead ten years my junior whom I had learned was a recent divorcee and a federal agent of some sort. She had moved into the apartment next door shortly after I had moved in, but I rarely saw her.

If the woman cop neighbor and I ever moved past the obligatory smiles and hellos and began speaking, I would find out just where this law woman worked and the story on the demise of her last marriage. I would share with her the sad story about the shrink I never should have gotten involved with, who had left me because of my commitment to the job. Maybe the lady cop would get that. It could be that we had a lot in common. I topped my cart with some healthy snacks: mixed nuts, protein bars of various assortments, and Coors Light. With the neighbor in mind, I glided over and browsed the wine selections. I picked a red and a white by name and price and hoped one or the other would be satisfactory should an emergency arise on the home front.

That was all I needed. Sometimes I wondered if I had completely lost my mind. I'd ask Floyd on our next long drive. I hadn't even thought of mentioning the new neighbor to him, but I was looking forward to doing so. It was always entertaining to get Floyd's opinion and advice on my romantic affairs and then completely ignore them and blow things up. Self-destructive was a word that came to mind at times of romantic contemplations.

After checking out, I decided there was one more stop to be made before arriving home. I pulled into the liquor store on the corner two blocks from my apartment that offered a quick and convenient in and out. I left with a bottle of Jameson. Irish whiskeys, scotch, and bourbon had replaced the gin after Floyd convinced me that the quinine in tonic water is what had been leaving me with headaches the following mornings. So far, it seemed to be a solid theory. Floyd, my personal physician and marriage counselor. He was batting about five-hundred.

My new apartment was a small, almost historic building tucked into the hills on the east side of Burbank. It was a two-story with twenty units, ten on either level. I was on the bottom floor at the far end which felt better to me than being sandwiched between the neighbors. Of course I had someone above me, but the tenants walked like mice and so far, I had never been disturbed. The apartment next door, the one with which I shared a wall, had been occupied by a young couple who appeared to be fans of punk. Not that I would be prejudiced toward a person for their choice in music, but the pair of orange- and green-haired, face-pierced, punk rockers were zealous consumers of medical marijuana, and for the few weeks that we were neighbors, I thought I'd made a serious mistake in relocating here. But soon they were gone—evicted by the landlord after spending all of their rent money at the head shop—and the carpet cleaners came, followed by handymen and painters and a team of Hispanic house-keepers that drove pink cars with their logos on the doors. And then the movers arrived, and I believed my luck had changed.

Until Sunday evening when I went to Josie's home and found that she was missing.

I walked past my new neighbor's apartment and saw the blinds drawn tight and the door shut. I hadn't yet figured out what she drove, so I didn't know if her car was there or not. I scanned the parking lot area on my second and final load of groceries and laundry that I brought in from the Crown Vic, but I didn't notice any vehicles that stood out as a fed car. I wondered if she had noticed the unmarked police car that was usually backed in to one of the dozen unassigned spots, and occasionally parked on the street in front of our small complex. A lady cop would take notice of such a thing, I would think, and then poke around to identify the other cop in her building. Or did only male cops do that?

I left the front door to my apartment open and raised all of the windows to let the fresh autumn air flow through. After changing into shorts and a t-shirt, I slid my bare feet into a pair of flip-flops and picked up my basket of underclothes and a box of detergent. I grabbed two beers from the fridge and set them on top of the clothes, and left my door open behind me as I headed down the walkway, past the front doors of my fellow tenants to the small laundry room at the other end of the building. After starting the load of whites, I moved outside and took a seat on the set of three steps that dropped down from the raised porch of the lower level apartments to a walkway that cut across a lush front lawn and ended at the sidewalk that paralleled the street. I popped open a can of beer and took a long pull of the cold beverage. It tasted good and went down easy. I set the can next to me and checked my phone for messages and missed calls; there were none. I then scrolled through my email and deleted the first dozen or so that were clearly junk. My work emails encompassed a variety of subjects including bulletins from the administrative offices of the sheriff, notices from our bureau admin, and several from a couple of prosecutors from the district attorney's office. I didn't bother to open those because I knew they would be requests for more discovery or additional reports or follow-up investigation on the various cases that were being prepared for trial. I would deal with those later in the week, from the office computer once I sorted out the more important issues in my world.

Birds sang as they hopped from branch to branch in the trees that surrounded our quiet courtyard. Traffic here was minimal; the sounds of an occasional passing car seemed less frequent than the pattering of a jogger's footsteps, the whispering sounds of a speeding cyclist, and the low chatter from pairs of mothers pushing strollers along the sidewalk. I tucked my phone into my pocket and propped my elbows on my knees as my mind drifted back to Josie. I wondered what Lopes and the lieutenant at Metro had in store for the operation that could jeopardize all involved. I trusted them both, unequivocally; they were two men with whom I would saddle up and ride straight through the gates of hell. Both would venture deep into the murky waters where there were no definitive rights and wrongs, blacks and whites, in order to be victorious when the odds were against them. They were the right type of men for the job, and a perfect fit for me and Floyd. It was the type of men and cops we were, unapologetically.

I finished my first beer. If my timing was on today, that would mean the first load of laundry was ready to be switched to the dryer. A second load would be started, and while it ran its cycle, the second beer would be consumed.

The sound of a car door shutting hadn't registered as I finished my duties in the small laundry room, but when I emerged with a fresh beer and headed back to my steps, I caught a glimpse of my new neighbor's shapely behind disappearing into her apartment. Damn my timing. As I sat sipping a beer and thinking about Josie and my new neighbor and about a mountain man who might come gunning for me and Floyd, I thought of strategies to meet the new neighbor: *Could I borrow a scoop of detergent to finish my laundry? I wanted to welcome you*—as if after a couple of months at the complex I was on the committee. *I heard you're a fed; how about a drink?*

But I talked myself out of all of my clichéd lines and held out hope that she would reappear while I was enjoying a cold beer in the shade of a camphor tree, many of which lined these old streets to create tunnels of shade as far as you could see. But this was no Hallmark movie and it didn't happen, so when I finished my beer and collected my laundry, I retreated into my quiet apartment and turned on the news while preparing a meal fit for a lonely bachelor. The Jameson beckoned but I silently declined, knowing that at any minute something could change with the case of my missing partner that would require me to be sober and at the top of my game. So, I stuck with Coors Light—since it was mostly water. Pure, cold, Rocky Mountain water. I was practically a health nut.

17

The morning came and I checked my phone just to make sure I hadn't missed any middle-of-the-night calls or texts. I knew I had slept hard as I couldn't remember tossing and turning or dreaming. There were no notifications, which meant no news. That could be good or bad, I knew, but nonetheless it caused me to rise in a somber mood.

Floyd and I were meeting in Santa Clarita at nine, which meant he would be there at eight and by a quarter after, he'd be blowing up my phone wanting to know where I was and when I would be there. We were meeting the flyboys at nine and we would be going for a ride through the sky above the mountains. It was bad enough riding in those helicopters in the city where you knew that if you went down, at least they'd find your body before it became bear food. I finished getting ready and left at seven-thirty, which would get me to Santa Clarita about eight or a quarter after when Floyd would begin his search for me. I would recommend meeting for a cup somewhere and bring him up to speed with whatever I was about to find out from the various calls I would make while traveling.

When I merged onto the Golden State freeway headed north from Burbank, Lopes was my first call. It was he who had come up with a plan to see if the Mexican mafia was involved in Josie's disappearance, and it was his operation. Metro was the supporting cast, and what a bunch of characters they were. Denny Michaels, the lieutenant, had been a tough and witty street cop who spent most of his career in South Los Angeles where he had also been raised. As he grew up, the demographics changed drastically, leaving him as one of few whites to remain. It was during those formative years that he learned to pick his battles carefully and fight like hell when it was unavoidable. I suspected it was also during that time of his life when he learned to use a knife—then or during his subsequent years in the navy. Michaels could often be found passing the time by sticking a fixed-blade knife into a tree trunk at ten yards with the precision of a ninja. His sergeant, Jack Smith, was a former Marine who had been assigned to our SWAT teams before spending a decade as a Narcotics detective. A fast-moving, fast-thinking, spirited man with the physique of a wrestler, Smith was perhaps best known for knocking out a captain after a colleague's funeral. The skipper had made the mistake of questioning the integrity of Narco dicks. Deputies Trujillo and Warren were "*The Odd Couple*" of Metro. A Mexican and a self-admitted redneck, the two would insult each other on a regular basis using terminology that would get either of them fired if ever reported by anyone who overheard it. Anyone unfamiliar with their relationship would think the two hated not only each other, but every person from the other's race. But they were best friends on and off the job and neither would ever allow an outsider to insult the other.

Lopes answered his cell after just one ring: "What do you want?"

He had been born grumpy and it never went away. His lack of tolerance for people rivaled that of a rattlesnake's, though the latter might make a better houseguest. Once you got to know him though, you could see through the hardened shell of the former Marine captain and realize that as long as you didn't cross him, he was harmless. I said, "Good morning, sunshine."

"The fuck do you want, Dickie? I've got about a hundred things going on and I just pulled into cha-cha's place to pick her up so we can get going with this deal and hopefully not get her killed today. By the way, I've got your sister with me too, and she says hi. Now, what the fuck do you want?"

"Tell my sis I said hello." Lacy Jones and I joked that we were siblings though our complexions were very different. "I just thought I'd check in, see what's up."

Lopes chuckled over the phone. "What's up? Are you kidding me, man? I'm about to turn an informant over to the mob and hope she doesn't get whacked before we can save her. I'm a fucking wreck, man. Your sister keeps telling me I need to chill but I swear to God I'm going kill somebody today. I can feel it. What else do you want to know?"

"How's this going to go down?"

"*Huero* from White Fence is one of the top shot-callers right now for the *Eme*. He's down at county from Pelican as a witness for one of his homies who's fighting a jailhouse murder beef. Anyway, they've got him locked down over at county in seventeen-fifty, high-power, but today he's going to get a little fresh air. He's about to catch a bus to Downey court."

"What's he got going on there?"

"Me, but he doesn't know it yet. He'll know something's up, probably be worried all day, looking out for a hit. But when I show up late this afternoon, he's going to shit himself. Every other time I've met with him it's to put another case on him. Anyway, that time of the day, lockup should be cleared out at Downey court and he will be secluded. They don't have much of a calendar. Then it's going to be showtime."

"How are you going to pull this off, brother?"

"Don't worry about it, man. I don't want to say too much on the phone anyway, but I think it's going to work. It will either tell us we're on the wrong track, or we'll be swinging into Plan B with my homegirl as bait. Just be ready to roll this afternoon. Michaels said for you guys to be at STARS at three, right?"

"He said four."

There was a pause and I could hear a female voice in the background. Lopes said, "Your sister said then meet us at Downey at three just in case. It's on your way."

I glanced at my watch out of habit. "Okay, three at Downey. See you girls later."

"Shut up, stupid," was all he said before signing off.

Next, I called Lieutenant Michaels at Metro and confirmed we were meeting at four. I told him we were going to stop by the Downey court-house on the way down and meet with Lopes and a Lacy Jones who was assisting Lopes today since he was transporting the female informant, Maria Lopez. Michaels said, "Yeah, that's fine. This will either be shut down by four or game on. I'm not sure what to expect at this point."

He was referring to the status of Josie and I knew what he meant. It would be bittersweet if the mafia test failed and they had nothing to do with it. Great, they have nothing to do with it. But then where do we look next? If they took the bait, we were going to play a very dangerous game called hostage swap. It could be a career-ending, deadly encounter, or it could end with Josie being recovered, the informant unharmed, and we would all walk away unscathed. It could happen, but there was a lot that could go very wrong.

A few years earlier, the same Metro team had gone into Mexico to recover a kidnap victim and the operation had gone hot. A shooting had occurred and it involved more than just the bad guys. There were Mexican cops on the opposition's side and the team had no choice but to defend themselves as they made their escape. It happened after I had left the team for Homicide, but I heard about it firsthand, the unadulterated version. The official version was that the team never went south, though gunfire had been exchanged at the border and the bad guys escaped into Mexico and were not pursued. This team took chances and the sheriff knew it but didn't want to know about it. It's why men like Denny Michaels and Jack Smith were handpicked to run Metro.

Floyd called in right on time, a quarter after eight. "Where're you at, Dickie?"

"Just coming into the valley. Want to get breakfast? We're early."

"Yeah, it's your turn to buy. Did you hear from Lopes or Michaels?"

"I talked to them both," I told him. "I'll fill you in over a stack of pancakes."

"Pancakes?! Jesus, dude, no wonder you're a fat ass. Go protein style, Dickie, bacon and eggs, a side of yogurt. Eat a Danish if you've got a sweet tooth, but stay away from all that starch and syrup. What's the matter with you, anyway?"

When my personal trainer finished his lecture, we agreed to meet at one of the new spots in town not far from the mall. Good food and drinks were served there all day and half the night, inside or on a patio around a gas fire pit. Santa Clarita had turned Bunny Luv and the other farms of my childhood into Yuppyville, USA.

Floyd and I finished our breakfasts and sipped coffee for a few more minutes before I glanced at my watch and suggested we head over to the station. Floyd was ready. Floyd was always ready. He pushed out of his chair, dropped his napkin on the table in front of him, and moved to a small gate that allowed direct access to the parking lot. I left cash on the tray to cover breakfast and a generous tip, and followed Floyd through the parking lot to our cars. The two were at the far end of the parking lot away from the other patrons, backed into adjacent spots. Without speaking we each pulled out of our spots and into the heavy Santa Clarita morning traffic.

At the station, we double-parked in the rear of the lot and headed for the back door. Each of us was dressed casually again today due to the nature of the work we had scheduled: a helicopter ride this morning and an under-cover operation this afternoon. We had no plans to be seen in the office. Our badges were clipped on our belts near holstered pistols, prominently displayed for easy identification. But the only thing badges would indicate is that we were deputies. Our executive-style name badges that boldly iden-tified us by name and assignment and were designed to be worn on suit jackets, were on the dashes of our vehicles where they would be easily seen if someone had a problem with where we had parked. Generally speaking, detectives from Homicide were treated with great respect throughout the county, especially at the patrol stations. We handled all of their murders and officer-involved shootings, the latter especially carrying significant weight.

Before we reached the back door that would take us in through the booking area and allow us access to the sergeant's office, the door to the detective bureau flew open. An overweight, gray-haired man wearing a short-sleeve dress shirt and a fat tie stuck his head out. "Hey, where are you guys from?"

I thought of the complaint that had come in the day before. "Forgery Fraud," I called out over my shoulder without pausing for conversation. Floyd hurried ahead of me to catch the booking door as a deputy came out. He held it open without looking toward the inquiring detective, and I walked in ahead of him. Floyd followed and closed the door behind him.

As I led the way to the sergeant's office, Floyd grumbled from behind me, *"Forgery Fraud.* Jesus, dude, why didn't you tell him Narco or something? That's fucking embarrassing, Forgery Fraud."

"We don't look like we're from Narco, dumbass."

I turned sideways to allow a pair of uniformed deputies to pass; they were clearly rushing toward the parking lot with purpose. They had likely been assigned a hot call or perhaps another unit in the field had requested backup. I watched them pass and then made eye contact with Floyd.

"You could have said we were from Major Crimes, or Arson, or the Office of the Sheriff, for that matter."

"House fairies? You want me to say we're house fairies?"

"I don't give a shit if you say we're from Internal Affairs. Just don't ever say Forgery Fraud again. Jesus, that's embarrassing."

I smiled and turned to continue my path to the sergeant's office. I glanced back at Floyd and said, "Well, it will keep him guessing for a while, anyway."

18

We stood in the hallway and watched through the glass partition of the sergeant's office as a young deputy seemed to be getting an education behind closed doors. The doors to the sergeants' offices were never closed unless privacy was needed, and we knew better than to knock. The man with stripes on his sleeves was black with short cropped hair that was mostly gray, matching his mustache. He leaned back in his chair, flagging a handful of papers that appeared to be a report toward the deputy.

"Somebody done fucked up," Floyd said.

I nodded and turned toward the sound of heavy footsteps falling on the tile floor behind us. A deputy in a green flight suit, his pant legs tucked into highly polished Corcoran jump boots, rounded the corner and met my gaze. "You the guys from Homicide wanted a ride in my bird?"

"Yes sir," I said, "that would be us."

He paused a moment, appraising the two of us skeptically.

We shook hands and introduced ourselves. A name tag sewn onto the chest of his olive drab-colored flight suit identified him as LASD Sergeant John Banks. He was the pilot I had spoken with the day before, though he didn't bother mentioning it when he shook our hands. He was a large man with deeply tanned forearms that showed scars and old tattoos of poor quality that had become blobs of faded ink over the years. A stubby, unlit cigar was propped in the corner of his mouth, protruding from a bushy salt-and-pepper mustache. He told us to follow him, then turned and headed in the direction he had come. His backside was wide from the spread of a middle-age man who spent too much of his time seated, but his shoulders were broad and thick, and I knew he was strong and powerful from the grip of his handshake.

We followed him down the hallway past the break room and past the restrooms. When we turned the corner, Sergeant Banks pulled an interior door open and stepped aside, motioning toward a set of stairs. "Stop up top and I'll lead the way out."

At the top of two flights of concrete steps we paused at a solid door and Sergeant Banks pushed past us, opening the door into a bright morning sky on the roof of the station. Floyd stepped through and lowered his sunglasses. I followed, removing my sunglasses from the top of my ball cap and placing them over my eyes. The sergeant closed the door behind us but didn't move. It was clear he was going to provide instruction, and neither of us bothered to tell him we'd both flown many times in the past.

"My partner took the morning off since you boys needed a tour, so you two can fight over who rides up front with me. I sit on the right side, opposite of what most people would think. So whoever's riding up front, you'll be on the left. The other one will sit on the left in the back. I can watch my side and will be better at it than both of you put together, because it takes some getting used to, seeing shit from a couple thousand feet above and knowing what you're looking at. Especially in the mountains.

"You'll always approach the helicopter from the front, even when it's not running. You build safe habits. You have to remember something around these birds: everything is dangerous and expensive. Anyway, you walk around the back of one of these jobs you get made into sausage from the tail rotor. Don't walk uphill away from a bird if we set down in the mountains, because that's how you get your head chopped off. Don't let your coats or anything else blow around freely. It doesn't take much to get sucked into the motor or the rotors."

Banks turned and walked hunched over as he approached the bird and we followed suit, building safe habits. I staged near the front seat and

Floyd went to the rear. It was my gig, my partner missing, and my murder on the mountain. We were on the same page and it didn't need to be discussed, which was the way Floyd and I had always worked as partners. Banks went around the bird and released its tie-downs. Once finished, he came back to where we were assembled at the left side of the helicopter where he went over the operations of door latches and seatbelts, and then headsets from which we would be able to hear radio traffic on the sheriff's frequencies. We would also be able to communicate to one another in the helicopter, he said.

"If you hear me talking on the radio, shut the fuck up. If it's quiet, you're free to speak and ask all the stupid questions you want."

Floyd grinned and hoisted himself into the back seat. I waited while Banks reached in to assist him in getting everything situated. I climbed into the front and prepared for flight without assistance, having watched closely as Floyd got set up. Going up in helicopters was a necessity from time to time for investigators, but the flights were relatively short and infrequent, so we lacked familiarity. After we were all seated, buckled, and briefed, Banks pulled a helmet over his head and adjusted a microphone close to his mouth. He fired up the bird and took several minutes to check instruments, the radio, and our intercom. "Test, test," he said into our ears. I gave a thumbs up and Banks looked into the back seat and nodded. I assumed Floyd gave him a thumbs up as well.

Moments later the bird began pulsating as the motor wound up and the rotors spun violently above us. The intercom hummed as Banks keyed his mic and said, "Okay, girls, we're off. If either of you ladies feel sick, there's barf bags in the front pockets of your seats."

The station below us grew smaller as we lifted slowly and steadily until we came to a stop. A hover they call it, but we were stopped in midair when I felt we should be going somewhere. It seemed to me if you weren't moving, you weren't flying. And if you're in an aircraft, you always wanted to be flying. Soon the back lifted, the nose dipped down, and the power of acceleration pushed me back against my seat as we shot off to the west. We climbed and accelerated and the traffic below us became smaller and slower than our travel. The bird seemed to settle once we were high above the trees and buildings and telephone lines. I figured we were a couple thousand feet up. Also, I was dying to start a conversation on the intercom.

"What are we at, about two-thousand feet?"

Banks glanced over as he answered through the headset. "Roughly a thousand; that's cruising altitude. About five-hundred if we're chasing bad guys or holding containment."

"No kidding. I would have guessed much higher."

"You did."

"Right," I said, and let off of the button that allowed me to speak in the headset. After a moment, I asked, "What's the speed capability of one of these things?"

Floyd's voice was distorted through the headset. "Dickie, shut the fuck up. I knew I shouldn't have let you ride up front."

Sergeant Banks grinned. I couldn't see Floyd behind me, but I gave him a one-finger salute over my shoulder. And I shut up.

A few minutes passed and Banks said, "Hundred and twenty in good weather, maybe a little faster with a tailwind."

It didn't take long before the sprawling city of Santa Clarita was behind us and our view below changed to the I-5 on our side of the bird, the left side. Beyond the snaking interstate I saw miles of hills covered in sage and rock, dried riverbeds, and Castaic Lake. Soon the mountains were shrouded with trees and scrub brush and a spattering of winding dirt roads. We passed Pyramid Lake and not long after, we banked to the right where I knew we would find Liebre Mountain.

The bird slowed and I started scouring the wooded ground below us. Suddenly we banked hard to the right and went in a circle. I looked down, being able to see past the pilot and straight to the ground. We must have been almost completely sideways. I didn't see anything and wondered what it was that the pilot might have seen that caused the sudden change in flight, but I didn't want to ask a stupid question on the intercom. I had been warned.

When the helicopter straightened and seemed to fly slow and easy again, Sergeant Banks spoke calmly to us through our earpieces. "There's a marijuana grow right back there. I circled around and recorded the coordinates, and I'll pass it on to the MET team."

I knew that MET was an acronym for Marijuana Eradication Team, but

I had no firsthand knowledge of how they worked. I craned my neck and searched behind us, but we had already traveled too far. I wanted to ask him to circle around but chose to remain silent.

He seemed to have read my mind. "I'd take you back around and show you, but it will scare them off and the MET team will end up with nothing but a lot of marijuana and no suspects."

"What about any cars?" I asked. "We're interested in finding a red Ford Taurus out here."

"No cars," the sergeant replied, "and no roads. These grows are set up miles from easy access and the equipment is humped in and out by the farmers, along with the marijuana."

Floyd chimed in, "Farmers? That's what they call these pricks?"

"Most of the guys they're finding up in the mountains are all wets. They come to farm. Marijuana in the mountains, or lettuce and strawberries in the fields, almonds farther north—what's the difference? They're not dope dealers or even affiliated. We're finding out that most of them are brought across and taken straight into the mountains without a clue as to where they even are. They have no way to get out, so they stay and work with the promise of being paid after the harvest. You have to feel a little sorry for the poor bastards."

Floyd said, "I thought they were getting a lot of guns off these grow busts. I know there was a shootout with one of the teams not long ago, somewhere in the Angeles National Forest."

"Sometimes they hit these deals at the right time and come across the guards who take the farmers in and bring them out with the product. Those assholes are heavily armed, and they *will* shoot it out with the cops. The farmers, though, they're just trying to make some money and have a better life.

I watched him as he spoke, and he glanced over when he finished and met my gaze. He knew flying and MET operations and probably a lot more, from being an old-time copper. I knew how to get inside people and read them by having conversations with them, from being an experienced investigator. It was never easy convincing someone that it was a good idea to confess murder to a homicide investigator. The way you did it was by breaking through shells and connecting with the person. The tough old cookie pilot had just allowed me to see past his shell, and if I needed to break him, I would have been able to do so. His eyes told me he realized it the second he finished speaking. We both knew that beneath his hardened exterior was a big fat marshmallow.

A few minutes had passed and we were now banking to the left where Floyd and I each had unimpeded views of the mountainous terrain below us.

"That's Liebre Mountain below us. That's where you said you wanted to go, right?"

"Yeah," I said into the headset, "I've got a murder scene just south and west of that peak, maybe a couple of miles by road, a mile or less as the crow flies."

"What would you like to see?"

"Well, the lay of the land—what we're seeing now—the proximity to any homesteads or camps, and the distance from the highway. Not really sure, to be honest, but figured being up here might jar something loose for us."

"What about a red car?" he asked. "You said you were looking for one. That your suspect's vehicle?"

I considered the question a moment before answering. "I'd say more of a person of interest."

He watched me as I finished answering.

Floyd said, "Tell him about the dickwad compound."

I chuckled into the mic. "Yeah, we came upon the Watkins outfit yesterday. I'd say anyone there is a potential suspect in our murder case."

"Yeah, I flew over you boys yesterday, you and the K twins, and a warden I believe. I'm familiar with the Watkins outfit. That's just over the peak there, a few clicks north. You boys seen all you need to see here? I can take us over and buzz the compound, see what's going on. Maybe stir up a little dust and piss them off."

"K twins?" Floyd said, "that's what you call Kramer and Kennedy?"

"It's what I call 'em; simpler than saying both of their names all the time. That or dumb and dumber."

"They seemed like good dudes," I said.

He pulled us out of the orbit and headed north, glanced over at me again. "They *are* good dudes. That Kennedy is a crazy bastard. You hear about the shooting he was in when the Watkins kid stole his ride?"

I chuckled into the mic. "He was telling us about that. Crazy. He said he got into another shooting not long after, and it was one of these grows."

I was thinking about Josie and all of the possibilities, and it seemed the mountains were a dangerous place to be. I hoped she hadn't come up here by herself, and I doubted that she had. But the images of Watkins and his band of bearded followers persisted in my head and I kept seeing Josie tied in a bedroom of one of the cabins. But where would her car be?

"Yeah, that was one of the only times I know of where a grow bust went hot," Sergeant Banks said. "Usually it's just a lot of hard working *mojados* they find manning them. But that's why they pay us the big bucks. You never know. Here's the compound. You want me to stay high or drop down and fuck with 'em?"

We had gained elevation going over the peak and were probably close to a thousand feet above ground, I realized, having been schooled in flight altitudes during the trip out.

"I say we stay high unless we see something of interest," I said.

"They're coming out of the shelters to have a look," Floyd said from the back seat. "Looks like they're all armed again."

"Probably always are," I said.

"You can count on it," Banks replied. "Long as they don't take any potshots at Irene, I won't worry about it. They're all show down there, wannabe warriors."

"Irene?" I said.

"That's what I call her," Banks said, "my lovebird, Irene. She reminds me of a girl I knew who was built for speed and always available for a spin."

"That's what I'm talking about," Floyd said.

"Anyway, they take a shot at Irene, I'll be crop dusting their asses while you boys are laying down lead. They'll only do that shit once."

I pictured the two hard-plastic rifle cases I had noticed in the back seat when the sergeant was getting Floyd secured before takeoff, and I imagined that they were likely AR-15s.

"Those AR-15s in the cases back there?" I asked.

"One's an AR, the other is a shotgun. It isn't easy shooting from a bird, but it can be a lot of fun. They have training once or twice a year for us out at Wayside, and all of the pilots and tactical flight deputies learn how to do it. Kick in the ass, to be honest."

We made three big circles over the compound, but I didn't see anything of interest. The structures were difficult to see through the trees, and the only vehicles I saw were the same ones that had been there the day before.

"Well, I'd say that'll probably do," I said over the intercom. "I've seen all I need to see for the day. What about you, Floyd?"

"Roger that," Floyd said. "Let's get back to civilization before something weird happens."

I craned my neck but couldn't see him behind me. "What do you think could happen when we're up here?"

"Who knows, Dickie. With my luck, you'll spot Sasquatch running across the mountain and insist we capture him. This whole place creeps me out. There's probably UFOs out here at night."

Sergeant Banks stared into the back seat, his face puffy from the fit of his helmet. After a long moment, he turned his attention back to where we were flying, and his voice came over the intercom: "I think you two need to get out of the city more often."

1 9

After setting down on the roof of Santa Clarita Station, Floyd and I waited for Sergeant Banks's instruction before stepping out and walking with our heads ducked low as we made our way back to the door. Quiet came as the door closed behind us, and the two of us walked side by side, in step down the staircase, through the station, and into the back parking lot. The detective sergeant was near my Crown Vic, looking it over as we approached.

"How ya doin', Sarge?" Floyd said as we went directly to our respective cars.

He nodded. "Where'd you boys say you're from?"

"Arson Explosives," I said.

I closed my door and quickly exited the parking lot, Floyd right on my bumper.

My phone rang.

"That's better, Dickie. Arson I can live with."

"I wonder if he saw my name plate on the dash. If so, we're screwed."

Floyd said, "Yeah, whatever. See you in Downey."

I disconnected and turned on the news station to catch traffic reports before the split—stay on the Five, or take the 210? That would be the question. Traffic was light so we sailed along in the fast lane, bumper to bumper, headed south.

When we arrived at the courthouse in Downey, Lopes was leaning against a black Ford Explorer with blacked-out windows, smoking a cigarette. I backed in alongside him and through my open window said, "I thought you quit."

"Shut up, stupid."

Floyd wheeled in beside me. Lopes looked past me in his direction. "I see you brought your girlfriend."

I nodded at the Explorer. "Where'd you get the hoop?"

"Michaels gave it to us for the operation. He didn't want us showing up in a Crown Vic. Besides, nobody can see homegirl inside."

I peered at the glass. He was right, you couldn't see anything. "She's in there now?"

"Her and your sister, Lacy Lou. I think they're talking girl shit or maybe changing clothes." He leaned back and looked through the windshield. "Nope, neither one of them is naked."

"Damn," Floyd said as he was getting out of his car. "Here I was thinking my day was starting to look up."

The three of us gathered under a cloudy sky at the front of the black Explorer. Lopes leaned on the hood and Floyd and I stood facing him, a view of traffic on Imperial Highway beyond his shoulder.

"So, what's the plan?" I asked.

Lopes blew a plume of smoke to the side, dropped his cigarette and mashed it with the toe of his brown, scuffed wingtip shoe. "*Huero*'s inside chilling, and he hasn't stopped asking anyone who'll listen why he's here. Nobody seems to know," he said, and grinned. "He wasn't happy when he missed the early bus back to county, according to the lockup deputy, and now he's going to be even more pissed when he misses the late bus. But once all of the other inmates are gone, I'm going in there for showtime."

"Yeah?"

"My plan is to go straight at him. 'We have something you want, and you have something we want. I'm not here to play games and I don't have time for bullshit. You want to trade or no?' See what he says."

"You think that'll work?" Floyd asked.

He shrugged. "I think it's worth a shot. I definitely think I can read him either way, so it will be interesting to see how he reacts. But I'm just going to put it out there and see if he bites. I'll tell him his girl, Maria, isn't that valuable to us, that she's been playing games, trying to work the system."

The back window of the Explorer came partly down, and Maria Lopez, with her oversized sunglasses and untamed black tresses, appeared in the opening. "Hey, watch what you say about me, Lopes."

The window went back up and Lopes snickered.

I nodded toward the closed window. "She's okay with this?"

"It was practically her idea," Lopes said. "They fucked up by putting the hit on her and failing. She's like a rabid dog now, a woman scorned. She's out for blood when it comes to the mafia, her former family."

Lopes began patting his pockets and a frown creased his brows. He seemed to be perplexed at his inability to find whatever he was looking for. He walked around to the driver's side of the Explorer, opened the door, and leaned in. When he came back around to where Floyd and I stood waiting, he was shaking a cigarette from an open pack. "Now I have to quit again. Maybe tomorrow."

Floyd shook his head, feigning disgust. I removed my cap and wiped sweat from my forehead while Lopes lit his smoke.

Exhaling, Lopes continued, "It can only go one of two ways: either he's going to have no clue as to what I'm trying to barter for, or this will be exactly what he wants to hear and the games will begin. That's when it's going to get dicey."

"How so?" I asked.

"He's not going to trust us on this; not at first. That's why she's here," he said, rolling his eyes toward the back seat of the Explorer. "He won't think I'm bullshitting if I tell him that the reason I brought him to Downey is because she too was here today for a hearing, and that I would see to it that both would ride the late van back to county if we brokered a deal."

"Jesus," Floyd said, "You're going to transport them together?"

"Yeah, that's the risk. But I don't think he'll make a move on her even if he has a key to get out of his cuffs and a shiv up his ass—which, most of the time, these guys do. I think he will talk to her, try to find out what she's given us, convince her she's welcome back and all can be forgiven." Lopes glanced at the closed window that concealed Maria from our view.

He lowered his voice and continued, "That's where the real risk is. She says she's down for it and will play it to the fullest for us, but I imagine there's always going to be a strong pull back. They *are* her family."

"Is she wired?" Floyd asked.

Lopes nodded. "Yep. That might be our saving grace. A reminder for her, you know? I told her she needs to badmouth the shit out of us and tell him that we're fucking her over with her kids, so she's been lying to us about shit. That will jibe with what I'm going to have already told him. The hope is that he buys it, and then he sees that I'm serious about trading her for Josie. Basically, I'm going to tell him that by the time the van drops him off at county, he'll have an hour before it lands at CRDF with Maria, the last stop along the line."

"Wouldn't he know she hasn't been housed at Century Detention?" I asked. "The mafia has to have all sorts of bitches there."

Lopes nodded. "Yeah, let me finish. I'm going to let him know that he'll have an hour to make whatever calls he needs to make, and Josie had better appear somewhere, safe and sound. If she does, Maria gets housed at Century where they can easily make a move on her, take her out. If not —if I don't have Josie in hand—Maria stays on the van and gets returned to the safe house. I tell *Huero* it will all look like a mix-up in transportation and nobody ever knows any different."

The three of us stood silent for a moment. This seemed like a farfetched scheme, and a dangerous one at that. I wondered how they would protect her at the Century Regional Detention Facility. To my knowledge, there weren't any "keep-away" cells there.

"How are you going to protect her?"

"That's the dangerous part. We figure we only need to keep her in there a couple of hours until Josie is accounted for. Metro has three female undercovers who are standing by with county jumpsuits and ready to be bused into Century the second we say go. We'll keep the four of them together, and the U-Cs are going to have pepper spray and a taser with them. Once we have confirmation that Josie is in pocket, we yank Maria out and the mafia goes crazy knowing we fucked them. Which means they will put a green light on me or maybe any one of us. But what's new, right?"

"What about during transport?"

Lopes took a long drag on his cigarette, his brown eyes seeming to smile. "Well, Dickie, that's the fun part. This particular transportation van is being driven by one of the SWAT guys, and we're going to have a helicopter tracking the van with a sniper on board. The rest of the SWAT team will be a mile behind but ready to move in if needed. Michaels is going to have a surveillance team with a close eye on the van at all times. They too have a green light to take him out if it goes hot in the van."

"Jesus," I said.

"That's where I want to be, in one of the U-Cs," Floyd said. "I'll put a cap in *Huero's* ass for him."

Lopes chuckled. "We might all be in prison when this is over. Or, they may pin medals on us too."

"I doubt that," I said. "Metro doesn't admit to half the shit they do. It's all black-bag ops shit. Never happened."

"The bottom line is, this may be all for naught. I still don't know how they could have grabbed her, or why they would go to that much trouble. Shit, it would be easier to try following one of us until they found the safe house, and then they could whack Maria there. This is a lot of work and risk for them, grabbing a cop."

I nodded and glanced at Floyd. He didn't say anything, but his eyes showed concern. I didn't know if it was because of the operation or a premonition he had about Josie, or something else.

"What's bothering you, partner?"

Floyd glanced at his watch. "I don't like any of this. You should be driving that transportation van with me riding shotgun."

I looked at Lopes. He shrugged. "You two goons look like anything other than transport deputies."

Floyd said, "Yeah, well, still. I'll kill *Huero* if he makes a move on our girl."

A HALF HOUR LATER LOPES WALKED OUT OF THE COURTHOUSE AND SLICED a finger across his throat indicating it was a no-go. *Huero* hadn't fallen for it, or the mafia had nothing to do with Josie going missing. Lopes smiled at a pair of attorneys he passed on the courthouse steps. They were a man and a woman, both dressed professionally and carrying attaché cases. The woman pushed a lock of hair behind her ear and smiled warmly as she watched Lopes pass by. The man seemed to frown. Floyd, sitting next to me in the Crown Vic, both of us with our heads back, resting, said, "Slut."

"Who, the lawyer?"

He sat up, popped his door open and paused. "Yeah, the lawyer. She's out there deciding if she's going to let that other asshole buy her drinks and maybe take her to bed tonight. She'll know before she agrees to the drinks how far it will go. Then, Lopes walks by, and she can't *not* check him out. A real man." He chuckled and stepped out of the car. I did the same. He looked across the hood and said, "Chick lawyers dig homicide cops."

"What's that, pretty boy?" Lopes said as he settled near our car. The three of us formed a circle. The girls—Lacy and Maria—were getting out of the back of the Explorer to join us.

Floyd said, "That chick lawyer back there looked at you the way a fat kid looks at cake. I was telling Dickie here how they dig homicide cops. Some of the lady judges too. All of 'em have the morals of alley cats."

Lacy punched Floyd in the shoulder. "You're a pig."

"Hey, I just call 'em as I see 'em, Lace. That one right there would drop her shorts for the Easter Bunny, guaranteed."

Lopes snickered and his eyes drifted toward Maria who stood silently, her shades now on top of her head to reveal lackluster eyes and a tightly drawn mouth. His expression changed to a somber one as if to match hers, and he said, "Well, bad news on the mob, boys and girls."

"What happened?" I asked.

"They don't have her."

He held my gaze, no doubt knowing I'd want more detail on the interaction. That I'd want proof, evidence, a sworn statement.

"How do we know for sure?"

"Trust me, I know. Guaranteed."

I nodded to indicate I wanted to hear more.

"He believes that I'm willing to trade Maria—he was willing to go for it. So much so that he tried to broker another deal."

"Like what?"

Lopes looked at Maria again before his eyes settled back on me. "Dirty cops. He says he will give us two deputies on the mafia payroll if we put Maria in general pop for twenty-four hours."

"What'd you say?" Maria demanded.

He grinned at her. "What the fuck do you think I said? I'm not going to get you killed to find out who's smuggling cell phones and dope into the jails for *Eme*."

"Thank fucking God," Maria said. "Thank you."

"Great," I said, "what do we do with that?"

"Nothing," Lopes said flatly. "It'll catch up with them. It's not our job to take down dirty cops—that's why they have the rat squad."

I nodded, and Lopes continued. "And that doesn't leave this circle. Ever."

After a moment, I said, "I'll call Michaels, tell him we're shutting this down. On to Plan B."

"Which is what?" Floyd asked, exasperated. "Back to the mountain?"

I looked at him before answering, then saw that each of them was watching me, waiting. "I don't know. I haven't a clue."

Lopes pushed his sleeve up and checked the time. "I'm going to get homegirl back to the safe house. You guys check in with Metro and let them know what's up, see if they have any ideas. After Lacy and I drop Maria off, we'll phone you to see what's new. If nobody has come up with anything, I say we go have dinner and some beers and come up with a new strategy. We have to be missing something. Cops don't just disappear. Not our cops."

Maria turned and stepped into the Explorer, resolutely closing the door behind her.

"She okay?" Floyd asked.

"She's fine. She's probably irritated about us dropping her off then going out. She thinks she's part of the team now," Lopes said, his gaze held toward the dark window that concealed her. "She had her chance."

I could see the pain in Lopes's expression as he said it, and I knew he had felt something for her before knowing who she really was. Maybe some of that feeling still lingered. I pushed off of the fender and moved toward my door, ready to go. That set others in motion, but before anyone ducked into their cars, I added a thought. "I think we'll also head to the office and see if anything has come from her laptop. Lonnie was going to hack in and see if there's anything of interest, maybe a new boyfriend or something."

Lopes nodded. "Good. We'll check in when we're headed back."

With that, the sound of four doors closing preceded three engines starting. Tires groaned against the asphalt as we each of us pulled out of our spaces, turning hard to the right to head for the exit.

When we were back on Imperial Highway headed west, I let out a long, exhausted breath. "Well, shit."

20

I drove to the office deep in thought and Floyd followed close behind, not allowing anyone to come between us. My thoughts were all over the place but the subject matter was women: Josie, Katherine, Valerie. And my new neighbor, the lady cop who lives next door. I wished I had her number and could call and let her know I'd be working long hours on this case. Tell her that my partner, Josie, was missing, and that we had a crazy murder going on in the mountains. I wondered if she would feel sorry for me and offer to have a drink later when I came home. Would she be impressed with my career as a homicide detective? Probably not, I reasoned; feds were brainwashed to think they were superior to all others, even though few of them ever did real police work on the streets. Maybe I could ask her to check on my fish, Cosmo, feed him and let him know I'd be home late again. I glanced at Floyd in my mirror and wondered what he was thinking about. Probably women also. I envied Floyd at times, his nice little family, and yet I knew he also envied the simplicity of my life as a single man. I guess you can't have it all: marriage could be a bitch, but freedom took its own toll.

I turned into the parking lot of our office and glanced at my watch. Not even five and the place looked vacant.

Floyd and I backed our cars in side by side as smoothly as synchronized swimmers turning a somersault under water. A single thunk resounded across the empty lot as both of our car doors closed together. We met at the fronts of our cars and were now walking in step across the lot toward the back door of the bureau.

"Doesn't anyone work long hours around here anymore?"

"New breed, Dickie. They do their eight and they're out the gate."

I shook my head in silent protest of the world—and my department—changing around me. I realized my thoughts had taken me far away and Floyd had been speaking to me while we crossed the lot.

". . . and if it's not the mob, then what happened to her?"

I looked at him but didn't answer. That was, of course, the million-dollar question, one to which I had no answer.

He continued, "It's either random—she was grabbed while jogging or something—or it's related to that goddam mountain. Or, she ran away from life."

I frowned at him.

"She wasn't suicidal, was she?"

We had stopped at the back door to the bureau and faced each other. I was fishing in my pocket for my keys, and I could feel my brows crowding my eyes as I stared at my partner who was watching his reflection in the mirrored door. Suicide had never once crossed my mind, and the thought of it seemed perverse.

"No, she wasn't suicidal. Not that I know of, anyway. Why the hell would you ask that?"

Floyd's head slowly turned until I was looking into his Ray-Bans, picturing his hazel eyes that were hidden behind them. "You never know with broads, Dickie. That's the thing."

I didn't respond. I had found my keys and turned away from him as I unlocked the door, seeing Floyd's reflection in the glass.

"Besides," he said, "working with you could make a person want to eat their gun."

I flipped the bird at his reflection and I could see his grin as I opened the door and stepped to the side, not bothering to hold it for him.

Inside, a short, robust man with thinning gray hair and rosy cheeks walked toward us with purpose. He held a large fast-food soda in one hand

and a thick file in the other. We made eye contact as he got closer, and he smiled.

"Hello, Lonnie, what'd you come up with?"

His eyeglasses, secured by a lanyard around his neck, sat crooked on his face. A row of pens and other cylindrical items were secured in his breast pocket protector—erasers, an exacto knife, a tire pressure gauge . . .

"Maybe a few things to work with. She was on a dating site, and of course she had lots of messages and requests related to that. I didn't go through it all, but I printed all of it for you guys," he said, raising the file in his hand to exhibit his work product.

I hadn't noticed how thick the file was until he held it up and identified it as the work from Josie's case. Now it was of great interest to me and I looked forward to digging into the two-inch-thick stack of papers. I reached out to accept the proffered file.

"That's a lot," I said.

"I'm not done yet. That's just the start, the easy stuff. Now I'm going to get into hidden files where data you think you've erased can be found. That takes more time. Maybe by the end of the day tomorrow?"

I motioned with my head toward the hallway behind us. "Let's get a cup and take a look at what you've got so far."

The three of us went into the kitchen and found a warm pot with an inch of thick, black matter cooking on the bottom. Floyd grabbed the pot and I took the filter of cold, wet grounds out of the machine. As he washed and rinsed the pot, I readied a new brew, and within minutes the teamwork had produced a fresh pot. Lonnie had gone to the vending machine and bought a Coke, and he added the contents of it to the fast-food cup he still carried with him. Topping it off, I supposed. The three of us met at a table where we pulled out chairs and set our beverages down before us. Lonnie reached for the file I had taken from him. "May I?"

"Of course," I said.

He opened the file and began removing its contents, placing papers in front of himself but upside down so that Floyd and I could see them from our side of the table. The stack of papers inside the file was separated into a dozen or so groups by paper clips. He fanned the first several stacks and said, "The first four or five groups are copies of emails from men she seemed to be communicating with the most, at least by email. As you go farther into the file—" he thumbed through the stack to get to about the middle "—you'll find others with whom she had only had a couple of contacts. Probably guys she wasn't interested in. The interesting thing is that the level of activity seemed to drop suddenly about a month ago."

"Like she dropped the site, or settled on someone?"

"Well, she didn't drop the site, but she seemed to stop using it. So yeah, maybe she met someone."

A pair of detectives walked into the kitchen and nodded as they went straight to the coffee pot and filled their cups. From the few words I heard exchanged between them, I knew they were talking about the fights. Over the weekend, our department had hosted the Fight for Life boxing tournament, an annual event for the last twenty-plus years in which officers from the LAPD go head-to-head with sheriff's deputies in a friendly but tough competition that benefited the City of Hope cancer research center. One of the two detectives, a stocky Hispanic with a scarred face, was a referee, and I knew he would have worked at the fights. Lonnie had paused while I watched the pair at the coffee pot.

"Who won, Manny?"

The referee detective looked over at our table. "The kids." He smiled, and they both walked out. I knew he meant there were no losers in an event where all proceeds went directly to cancer research with an emphasis on children.

I turned my attention back to Lonnie, who waited with the papers still propped on the table between us. He continued to go through the remaining stacks and provide us with an idea of what we would be viewing and from where the information had come. I was thinking about Josie, knowing she had been a big fan of the fights, and I wondered if she had gone Saturday night. It occurred to me that we were at the point where this could no longer be kept quiet, nor should it be. Maybe a department teletype with a brief statement of the facts and a call for information from anyone who might have seen her over the weekend would be appropriate. I pushed out of my chair and hurried to the hallway, and I heard Floyd behind me asking where I was going.

At the doorway I called out, "Manny" to the back of Detective Manny Lucero. He and his partner had just started around the corner into the squad room. He stopped and looked back.

"Did you happen to see Josie at the fights?"

"Oh, good thinking, Dickie," Floyd said, stepping up to my side.

Manny shook his head. "I don't remember seeing her. Why, what's up?"

It occurred to me that few knew of the situation with Josie missing, even though at times this place was worse than a hair salon for gossip. With the investigation being led by Metro and having been moved to the STARS center in Whittier, she—and we—were out of sight and out of mind. Which had been the intent. I walked toward him rather than shouting down the hallway, and he moved toward me. We met in the middle, each with our partners at our sides. I said, "She's missing."

Manny frowned as if he didn't understand what I said.

"We have no idea what's happened. She's gone."

"Jesus," he said, and looked at his partner who stood shaking his head. Each of them now had intensity in their expressions, the faces of men who met challenge and danger head on, and whose claws came out rapidly when a loved one's safety was threatened. Almost all of us were made up this way, cops and most parents too.

"She was always a fan of the fights," I continued, "and I'm curious if she was there. She lives with her mother who said she hasn't seen her since Saturday."

He was nodding while listening. "She used to fight. I remember a few years back she had that epic fight with the LAPD chick who looked like a man. She won—Josie did—and the girl went after her again when I raised Josie's hand as the winner. I refereed the fight and then had to break up the post-fight fight. That LAPD bitch was nasty, fought like she was off the street, if you know what I mean." He took a sip of his coffee and his eyes seemed distant as if he was recalling that night from several years ago.

"Put the word out with the fighters and anyone you know who was there. We need to know if Josie went to the fights Saturday night. So far, we can't find anyone who's seen her since she left home that afternoon."

Manny Lucero nodded, then he reached over and put a hand on my shoulder. I could feel his strength through the slight squeeze he offered as a way of embracing me. "I'll check it out, brother. Let me know what else we can do."

I thanked him and the two of them turned away.

I turned to Floyd. He lifted the file to show me it was in his hand, and I saw Lonnie walk out of the kitchen and take the hallway in the opposite direction toward his office.

"We're done?"

"Yep. How do you want to do this?"

"Over cocktails," I said.

21

Floyd and I had two beers each and shared a plate of quesadilla appetizers at a local Mexican restaurant while sifting through the private internet life of Josefina Sanchez. We were waiting for Lopes and Lacy Lou to meet us, which they had planned to do after dropping Maria Lopez back at the safe house in Huntington Beach.

"Is she gay?"

I looked away from the stack of papers that sat on the table in front of me and frowned at him. "I don't know. I don't think so. But, I mean, who knows? Why do you ask?"

Floyd was still studying his papers and didn't bother to look up as he took another swig of beer. "There's nothing so far that shows any relationship stuff. Everything I've seen so far could be written by her brother. This one guy is a friend from the gym, someone it seems she works out with and maybe even spars with. There's another dude here who's obviously a cop, and might be an old partner. Tom, no last name. But nothing that sounds like romance, to me. Can Lonnie figure out where these emails come from? Do you know?"

I shook my head. "He can get IP addresses, which I think narrows the search to a region, but that's about it. We can have the girls over at Major Crimes research email addresses through their data providers, but there's no guarantee they'll come up with matching IDs. The problem with email is I can create an address right now, 'Bob Bitchin' at Gmail,' and register it to Bobby Brown. There's no verifications involved."

He reached for a slice of the quesadilla and paused with it over the glob of sour cream on the plate. "It's probably already taken, Dickie. But you could maybe go with Dumbass Dickie at Gmail dot com." He shoved half of the quesadilla into his mouth and smiled while chewing it.

My phone vibrated on the table and I saw it was Lopes calling in. I pushed the green button and lifted the phone to my face. "What's up, buddy?"

"Lacy got a break on a case she was working with Norris, so I'm going to roll with her to Twin Towers to talk to an inmate. We can catch up with you guys later or tomorrow. I don't know how long we'll be."

I looked over at Floyd. "They're going to county to interview someone. How long are we going to be here?"

Floyd glanced at his watch while Lopes said into my ear, "That's right, check with your sister."

"I'm about ready to go now," Floyd said. "I can look at this stuff at home and see the wife and kids before Sancho moves in and they start calling him 'Daddy.'"

"Let's catch up tomorrow," I told Lopes. We disconnected and I looked at Floyd. "She probably already does."

He frowned, not catching it.

"Cindy. She probably calls Sancho, 'Daddy.'"

He flipped me off and went back to reading and drinking his beer.

After finishing our beers, Floyd and I parted company and each of us headed to our homes. He was going to spend some time with the kids, and if the wife was in a better mood, he thought maybe it would be a good evening for a nightcap in the Jacuzzi. I was going to check in with Metro while making the trip north to my apartment where Cosmo would be swimming around waiting to be fed. He wouldn't gripe and complain about the hours I kept, nor would he judge me for my interest in the new neighbor. Fish were good companions like that.

Sgt. Jack Smith answered the phone that had been designated as the hotline for the Josie Sanchez missing person case. He told me he would be there until midnight, then a sergeant from Human Trafficking would take the helm. A couple of investigators from that unit would spend the night running down and leads that might come in, and they would be available to roll out if needed. The Human Trafficking Bureau was relatively new in name, but in reality, it was the Vice Detail reincarnated with a few additional responsibilities and focuses, and a modern, politically correct name. After all, nobody gave a shit about vice laws now. Smith said if we had anything they could do to keep them busy through the night, to make sure we utilized them; they were all making overtime on this operation. It gave me the idea to call the command post later with all of the email addresses Floyd and I now had, and have them try to match names to as many as they could. So far, none of the emails had offered any leads or even hope, but a list of corresponding names might come in handy. Maybe someone on that list had seen or spoken with Josie over the weekend.

Before we hung up, I told Sergeant Smith about the Fight for Life event and my idea about getting the word out to those who participated or attended to see if anyone had seen her. Jack Smith knew just about everyone on the department, or so it seemed, so I wasn't surprised when he told me he was friends with one of the coaches of the boxing team. He said he'd call him and get the word out through the team.

I disconnected the call, turned the air conditioner off, and rolled down the windows to take in the cool evening air. As I neared downtown, I could see the glow of Dodger Stadium and was reminded that life went on in the City of Angels in spite of the devilish deeds committed by those who lurked in her underbelly. I tuned the radio to pick up the game and listened to Rick Monday broadcast the play-by-play, anxiously waiting to hear what inning they were in. Once the seventh began, hordes of "loyal" Dodgers fans—who had arrived only four innings earlier—would file out of the stadium in order to beat the rush of traffic home. The arteries leading in all directions from Chavez Ravine would soon be clogged by those who would join me in taking in the game audibly, while mobile. I enjoyed listening to Rick Monday and would always have a special place for him in my heart because of the night he saved an American flag from being burned on the field by some foreigner protesting our country. But as much as I liked Monday, I missed listening to Vin Scully and Don Drysdale. As for Ross Porter, I'd just as soon have listened to the Korean station broadcast.

I was a few miles from the East L.A. interchange when Monday announced the boys were headed to the bottom of the seventh. I would likely beat the Dodgers traffic and be home before the game was over.

When I arrived home I immediately noted that the neighbor's lights were on but the shades were drawn and the front door was closed. So I traipsed past, making sure my footsteps could be heard in the event she had been thinking about meeting the cop next door. I envisioned her tapping on my door a few minutes after I went inside, having left it open behind me, and asking to borrow a cup of sugar. Or maybe getting straight to it by asking if I was up for a drink and some company.

The fantasy that had played out in my head never materialized, and the night breeze quickly cooled, so after an hour of diminishing hope, I shut the door and windows.

In that hour I had listened to the game on TV while organizing a list of email addresses to provide to the night crew at the command post. Once finished, I called the command post and spoke with a Sergeant Woo from the Human Trafficking Bureau. She said she and two of her investigators were there until six in the morning, and they would be happy to work on the list. They would run the accounts that produced legitimate names through various databases to come up with information such as employment, licensing, histories of residency, relatives, liens and judgements, and of course, criminal histories. I jotted her email address in my notebook and thanked her in advance for their work. When we disconnected, I sent her the data.

That handled, I dimmed the lights and drank another beer in the glow of a muted television where sports announcers appeared to be analyzing highlights of the day's games. Baseball was headed toward the final few weeks and football was now in full swing. Between great sports and cooling weather, this would normally be my favorite time of the year, but dread washed over me as I sat in the darkness and imagined the plight of my partner. In the blood business, finality was compassionate. The dead no longer suffered pain, and the terrors of their final moments were behind them. For the survivors, a sense of peace could accompany the scenes of unspeakable violence, in the way gentle winds persisted against the black-green skies over the ruins of a tornado. The destruction, the pain, the death that was left behind, those were manageable things that required sensible and logical responses, plans, and actions. Perhaps the tasks to recover and rebuild were only distractions from the terror that had struck when the winds roared like trains and giant hailstones crashed through the darkening skies and earthly possessions were mercilessly uprooted and hurled from one place to the other. Those were moments that seemed like lifetimes as the battle had yet to be measured and survival was uncertain. Death, though, is finality. Certainty.

I switched off the television and sprawled onto my couch, content where I lay for the time being, and likely for the night. In the darkness I could hear the sounds of light traffic and the movements of neighbors, soft steps scurrying through living spaces, the muted sounds of televisions, the occasional opening and closing of doors, the running of water. I thought about my neighbor and wondered if she was alone or had company, and whether she was getting ready for bed or going to work. You never knew with cops. Again I wondered where she worked, if she was in fact a cop. In years past, I would have noted the license number of her vehicle and made a simple inquiry through DMV files which were accessible to all police officers. Cops were allowed to register their personal vehicles as "confidential" by simply filling out a form and submitting it to the DMV. The confidential registration would withhold the home address of the registrant and note the agency of their employment in its place. *Richard Jones, Los Angeles County Sheriff's Department.* But no longer could a police officer run the license plates of neighbors and motorists without good cause, and to identify an attractive woman was the antithesis of that. The computers had long ago been altered to require all users to log in, and all inquiries required a reason for the search. As investigators, a simple file number of the case we were working would suffice. In the event of an audit, you wouldn't want to try explaining how an attractive neighbor fit into your murder investigation. Besides, I hadn't yet identified her car.

In the darkness I closed my eyes, thinking the last thing I needed in my life at this moment was a woman. The glow of a light in the room drew my eyes open, and I recognized the source as my phone. A wave of shock rolled over me when I reached to retrieve it. In the instant before the screen darkened, I thought I saw that I had received a text message from Josie.

22

Wiping the sleepiness from my eyes with one hand, I thumbed the phone back to life with the other. My heart beat faster when I confirmed that I hadn't imagined it. A text from Josie awaited me, and I only knew one Josie. There was only one Josie in my contact list. I opened the message.

902t on mtn help

It was the radio code for a traffic accident. I responded immediately: *Where are you?* Five seconds later: *Are you okay?*

Another ten seconds passed without a response. I screenshot the message and sent it to Floyd while moving quickly to the kitchen where the attaché containing my notebooks sat on the table. I grabbed the notebook I had started for Josie's case and flipped to the inside front cover where I had important numbers noted. As I began punching in the landline to the command post, it occurred to me I could have looked at my call log and found it there. Before I hit send, my phone lit up again, only this time a picture of shirtless Floyd with a snorkel and mask populated the screen. I took the call.

"You saw the message?"

"Yeah, what the hell? Where is she? Did you message her back? Has she said anything—"

"That's all there was," I interrupted. "Just what you saw, and it came in as a text, not an iMessage, so I can't even tell if she's read my response or not. But an accident, on the mountain. That's what I get out of it. "

"If it's not coming through as an iMessage, it's because she's barely got a signal. That explains why they haven't been able to track her phone."

"That makes sense. There's only one place on the mountain I've ever found a signal."

"What now?" Floyd asked.

"I need to call the command post and make sure they're tracking her phone. Meet me at Santa Clarita in thirty—make it forty-five. Bring your survival shit."

He started to speak but I disconnected the call and rang through to the command post while rushing to start a pot of coffee.

"Sergeant Woo—"

"Sarge," I interrupted, speaking rapidly, "it's Jones from Homicide. I just got a message from Josie's phone saying she's been in an accident on the mountain. Can your team start tracking her cell? My partner and I are headed that way."

"I'll call the lieutenant and let him know. I'm not sure who—"

"Okay, whatever it takes. Shit!" I said, dropping a mug on the counter-top. It shattered and I left it there, reaching for another. "Sorry about that, broke a mug. Listen, Sarge, I don't mean to be abrupt, but yes, do whatever it takes to get someone tracking that cell, and do so as quickly as possible. Call me if you need anything; otherwise, I'll check in before we go out of range."

I set my phone among the debris of a broken blue ceramic cup that previously boasted a gold star, one of my department mugs. I hoped it wasn't an omen. I finished getting the coffee started, grabbed my phone, and checked my messages again while hurrying into my bedroom for a change of clothes that would be suitable for sustained mountain dwelling. I made a mental checklist, picturing the items in my trunk: boots, water, first-aid, AR-15, extra ammo, county blanket . . . What else? Of course all of my crime scene processing equipment and material, but I wouldn't be needing any of that—or would I? I forced the thought from my mind and continued on with the mental inventory: change of clothes, extra hat, gloves, rope . . . I stood for a moment and looked around my room in the event something would trigger a thought. Nothing did, so I went to the kitchen and poured fresh coffee into a thermos. I grabbed a plastic grocery bag and filled it with protein bars, what few pieces of fruit I had, and a plastic jar of mixed nuts. I holstered my gun and extra magazines and wove my belt through each, grabbed my attaché and hat and started for the front door. I stopped and flung open the hallway closet and grabbed my North Face down jacket.

After I pulled the door shut behind me, I stopped and tucked the thermos of coffee under the arm that held the bag of food, my attaché, and coat. I briefly fumbled with my keys to bolt the door behind me. As I began to step away, I was startled by a woman standing in the light that spilled from her open door. Next door. *The cop.*

She wore shorts and a loose-fitting t-shirt, and her hair was pulled up on her head. It was the closest I had been to her and was mesmerized by her auburn hair and light green eyes. Irish, I supposed. She was in her forties: mature, confident, watchful. "Is everything okay, Detective?"

It surprised me that she knew I was a detective. Words bounced around in my head before I could form a response. "Yes, it is. Sorry about the noise; I broke a mug."

She shook her head. "No problem, just checking. It's good to know I've got a cop for a neighbor."

I held her gaze without responding until it felt uncomfortable and I looked away.

"You're in a hurry," she said, pulling back from the door. "When you're not, we should chat."

"Yeah, you bet," I stuttered. "I'll, uh, be seeing you around, neighbor."

She smiled and disappeared behind the door, closing it lightly.

I keyed open the trunk of my Crown Vic and put the jacket, change of clothes, and bag of food in with the rest of the equipment. Inside the car I checked my phone messages again. Nothing. I had no way to see if she had received or opened my reply. It occurred to me to check the time her message was sent, and it indicated that it was sent just as I received it, shortly before eleven. I wondered if that was when it was actually typed, or just when the phone finally found a signal. It seemed she no longer had the signal, or maybe her battery was dead. I pictured her outside of her car in a brushy draw that we hadn't been able to see by driving on the mountain roads. Maybe she had a broken leg and it had taken her three days to crawl out of a hole and high enough to find a cell phone signal to get help. I prayed her battery wasn't dead, and that it was a case of the signal coming and going. I plugged my phone into its charger, placed it in its cradle on the dash, and fired the engine.

After pulling away from the curb, I began racing through the streets of Burbank hoping the cops wouldn't see me. If they did, I'd hit the blue and amber "*excuse me*" lights on the rear deck and hope they left me alone. I didn't have time to explain who I was and what I was doing, and I was in no mood for a lecture. So far, all of the cops I had met here were cool, with the exception of one: a big-headed white guy with an Italian last name. I had stolen a glimpse of his name tag once when I walked past him, but now I couldn't recall it, only that it sounded Italian. He worked the graveyard shift and seemed to always be parked at the 7-Eleven sipping coffee and chewing seeds. He was a salty patrol cop who usually had a younger cop with him who would sit sheepishly in the passenger's seat of their patrol car while Officer Salty leaned on his hood and visited with other cops to pass the time. He had eyeballed me once when I stopped to buy a box of beer on the way home one night. Though he was well aware I was a cop—or otherwise the least observant cop I ever knew —he offered nothing other than a fatheaded nod when I walked past him and said hello. The 7-Eleven that served as his substation happened to be along my direct route to the freeway. I flew past it and glanced over to see no cops in the parking lot. *Whew.*

Floyd was calling in. I answered the phone with, "Let me call you right back," and disconnected. I pictured him alone in his car cussing his phone—rather, cussing me *at* his phone. I called the command post and told Woo to make sure to advise whoever would be in charge of tracking Josie's cell phone not to give up if they didn't find a signal. I wanted them checking constantly, every five or ten minutes. I hung up and returned Floyd's call.

"Sorry about that," I said. "I needed to check in with Woo at the C.P."

"What exactly is a Woo?"

"It's a female sergeant from Human Trafficking."

"I bet she's hot."

"Who knows," I said.

"So what's the word? Anything? Any more messages?"

I checked my mirrors as I brought it up to eighty on the northbound Golden State. "Nothing. I have no idea if my message even went through. There's no way to know."

"I've been thinking about the message—"

Floyd analyzed and reanalyzed every action, statement, and shred of evidence, in any case, situation, or setting. It was what he did. Nobody did it better, either. I may have been close, but I honestly felt he was burdened with a sickness that would never allow him to reconcile anything that wasn't as plain as day. Sometimes it could be tiresome but most of the time it was helpful. This would be one of those times. I needed to hear his thoughts on the succinct text message I had received.

"Of course you have," I said. "Let's hear it."

"Well, first of all, you were right that she may have gone back up on the mountain without you. The *why* is anybody's guess. It's fucking stupid, if you ask me, but I digress. So she must have gone back during the day Saturday because there would be no reason to go at night. I don't think anyone from the fights is going to respond to the request for information; she wasn't there. She was back on the mountain, and as I said, it'd be stupid of her to go there by herself."

"You said that," I said, aware of the irritation my tone revealed. "I got it. What's your point?"

"That she didn't."

"What? Wait, what are you saying? She didn't go up there, or she didn't go alone?"

"She didn't go alone."

I pondered that for a moment. "Well, who the hell would she have gone up there with?"

"I don't know, Dickie. That's why those emails are important and why we need to get the records from her cell. Maybe she has a boyfriend that she's kept quiet around the department—you couldn't blame her for that. Or, maybe she just started seeing someone. Maybe he's a cop too, but he works Gangs, or Narco, or someplace other than Homicide. Maybe someone who wants to come to Homicide, and maybe she's showing him the ropes, or showing off."

There was silence as I considered what Floyd was suggesting. It made sense, more sense than to think she went up there alone. Then it hit me. "They might not be in her car."

"That's another possibility," Floyd agreed. "But why take a personal ride when you have the county hoop? It makes more sense that she did take her car, and then she could have filled up at Gorman or in Santa Clarita with county gas if she needed it."

"Unless he has a county car as well."

"That's a thought, too; we need to check the gas logs at Santa Clarita and Gorman. Shit, for all we know," Floyd said, "she's doinkin a commander or a chief. One who's married so they have to keep it on the down-low. They've all got cars, better ones than what we've got."

"We get their hand-me-downs," I added.

"Just a thought."

"I don't know how helpful that thought is, unless the car is camouflaged; that would explain why we haven't found it."

I gunned it to swerve around a drunk doing sixty in the fast lane, the asshole keeping it nice and slow to not attract any attention, having no idea that's exactly how you draw attention. Where were the goddam chippies when you needed one?

"Anything other than red is going to be harder to see, so maybe it does matter. Plus, that's what we've been looking for, which isn't helpful either. But truthfully," I said, "your hypothesis brings up a whole lot of other questions. Who is he? What's *his* cell phone number? As you said, what's he driving? Why hasn't someone else on the job been reported as missing?"

"It's also just a hunch, Dickie. I could be wrong. You know her better than I do; would she go up there alone?"

I thought about it for a long moment. "I can't say. Part of me says that she would, because she is strong and smart and confident—"

"But always looking to prove herself."

"Maybe," I conceded. "Another part of me says she's smarter than to go up there alone. Also, she knows I'd go if she had something that needed to be checked. She realizes I have no life outside of this job. Why wouldn't she have called and asked me to go? That's the part that has me thinking you may be on to something. That right there. She didn't call me because she didn't need me. She made a date out of following up on a homicide investigation. Maybe this dude she's seeing has some type of special skills that she doesn't think I have."

"Could just be that he has a personality, Dickie. That's something you don't have."

"Maybe it's someone from SEB, some stud deputy who can rappel from helicopters and track killers like an Indian. Chicks dig the Special Enforcement Bureau. SWAT cops."

"If that was the case, you'd think she would have been rescued by now. I say it's some pogue who's wearing dress shoes and slowing her down. Shit," he said, "you and I could survive out there on the mountain before any commander could."

I was pulling off the freeway. "How far are you from Santa Clarita?"

"I'm sitting here waiting on you, Dickie."

"Holy shit, how'd you beat me there?"

"When it comes to fucking around, Dickie, I don't fuck around."

2 3

At Santa Clarita we checked in with the watch sergeant and asked what time the Gorman deputies normally started their shifts.

"Six a.m., but technically they're always on call," said the sergeant. She was a plump black woman who wore her pants high and had big hoop earrings. "Washington" was on her name tag, and I thought I recognized her as someone who had worked Compton Station and then Narcotics back in the day. She carried herself with confidence and had a take-no-shit air about her.

"Did you work Compton?" I asked.

"Worked there and lived there too. Whatchya wanna know?"

I shook my head. "No, just thought I recognized you from there." I nodded toward my partner. "We worked Firestone back in the eighties, early nineties, and then Century Station after that. We spent a lot of time in Compton back in those days ourselves, but we didn't live there."

She smiled. "No, I wouldn't imagine you did."

Floyd said, "Sarge, what about Aero, are they on call also?"

She shook her head. "Not technically, but in an emergency, we might be able to roust a pilot and get him to come in for the overtime."

I looked at Floyd. "Are you thinking we need to go up?"

He was shaking his head before I finished asking. "No, but we're going to need them out there at first light."

Floyd was right. I glanced at my watch. It was just after midnight. "I guess if we set it up now, they can get some sleep and come in an hour before daylight, be up on the mountain when it gets light."

A deputy popped his head through an open window that divided the watch sergeant's office from the hallway. "Sarge, a complaint on line two."

She rolled her eyes. "Tell 'em we're closed."

"Yes ma'am," he said, and turned to walk away.

She leaned toward the window and called out to his back. "Tell 'em they can hold for ten minutes or call back. I'm busy." She settled back in her chair and looked back at us. "Don't promote, whatever you do. You boys have the best job in the department and this sergeant shit is for the birds. I never wrote so much goddam paper in my life."

We finished with the arrangements inside, then gathered outside the back door of the station near a line of black and white patrol cars all backed into their spots, frost settling on their tops and glass. I realized it had cooled off quickly tonight, and thought about how cold it would be on the mountain. I was glad I had my good coat in the trunk. The deputies in the north county were issued parkas rather than the typical type of uniform jackets the rest of the department wore. In the ghetto, nobody wore coats. Long-sleeved shirts with thermals beneath your uniform on cold nights. We'd drive with the windows down and the heater on high. But you couldn't chase bad guys with heavy coats and you sure didn't want to end up in a fight while wearing one. The men and women you fought in the ghetto knew how to fight, and there were no rules. These people fought every day of their lives just to survive, and they got down and dirty. If someone wore a coat, it would quickly be pulled over the person's head, which would tie up their arms, blindfold them, and bend them forward for a proper whaling.

Floyd looked at me and said, "What the hell are we doing here?"

"What do you mean?"

He glanced at his watch. "There's no sense in us getting up there before daylight. That makes no sense."

"Right, I know. But I wasn't going to sit home either. We can work the phones and the computers for the next couple of hours and even keep going through those emails. We'll head up the mountain an hour or so before it starts to get light. Once we're up there, we'll have no communications, so I'd like to get a few hours of work done before we leave. Make sure everything on this end is going in the right direction."

"Michaels will have it covered, dude; you know that."

I nodded, realizing I had been irrational in my planning. But in my defense, I wouldn't have slept if I'd stayed home. At least now I was close to where she was, and I could work until it was time to get up on the mountain.

Floyd seemed to realize I was second guessing the decision to be here all night. "But since you ruined another night's sleep for me, let's see if we can figure out who she went up there with. That could be some invaluable information. Besides, there'll be plenty of time to sleep when we're dead."

We made ourselves at home back in the station's detective bureau where it was dark and quiet this time of the night. Floyd flipped a switch and the fluorescent lights began humming as they came to life. We had both gone back to our cars and grabbed our laptops. The desks in the bureau were all situated with computers, but the detectives would log off and lock them before leaving for the day. The computers along the wall allowed anyone with a password access to law enforcement applications: DMV, DOJ, and FBI files, but that's all they were good for. We had a lot to do and before we knew it, we'd be headed up the mountain. So before we got deep into the work, I helped myself to the detective bureau coffee supply and stuffed a five into the donation can knowing we'd get our money's worth before we left.

At half past three the station was quiet except for the occasional jingling of jailer keys down the hallway and the sheriff's radio broadcasts that played in the background over speakers in every part of the station other than the secretariat. Floyd and I hadn't spoken much over the last hour or so, both of us with our noses buried in our files and staring at data on computer screens. I got up to stretch and Floyd leaned back in his chair, spinning it away from the desk he was using as his work station.

"Dickie, this is a wild goose chase, these emails. We need text messages; that's where you get the dirty secrets shit."

"Yeah, I know. We're waiting. I guess it's not that easy to get those from the county phones. If she had a personal cell, it'd be a breeze."

He frowned. "Do we know that she doesn't? A lot of us have two cells, those of us with lives outside of the job."

I shrugged. "I'm assuming she doesn't. I would think after being partners for six months and now sleeping together, I'd know if she had a second cell phone."

Floyd didn't bite, not even for a moment. "You wish."

I chuckled. "Right. But anyway, no, I don't think she has a personal cell. Remember, there was an old one in her room that wasn't being used. If she has another, it must be top secret. And if it's top secret, it's probably a burner."

"For talking to the commander or chief. He has one too, one the wife doesn't know about."

Something about Floyd's idea on the affair hadn't set well with me from the start. Probably because I didn't see Josie as the type of person who would sleep with a married man. Why would she? She had so much going for her she could have her pick of successful men. Yet she seemed to be a bit like me, married to the job. Maybe he was partly right; maybe she did have a secret relationship, though I doubted it would be with a married chief or commander. Maybe she was just smart about keeping her private life private. In the days of social media and everyone in everyone else's mess, I found the idea of it refreshing. All I could think of to counter his idea was that she had sent the text from the county phone.

I added, "And short of taking county counsel hostage at gunpoint, I don't think we're getting those text messages anytime soon. They're more worried about legal issues, lawsuits, and privacy, than they are about a missing deputy sheriff."

Floyd nodded and stood up to join me as I moved toward the coffee pot.

"I'm hungry," I said.

"Santa Clarita. Probably nothing open here this time of night."

"Maybe. I'm sure there's a least a Jack-in-the-Crack that stays open, probably one of the ones up by the freeway."

Floyd shrugged. "I'm game. I need to get the hell out of here and get some fresh air before I fall asleep."

When we walked through the back door into the parking lot, the cold wind washed over me, chilling me to the bone. "Holy shit."

"Yeah, freezing up here."

I thought about the mountain. "Imagine what it's like up there."

We both paused and looked to the northwest. A long moment passed before Floyd bumped my arm with his and said, "Come on, buy me some grease."

In the drive-thru we sat behind a pickup with two young men with long locks of hair who wore their hats so that we could see their logos from behind. Very clever of them. Their truck's engine rumbled and sputtered, and spewed blue-gray exhaust that rose from a tailpipe and blended with plumes of smoke leaking from both sides of its undercarriage. Its mirrors vibrated, and the relentless pounding of stereo bass shot waves of sound through me. For the second time in a few short hours, I wondered where the hell the chippies were when you needed them.

"This is why I need a grenade launcher mounted on my hood."

We picked up our food and large cups of coffee and headed back to the station where I called to check in with the command post. Sergeant Woo said that the tech crew was actively pinging Josie's cell phone every few minutes, but so far, they had not picked up a signal. I said nothing, so after a brief moment of silence, the sergeant continued: "I talked to Lieutenant Michaels just a few minutes ago. He's calling his team out early and sending them up to Gorman to assist you guys. He said to let you know that Sergeant Smith would be getting ahold of you before daybreak. I'm waiting for a call back from SEB. We'd like to get ESD out there or at least standing by."

The Emergency Services Detail was the SEAL team of the sheriff's department. The Special Enforcement Bureau (SEB) comprises six SWAT teams, the Canine Detail, and the Emergency Services Detail. All members of each detail are SWAT trained, and the deputies assigned to ESD are additionally skilled in advanced search and rescue, and they are each certified as divers and paramedics. They could do it all.

Floyd had leaned back in a chair, propped his feet onto a desk, and closed his eyes. My eyes were heavy as well, and as I listened to Sergeant Woo, I glanced at a clock on the wall and wondered if we had time for a quick nap. Maybe, if I could get her off the phone. I said, "Sounds good. We have some more leads to follow. I'll check back with you in a bit."

When I disconnected, Floyd looked at me through half-open eyes and nodded.

"We're all set," I told him. "Let's get a nap."

His eyes fell closed again, heavily. I got up to shut the lights off and thought about how little sleep we'd had the last couple of days. Floyd's vacation. I rolled a desk chair out and plopped down not far from Floyd in the darkened detective bureau. I glanced at my phone once more. No messages. I propped my feet on a desk, leaned my head against a file cabinet, and closed my eyes.

It seemed like only five minutes had passed when the lights came on again and I woke to see the gray-haired detective sergeant glaring at us. I wondered if his short-sleeve shirt and fat tie were the same ensemble he had worn yesterday. I didn't remember the stain on the tie, but everything on him appeared rumpled and worn as if he had worked all night. I didn't think he had. This was Santa Clarita, and it was very unlikely that the detectives here ever deviated from their straight dayshift schedules and afternoon tee times.

I had assumed he was a sergeant since he was old and crusty and worried about little things like who parked where in back of the station. Now I was convinced of it since he was the first to arrive. I glanced at my watch: 5:45. The station seemed to have more of a buzz down the hallway as it came to life on a Wednesday morning. I dropped my feet from the desk and sat up. "Good morning."

"Fraud guys, right?"

I glanced to see Floyd had opened his eyes but remained as horizontal as one could be in a reclining desk chair, unmoved by the lights or the presence of someone whose turf we had occupied.

"Right," I said, "Forgery Fraud."

He turned to the coffee pot that sat on the warm burner, indicated as such by a lighted orange button. He lifted the carafe to see the remnants therein had taken on the consistency of used motor oil. Holding the carafe in his hand, he turned to frown at us.

"Would you look at the time," Floyd said, exaggerating a glance at his watch as he rose from his chair.

I pushed out of my chair and the two began gathering our files.

"He's Forgery Fraud, I'm Arson," Floyd said, starting past him toward the back door. "We're teamed up chasing a check bouncer who sets shit on fire."

I didn't glance back to show the sergeant the grin on my face.

In the parking lot the sky showed its first signs of dawn. We climbed into my Crown Vic and I fired it up. I looked over at Floyd and shook my head, grinning still.

"Where do you come up with this shit?"

Floyd thumped the lid of his Copenhagen and met my gaze. "I had to clean you up—again. One day you say Forgery, the next you say Arson. Even an egghead like that idiot is going to start to wonder."

I pulled out of the parking lot. "Well, his timing is good, if nothing else. This should put us up on the mountain just as it's getting light enough to see."

"Great," Floyd said, resting his head against the seat. "Wake me up when we get there."

2 4

Before we were out of range I had made a series of phone calls in order to be confident the search efforts were coordinated and also to check on the status of Josie's cell phone. There was still no signal from the phone, and Michaels had come in early and taken charge of the operation from Whittier. A search and rescue team had been called out and they would assemble at Gorman Post Road and the 138, or Lancaster Road. Michaels said he was told by one of the search and rescue personnel that there was a large dirt area off the highway where they could stage, and that you could usually get cell service there. They would need ample parking for the mobile command post—a motorhome equipped with radios, televisions, grease boards, tables, chairs, awnings, portable generators and auxiliary lights, and large supplies of water and food—as well as numerous pickups pulling horse trailers and an assortment of county and state vehicles. They could even set a bird down if needed.

When I disconnected with Lieutenant Michaels, I gave Floyd the Reader's Digest version, but he seemed uninterested, his eyelids sporadically bouncing open but staying mostly closed.

"Search and rescue has horses, motorcycles, and four-wheelers," I elaborated.

No response.

"Ted and Joe are coming up with their tracking dogs."

Nothing.

"SWAT's going to be there, ESD too."

"Good for them," he said in his sleep.

I started to feel contempt as I glanced back and forth from the road to my sleeping partner. Nothing bothered me more than trying to stay awake while driving, when your partner—or passenger—thought nothing of having a snooze. I recalled coming back from San Diego one morning and having yet another brush with death, this one due to fatigue. I had started work early one morning and picked up a double murder in the late after-noon when two men were gunned down in daylight at the busiest intersec-tion in Carson. A bus had just pulled over to a stop and there were dozens of witnesses to the shooting. Many of them had descriptions of the lone shooter, and others had descriptions of a woman behind the wheel of a black Escalade, with whom the suspect fled. One witness had obtained a license plate number. The registration of that vehicle had come back to a female who lived in San Diego.

I had been partnered with "Slow" Joe Herrera for the on-call period, as Floyd had been sent to a weeklong blood spatter analysis training course in San Jose. Which meant he would be spending about six hours a day in a classroom, two hours a day by the hotel's pool, an hour or so running or working out, and every night at the hotel bar or wherever he could find women and trouble. That was part of my irritation about having been assigned to work with Slow Joe. The other half was that Joe—as good a cop as he was, and as nice a guy as he was—would drive you crazy with his slow ways. He walked slowly. He talked slowly. His interviews lasted for hours, even with those who had nothing to say. God help you if any of your witnesses were Spanish-speaking. He would go on and on and on with the world's longest question, in Spanish, and the witness would reply in kind, going on and on and on in high-speed Spanish, and when the two would stop for air and you asked what the witness said, Joe would look over at you with a straight face and say, "He said 'No.'"

That afternoon, as soon as we had identified the owner of the getaway vehicle, I had dispatched a surveillance team to the San Diego location and had San Diego cops watching it until they arrived. Everyone was on the lookout for the vehicle, including all chippies between Los Angeles and San Diego. The Border Patrol had been alerted. We asked for several teams of homicide investigators to assist us with the many interviews we had to do, and I designated another team to process and document the crime scene for us while we interviewed the most relevant witnesses. It was always a long process, but on that day, it was imperative that we shorten it without cutting corners as we had good, workable information, and a vicious killer on the run.

We finished up at Carson Station in the wee hours of the night and learned that the suspect's vehicle had in fact arrived at the home where it was registered in San Diego. The sole occupant was the female driver. I asked that the surveillance team remain in place, and told them we were headed their way. The plan was to "knock and talk" to the female, and if that didn't work, we'd get a search warrant for the place. We arrived just as the sun came up, which put me right at twenty-four hours without sleep. The woman was uncooperative—to say the least—so we detained her, secured the location, and wrote a search warrant.

By the time we finished in San Diego it was evening and Joe and I were both beat, having been up and running for thirty-six hours straight. We loaded into my Crown Vic, but before we headed north, Joe insisted that we grab a bite to eat. I told him I didn't think it was a good idea; it would take too much time and make us even more tired. I suggested we grab coffee and hit the road. He insisted, so of course we stopped and filled our bellies with authentic Mexican food from a bus with a picnic bench at its side that sat on a dirt parkway near the highway.

After we finished, we got into the car for the drive north. As always, I quickly navigated to the fast lane and brought her up to about seventy-five for the ride home. Joe, his belly full, his slow-moving life content—not a worry in the world—leaned his head back against the seat.

"Don't go to sleep, Joe," I demanded. "You need to keep me awake."

Joe promptly went to sleep. He was probably dreaming of moving sheep across the vast plains of a faraway land with a slow-moving dog at his side, until he settled at a campfire under a blanket of stars twinkling in the black of night. Soon, he was fast asleep, snoring in his dreams and in my car.

Soon, I too drifted off to la-la land.

I awoke abruptly to the sounds of horns and screeching tires to discover our vehicle traveling diagonally across the five lanes of the north-bound San Diego freeway. I grabbed the wheel and jerked us into one lane of travel, the back end fishtailing until I gained control of the car.

It had been the only time I had ever seen Joe move quickly. He went from a slumber to a straight-postured, hands-against-the-dash brace, his eyes wide with shock and fear. He uttered an obscenity or two, and when we safely settled into one lane, he let out a breath that could have pushed a pirate ship across the Panama Canal. He scrutinized me angrily until I finally barked at him: "That's what happens when you go to sleep on your partner, asshole."

That we hadn't crashed and died was a plus as it allowed me to now tell the story as yet another near-miss brush with death, but a somewhat humorous one. More than anything, it had taught me a lesson, and although the nature of our job would cause us to push our luck as far as fatigue went, there were certain precautions I would take from that day forward. Primarily, I wouldn't let my partner sleep.

I glanced again to see Floyd's mouth parted and his head bobbing.

"Desi Velasquez is going to be in charge of the command post."

Floyd's eyes popped open and he lifted his head. "No shit?"

"She's the captain over at SEB now, been there a couple months."

"Holy shit! We love Desi."

I didn't have the heart to tell him yet that I was bullshitting him. Both of us had known Desi from a kickboxing gym we belonged to in East L.A. before she had hired onto the department fifteen years earlier. She was a champion kickboxer and we had become friends at the gym. Desi was interested in law enforcement, and she had an uncle who worked for LAPD, so she had planned to apply to that department. Floyd and I talked her into going with the sheriff's department instead. It would be difficult to find a tougher female recruit, and neither of us could bear to see her going to work for our friends in blue.

Floyd said, "I should probably stay at the command post while you guys search, be there as a liaison, keep the communications flowing smoothly."

"Oh, I'm sure you'd be smooth."

"I haven't seen her in years, Dickie. I'd love to see Desi, hang out for a while. She loves us."

"Uh-huh, that's just what I need, you at the command post with a hot SWAT captain."

"How'd she get to SWAT so fast? I didn't even know she'd made captain. I guess if you're going to have a woman run SWAT, she'd be the one to have do it."

He was wide awake now, excited, and he remained so for the entirety of the forty-minute drive. When we arrived at the location where the command post was meant to be, we were all alone. I glanced at my watch: quarter to seven. I leaned my head back on my seat. "Well, maybe I'll take a little catnap while waiting for the cavalry."

Floyd said, "I'm not even tired now. I think I've caught a second wind."

"Or something," I said.

I closed my eyes while Floyd talked about the gym in East L.A. and how he wished the owner hadn't moved it farther east and that it would be good to see Desi and he wondered if she still boxed at the gym or for our department. I was vaguely aware of him changing topics to a heavyweight from the same gym named Frank, but I drifted off and dreamt about finding Josie at the bottom of a brushy draw, her car upside-down among the shrub and pines, windows broken and metal bent and twisted from a violent descent.

The sounds of screeching brakes and a diesel motor winding down jarred me from my sleep, and I awakened refreshed from the twenty-minute nap. Floyd popped out of our car as two pickups pulling horse trailers wheeled into the other side of the vacant lot and came to rest with twenty feet between their rigs. As I stepped out, I saw the mobile command post coming up the road, followed by a line of sheriff's vehicles, some of which I recognized to be those assigned to SEB. I walked around the front of our vehicle and stood at Floyd's side in the burgeoning daylight.

"I'm pretty sure they said it was Desi's team that was coming," I said. "I'm trying to remember now."

He glared at me and I just shrugged, my bases now covered from the inevitable letdown coming to Floyd.

2 5

Josefina Sanchez, for all of her strengths and her display of raw
courage in the face of grave danger, had her insecurities, no different
from anyone else. She didn't like being alone. Her mother lived with
her to fill a void as much as for the aging woman's benefit. Josie had never
married, nor had she even lived with a man. As she watched the years sail
by, the idea of matrimony waned and the prospect of children became but
a fleeting notion. As was the case with many women in law enforcement,
Josie found dating outside of that community a strain. Attorneys, firemen,
businessmen, a professional motocross rider—it wasn't as if she hadn't
tried. But men outside of law enforcement seemed threatened by a strong,
confident woman, one who packed both a piece and a punch.

But cops were dirty dogs.

Maybe not all of them, but many had difficulty resisting all of the
opportunities which were plentiful for men who wore uniforms *and*
carried guns. There were groupies everywhere, and Josie hated them. She
would sometimes confront the nastier of the lot and chase them from
watering holes or other cop gatherings, as if she were protecting her little
brothers from known carriers of communicable diseases. The good Lord
knew the boys wouldn't think for themselves once they had started
drinking.

She thought of her partner, Dickie. He was different than a lot of other cops, almost to an extreme. If he weren't so rugged and manly, she'd wonder if he was gay. He didn't seem to need the company of women, but Josie had come to realize he was just the odd type who was comfortable being alone. The perfect bachelor. Floyd, on the other hand, was a bit of a tomcat, she had noticed. Or at least a big flirt who craved the attention of women. He too was rugged, but he could at times seem a bit metro with his acute sense of fashion and style. He was the type of man who would spend fifty bucks on a haircut and he probably got pedicures. Josie had grown to love them both—in a partner-like way—and she would give anything to have either of them with her at this moment.

Then there was Lopes. He was her favorite among the homicide guys, and he had become a reliable drinking buddy. She had learned early in life not to ruin a perfectly good drinking buddy by sleeping with him. But she would sleep with him now—hell, she'd sleep with them all—if given just one more opportunity to see them. To see the three of them come through the door when the asshole came to feed her again. Lopes, Floyd, and Dickie, the three of them barreling in with guns blazing and fists flying until the floor was covered in bodies and blood. She could see them doing it, three of the best cops and toughest men she had known.

What would they be doing now to find her? Josie knew they would be working long days and nights and pulling out all stops to find her. Unless they hadn't even realized she was missing.

Missing, hmpf. Being held captive was more accurate. Jesus, to even think of herself as a victim. But she was. Her injuries had left her vulnerable. She didn't even remember being brought to this place. She remembered the crash, sailing through the air off of the mountain road. She remembered crawling away from the car and searching for Tom. But then there was a blank space, a lapse in her memory, because the next thing she knew she had been bound and gagged and left alone in the dark. But why? What did they want? Who were they and what was the end game? Death, of course. There was no other way it could end. They had to have known she was a cop. This wasn't a case of ransom. Or was it?

She wondered if they would use her as a bargaining chip. No, that was only in the movies. There would be no exchange of prisoners for the release of hostages. Revenge? That seemed more likely the case. But from whom? And why? She didn't know. Josie kept thinking about the murder on the mountain—the latest case she and Dickie had been assigned—and she wondered if the killer had seen her and Tom visiting the site. Maybe the killer didn't even know she was a cop, just saw the two of them snooping around and he panicked.

Josie shivered against the cold, damp floor beneath her. She thought of her mother at home. Esmeralda. A woman who appeared frail but had the energy of someone half her age and the spunk that ran through Josie's veins as well. Mama would be worried, and she would be praying and lighting candles and going to church every morning and again each evening until—

Until.

Her arms ached and her legs were terribly cramped. She drew a deep breath and silently assured herself that she would survive. Her partner, and the others, would be coming for her soon. They were the best detectives she knew, and they would figure this out. They would come and find her, Josie told herself, over and over. She almost pitied the sons of bitches who held her. Almost.

26

Among the search and rescue teams and SWAT teams and canine search teams and Gorman deputies with their dogs and trucks full of emergency gear, there was a group of a dozen men and one woman who had arrived in unmarked cars and pickups and had assembled together separately but near the others. Most had arrived wearing jeans and t-shirts, and now they stood near the open trunks of their cars pulling on green jumpsuits with sheriff's insignia. Some of the men were bald-headed; others wore their hair long. Some wore goatees and beards or long, bushy mustaches; a few were clean-shaven. Tattoos seemed to be popular among the group, and one man had full sleeves of colorful ink. None of them was the clean-cut type you would make for cops.

"Who the hell are they?"

Floyd and I had gotten out of our car and both of us were leaning on the warm hood. The morning air was crisp and clean with a dampness that numbed my nose and ears. The sounds of quail moving out for their morning forage mixed with the hum of distant traffic and the increasing chatter of the assembled cops.

"I'd guess Narco," Floyd said, and spat a stream of tobacco to the side of his boots.

I nodded. "Maybe the MET team?"

"Could be, Dickie. I don't recognize any of them. Other than the broad. Isn't she the girl they used to bring down to Firestone to buy dope? Looked like she was fifteen at the time."

I shrugged.

"She's cleaned up since then. Remember? She used to look like a crackhead straight out of the projects, as long as she didn't smile."

"What's her name?" I asked.

Floyd shrugged and pushed off of the car. "Let's go find out."

We approached the group and offered morning greetings. I introduced us and asked where they were from. One of the men in the group confirmed that they were in fact narcotics deputies who were assigned to the Marijuana Eradication Team. He said they had been called out to assist us, and then he introduced himself as John Brady, the sergeant of the crew. He was tall and lean with long blond hair, and he was one of the few in the group whose face was clean-shaven. His blue eyes had a hardness that contradicted his otherwise youthful appearance. The others in the group continued with their preparation of weapons and backpacks that were scattered about like sleeping bags and luggage outside a summer camp bus. Only everything here was green or black or camouflaged, and narrowly purposed for either saving or taking lives.

The sergeant offered me a cup of coffee from his thermos as he poured one for himself. I accepted, and while he poured me a cup I turned my attention to Floyd, who stood just a few feet away talking with the only woman in the group. Her brilliant white teeth glowed against her dark skin. She glanced over to see me paying attention and said, "Yeah, I remember both of you from Firestone. I used to buy dope down there when I was straight out of the academy. I was just a kid and hadn't ever even been to the ghetto before. Hell, I grew up in Sierra Madre. Talk about an education."

Floyd said, "I thought I remembered you."

"You and him," she said to Floyd, and then nodded toward me. "You two were pretty young back then yourselves. But everyone seemed to know you."

"I'm famous," Floyd said matter-of-factly. "Nobody's even heard of Dickie."

She chuckled and I turned back to Sergeant Brady who was handing me a fresh coffee. He nodded toward the woman. "You guys know my lieutenant."

She and Floyd stopped talking and turned their attention to us.

Brady smiled. "Anna-banana McCravy. A-mac, our dark little Irish girl. She's the boss but I'm the team leader. We mostly keep her around for entertainment."

McCravy glared at her sergeant and held it for a moment, then smiled when she told him to check himself. She turned back to Floyd and said, "This is the abuse I take."

Brady, not looking up from a bag of equipment he was searching through, said, "I'll show you abuse."

It was clear to me that like other great assignments on the department, there was a close-knit relationship among the personnel assigned to MET. A black female lieutenant, a white boy sergeant, a crew of whites, blacks, and Hispanics, and you had the feeling that any of them could joke with and about the others without concern for political correctness. They were a team who trained together, worked together, and got in and out of the shit together. No policy manual would dictate how they interacted with one another. It was that way at Homicide—to a degree—and it had been that way at Major Crimes Bureau when Floyd and I worked for Michaels and Smith.

As the sky grew lighter and chatter and laughter now filled the brisk morning air, I looked around the command post and realized that the job I had—being a deputy sheriff in the County of Los Angeles—offered me the opportunity to know as friends, some of the best men and women society had to offer.

A few more cars arrived and the mobile command post came to life as the sun peeked over the eastern mountains, casting long shadows across the valley floors. Brady had finished his preparation and pulled a sweat-shirt over his head. McCravy had wrapped herself in a parka and stood with her legs pressed together and her arms crossed, shivering against the cool mountain air.

Brady saw that I had finished my coffee, and held his thermos out as a gesture. I accepted and as we both watched the steaming dark liquid cascade into my cup, I asked, "So how do you guys work these grows?"

"Basically, we get the information from Aero Bureau or hunters or sometimes anonymous calls, and we go in and take them down. If the information came from Aero, we'd have coordinates to put us right in the spot. Otherwise it can be a needle in a haystack type of deal. You'd be surprised how big this country is when you get out there in it."

I noticed that Floyd and the feisty lieutenant had faded a few feet away and were chatting as if they were two old friends. I was more interested in Brady and his MET team operations. "Do you hike in or fly?"

"Both," he said. "The thing about the mountains is you can hear everything, and from long distances. We usually get choppered in, but miles away from a suspected grow site. The bird drops us fast and moves off to keep the farmers from spooking. When the helicopter's gone, we settle in, prepare our gear, and begin a long, slow, methodical approach on foot. The closer we get, the slower we go. For one, they can hear you coming. And two, we have to be careful to watch for boobytraps. I swear I feel like I'm in Vietnam sometimes doing this shit. Or Colombia, or whatever. I was never in the service, but when we're out here doing these maneuvers, I get the feeling that it's what it must have been like over there."

I pictured the drop of a dozen commando-types and wondered if I had missed out on a great opportunity in working narcotics. "So do you guys rappel from the helicopters, or do they find somewhere to set you down?"

Brady had gone back into his duffle and came out with a military-style jacket. He punched his arms through the sleeves and zipped it up, and took a seat on his bag. "We generally fast-rope in from about thirty feet. Air Five, the big Sikorsky, brings our whole team at once. Anywhere from twelve to fifteen of us. We can all be on the ground in less than a minute and the bird is gone before anyone thinks much of it. Just another fly by. The first time I went out on a mission, that bird leaving was a weird feeling. When the engines and rotors faded, it all of a sudden felt lonely on the mountain, even in the company of a dozen guys. I don't know why. Maybe just that we were miles away from civilization and in unknown terrain."

"You guys get a lot of specialized training for this stuff? Survival training and whatnot?"

"Yeah, they teach us how to walk in the mountains, how to use camouflage, how to navigate. Advanced first aid, advanced weapons training—"

"SWAT?"

"And military. We've gone down and trained at Pendleton with the

Marines, gone to Coronado and trained with the SEALS. It's a cool gig if you don't mind sleeping on the side of a mountain. It's creepy out there at night, all the weird sounds you hear. Especially for a city boy like myself. I'd never done anything like this before. Never camped or hunted or even did scouts."

The idea of it still fascinated me, though I wasn't sure I'd want to spend very many nights out there on the mountain. Maybe with buddies, but not alone. I thought of Josie and wondered how she was faring. I knew in my heart that she was alive. I could feel it now. I hoped she knew we were coming. I hoped she would soon hear the helicopters and feel invigorated and find a way to signal her location to us. I wondered if she had stumbled upon one of these grows and was in more danger than any of us realized.

"What happens when someone, say a hunter, comes across one of these grows? What do the farmers usually do?"

"These guys normally are not very aggressive. If they hear someone coming toward their camp, they usually hide and hope they're missed. Also, most hunters around these parts are aware that there are grows, and they're usually smart enough to avoid walking into them. Most times they will retreat and call it in."

I nodded, picturing a camp with a group of illegals sitting quietly while hunters tromped across the hillsides having no idea they were there, the dream of a big buck the only thing on their minds.

Brady continued: "When they know it's us who's coming, they try to flee. But most of them are wets, brought here by coyotes and dropped in the middle of nowhere in an unfamiliar country. They won't go far from the camp because they don't know where the hell they are. A lot of times we'll find them a hundred yards uphill in the brush. When we do, there's usually no resistance."

"So what do you do if you don't find them? Just the camp, or farm, or whatever you call it."

"When the camps are abandoned, we confiscate the plants and load them out. Helicopters take it all out in nets. Then we just write it up as a find. Not much else we can do with it."

My mind was still on Josie. I saw her tied and gagged against a tree with a bunch of dirty marijuana farmers sitting nearby sipping tequila and showing their gold and silver teeth when they laughed at their own jokes.

"Okay," I said, "but take the average hunter, or hiker—whatever—and say he or she stumbles right into one of these camps—"

"It isn't likely. These camps have a lot of signs before you're in the thick of them. Sometimes there are miles of hose running down a draw, feeding water from a natural spring to the camp for irrigation. There are fresh kills in the area, deer and birds and whatever else the farmers can eat. There's trash scattered about—there's always a shitload of trash left behind—and once you get close, there's always something cooking on a small fire. You can smell it. You're thinking about your partner."

I nodded.

"If she's up here, we'll find her."

Lieutenant Michaels arrived, driven by Jack Smith. They called for a briefing near the mobile command post that now had two folded tables beneath a pulled-out awning. There were boxes of donuts and vats of coffee and rosters where all in attendance would sign in. Two ladies on the other side of the tables sat in folding chairs with radios and pads of papers and pens at the ready.

The plan was to cover a ten square mile area that encompassed both the location of William Lance Brown's execution and the nearby Watkins compound. There was a lot of conversation about how we would deal with the residents therein, and considerable focus on their property and the immediate area. While this was being discussed, I looked around for the game warden but didn't see him. I would mention to Michaels after the briefing that Spencer might be able to get us back onto the property, and we should see if he could assist us.

Some of us would be divided up into teams of mobile search parties that would crawl the woods by roadways in cars and trucks and motorbikes. The mounted posse would ride their horses into the deep draws that were inaccessible to vehicles and invisible from the roads and trails. There would be two helicopters and a fixed-wing plane scouring the chosen grid and perhaps beyond from the sky above. A Sikorsky stood ready to transport and drop the MET team members, or SWAT, or both, into any areas of interest identified by scouts on the ground or eyes from above. We were all given starting points and directions to travel in our searches, and then Michaels asked if I had anything to add.

I stepped forward into the semi-circle of personnel and looked left and right at the faces of those who were there to help me find my partner. Emotion crept into my throat as I began to speak. I excused myself, downed the remainder of my coffee that had grown lukewarm, and took a moment to compose myself while hoping nobody had noticed. I thanked everyone for being there and then provided some of the details about the murder we had been sent to investigate on the mountain, the background of the victim, the dynamics of the Watkins compound, and a description of Josie and her vehicle. I told them about the text message I had received, and interrupted myself to ask Michaels if there had been any news on additional cellular activity from it. There hadn't been. It looked like we were going in blind.

27

Josie awoke to dim light seeping in through cracks and crevasses from the log siding that showed minuscule particles of dust floating in the damp air. She realized she must be in some kind of rundown cabin or shed. She shivered beneath the wool blanket that covered her, and then pulled with her arms and legs at the restraints that held her. Pain shot through her right leg above the knee where she knew from the swelling that something had been broken. Fighting the restraints was no use, especially since it hurt so much to do it. She went limp against the cold, damp, wood plank floor, from which she was separated by nothing more than a second wool blanket. She had noticed the "U.S." imprinted on one of the two blankets, and she assumed they were military surplus. She rolled her head violently from side to side until locks of oily hair were out of her eyes. She blew sharp breaths at the remaining strands.

How was she going to get herself out of this? Usually once or twice a day her captor would come by and check on her, provide her with some water, and allow her to relieve herself in a five-gallon bucket that he would take somewhere outside and dump, bringing it back inside and storing it not far from where she lay. When the cabin—although that was really too grand a word for what was nothing more than a broken-down shed—warmed in the afternoon sun, flies would buzz through the cracks and holes in the structure and concentrate on the bucket. It made Josie think about what her grandpa had said about how a bucket of shit in the corner could draw the flies away. He told her before she entered the academy that there would be those in the class who would constantly mess up and draw the attention of the instructors away from the others. The proverbial buckets of shit. It made her think of Sandoval, a cadet in her platoon who stood next to her during formations due to the alphabetical order of their names. He couldn't seem to get anything right. The drill instructors would scream in his face daily. One day, his hair was too long, the next day it was too short. His uniform appeared as if he had slept in it. Her grandfather's words echoed in her head while the instructors surrounded Sandoval, berating him as he stood only a few feet from where she remained at attention, her eyes locked straight ahead. It was as if the drill instructors didn't even know she was there; they were all over the bucket of shit. She wondered what had become of Sandoval, who had resigned in the second week of the academy. She never saw him as a bucket of shit, and she had felt sorry for him. She hadn't thought about her grandfather's words since those days, at least not that she could recall, and she didn't remember thinking of Sandoval much after he left.

Josie had nothing but time to reflect when not planning her escape, which she had concluded would have to be during the bathroom break. It was the only time that her hands were freed, though her ankles remained tethered by coarse, wiry ropes. The rope was tied tightly, but a few feet of slack had been left in each length, allowing her to room to roll over on the so-called bed and to straddle the bucket when her hands were untied. After her break, he would come back in—he was at least decent enough to allow her that moment of privacy—and that is when he would supply her with something to eat, and water. He would flip the bucket over and use it as a seat while he waited for her to finish the sandwich or piece of fruit or other small ration of food he had provided. Once, it had only been a piece of jerky. During the bathroom and feeding periods he left her hands free, and he would always offer her use of the bucket once more before he left. She had never taken him up on it to this point, but now she intended to use that time to prepare for her planned assault and escape from this prison.

That's what it would have to be, an all-out assault. She would have but one opportunity, and she couldn't mess it up. She prayed her idea would work, that he was like all other men and could be easily distracted by the sight of a woman's cooch. Josie thought back to her academy training when she was introduced to "Laser Village." Life-sized video was projected onto a screen in a darkened room, introducing various situations that one might encounter on the streets. These setups were commonly called "shoot/don't shoot" scenarios, and they were eerily realistic, causing one's heart to pound as it would during actual dangerous encounters. One such episode involved deputies making a traffic stop and encountering an attractive woman at the subject vehicle's driver's window. The woman wore a short skirt and had her blouse unbuttoned revealing most of her sizable chest. She also had a gun clutched in her right hand, and many of the male cops had significant delay in their reaction to the threat. Josie had quickly blown the bitch away, two laser beam shots to the head while retreating from the kill zone.

Two seconds is all she would need. She would allow the roll of toilet paper he always provided to fall beyond her reach, and as he moved toward it, she would open her legs and show him the goods. And while the blood drained from his brain, she would strike out as if her life depended on the outcome. It did, she knew.

Her plan was to utilize a move she had learned practicing the art of Brazilian jiu jitsu: she would thrust her hand into one shoulder while pulling his other shoulder toward her, spinning him away from her while wrapping one arm around his neck. She would lock one arm with the other for what was called in mixed martial arts, a rear naked chokehold. Then she would hold on for her life for the few seconds it would take to put him out. Once he went unconscious, she would find the knife he carried, the one he had used to cut lengths of rope one day to reconfigure her restraints. She would then either cut his throat, or quickly free herself and put restraints on him. It would depend on how much time she believed she had, how strong he felt to her once she started on him, and how much fury she felt when she acted. But she reconciled within herself that cutting his throat had to be an option.

Josie had used the chokehold on numerous occasions both in the gym and on the streets. She had become proficient with it and considered it her great equalizer in dealing with stronger men. She knew better than to think she could stand toe-to-toe with an accomplished fighter, or even an unaccomplished, brawny barroom brawler. Knowing her limitations was something she viewed as great knowledge and an edge in survival. She who didn't recognize her weaknesses was bound to have some tough sonofabitch reveal them to her. But Josie knew she didn't have to be a brawler to choke someone out. She had, on many occasions, done just that, and after doing so had been able to restrain her opponent with handcuffs before he regained consciousness. She pictured her bag in the car with her gun and handcuffs among other tools and weapons. She would give anything to have access to those now.

She felt strength through her resolve, having played out the scenario many times in her head to include the more gruesome idea of cutting the man's throat. It was mental preparation for something she hoped she wouldn't have to do but embraced it as an option. She set her mind to doing whatever it took to overcome the man and to win what would likely be her most critical confrontation, and she promised herself she would never weaken nor quit. Death was the ultimate conclusion to the game; of this, she was certain. Maybe she was wrong, but she had to assume that she wasn't. She believed her life depended solely on her ability to escape by any means possible.

Josie thought back to Saturday when she drove Tom up to the mountain to show him the site of her latest murder investigation. Tom was a hunter, and he was particularly interested in this recent case. He questioned her nonstop about every detail of the terrain, its surroundings, the foliage and habitat. He wanted to know if there were game trails. How far from the nearest road was the victim? Had you found his vehicle? No? Well how did he get there? Had you found and followed his boot tracks? He was wearing boots, right? What kind of boots? Hunting boots, hiking boots, or cowboy boots?

Tom, also a cop, seemed determined to help her solve this case. Maybe he only wanted to impress her. Though he had never worked a murder case, he had hoped to someday promote from Gangs to Homicide. He continually tried to prove himself to her by asking about her cases and coming up with theories or suggestions for investigative processes. Showing her how smart he was, what a great cop he was. Though she would mostly humor him by playing along with his games of Clue, at one point she finally had said, "Tom, I want you for your body, not your mind."

The birds were chirping loudly outside, and she wished she knew what it meant. Was somebody coming? Or were they only chattering amongst themselves, talking about the weather or juicy worms or insects that could be found in a rotting stump? Maybe they were just happy for another day of sunshine, a day to bask in the warmth to counter the long, cold mountain nights. She wished she could go warm herself under the sun, and she shivered once again at the thought of it.

But the sounds of singing birds didn't keep her from the nightmare she lived day and night as she stared at the rusted metal above her that provided the shelter of her prison. Something bothered her about the truck that ran her off the road, its bright lights blinding her and sending her off an embankment and what, a hundred feet down? She thought about the moment before the lights of the truck appeared, having been suddenly switched on, seemingly with the intent to blind her. She had been driving along on the dark road chatting with Tom when suddenly the truck appeared in front of her, as if from nowhere. She had jerked the car hard to the left, desperately trying to avoid a collision. Had it been driving without its lights? Or had it been parked, waiting at just the right location for the right moment where it would force her off the side of the mountain?

Tears formed in her eyes again as the image of Tom being ejected from the car played over and over in her mind. An eerie silence had blanketed them when the car launched from the road and sailed through the air. The plunge seemed to last a lifetime as memories of her childhood flashed before her, and the voice of her mother spoke to her, telling her *te quiero, mi hija*, I love you, my daughter. Then the car ricocheted off the rocky mountainside, and in an instant, they were airborne again, the steel-crunching impact having twisted the frame and body of the flying mass of steel, plastic, rubber, and glass, shattering windows and blowing the passenger door from its frame as if it was a cork released from a bottle of champagne. Tom had bounced back and forth like a crash test dummy, and on the next impact he disappeared from his seat. Josie never saw him leave, nor had she heard him scream or cry or call for help. Later, as she crawled from the wreckage, dragging her broken leg, she had stopped several times and called out for him. But Tom had never answered.

When the first morning came, she had awakened in her new housing arrangement, bound, cold, and hungry, and dying of thirst. Her body ached all over, but the pain in her leg was nearly unbearable. She passed out only to wake hours later in the company of her captor. Her *caretaker*, he would say. He provided her with pills for her pain, water, and food. And he allowed her privacy for potty breaks.

But why?

She asked, she begged, she cried out for mercy. She assured him he would be rewarded for saving her life, and she told him about being run off of the road by some asshole, but that she never saw who it was nor could she say what type of vehicle the person had driven. This, of course, was to convince him that he wouldn't be held accountable, though she knew in her gut that it was he who had sent her plunging down the mountainside.

She had asked about Tom. The captor would only shake his head and shrug his shoulders, and the most he ever said was that he had no idea; he hadn't seen anyone but her, he would say.

In her heart, Josie knew Tom was dead. How could he have survived the crash? She knew from the many fatal accidents she had seen throughout her years on the streets, that when one is ejected, it is almost certain death. Seatbelts mattered. Why hadn't Tom been wearing his? She remembered him turning in his seat to grab a beer from their cooler, telling her that hey, they were off-road, and the open container laws didn't apply. They both knew better, but each partook nonetheless as they drove the winding mountain roads until the sun had set and darkness covered them like a blanket. They had finished at the site of the murder scene and were only a mile or so down the mountain when the truck appeared with its blinding lights and blaring horn, and she had panicked and jerked the car hard to the left, unwittingly. Maybe the beers had played a part in it, she considered, regrettably.

Just as she shifted her thoughts to the caretaker who would soon be coming with food and water—and if she was lucky, another pill—a distant sound made her stiffen. She willed the birds to be quiet so she could better hear, but they wouldn't comply with her wishes. She lifted her head slightly from the ground beneath her and strained to listen until she heard the sounds again. It wasn't a passing helicopter, she thought, as tears welled up in her eyes.

But they were tears of joy. She smiled slightly as she felt a tinge of hope, knowing it was two helicopters, and they were circling, not passing by. They were looking for her.

28

As the helicopters circled above the compound, men came out from various structures and gathered at the meeting spot, a clearing with a fire pit encircled by logs and folding chairs. Broken glass from previous firelight gatherings crunched underfoot while more recently discarded whiskey and beer bottles—amber, brown, and clear—still whole for the time being, lay scattered on top. Cigarette butts, perhaps accumulated over several months, bloomed from the soil along with rusty beer cans and broken glass and the black ashes in the pit. The smell of smoldering ash and stale beer reminded Junior of last night's shindig.

He and the others stood looking toward the sky as two birds circled, one above the compound, the other not far off. Sheriff's stars were visible on both from their vantage point.

Johnny Watkins, Sr. held his hand out to shield his eyes from the sun, a Marlboro dangling from his lips. The old man seemed unaware that the inch-long ash at the tip of his cigarette threatened to drop.

"Junior, you been poaching again?" the old man asked, his eyes not leaving the helicopters.

The ash fell into his beard as he said it, but he didn't seem to notice or care. Junior pictured his dad's face going up in flames and grinned at the thought of it.

"No, I ain't been poachin'. You tole me not—"

The old man turned his head from the sky and set his eyes on Junior. "There a reason you're grinnin' like an idiot, boy?"

Junior shut up. He knew better than to even answer the question posed. The old man was already pissed off—the presence of cops tended to do that to him—and he would be looking for any reason to backhand him, or worse. Truth of it was, the old man had been uptight the last week or so—more so than usual—and Junior didn't know why. Real uptight. Probably just the cops nosing around and coming onto his land without a warrant under the guise of searching for wounded game animals. If there was one thing Johnny Watkins, Sr. couldn't stand, it was government intrusion into their lives. Especially on their privately-owned property. Junior dropped his gaze to the toes of his dust-covered cowboy boots and waited.

The old man turned his attention back to the sky. After a moment, Junior said, "Maybe they're after the Mexicans," downplaying the activity that had his father out of sorts.

Old man Watkins held his skyward gaze. "Wetbacks, boy. Fucking wetbacks." After a moment, he turned to the half-dozen men who had gathered at the pit. "Anyone here see any grows up around these parts lately?"

Everyone in the group but Junior shook their heads. Junior knew of one marijuana grow, but it wasn't close to their land. He had seen the signs of one while riding his dirt bike through the mountains. He had started to explore it until he saw the warden's truck snaking its way up the mountain road, appearing on some stretches, then disappearing as the road turned. Junior had run from the warden and local cops so many times he had a keen eye for spotting them, and he knew to head back to the compound any time they were around.

Watkins directed the question to his son. "Well, boy?"

"I seen sign of one, but I don't know if it was an active camp or not." Junior turned to face south and indicated the direction with a wave of his hand. "It was down there, 'bout five miles or more, down past Lookout Ridge. I seen trails going into that draw on the west side of the lookout, and I thought I smelt a little fire though I never seen any smoke."

The old man dropped his cigarette at his feet and ground it into the dirt with the toe of his boot. "When was this, boy?"

"Last week, couple days ago, I don't know."

Johnny Watkins stared off to the south as if he were trying to see for himself. After a moment, he said, "You didn't check it out better? I've tole you—" he waved his hand across the direction of the others in attendance and looked each man in the eyes "—*all of you*, if you see them wetbacks 'round here, you're to run 'em off. Or kill 'em, one of the two."

"The warden was out, Dad. I had to get back to the property."

Watkins was silent as he tapped another cigarette from a package and held it in his mouth, searching one pocket and then the other before coming up with a lighter. Contemplation and contempt were both obvious to anyone who knew him. Especially Junior.

Junior said, "I can go back out and look for it, you want."

A gray-bearded man with a ponytail cleared his throat and waited for the old man to look at him. "How 'bout I take a four-wheeler, go have a look-see?"

Old man Watkins seemed to be contemplating it.

Junior too was staring at the man he knew as Uncle Pete, the one who every day wore the same flannel shirt and olive drab boonie hat with its Vietnam veteran button and crooked peace sign that had been drawn with a marker.

Watkins shook his head. "No, I don't think so, Pete. You best stay put. In fact, go get your long gun and take a sniper position back there in them woods where you can watch our backs, should those pricks come on my land again. I'm not so sure it won't get bloody this time."

Without replying, Pete turned on his heel and moved out. The others seemed to wait for instruction but Junior was next to get his orders. The old man pointed his finger at him. "You, boy, you go get on your motorbike, and take a ride. See if you can figure out what they're looking at. These hills are probably crawling with pigs if they got two birds up. I ain't never seen 'em have two birds out here at once."

A plane flew overhead, and they all paused to watch.

"And a fucking plane," Watkins grumbled.

"That the sheriff?" one man asked.

"Gotta be," he said.

Junior started for the tree line where his fifteen-foot camp trailer sat among the Ponderosas fifty yards beyond the clear cut. His dad called out to his back, "Don't get caught."

Junior didn't bother to answer. He walked briskly back to the trailer and went directly in to get his coat and the beanie that could be pulled down over his face like a ski mask when it was cold or when he wanted to conceal his identity. His Husqvarna 250 sat parked between a stump and the Ford pickup he'd drive when he had to go to town. Two fuel containers were bungeed in the bed of the truck, which was littered with empty beer containers and Copenhagen cans. There was a shovel, a floor jack, a tire iron, and several lengths of rope scattered about. A spare tire mounted on a rusted wheel lay in the center of it all. Junior pulled one of the containers of gas out and filled the tank on his motorcycle, placing it back in the truck before kickstarting his bike. He pulled a helmet over his beanie and took off through the woods, the motorbike sputtering and spewing a bluish plume of smoke behind him. He fiddled with the choke until the motor smoothed out, and then he throttled it, pulling the front wheel off the ground as he headed up the trail.

Junior would use game trails today and avoid the main roads. He spent the bulk of every day riding through these mountains, and he knew his way around better than anyone, he reckoned. Half of the trails he rode showed evidence of his previous travels, fresh dirt turned up on the corners where his nobby tires had torn through the soil like a chainsaw, flinging rooster tails of dirt through the air. Sometimes he would spot a doe and try to run her down. You couldn't catch them if they ran, he had learned long ago; they were too fast with their changes of direction, and they could go places you couldn't take a motorbike. Sometimes they'd freeze, and stand broadside looking at you. That's when he'd take a shot with his 9mm. You could hit a deer in the side and it'd take off running and sometimes you'd never even find it. Usually, Junior didn't bother to look. On the rare occasion one would drop close by, and if it wasn't too much work and Junior was in the right mood, he'd carve out the back-straps—the best meat on a deer—and leave the rest for the bears and coyotes. Everyone had to make a living.

The sky brightened as the trees thinned and he came to the top of the lookout where he'd be able to see for miles in the direction of all the activity. He left his bike beneath a stand of trees where it wouldn't be spotted from the air, removed his helmet and hung it on his handlebar, and moved to the edge of a clearing with a pair of binoculars in his hand. He wondered if the cops had spotted a grow and were rounding up the wetbacks. He also considered that maybe another body had been found. They had found the rapist against the tree, but so far, nobody had found the woman.

"At some point, I'm going to have to do something with my murder case."

We were barely moving along the mountain road, scouring the terrain for any sign of Josie, her car, or anything else that might give us a clue as to her whereabouts. One of the search and rescue members had wisely instructed us to look closely for any disturbances where a car might have left the road and taken a plunge. It seemed obvious when he said it, and it made me wonder if I would have thought of it myself.

Floyd had his head turned watching the landscape from his side of the car. That's the way partners worked. It didn't matter if it was in the city or on the side of a mountain, whether you were searching for crooks or lost children or a missing homicide detective and her vehicle, the rule remained the same: everyone was responsible for his or her side of the car. I glanced over to see his brown hair fluttering against the gentle breeze that passed through our open windows.

"You still feel the rape victim's father's your best bet?"

"Or his brother, the girl's uncle."

"The girl still around?" he asked.

"The one he raped?"

"Yeah, Dickie, the one he raped. Who else would I be asking about?"

I stopped the car and shifted into park. "Let's go out on that peak and glass this area. I can't see shit from my side of the car."

We both got out with our binoculars and met on his side of the road where the mountain dropped steeply into a deep draw between the ridge we were on and another across from where we stood. I lifted my binoculars to my eyes and began searching the brush below us. In the background I could hear helicopters buzzing through the sky only a short distance from our location. Down in the draw there were clumps of green vegetation that indicated a spring or creek in the bottom. The growth made excellent shelter and cover for animals, and I pictured a herd of lazy deer enjoying the morning on a patch of green grass beneath the canopy.

"Did you bring anything to eat?"

"I've got some snacks in the trunk, and water and coffee. They're going to have chow at the command post too."

Floyd lowered his glasses and sat down on the edge of the road, his legs aimed down the mountainside. "I'm starving."

I joined him, taking a seat next to him. When I stretched my legs out, the ground beneath my feet crumbled, sending loose dirt and small rocks down the steep terrain. Floyd began picking at the gravel near his side and tossing stones down the mountain.

"I figured we'd go till about one, then report back to the C.P. and get some grub, see if there's any news."

He cocked his arm and tossed a larger rock straight out from where we sat, and we both watched it plummet downward, crashing into the brush. Nothing stirred. I figured if you could get a rock down to the bottom where those green trees were, you'd kick the lazy deer out of their hole. I was convinced they were there because it was where I would be if I were one of them. Green grass and leaves with a source of water, and virtually inaccessible by two-legged predators. I thought back to the buck that was shot out of season and left for dead, and I wondered who would shoot an animal just for the thrill of killing it. For some reason, it made less sense to me than why a child molester would be executed against a tree in the woods. I could reason through that quite easily, even though such an act of vigilantism was contrary to the fiber of a civil society.

The sound of a helicopter hovering behind us drew my attention. There was a different cadence to the blades chopping through the air, and it was a sound I had become familiar with as a result of my many years working the streets of South Los Angeles. Without looking up I could tell if a bird was flying by, circling, if it banked hard, or if it had settled into a hover.

I stood up and brushed the seat of my pants while searching south toward the lookout, a high peak that offered miles of unobstructed view. I could hear Floyd moving as I glassed the terrain beneath the bird, and soon I became aware of him standing next to me. I lowered my glasses. "Wonder what they're looking at over there."

He walked toward the car. "I'll grab the radio and ask."

The bird began moving, flying a tight circle in the area above the lookout. I reflected on the ride we had taken in that bird the day before—or another one just like it—and the feel of being up in the air above the mountains came back to me. I was glad my feet were planted on the ground at the moment. I always enjoyed going up in a bird, but being back on solid ground always felt good, like you had gotten away with something.

Floyd keyed a handheld: "Air unit above the lookout, do you have something? This is david five adam six, Homicide."

The radio squelched in return, and a woman's voice came over clearly. "Roger that, david five unit, this is Air Twenty-two overhead. We thought we saw some movement just inside the tree line up here, but we aren't seeing anything now."

Floyd looked over at me. "They've got a chick observer."

It was a statement, not a question. A joyous statement. Floyd was likely picturing a beautiful woman in her green flight suit stepping out of the bird and jogging toward him, seeing it in slow-motion as she pulled her helmet from her head and shook her hair until it fell into a perfect evening look. No helmet head for airborne beauties.

"David five, did you copy?" she purred.

Floyd stared toward the bird and batted his eyes as he answered. "Roger that, twenty-two, thank you, ma'am."

"How do you suppose we get up there?" I asked, indicating the top of the peak the bird was circling.

"Into the helicopter?"

I frowned.

Floyd smiled, and then looked off to the left. He walked twenty paces south and stopped. After a moment, he turned back to me. "I don't know, Dickie. Probably just get back on this road and head that way, keep veering south."

I turned toward the car. "Let's go check it out. I want to see what caught their eye."

"I want to see that broad in the bird, Dickie. Tell her she better set it down and give us a hand. She sounded hot."

"You amaze me," I said.

"I'm not going to lie, Dickie; I am rather amazing."

JUNIOR HEARD THE HELICOPTER BANK AND HEAD BACK HIS DIRECTION. HE panicked, thinking maybe it had picked up a reflection from his binoculars, or from his motorcycle that sat twenty feet away beneath a canopy of ponderosas. He scurried into the trees and grabbed the handlebars of his bike, kicked the shifter down twice and up half a click to put it in neutral. He quickly pushed the bike farther into the dark timber and stopped, listening to the chopper while trying to catch his breath. Surely they hadn't seen him, he thought. Or had they?

The bird circled several times and then faded away. He waited and listened until he was sure it wasn't coming back. He started downhill, first pushing the bike and then jumping onto the seat. He pulled the clutch lever in, kicked the shifter into second gear and popped the clutch. The bike came to life and he throttled it, leaning to one side and turning slightly so that the rear wheel would spin against the ground and throw a wave of dirt behind him.

A mile or so away, when he came to the clearing above Miner's Gulch, he cut the engine and coasted to the edge of the woods. He sat on his bike and peered down through brush and rock to the rusted tin roof of the old miner's shed. With all the activity in the area today, he hesitated to go check his stash, but he couldn't just leave it unattended. He looked up at the sun and realized it would be hours before darkness came, but that was when he would come back. Whatever the cops were doing would likely be finished, if for no other reason than it got darker than a cave around here once the sun went down.

Junior rolled backward several feet, turned the bike away from the clearing, and kicked the starter down twice before it fired up. He pulled his helmet on and rode away, headed back to the compound.

THE ROAD DIDN'T REACH ALL THE WAY TO THE LOOKOUT, SO WE PARKED AT its end, each grabbed a bottle of water, and set off on foot. The trail wound up the mountainside and was beaten with hoof prints of deer and cattle. In some places along the soft edges you could see the tracks of quail left by a covey out for their morning or evening strolls. They were birds that preferred not to fly other than short distances and with purpose, motivated usually by the threat of predators.

Predators were everywhere, I knew: in the cities, around small towns, up in the woods, and across the deserts and seas. A bird's instinct was to avoid them at all costs. Streetwise civilians knew the same principle applied to surviving in the inner cities and even in jails and prisons. I stopped to look at an impression of a canine paw that partially covered some of the quail tracks. A coyote tracking the quail. Predator stalking its prey. No place was free of conflict. The coyote trots across the hillside with feathers in his mouth and his head held high until a lead projectile tears through his side, boring a hole through both lungs and his heart before exploding from the other side of his hide. A young man overpowers a younger lady and has his way with her and leaves her weeping and bleeding as he walks away relieved, satisfied, enjoying a conquest completed. Until he's backed against a tree in the woods and a projectile cracks through his breast plate and blows his heart apart before tearing through his spine and lodging in the bark of a hundred-year-old pine.

Floyd was saying, "I've never seen any cows around here. Have you?"

I looked up from the trail, across the open range that was brown and barren in the early days of autumn, a vast land that few knew existed within the boundaries of Los Angeles County. On the peak, the wind blew stiffly, and I figured it always did whether or not two homicide detectives were here to notice it. I drank in the coolness against my sweaty skin while catching my breath from the hike, and I finished off my bottle of water. Floyd had turned and seemed to be studying the terrain which faded away toward the tree line. I walked to the south of the point, took a seat on a rock, and began glassing into the draws that ran like bony fingers toward the basin.

Floyd said, "Fresh tracks, partner."

I continued glassing and raised my voice against the wind. "Cows?"

"Boots."

I lowered the binoculars and turned to watch him studying the ground. "What kind of boots?"

"I don't know, just boots. Kind of smooth bottomed, like cowboy boots. Something with a heel. Definitely not hiking boots. More like work boots or biker boots."

"What are biker boots?"

"Hold on, Dickie. We've got tire tracks."

I was now walking briskly toward him. "How are there tire—"

"Motorcycle tracks. Dirt bike." He stood and looked into the woods, in the direction of a well-beaten path, a game trail that appeared torn up from nobby tires and horsepower. "That's what Aero saw, Dickie, a dirt bike. Someone was up here on a motorcycle."

I looked around. "Where'd it go?"

"What was it doing up here? That's a better question." Floyd now looked back to the north. "You can see where we were parked from here."

I followed his gaze. "Interesting. You think he was watching us?"

He thought about it a minute. "He or she. Somebody's creeping around here keeping an eye on us."

"Watkins," I said.

Floyd nodded. "Most likely."

We walked down the trail twenty paces before stopping, following the tracks. I looked back up the trail that we would have to climb before heading down the other side where our car was parked. "We're giving up a lot of elevation, partner."

"Yeah, and for what? He's long gone."

"Let's get back to the car and radio in for the mounted posse to come up. They can use their horses to track this asshole to wherever he went, see what he's up to."

Floyd seemed to consider it for a long moment. "It's a distraction."

"What do you mean?"

"It's Watkins keeping an eye on us; that's no surprise. We've already been to the compound and we didn't see anything that interested us as far as Josie goes. I'm afraid we go down there and we'll get off in the weeds with that anti-government, resistance bullshit, and we'll end up having to kill someone. I say we keep our eyes on the prize. Let's find that car. Let's find Josie."

I nodded my head and kept it going as if following the beat of a song in my head. The only tune I heard though was the one Floyd was singing, and he was right on the mark with this one. "You're right. Okay, good thought. Let's go back up top. I want to keep glassing for a while. You can see for miles from up there."

3 0

We glassed for what seemed like two hours. In reality, it was less than half of that before we decided to hike back down to the car and keep moving. We felt it was better to cover more ground rather than to analyze every draw, every cluster of trees and brush, every mountainside. We weren't looking for deer. I had hunted enough to know the magic of glassing for hours and being patient. An area that seemed to hold no game could come to life at any moment, and only the patient hunter who waited and watched would see it. But there was a red sedan to be found, and according to the message Josie had sent, she had been in an accident *on the mountain*. It had to be this mountain. Where else would she have gone? If not here, would she not have provided more information? Maybe she hadn't been able. But the point was, Floyd and I agreed, we needed to find the car in order to find Josie. The plane and the birds continued their searches, but not all terrain could be seen from above. The mounted posse had pulled their trailers halfway up the mountain and parked, offloaded their geldings and mares, and plunged into the woods with the intent of side-hilling from the west to the east, covering much of the land by utilizing game trails. It was estimated they could cover twenty miles or better in a day depending on the terrain and whether or not they found natural sources of water for their steeds.

Others were doing just as Floyd and I were, driving the roads and stopping to glass the hillsides and draws from various vantage points.

When we reached the Crown Vic, I popped the trunk and pulled out two cold bottles of water. I handed one to Floyd and propped the other on some of the equipment in my trunk so I could shed my coat and the sweatshirt beneath it. Floyd said, "Good idea," and followed my lead. As I started to close the trunk, Floyd stopped me. "Hang on, Dickie." He reached into the trunk and opened my cooler. He pushed a few bottles of water aside and dug into the ice until he saw the shiny tops of what he knew would be cans of Coors Light. "Good thinking, dickhead."

"Of course," I said. "This isn't my first rodeo, pal."

We drove off with cold water between our legs, and I imagined we were both thinking about the cold beer that awaited us, wishing it were beer time now. We soon came to a crossroads and I paused, considering my options.

Floyd pointed left. "That way, Dickie."

I took a moment to consider the options. Left meant heading back the way we had come, and that was likely what Floyd had in mind, either letting me know that it was the way we had come—in case I had forgotten—or letting me know he was ready to go back to the command post to check in and grab lunch. I turned right.

"Wrong way, Dickie."

His shades were locked on me as his hair blew across his forehead in the breeze that pushed through our windows.

"I'm thinking this takes us to the other side of the lookout, and I don't think we've been that way. I figured we'd take a look before we head down."

"You realize," he said, "that you always do this."

"Do what?"

"You always manage to think of more to do before. Before we grab a bite, before we wrap up a crime scene, before we end an interview, before we can go home or start drinking beer."

"Do you want a beer? Do you need a beer? Is that what this is about?" I glanced at my watch. "It's almost noon, buddy, I'll gladly get you a beer."

"Don't tempt me."

I veered to the right again at another split and nodded to indicate the other direction. "I think that's the road that gets us back toward the wad compound."

"Yeah, so go the other way."

I glanced in the direction of the compound, looking through my sunglasses into my sideview mirror, picturing Watkins coming over the top of the hill on his four-wheeler the day Floyd had knocked him on his ass. "You don't want to go another round with Watkins?" I looked over and smiled at my partner.

"I'm about to go another round with you, if you don't feed me."

"There was a sign down below, 'Don't feed the bears.'"

He flipped me off. I chuckled while moving slowly along the dirt road, guiding the sedan around some potholes while being unable to avoid others. Our heads swayed back and forth with the motion of the car, and we continued for the next couple of miles in silence.

"Wait," Floyd said, excitedly.

I stopped the car. "What've you got?"

He had lifted his binoculars to his eyes and was looking into a draw on his side of the car. He didn't answer. I threw the shifter into park and popped my door. As I jumped out, I asked again. "What've you got?"

When I came around the back of the car, Floyd had popped his door open and had stuck one foot on the ground, still seated in the car, glassing below the road. I stopped near his open door and began glassing in the direction he seemed to be focused. I heard and felt Floyd stand up and come out of the car, and he was near me now as he finally spoke.

"There's some kind of a shed down there. An old building of some sort."

I lowered my glasses and hurried to the edge of the road, sat down on the dirt embankment, and lifted the binoculars back to my eyes while pressing my elbows against my knees to steady my gaze.

"But I don't see any cars," Floyd said softly.

I kept looking, beginning at the shed and moving up and down the draw in both directions. It was an old wooden structure with a rusted tin roof, and it seemed to lean to one side as if it could collapse at any moment. I kept going back to it with the glasses, but there was no movement in the area, nothing of interest. There were no cars or any debris to be found anywhere near it that might indicate it was worth looking at. I lowered my glasses and sighed. "Nothing."

"It'd be a good place to shelter up if you were stuck out here."

I pictured the interior: warped, rotted wooden planks, rusted nails failing to keep them anchored. Rats pitter-pattering across the uneven surface or nesting in the corners, unaware of the snakes slithering against the dark damp ground beneath them, quietly searching for openings in the slats while following their flickering tongues that guided them to their prey. Maybe there was an old camp stove, a rusted coffee pot abandoned on its surface. Sticky strands of spider webs with shells of old insects that had been trapped but never consumed, and small particles of dust glimmering in the few rays of sunlight that seeped through the south-facing wall. For a moment I saw an old cot, and I pictured Josie resting her broken body, unable to get any farther and choosing the dingy shelter over exposure as she waited for help to arrive. I glassed down the draw again, wondering if it could be. Her car would be nearby if it was even remotely possible, and there was no sign of it. Nothing I could see.

Floyd had moved back toward the car, his voice trailing off with his back to me. "Come on, Dickie, let's head back. You're killing me."

I continued glassing as Floyd drifted away. The car door shut behind me. After a long moment, I conceded, and joined my partner in the comfort of the Crown Vic. Soon we were headed down the mountain road toward the command post.

It was nearly three in the afternoon when we arrived to find many of those who had been sent out to search had returned and were waiting. Waiting for what? I fooled myself into thinking the search had been called off because she was found, and I clicked the mic of my radio to make sure it was on and receiving a signal. It was, yet I had heard no such broadcast over the airwaves. Still not ready to let go of the fantasy, I told myself we could have been out of range, especially on the far side of the mountain where we had stopped and glassed the draw that held the old abandoned shed. But as we drew nearer, the faces of those who waited in folding lawn chairs or leaned against vehicles, many of them reddened from the afternoon heat or exhaustion, revealed there was no sign of good news. If anything, the searchers appeared spent and disappointed, maybe frustrated. I heard the sound of diesel motors and squeaking brakes, and glanced in my rearview mirror to see that two pickups pulling horse trailers were now coming in behind us. Additional searchers ready for a break and maybe another game plan.

It didn't take long after we joined the group to feel the collective letdown after the day's efforts. I realized then that the helicopters had gone, as had the fixed-wing sheriff's plane. The mounted posse unloaded their horses and tied them to the sides of their trailers where they stood with their heads hung low and their hind legs cocked. Buckets of water were hung from the sides of the trailers within the horses' reach, though none seemed interested. Their black and gray and sorrel hides were lathered in sweat from a hard day packing men and women through rugged terrain. Just another day in a horse's life.

Michaels and Smith came out of the mobile command post with solemn expressions on their faces. The lieutenant made eye contact with me and nodded. I bumped Floyd's elbow and started for them, and saw that they began walking toward us. We met halfway and stood silent for a moment.

"Well," Lieutenant Michaels started, "I had sure expected to find something today. We had enough goddam people looking."

"Is that it?" I asked, an unintended edge to my tone. "We're done here?"

Smith held his eyes on me as Michaels answered. "For today, buddy. But we're going to try again tomorrow, though likely with a smaller group."

"Unless we can scrounge up some new blood," Smith added.

I glanced at my old sergeant from Major Crimes and saw the resolve in his eyes. He added, "Or the four of us will be out here searching these fucking hills ourselves. How's your horsemanship?" he said, chuckling.

Michaels said, "Everyone has covered the grids they were assigned, and none of them has the energy left to start anew. Even the horses are worn out, apparently."

My gaze drifted to the horses but was quickly drawn toward the highway at the ring-ding-dinging of decelerating dirt bikes. Two riders turned in to camp and coasted their bikes to a stop. They dismounted, lowering them onto kickstands, and quickly removed their helmets to reveal sweat-soaked heads of hair beneath.

"What about the bikes? They aren't tired."

"You know how to ride one?" Smith asked.

"How hard could it be?" I answered.

Lieutenant Michaels said, "By the time we all get fed and debriefed, there's not going to be much daylight left. I know you don't want to hear it, but we would all be better off starting fresh in the morning. We don't want anyone not making it back before dark and having a second emergency to deal with."

I sulked for a moment though I knew he was right. Lieutenant McCravy appeared at Floyd's side and handed each of us a bottle of water. I saw her sergeant, John Brady, not far behind her at his car. He now wore only his cargo pants and boots, and a sweat-soaked brown t-shirt. He finished a bottle of water and tossed it into the open trunk.

"Thanks," Floyd said to McCravy.

I held the bottle up as a gesture and also thanked her. "Anything at all?"

She shook her head. "Not where my crew went. Nothing."

"We appreciate your efforts," Floyd said.

Michaels cleared his throat. "Let's get everyone together for debriefing and wrap this up for the day."

Floyd drifted off and I stood silently waiting as the others gathered in a semi-circle, everyone facing Michaels. The chatter paled in comparison to the morning briefing, a sign everyone had put in a hard day's work, and all likely shared in our disappointment. Michaels began to speak, then stopped and smiled as he looked past me. I turned to see Floyd returning with two beers. He handed me one as he stopped next to me. He nodded to the lieutenant and said, "Beer time, boss. That's how we roll at the bureau."

"I hope there's more where that came from," he said before turning to address the group, his smile quickly disappearing from his face. "I need each team to check in before leaving, give us a quick summary of what you were able to cover today, what, if anything, you came up with, and which, if any, other days your teams are available this week. We plan to be back here tomorrow and the next day and however long it takes to find Detective Sanchez or prove she's not here. We would appreciate any help we can get."

He panned the group as he said it, an assembly of men and women of all shapes and sizes, ethnicities and backgrounds, all on the same team, each willing to risk their lives to save another. As I studied the dirty and sweaty faces beneath brimmed hats and behind sunglasses, each attentive and sober, it again occurred to me how blessed I was to be part of this organization. I briefly reflected back to the year after I had been shot when many times during my recovery I had considered not returning. I was glad that I had.

When Lieutenant Michaels finished, the group slowly dispersed, some moving toward the table outside of the command post where they were likely headed to report in and check their teams out for the day as Michaels had instructed them to do. Others began policing their gear and reorganizing their equipment into the trunks of cars and beds of trucks. Horses were unsaddled and brushed and then loaded into their trailers so they could be hauled back to their stables.

The first to depart was Jacob Spencer, the game warden. His dusty white truck with a four-wheeler loaded in the back caught my attention as he pulled out of the far end of the lot and turned east, toward the mountains, not west to the freeway. I considered it for a moment, wondering if he was going to make one last sweep. None of us knew those mountains as he did.

Good guy, I thought. I hadn't seen him at the command post this morning, but seeing he had come at all reinforced the instinct I had for him. I had known from the moment I met him that I liked him.

3 1

W hen the mountain had grown quiet and the pale blue sky had
been free of flying pigs for several hours, Junior Watkins rolled
off of the hammock that was strung between two trees at the side of his
trailer. The compound was still, and he assumed most of the men were
taking their afternoon naps so they would be fresh for the evening festivities of drinking around the fire and plotting to overthrow the government
—or at least putting up a strong resistance to its overbearing encroachment
on their personal liberties. It was the same agenda every night.

Sometimes Junior would participate for a couple of hours and then
sneak off into the woods, pushing his motorcycle over the hill until he
could jumpstart it at a low rumble in third gear, sounds that wouldn't pene-
trate through the woods and over the laughter and music and a crackling
bonfire. Other nights he'd take off before it began and miss the festivities
altogether, taking his chances on how the old man might react when he
returned. Usually, he could avoid him by sneaking in similar to how he
would sneak out, but using a different route that would have him coming
in downhill so that he could cut the engine and coast. The last thing Junior
wanted to deal with was his old man on a mean drunk. Sometimes he
wanted to leave the property for good, be done with his old man, his
"uncles," the various drunks and drug addicts, self-proclaimed killers of

men, revolutionary soldiers. But because of his mother's death, he hadn't had the courage to leave. She would be alive to this day, had *she* not decided to leave. So, he was stuck, and each day Junior would contemplate pulling his nine or his knife on the old man and being done with him. Be done with all of it. If not for the old man's allies—the loyal dummies with whom he surrounded himself and who hung on his every aggrandizing word—Junior may have already made his move. Soon, though. One day . . .

He stretched, then shivered as the mountain air—cooling quickly in the waning sunlight—washed over him. Junior stepped into his trailer and gathered his hoodie, a leather jacket, and some of his deer jerky and dried fruit. He placed those items in his backpack with other supplies such as tools for survival: fire-starting materials, water filters, space blankets, a small flashlight, a compass, a first-aid kit, and protein bars. He checked his pistol to see that it was fully loaded, and placed it back into its holster he wore on his right hip. His hunting knife was worn on the left hip, backwards, in a cross-draw configuration. Junior grabbed his canteen on his way out the door. He would stop by one of the springs along the way to fill it with fresh water.

A chainsaw idled somewhere nearby. Junior figured it was one of the others in camp cutting firewood, and he pictured the sharpened teeth of the saw's blade ripping through timber as the high-pitched revving pierced the quiet woods. As long as the lumberjack continued his work, nobody would notice the sound of Junior's bike putting away. He hurried to top off the fuel tank, then strapped his pack to the seat where it would ride securely behind him. He pulled his helmet onto his head and kicked the starter three times until she fired. Moments later he was gliding through the woods on narrow game trails of loose dirt, softened from his frequent travels.

He was headed to the lookout where he would wait and watch until darkness swept over the mountains, and then he would go down to the shed to check on the woman.

FLOYD AND I BELLIED UP TO THE BAR AT THE *FIESTA COCINA* IN SANTA Clarita where Lieutenant Michaels and his trusted sergeant Jack Smith had told them they were going to stop and have a couple of cold ones while rush-hour traffic died down. It was a popular restaurant where businessmen and -women gathered in the afternoons for end-of-the-day trysts before heading to their homes, where golfers gathered to lament their games at nearby courses, and where cops, whose anxieties were greater than triple-bogies, huddled behind frosted glasses of beer or tumblers of scotch and bourbon while scrutinizing everyone who entered the bar. Later, the dining room would fill with families, mothers and fathers having their margaritas while children sipped sodas and all feasted on fine Mexican cuisine, unaware of the troubled adults in the adjacent room who were resolutely self-medicating.

Michaels had started a tab and kept insisting the bartender put all our drinks on it, arguing he was the lieutenant, the ranking officer among us with the highest salary. Floyd assured him we'd surpass his fixed income by the time we finished lying about how much overtime we worked, and in the end each of us had cash on the bar. Smith kept lighting cigarettes and being admonished by the bartender about smoking in restaurants, a violation of California law for more than two decades. A pair of college girls, who sat nearby, had wrinkled their noses and fanned the air in protest, and finally they moved to the other side of the bar. Smith lit another smoke.

Floyd was asking Smith if he knew the identity of the female deputy in Air 22, and Smith was saying who cares, aren't you married, like you need more headaches in your life. He then went on to give him a fatherly talk, telling Floyd that the goal in life was to get through life with one woman you can manage, that it made no sense to keep starting over as if the next marriage would be better than the last. "We have enough trouble with one," he said, speaking generally of cops, "why would you want more?" He was speaking from experience and Floyd appeared to be heeding his advice, though God only knows what was really going on in Floyd's head. When Smith finished speaking, Floyd chuckled and thanked him for the sage advice, assuring the old Marine that he had no intention of trading in for a new bride. Floyd said, "I just happen to be a serial window shopper."

"You're a glutton for punishment, kid," Smith advised.

I turned to Michaels and asked what the plan was for tomorrow, while the veteran sergeant began telling Floyd that when you're on a diet, you don't stand around outside the bakery, and continued on with some other words of wisdom that would fall on deaf ears.

"Aero Bureau is concerned about flying in the morning," Michaels said. "Apparently there's a report that it's going to be soupy up there tomorrow. They were thinking it might be late morning before they could be up for us, if at all. I guess you never know."

I glanced outside at the clear late-afternoon sky. "Weird."

Michaels shrugged. "It's what they're saying. The fuck do I know?"

"I guess that's why they call it the Gorman triangle."

I noticed Floyd and Smith had finished their conversation about Floyd's love life and were paying attention to our conversation.

Michaels said, "Gorman triangle?"

I took a sip of my beer and nodded. "Steve Kennedy, one of the resident deputies up there, told me about it. Apparently, there's a shit-ton of plane crashes due to the low clouds and fog that roll in. They disappear in the triangle, the pass surrounded by high peaks."

Sergeant Smith interjected: "The problem is, some of these single-engine pilots aren't instrument qualified, and they get themselves in over their heads."

"That's what Kennedy was saying," I continued. "Apparently, there's IFR—Instrument Flight Regulations—and VFR—Visual Flight Regulations—and a lot of small plane pilots only fly VFR. So they take off out of sunny Southern California and suddenly they're socked in while flying through the Tejon Pass, headed to Bakersfield. Or vice versa. Kennedy said what happens is they keep going lower, trying to stay under the clouds, and bam, they crash into the side of a mountain."

"I can imagine," Michaels said.

"He said one time, he was up near the top and a plane buzzed over his head, apparently trying to stay under the clouds. The dude missed the summit by five feet."

"Fuck that," Floyd said. He then gestured to the bartender for another round.

Michaels said, "Not for me, bud, I need to get going."

"Come on, boss," Sergeant Smith said, "don't be a pussy. One more and we'll all head out."

I shrugged. Michaels stood up and said, "I'll see you boys tomorrow. Stay under the clouds when you fly home." He grinned and motioned for the check. The bartender brought it to him and he scribbled his signature on the receipt and put his card back in his wallet. "I'm getting to be too old for this shit."

Michaels left and another round was placed in front of us. I was still thinking about the summit and the planes and the stories I had heard about this crazy outpost called Gorman Station where planes lost their ways and crashed into mountains. It was a vast land comprising thousands of acres of forest and mountainous terrain, untamed and oftentimes occupied by a variety of people: hunters, hikers, motorsports enthusiasts, and the lovers of nature. Then you had the residents: throwbacks, societal dropouts, survivalists, anti-government revolutionaries.

Smith had stood up from his stool and was leaning on the bar taking swigs of his beer. Floyd seemed preoccupied by his phone, his thumbs vigorously pecking at the screen. All of us alone in our thoughts or devices. A thought came to me and I announced it flatly. "How do we know it was a car accident?"

Floyd squinted at me.

Smith said, "What do you mean?"

"The message said there had been an accident. Maybe she was in a plane."

"Does she fly?" Smith asked.

"No. I mean, not that I know of. I guess anything is possible, but we've been partners for six months and she's never mentioned it."

"She have any friends who fly?" Floyd asked. "Maybe she talked someone into flying over the mountain so she could see the area from above, get a better perspective of the area like we did."

"I'm not sure," I said. "I guess it would be easy enough to figure out though. Don't all pilots have to file flight plans? We can get Aero Bureau to inquire if there are any planes missing since the weekend, anything that didn't come back in. If there are any, cross-reference the pilot with names from her emails, see if anything pops."

Smith shrugged, then finished the rest of his beer. "Seems like a long-shot. Either way, I'll see you boys in the morning at the C.P."

"You're out of here?" I asked.

He clapped me on the shoulder. "Yep, gotta go, buddy. You boys be safe."

Floyd and I finished our beers in silence and then looked at each other for a long moment. I was wondering about another beer and he was likely doing the same. His drive home was farther than mine, and his wife wouldn't be happy with him putting in the extra hours after our shift to "debrief" at the local watering hole. I figured he would opt to go, so I thought I'd make it easy for him.

"We better hit it, partner."

"Yeah, I guess so." He stood up and dug into his pocket. "Are we all squared up here?"

"I think so." I caught the bartender's eye, and when he sauntered over, I asked, "Are we good?"

He nodded, unenthusiastically, and gave me a weak "yep." I got the feeling he didn't care for our group.

We left the restaurant and drove to Santa Clarita Station where Floyd had left his car for the day. I dropped him off and confirmed our meeting time for tomorrow, and then pulled out of the lot. In the silence of my car, my thoughts were back on the mountain. The shed still bothered me, and I couldn't stop seeing Josie holed up inside it. There was no logic to it—her car was nowhere to be found, the terrain was steep and brushy, and it wasn't a place you would easily find or access—but it bothered me still that we hadn't checked it out.

Just before I passed under the interstate where I would access the southbound onramp from the other side, I jerked the car to the right and turned onto the northbound onramp instead. "What the hell are you doing?" I asked myself, rhetorically. For I knew exactly what I was doing, and I knew it was a foolish thing to do. I let out a long breath and settled into my seat as I brought the Crown Vic up to seventy-five on the freeway. I could be back to the road above the shed before dark if I hurried.

3 2

Junior waited where he had views of the shed at the bottom of Miner's Gulch and of the main mountain road coming in from the highway.

He would ride his motorcycle to the shed, though it would be the long way to get there. Still, he preferred that to climbing down the steep, brushy hillside. It was hiking back up that he wanted most to avoid.

But he wasn't the only one who knew how to get to the old miner's shed from the bottom. He had seen four-wheeler tracks going in and out of the area, and he wondered if the tracks had been made by his father, or by one of the other men in camp. It could have been any of them, as there were several four-wheelers in the compound and everyone was welcome to use them. Or, it could have been anyone else. Because of the tracks, Junior knew he had to be cautious when visiting the lady, and he knew to only go at night now. Especially with all the cops that had been around lately.

Junior had to do something; he couldn't just leave her staked out on the floor indefinitely. At times he wondered if he were to free her, would she be grateful to him for it? She was an attractive woman, and he had many times fantasized about being with her. But not tied to the ground, unable to participate. He was no savage. He wanted her to love him—to make love to him—and he couldn't shake the idea that if he freed her, she would give him the love he so desired. Why would she not? After all, she would still need help getting out of the mountains. She would have to rely on him. He would be saving her. To try to get out on her own would be a death sentence, given her current condition and with no access to water, food, and warm clothing. He could offer her all of that. Hell, he'd ride her out of here on his motorcycle if she would make love to him first.

He detected movement far below on the mountain road and lifted his glasses for a better look. He only caught a glimpse of the pickup before it disappeared around a corner, winding its way up the mountain. But whose truck was it? It was white, which seemed to be the most common color of trucks. At least it wasn't black and white.

It was time to start heading down to the shed. It would take him a half-hour or better from where he sat, and it was close enough now to being dark. The sun would be down by the time he arrived, or soon thereafter. He glassed the mountain road once more before moving from his perch. He didn't see the truck and decided not to be concerned with it. There were many forks in the roads, and only one led to the area above Miner's Gulch. Few vehicles ever traveled that route because the road eventually ended. Mostly hunters used that road to get to the end where they would park and then hike into the woods.

Junior stuffed his binoculars into his backpack, zipped up his coat, and took off for the shed.

———

WHEN THE SOUNDS OF HELICOPTERS AND MOTOR VEHICLES HAD FADED FOR good, and only the birds chirping and the chipmunks scurrying through the leaves and branches outside of the shed remained, Josie went limp against her wool blanket, deflated. Tears welled up in her eyes as she pictured the helicopters flying away and the search and rescue teams packing their equipment into their vehicles and driving off the mountain, doubtful. She prayed they hadn't given up, that they would try again tomorrow, and the next day, and the day after that. She wondered if they had found her car. She assumed that they had; how could they not? And if they did, they would never give up the search for her until she was found—dead or alive.

Josie could feel the mountain air cooling as the scant light from outside had all but disappeared, and she shivered at the thought of another long, cold, lonely night. Unless.

She summoned her inner strength and recommitted her resolve to overcome—and kill if she must—her captor. She wouldn't leave her fate in the hands of others. She didn't know how much longer she could survive without medical aid, proper nutrition, and adequate water. But would he come tonight, or had the efforts of the searchers driven him away, if only temporarily? He usually came during the hours of daylight.

Her eyes grew heavy and fluttered as she tried to remain awake while listening for the sounds of the motorcycle. She thought about her partner and pictured him driving off the mountain. Surely he and Floyd would have been spearheading the search that had clearly taken place today. Were they finished? Most likely. There would be no reason to continue searching into the dark. Now she saw Dickie and Floyd driving back into the city—God, what she would give to see the city life again, to fight traffic, to wait in long lines for Starbucks. The boys would probably be looking for a place to stop and have dinner after a long, disappointing day on the mountain. Maybe a place where they could get a steak and beer— several beers. They were simple like that. Emotion welled up inside her as she thought of Dickie worrying about her, chugging his beer and staring across a room wondering if she was alive or dead. No, she decided, he would know she was alive. It's how he was wired.

Her mother would be a mess. But she would be surrounded by family, and she wouldn't give up hope and she wouldn't stop praying. Josie pictured her mom lighting candles and saying her prayers.

Josie began to think of Tom but forced herself to move beyond those thoughts. It pained her to think of what had happened to him, and it devastated her to picture his broken body somewhere on the mountain being ravished by animals.

She had to stop thinking this way. It was weakness. To survive she had to be strong. She closed her eyes and again rehearsed her plans for an escape. It had to be tonight. If he came.

"WHAT IS THAT LITTLE SHITHEAD DOING DOWN THERE?" JACOB SPENCER said.

He leaned into his binoculars and strained against the fleeting light to see the man on the dirt bike headed toward Miner's Gulch. It had to be the Watkins kid, he knew. He had chased him enough on that Husqvarna of his to know it by sight, even at a distance at dusk. Hell, he practically knew it by sound, the way the boy rode, how he would double-clutch when shifting, revving it up and throttling it to raise the front end or spin dirt from the back tire. He knew the boy the way one might know his mortal enemy, observations seared into his memory by hatred. Spencer lowered his glasses and smiled. Tonight could be the night he nailed that Watkins kid.

Jacob Spencer slid down a dirt embankment to the road below him as if riding a wave, his feet positioned as if propped on a surfboard. He held his left hand out for balance, while his right instinctively gripped his holstered pistol. He had climbed above the road in order to glass the area of Miner's Gulch, but he never expected to come across Junior Watkins out and about after dark. Well, it'd be dark by the time he got down to him, snuck up on him, and nailed him. Normally, Spencer would unload his state-issued four-wheeler out of the bed of his game warden truck and take the long way into Miner's Gulch, rather than hiking down and having to hike back out. But tonight, he would sneak down there and get the drop on the kid. He knew what Watkins was up to. Spencer now knew for sure that it was Watkins who had been visiting the woman. It was his motorcycle tracks that Spencer had seen coming in from the bottom. He had assumed it might be, but Watkins wasn't the only kid to ride a bike around these mountains. Now he knew for sure. Now he could do something about it.

Spencer drove with his lights off, using the last of the day's light to navigate the roads that he knew like his own backyard. Gravel crunched beneath his tires as he crept toward the spot where he would park and start down the steep grade into the brushy draw, down to the shed. He thought about using rope; it would make it easier to come back up, and he could anchor one to the heavy-duty brush guard that covered the front grille of his truck. He wouldn't need his rifle, and he knew he could travel faster without it. As he came to a stop, he pulled his flashlight off of a charger that plugged into the power outlet of his truck, and cupped his hand over the lens and checked it before getting out. It was fully charged, a bright beam turning his hand a translucent red against the thirty-thousand candle-power light.

Spencer opened the door and closed it quietly. He pulled his leather gloves from a back pocket and stretched one and then the other over his hands. After he secured the rope to the truck, he began his descent. He lowered himself slowly down the embankment, trying not to dislodge the loose soil and rocks, careful to move quietly. He kept a tight grip on the rope, feeding it out carefully as he worked his way down. He glanced at the sky to the west and realized it would be completely dark before he made it to the shed. He had lost sight of Junior Watkins, and he no longer heard the bike. He wondered if he was already there. With her.

GRAVEL SHOT OFF THE GRADED ROAD, PELTING THE UNDERCARRIAGE OF MY county-issued Ford Crown Victoria that had been beefed up at the factory with heavy-duty suspension and power plant and sold as a police package. It handled like a Corvette rather than the family sedan it was designed to be, and I was thankful for it as the back end slid around the first corner and fishtailed before straightening. I had just left the pavement where normally I would have slowed, but this was anything other than normal circumstances. I had now convinced myself that disregarding that shed had been an egregious error and something that needed to be addressed before my partner spent one more lonely night on the mountain. I pictured her there, alone and scared, and until I proved that she wasn't there I wouldn't be deterred.

I thought I would have been able to arrive before dark, but it was dusk already, and without light I might never find the shed from the road. If I found it, I would inspect it tonight. I didn't care if the trip down the mountainside in the dark was treacherous and dangerous and creepy; I had a flashlight and a pistol and the resolve to find my partner.

But could I find that spot?

I was fairly certain I remembered which direction to turn at the various forks in the road, and I had a general idea of where we had stopped and glassed and found the shed below; but I had been on mountain roads at night enough to know that nothing looked the same once darkness arrived and smothered the vast land, and landmarks could no longer be seen. I cringed at the thought of spending nights out here alone, and the thought that my partner was out there somewhere only made me more determined.

As I continued on, I slowed for the corners, knowing a mistake would compound the problem at hand. It was like the days of patrol: when responding to an officer needs help call, you failed your partners if emotions got the best of you and you crashed along the way rather than arriving to offer assistance. But on the straightaways, I opened it up.

Soon the road leveled, and with the occasional glimpses of city lights far off on the horizon I knew the top of the mountain was near. I had come to three forks and felt confident that I had made the right choices along the way. Now it was time to slow down and figure out where Floyd had spotted the shed deep in a draw below the road.

I had just begun to question my location, wondering if I was even close to where I needed to be, when I rounded a corner and my headlights reflected off of something a half-mile down the road. I slowed and continued cautiously, my right hand gripping the butt of my pistol that rode high on my right hip. Soon I was close enough to see that it was a pickup parked on the side of the road. Its lights were off. As my high beams flooded the vehicle with light, I realized it was the game warden's truck. I stopped and considered the possibilities while scanning the sides of the road to the degree that I could in the darkness. There was nobody around.

Where was Officer Spencer?

33

J osie's heart thumped when she heard the sound of a motorcycle drawing near. Her body temperature rose and perspiration beaded on her forehead and nose though she had been chilled to the bone moments before. She tried to rub her itching nose against her shoulder, but it wouldn't reach. She took deep breaths and focused on the task at hand. This was it, she told herself. Do or die. Tonight. Now.

She ran the plan through her mind again and saw it unfold the same way it had the hundreds of times she had rehearsed it before. She would be victorious; there was no other option. Well, that or die. But dying wasn't an option either, she decided. When she reflected on her academy training, her patrol training, and her life-and-death encounters on the job—of which there had been many—she knew she had the will to survive. She thought of a plaque that hung on the wall in her home gym. It wasn't cute, it wasn't part of some larger theme, and it certainly wasn't *décor*. It might have looked a bit stark alone on that wall, but that was okay; it was a stark reminder. "*Don't let them waste you in some dirty, stinking alley.*" The words were burned into her mind, and she would never let that happen.

The motorcycle grew nearer, and as before, it seemed to approach slowly, the rider methodical, maybe even cautious. When he would leave, the sounds were different. The motor was revved higher and his speed was greater. She wondered if he thought he could sneak up on her, if that was why he was always tentative in his approach. He seemed to be timid, careful, maybe even afraid when he was near her. She hadn't been able to figure him out. Why had he never harmed her? Why was he keeping her alive and nurturing her? Why hadn't he made any attempts to sexually arouse and satisfy himself? She saw how he looked at her, his unblinking eyes peering through the holes in his ski mask, taking her in from head to toe. She had even seen the pulse in his throat, revealing his excitement of being near her. She thought about that and envisioned blood shooting out of his artery when she pulled the blade of his own knife across his neck, his eyes opened wide as he realized what was happening to him.

There was a rumble above her, coming from the area where she assumed there was a road. She had heard vehicles moving above her on many occasions, their motors idling as tires turned slowly on gravel. It amazed her how keen her hearing had become in the days she had been deprived of seeing anything beyond the dingy walls and rusted roof enclosure. Her imagination, too. She wondered if this was what it would be like for a blind person, the heightened sense of hearing, the amplified processes of deep thinking and concentration. Perhaps it wasn't such a handicap at all.

She wished the motorcycle would stop so she could better focus on the sounds above her, but it wouldn't. It continued slowly toward her, and she estimated she had ten to fifteen minutes before he arrived. There were no more noises from above, and she wondered if she might have only imagined hearing something. She wondered if the shed she was held in could be seen from the road above. She assumed that it could not. She reasoned that if so, someone would have noticed it and thought to check for her there by now.

The motorcycle drew closer, but it seemed to be moving slower than usual. Was it because of the darkness? She watched the south wall for glimpses of a headlight. Maybe the bike wasn't equipped with one. Or maybe he was being extra cautious due to the activity of the day. He might be unsure of what he would be walking into.

Jacob Spencer had made it nearly halfway to the shed at the bottom of Miner's Gulch when he stopped to rest and drink some water from one of the two bottles he had brought with him. He saw the Watkins kid coasting down the trail at the bottom of the draw. He had shut the engine off and was approaching stealthily, but Spencer didn't know why. He hoped it wasn't that the kid had seen him coming in on the road. Though he couldn't hear the bike's engine, he heard it coasting along, its parts rattling and the shocks occasionally squeaking. Twice he had caught a glimpse of movement that he knew was the kid on the bike, a blob moving in the darkness suddenly silhouetted against barren ground that reflected the scant light from a rising half-moon.

Spencer strained to see the red car that had gone off the cliff, but it was too dark. He knew it was nearby, not far from the path he was taking down. The morning after he had run it off the road, Spencer had roped down to the bottom and found it stuck nose first into a thicket of brush. Only the back end of the car had been visible, but it too was now covered and concealed. He had ridden his four-wheeler down to the shed that next day, and with his chainsaw, hiked back to where the car had come to rest. He had cut lengths of brush and limbs and covered the exposed back part of the car so that nobody would see it from above. Now it would be difficult to see even if you hiked right by it. He was pleased with the job he had done, thus far.

Now it was time to wrap it all up.

He finished the bottle and continued on, moving carefully as to not make any noises. He didn't want to scare away the boy because all of this was coming together nicely now. He thought about that night, finding the lady unconscious a hundred yards from the car and conveniently near the shed. She was alive, though he didn't think she would last long. Still, he couldn't leave her lying and take his chances. He remembered standing, pointing his pistol at her head—her pretty little head—and he hadn't been able to pull the trigger. He still didn't know why he had taken her into the shed and tied her up. He never did come up with a plan. Let her starve to death and become bear bait? He knew he couldn't execute her. The poacher had been easy. Spencer hated poachers and this one had been a rapist to boot. But the woman, she was another matter. He didn't think he would be able to look her in the eyes and shoot her the way he had backed the poacher against a tree and sentenced him to death.

Spencer had gone back to the shed two days later, but he hadn't checked on her then. There were tire tracks leading to the shed that hadn't been there the day before. Motorcycle tracks. He had looked around and wondered if he was being watched. If he didn't go to the shed, they'd never know for sure if he knew about the woman inside. He departed and never came back, and he assumed she wouldn't live much longer. Now he knew that the Watkins boy had found her, and he was probably visiting her daily, raping her and trying to keep her alive to fulfill his sick desires.

Now Spencer saw an opportunity that he never could have imagined. The Watkins kid would take the rap for the murders of the woman and the poaching rapist. And he would not live to dispute the facts that Spencer would neatly present to the homicide detectives. His new buddies.

BEFORE GETTING OUT OF MY CAR I WOULD NEVER HAVE IMAGINED THAT the game warden would be off into the brush after dark, but after checking the cab and seeing it was unoccupied, I went around the front of the truck and saw a rope tied off to the brush guard and dropping down the steep mountainside into the draw. I felt this was where the shed was located, and I wondered if Spencer had had the same gut feeling that I had had about it. I remembered seeing him heading back up the mountain as the rest of us shut down the operation for the day. While we had returned to civilization, Spencer drove back into the wilderness. I figured it was where he felt the most comfortable. He was one of those types you knew could be stranded in the mountains for days by himself and easily survive and not miss companionship or modern comforts. He was the rugged sort, a son of the pioneers. Now he had gone off a mountainside—I might argue that it was more of a cliff—and likely in search of my missing partner. It was at times like this that I was proud of the brotherhood that was the family of law enforcement. The thin blue line.

I listened while staring into the darkness, but I heard nothing below. The rope seemed taut, and I wondered if he was coming back up. I shined my light down the length of rope, but the beam stopped a hundred feet down at a clump of vegetation. There were broken branches and a path through the brush where the rope disappeared from my view, and I imagined that Spencer had gone straight through it. He was a mountain man. I was not, but I knew I could follow the rope down and join Spencer at the bottom. I hoped he was in the shed providing care to my partner as we spoke.

I hurried back to my trunk for a pair of leather gloves. I had experienced rope burn before, and it hadn't been pleasant. While searching for the gloves, I wondered how we would get Josie back up to the road if she was found in the shed. She had mentioned an accident, and since she hadn't emerged from the woods on her own, I had to assume she was badly injured. I thought about our Emergency Services Detail and wondered how long it would take them to deploy here. Could they retrieve her in the darkness? It was routine for them to rappel from the helicopters for mountain rescues, and it might be our only option. I found my gloves and slammed the trunk closed and headed back toward the rope.

———

THE SOUNDS OF THE MOTORCYCLE HAD DISAPPEARED, BUT JOSIE COULD hear activity from several directions, and this puzzled her greatly. Something or someone was moving toward the shed from the direction the motorcycle had always come. But there was no sound of an engine, and she didn't hear anyone walking. Nor did it sound like an animal. There would be the occasional squeak as if it was something mechanical, something that needed oil. Then something else had scurried through the brush behind and above her in the opposite direction. Her eyes rolled up as if searching the top of her head as she listened carefully in the direction of that noise. It could have been an animal, she thought, but it would have been a large one. Maybe a deer. A bear? She hoped not. And then a door shut from above, up on the road. A solid clunk that was unmistakably a door—or a tailgate or a trunk lid. Somebody was up on the road, and somebody else was approaching the shed. And *something* was in the brush behind her.

The shed door flung open and she saw the outline of a man against the moonlit night.

34

"Who's there? What do you want?"

"I thought you'd be hungry."

Josie recognized the voice and at once felt disappointment that she wasn't being rescued, but also relief that it was the one who came daily. So far, he hadn't hurt her, nor had he tried to violate her. Besides, he always fed her and allowed her a bathroom break when he came, and she desperately needed one now. She had wet herself a few hours earlier, unable to hold it any longer when nobody had come during the day. It hadn't been the first time.

"Why don't you let me go? Why are you holding me?"

"I'm not holding you," he said. "I'm helping you."

He was crazy. What type of insanity would it take for him to say that, she wondered. *He was helping her.* Jesus. Her resolve to escape tonight was strengthened as she realized how insane he was.

The man turned on a dim flashlight and approached her slowly while looking around the interior of the shed, the dull beam of light leading the way. He seemed to look at the ropes that held her in place, perhaps making sure she hadn't been able to free herself before he came closer. She could see that he hadn't put on his mask this time. Maybe because it was dark.

Or maybe because it was over, that this was the last she would see of him. Of anyone.

She had a surprise for him though. It wouldn't be that simple.

"Do you know who I am?" she asked softly, almost pleadingly. As she did, she wondered if that was the wrong thing to do. Would it help her situation or make it worse if he knew she was a cop? It didn't matter, she decided. On with the plan. This man was never going to let her go, so it was up to her.

He didn't answer her.

"I need to use the bucket," she said. "Badly."

He still didn't say anything, but he moved toward her and knelt down at her left side. He used a knife to cut the rope on that wrist, and then he stepped around in order to remove the other. While he was cutting the rope that held her right wrist, it occurred to her that she might have to make a change to her bathroom break assault plan. She realized that in the dark, he would have to put the light in just the right place—at the right moment—in order to catch the glimpse that she planned to offer him. It might not work.

"I'll need light," she said.

He freed her right arm and stepped back toward the door, keeping her in the beam of weak light. After a moment, he took the bucket from the corner and brought it to her, placing it near her feet.

"You'll have to do it by feel. I need my light."

"Stay in here with me," Josie said. "Please. Maybe we could just be friends."

In the following silence she could hear him breathing, almost panting.

She wondered if he was a virgin, if he had ever seen a woman naked. He was young, she knew now for certain from the little she could see of his face in the darkness. She had already assumed as much from his voice —the uncertainty, the lack of harshness—and from his lanky build. He looked like a high-schooler.

"Come on, I need the light," she told him. She realized that she had sounded authoritative, and that she needed to soften her tone. "You've been a gentleman, and I appreciate that. Just stay and hold the light, please. And try not to look."

"I can get you out of here," he said. "I want to help you."

What kind of a sick freak was this kid, she wondered? He had tied her up and held her captive for God knows what purpose, and now he wants to help? Was he sincere? Had he lost his appetite for whatever it was he had planned for her?

Fine, Josie thought, this would be better than cutting his throat—if she could believe him.

"Did you bring me more pills? I am in terrible pain. I need to get to a hospital. Can you help me do that? I will be forever grateful to you. I will never tell anyone what you've done."

"What I've done!"

His tone startled her, and suddenly she saw an explosive side to the quiet kid. Now she had probably ruined any chance of getting him to help her out, and had most likely blown the plan to lure him in and cut his throat. Her mind raced for another option or a way to patch things up.

"I mean—I just mean that you left me here and didn't free me sooner. You've been very kind to me, and I want—"

"You have some nerve, lady. I been helping you and trying to figure a way to get you out of here before—"

He stopped, whipping his head around to see behind him. His body followed, and the beam of light in his hand washed across the rotted siding of the shed, through the open doorway behind him, and across the stern face of a man who stood defiantly a few feet away, facing him down.

Josie held her breath, her eyes wide. She didn't recognize the man outside, though he seemed familiar. Her hands were free, and her captor was no longer paying attention to her. She began pulling at the ropes that bound her legs, trying to untie the knots. Suddenly, it occurred to her that the kid had cut the ropes from her arms. It was the first time he had done so, and she realized that it was, indeed, meant to be their final meeting.

"Drop it!" shouted a voice from outside.

Josie looked up, the knot she was working to untie held in her hands. There was a burst of light, a single flame erupting from the outreached hand of the man who stood outside. An explosion echoed through the night.

The kid fell backward and nearly landed on her.

She cried out. It wasn't a scream, more of a yelp.

The young man's head slowly rolled to the side until he was looking directly at her. He coughed, and blood sprayed out of his mouth. There was silence for a long moment.

"I wanted to help you," he said, weakly. His eyes, showing both fear and sadness, perhaps regret, became fixed on something beyond. Slowly, his gaze became distant, dull, and clouded. And finally lifeless.

He was gone.

Josie stared at the dead kid next to her for a short time before she finally looked away. Her eyes drifted up to the man who now stood filling the doorway.

He directed a beam of light to reveal a knife that lay on the floor not far from the dead kid's body. "He was coming at me. I did what I had to do."

Josie didn't respond. She didn't know who the man was. She couldn't see his face nor his clothing. She didn't recognize his voice, and she wondered who he was and what he had in mind for her. The knife was within her reach, and she now had both hands and one leg freed from their restraints. She glanced from the knife back to the figure of a man, and took a deep breath, readying herself for what might come, preparing herself for what she might have to do.

"Spence!"

Josie recognized her partner's voice. A flood of emotion rolled over her as the man in the doorway turned toward the voice. "It's your partner," the man said, his speech directed to Dickie who Josie now knew was outside though she couldn't see him. "She's inside," the man said. "She's going to be okay."

35

The temperature dropped as the cloudless sky showed its first signs of light and the twinkling stars began to fade, their work done until the next evening. Our work had continued from yesterday into today and the entire week felt surreal, a blur of a bad dream.

Josie had been air-lifted to Newhall Memorial and Spencer had been driven to Santa Clarita Sheriff's Station where he would wait to be interviewed by Homicide. I had driven down to the hospital to be with Josie. A patrol unit from Santa Clarita was stationed on the road above the gulch to preserve the scene until daylight. The game warden's truck with a rope trailing down the side of the mountain was considered part of the scene, but the bulk of the investigation would take place at the bottom of the draw. A motorcycle sat in plain view twenty feet from the old miner's shed, and the body of the Watkins boy grew cold and rigid on the dirty wooden floor inside it.

Josie was in surgery most of the night for compound fractures of her leg and hip. I slept for a couple of hours in the waiting room, off and on, until I learned she was in recovery and all seemed to be going well.

I left the hospital and drove back up to the mountain where I spoke briefly to the two deputies who sat guarding the scene from the warmth of their vehicle. It had been a quiet night, they said, nothing to report. I moved over to the edge of the road and stared down at the shed, replaying the events of the night in my head, and thinking about my partner having been held captive in such a rathole for four days. I hadn't been able to speak much with Josie—it seemed she was in shock when we found her—and I wondered what she had been through during those long days and nights. Some of the possibilities made me cringe. Though the man who lay dead on the floor was not much more than a boy, I was glad he was dead, and thankful for my new friend Jacob Spencer who had put him down. The healing process would be less complicated without legal proceedings where a victim is forced to relive the horror of such an event.

I got back in my car and started it, turned the heater on high, and leaned my head against the seat. My heavy eyes closed but my mind still raced, replaying it all over and over again.

It wouldn't be much longer before the mountain buzzed with activity. Once it was light, the investigation would begin. A team of homicide detectives would be accompanied by crime scene techs and a coroner's investigator, and the scene would be examined and documented, and evidence would be collected, and eventually, the remains of Junior Watkins would be tagged and bagged and sent to the coroner's office downtown.

I knew that there was also a very good chance that at some point before that happened, Old Man Watkins would arrive with his posse in search of the boy. As soon as he got a glimpse of the scene below with the boy's motorcycle within the area cordoned off by yellow tape, he would know instinctively what had happened. And the war might then begin. It would at least be sparked. Anticipating it, I had asked for two additional patrol units to be stationed on the road near our vehicles at first light.

When my eyes bounced open, I was surrounded by vehicles, and the sun was up in the eastern sky. A coroner's van, two crime scene vans, and several SWAT vehicles containing Emergency Services Detail deputies had arrived. They appeared to be preparing ropes and harnesses at the side of the mountain. Floyd had just parked and was walking toward me. I shut my car off and met him halfway.

"What the hell, man?"

I glanced at the SWAT cops who stood at the side of the road, and shrugged my shoulders. "It's a nightmare. I can't yet wrap my mind around it."

"The word I got is you were here when the warden dumped the kid."

I nodded, my gaze now beyond the activity at the side of the road, my mind far away.

"How'd that go down? And why didn't you let me know you were coming back up? That's bullshit, man."

After a moment, my eyes drifted back to meet Floyd's gaze. He had showered and shaved, and he appeared to be refreshed. He may have had a near-full night's sleep.

"I don't know, man, it was just a hunch. The shed bugged me and I couldn't let it go."

"Do you realize how stupid that was, coming back by yourself? Without anyone even knowing. I'm kind of pissed off at you right now, if you want to know the truth."

I drew a breath and waited. "Look, I get it. It was stupid. I'm sorry; there's nothing else I can say."

I looked back to the activity at the edge of the road. Two detectives from our bureau, dressed in jeans and boots and warm jackets, were talking to the ESD members. They all appeared to be focused on the draw below, maybe talking about how to best get everyone down to the bottom safely. I recalled a murder Floyd and I had investigated on a cliff high above the ocean in Pacific Palisades, and how ESD had assisted us on that case too, harnessing us so that we could safely approach the cliff's edge to document the scene. One of the ESD deputies eventually rappelled to the bottom, searching the entire face of the cliff for evidence. It dawned on me that it had likely been Floyd's idea to bring them out this morning.

"That your idea?" I asked.

"Yeah. When I got the call a few hours ago, it was one of the first things I thought of. I wasn't going down that hillside without a harness."

"Who's doing the interviews?"

Floyd zipped his coat up the last inch and pulled his head down into the collar like a turtle. He then stuffed both hands in his front pockets and shivered.

"I think Farris and his partner, what's-her-ass."

"Marchesano."

"Yeah, Lizzy."

"Is my lieutenant coming out?"

"Should be here any minute," Floyd said. He pulled his hand out of his pocket and glanced at his wristwatch. "Let's wait in your car, Dickie. I'm freezing."

An hour later, two helicopters circled above. One was ours, clearly marked with the sheriff's star on the side, the other had the Channel 7 logo prominently displayed against the bright blue bird. Two news vans were parked a quarter-mile north with a limited view of the action. One of the patrol deputies had used his vehicle to stop traffic at that point, allowing only official vehicles beyond it.

Lt. Joe Black arrived and asked that I head back to the bureau so that I could give a statement to Farris and Marchesano. They were handling the interviews while another team of investigators would oversee the crime scene, and yet another team prepared a search warrant for the Watkins compound. Lieutenant Black said this warrant was going to be executed by SWAT. He then said, "I think it would be best if you two weren't part of it, or even around when it happens." He winked at Floyd after he said it, letting us know that he knew. Somehow, he always knew. I grinned and Floyd just shrugged. No big deal.

I had turned and started for my car when Floyd called out for me to hold up. I looked back to see him walking toward the side of the road and motioning for me to join him. There were others lined at the edge, peering down the mountainside. As I came up to join them, Floyd faced me and said, "They've got her car."

It was nearly at the bottom. There were two ESD deputies dressed in green tactical pants and shirts and wearing orange helmets on their heads, rappelling harnesses around their bodies. They were no longer attached to any of the several ropes that were staked at the top not far from where we stood. The deputies were pulling branches away to reveal the back end of a red sedan.

We all watched and waited, likely for the same reason, to see if anybody was inside.

The ESD deputies worked like beavers disassembling a dam until they were able to see inside. Each of them moved around the pile of wreckage and brush, looking in from different angles. Finally, one of the two looked up the hill and shook his head. It was empty.

Floyd grunted.

"Uh-huh," I said, and walked away. It was time to get off of the mountain. I needed to give my statement to Farris and Marchesano so that I could go back to the hospital and wait.

———

Before I arrived at the bureau an hour and a half later, Floyd called to give me an update. He was going to be headed down from the mountain himself, but before he left, he went up to the lookout so he could make a call. He didn't want to wait until he was back in civilization to let me know they had found the body of a white male adult not far from where Josie's vehicle had been found. It appeared there was major trauma that would be consistent with an ejection during the crash, and they had found that the passenger's door of Josie's car had been torn off, probably at impact.

"Any idea who he is?" I asked.

There was a pause. "Yeah, he had I.D.—sheriff's I.D."

"Oh shit."

"Uh-huh. Tommy Zimmerman from Gangs."

I had just exited the freeway and was only a few minutes from arriving at the office. "Jesus, man, Tommy Z?"

"Yep."

"Does anyone know yet, anyone down here I mean?"

"Black notified our captain, and then he called the captain of the gang unit, George Dennison. Apparently, Tommy was single, and he was on vacation, so nobody noticed him being gone for a week. Nothing was ever reported."

I didn't respond. I was thinking about Josie and picturing her with Tommy, and I thought that the two of them would have been a good match for each other. Then I wondered how long they had been seeing each other and how hard Josie was going to take the news.

Floyd said, "We cleaned up some beer cans too, kept them out of the scene photos and description. I'm sure some goddam hunters tossed them out their windows while driving along the road up there."

"Yeah, I'm sure of it."

"Anyway, I wanted you to know."

"I'm pulling up to the office right now. I'm not going to say anything to anyone about Tom for now."

"Probably best, Dickie."

"Okay, man, thanks," I said, somberly.

Floyd picked up his tone, likely trying to get me out of the dark place he knew I easily retreated to. "Hey, and don't go snitching me off about Old Man Watkins."

I cracked a slight smile. "It'll cost you a steak, maybe a few beers."

"Deal, Dickie. Now get crackin'. I'll meet you at Newhall Memorial when you're done. That's my next stop."

"Roger that," I said, and disconnected.

I arrived at the office and checked my eyes in the rearview mirror before getting out. I had hoped they showed no sign of the tears I had fought during the long drive that had allowed contemplation and reflection, which had weakened my emotional dams.

36

O f course I ran into Captain Stover as I entered the bureau, exhausted, dirty, an emotional wreck, and dressed in blue jeans, a hoodie, my Dodgers ball cap, and hiking boots. He stood at Ricky Welker's desk near the back door with a file in his hand, apparently discussing a case with the veteran detective. There was no way to avoid him unless I turned around and walked back out, which I actually considered, but of course wasn't about to do.

He held up a finger to Welker and took a step back to block my path. I stopped.

"Mixed bag on the results, huh?" he said, somberly.

"Yeah, you bet."

He clapped me on the shoulder. "I'm glad we found her."

I nodded.

"Farris and Marchesano are on their way back from Santa Clarita. Why don't you go relax in the conference room until they get here. Give them your statement, and then I don't want to see you around here until next week, or the week after. Take some time off, Richard."

"Okay, Skipper," I said, though he and I both knew that I wouldn't, "will do."

An hour later, Rich Farris and his partner, Elizabeth Marchesano, came into the conference room. Farris pulled out the big leather chair at the end of the table and sat down. Marchesano took a seat next to him and immediately began writing in a notebook that she had set on the table in front of her.

"How ya doin', Dickie?" said Rich Farris. He leaned back in his chair and began nibbling at the end of a pen while he watched me.

I knew what he was doing. He wanted to get a feel for my state of mind before asking the tough questions that needed to be answered for the case file. He was reading me. It's what he did. It's what we all did, but not often to one another.

"I'm tired, Rich. How are you?"

"I can't complain, brother." He glanced at his watch. "You good to go for the interview?"

I nodded.

"Okay then. You're our last one for this deal, and then I can scoot out of here a little early and head downtown for a scotch."

Marchesano set her pen down and looked up, a cue for her partner that she was ready to start. She had probably written in her notebook the date, time, location, and subject of their interview. I would be that subject.

I said, "How are you, Liz?"

She smiled. "I'm good. How's Josie?"

"I haven't seen her since they took her in for surgery. I'll head back up to the hospital when we're done here, stay there until she's stable. Maybe longer."

For the first time since she had come to the bureau nearly a year ago, I realized what a powerfully expressive woman she was. Farris had told me she was great during interviews, that people couldn't shut up in her presence no matter what crimes they might have committed. I could see it. There was an understated allure in her dark brown eyes that seemed to sparkle as she watched me.

I looked away, and nodded to Farris. "You guys interviewed Jacob Spencer, the game warden?"

"Conservation officer," Farris said, and smiled. "Yeah, we talked to homeboy. He's a little different, huh?"

I felt my brows crowd over my eyes, perplexed a bit by his statement. "What do you mean, Rich? I thought he was a pretty good guy. And that was *before* he saved my partner and killed the asshole who had taken her. Now I love the guy."

Farris dropped it, but I sensed from the way he averted his eyes, he had something else to say. He sat up to the table and readied a recorder. "You ready?"

I nodded.

He started the recording, introduced the three of us for the record, and he took my statement.

I provided an account that could have been presented to a grand jury for its tone and formality. I began with the murder on the mountain and Josie's and my decision to put it down for the weekend and take our days off to avoid submitting for overtime. I told them we had planned to meet Sunday at Josie's home and that we were going to take care of a detail for Davey Lopes which involved checking on an informant in Orange County. I briefly mentioned my concerns about the mafia connection to the informant situation, and that we had considered it possible that they might have had something to do with her disappearance. I then told them that Lopes had been able to eliminate their involvement, and left it at that.

I moved to the topic of Gorman and how we came to focus our search efforts there. "It was the only thing that came close to making any sense. Turns out, that's exactly what happened. They—*she*—went up there Saturday to poke around on our murder case, even though we were supposed to be off for the weekend. I guess you can't fault her for that; all of us have done it, worked cases on our days off, and kept it off the books."

Farris spoke for the first time since I had started. "We know about Zimmerman too, just so you know."

A long moment passed before I spoke. "Okay, yeah, she apparently went up with him. *They* went up to the mountain. Of course, none of us has any idea what happened up there, how she ended up going off the road, how she ended up tied down in that shed, or what might have happened over the week."

I stopped and looked away to keep my emotions in check as I imagined what might have happened to Josie as she was held captive for four days. What that little Watkins asshole might have done to her. I could feel them both watching, but I wasn't about to look up. I certainly wasn't going to make eye contact with Lizzy.

"She didn't give you anything out there," Farris asked, "when you found her last night?"

I shook my head while staring into my lap. "I think she was in shock. She wouldn't talk about anything. I tried to hug her and she pushed away from me. That worries me. God only knows what she's been through."

I thought about the Watkins kid lying in the pool of blood that seeped from a chest wound, his eyes clouded and dull, fixed on something far beyond the confines of that shed. Bubbling blood, pinkish red—the color dead—coated his tongue and oozed from his gaping mouth. I glanced at the recorder and refrained from telling how much I had enjoyed the sight of it, and how it reminded me of the innocent deer that had been killed a few days before, shot through the lung, likely by him. The irony hadn't escaped me.

Farris cleared his throat, jolting me from my deliberations.

"So no, we don't have any idea yet what happened out there, or why. All we know for sure is the ass—the *individual* who is responsible has been killed."

Farris waited, watching me carefully with his steely brown eyes as if he measured every word. He was known as a top-notch investigator and one of our best interviewers, and as I sat across from him, I understood why. Between Farris and his partner, I wanted to confess to previous indiscretions just to get the weight off of me.

After a moment, I continued, telling them about the gunshot we had heard that morning, and then the deer that was killed, and how we had gone onto the Watkins property with the game warden. Farris blinked at the mention of the warden, and it gave me pause again.

I went on. "We had previously spotted a red sedan on the property, and now that we would be justified in going onto the compound—because of the gunshot from that area and the deer that had been shot out of season—we did. Nothing much came from that other than seeing the dynamics of the outfit."

Farris looked over at his partner and waited until she caught up with her notes. I kept my eyes on him, wondering if there was something I didn't know. Farris was a straight shooter, and a man for whom I had great respect. I wanted to know what his problem was with Jacob Spencer, but it wasn't the time to ask. Not while the recorder ran.

I took them through the remaining days on the mountain, the search and rescue effort, and I closed with how and why I ended up going back up there to check that shed after some of us had debriefed at a watering hole in Santa Clarita. "It might not have been the smartest move on my part, but that shed bothered me. I had to check it. She must have been sending me the vibes."

Then I closed it out, telling how when I had arrived in the vicinity of the shed, the warden's truck was parked on the road above it, with a rope tied to the bumper and trailing down the mountainside. And that I looked but didn't see anyone, so I went in search of Spencer, assuming he too was checking the shed. He was, I concluded. "And it was right before I got to the bottom when I heard the gunshot."

Farris avoided eye contact with me while his partner finished her notes. A moment later, Marchesano set her pen down and shook her hand.

"I don't have anything else," Farris said, still looking at his partner. "Do you have anything?"

She shook her head. "I don't think so, Rich."

"Okay," Farris said, looking at the recorder and speaking directly into it, "that concludes this interview with Los Angeles County Sheriff's Homicide Detective Richard Jones." He mentioned the time and clicked the recorder off. Then he settled back in his chair, and his eyes wandered over to meet my gaze.

"What's up, Rich?"

He shrugged and looked away. After a moment, his eyes came back to mine.

"Nothing, man."

"There's something, Rich. What is it? What bothers you about Spencer?"

He let out a breath before continuing. "I don't know about him, man. I had a bad feeling for the kid when we interviewed him. Something seems off with him."

I had tremendous respect for Rich Farris, and most everyone else did too. Everyone but maybe his ex. He had gone through a rough divorce some years earlier and the fallout had become the topic *du jour* around the office. She had filed complaints with the department alleging mental abuse. She demanded of our captain that he be sent to rehab for alcoholism. She had filed a restraining order against him, citing that she was in fear for her physical safety. She had hired a snake of an attorney who managed to get her more than half of everything, including his pension. Rich had had a rough go, and it had taken its toll. But he rebounded quickly and seemed happier now than he ever was when married, and he was living the life of a consummate bachelor. He was easy to get along with and always had a smile on his face and a twinkle in his eye that left you wondering what he might be up to. But at this very moment, I felt anger welling up inside me. I liked the young warden, Jacob Spencer, and to me he was now a hero. He had gone back up that mountain by himself, and into that gulch in the darkness, and by doing so, he had saved my partner's life and had taken the life of the piece of shit who had tormented her.

"Rich, I don't get it, man. What are you talking about?"

He sighed and ran a hand across his head, rubbing his short cropped natural hair that I noticed was starting to show gray on the sides. He never blinked; he just held my gaze while I waited, impatiently.

Finally, "I've talked to a lot of cops that have dumped people, Dickie. Know what I mean?"

I nodded. "Sure. We all have."

"You know how you get a feel for these things, man, how cops process taking a man's life. I mean, there's a wide range, but there *is* a range. Parameters. Common denominators. This guy was off the range, to me, man. Like there was something he was hiding. I didn't feel like I was interviewing a cop. It felt more like taking on a suspect. You know what I mean?"

I didn't respond. What could I say? I wasn't going to argue with him because we all have a right to our feelings. So he had a bad feel for the kid. Who knows, maybe Spencer is uncomfortable around black people. Some people are still that way, the ones who have lived sheltered lives. Probably the ones who spend their lives in the mountains where human interaction is at a minimum and interaction with minorities is almost nonexistent.

Farris looked back to his partner. "What do you think, Lizzy?"

She shrugged, indifferent. "He was interesting. I'll say that."

An awkward silence hung in the room. Rich Farris and Elizabeth Marchesano watched me as I waited, considering. I thought about all of the things I wanted to ask, but it boiled down to the fact that they had their opinion of the young game cop, and I had mine.

"Well, in his defense," I said, "he's not really a cop. I mean, he's a fish cop, for Christ's sake. And just a kid. Jesus, he probably went home and hugged his mother after this."

Neither spoke. They watched me as if waiting for me to finish. Rich probably just wanted to go, I realized. It had been a long day for all of us.

"I wouldn't be surprised if it ends his career," I added. "Like that young deputy years ago who shot and killed a guy in a church. That dude was a mess after that. I wouldn't be surprised . . ." I stopped and left it there, realizing there was nothing else that needed to be said. At that moment, I wished I hadn't asked. I wished I hadn't pushed him to tell me his concerns.

After a moment, Farris said, "Are you aware that the dead kid had a pistol on his hip?"

I shook my head, and frowned.

"That's the word I got from the mountain before I interviewed your boy, Spencer. The kid had it holstered on his right hip, concealed by his jacket."

Now I knew what bothered Farris. If Watkins was going to take on the warden, why do it with a knife when he had a pistol? On the other hand, if the kid had a pistol, why not say he went for it if you're trying to justify a shooting that might have been questionable? Unless you didn't know he had it.

"Spencer never mentioned the gun?"

Farris curled his lip and shook his head. "Nope. I don't think he knew about it."

I looked away, thinking about the possibilities but always finding my way back to center. My center was that Josie was rescued and the man who had taken her was killed. If the warden had over-reacted to a perceived threat, who was I to judge him? Even if he was overly zealous, or scared, or even vengeful, why should I care?

"Well," I finally said, "that's interesting, but it doesn't change anything. Does it?"

Farris shrugged. "Nope, I guess not." After a moment, Rich asked, "What does he know about the murder you and Josie were handling up there?"

I shrugged.

"He told us the dude is probably good for it, the Watkins kid he blew away."

"Well, someone on the mountain most likely is. Watkins is as good a suspect as any other."

Rich Farris stood up from his chair and Lizzy followed suit. He offered me his hand, so I pushed out of my chair and stood to shake it.

"Thanks, Rich."

"No problem, man. Get some rest, my brother. And tell your partner we're all thinking of her."

I nodded, then looked at Marchesano. "Thank you, Lizzy."

She smiled.

I turned and walked out of the room, wondering how two good detectives could be so far off about a person.

T he waiting room at Newhall Memorial had overflowed from visitors of various patients, and I found Josie's mother, Esmeralda, waiting outside with her sister and a niece. Her eyes were swollen and red. When I approached her, she dabbed at the corners of her eyes and then stuffed a handkerchief into the pocket of the sweater that she wore over a flowered dress with white sneakers. I hugged her and held her tightly but didn't speak. I could feel her body jerking and knew she was crying on my shoulder, so I didn't let go until I felt her pull away.

"She's going to be okay," I said, stooping to bring my eyes level with hers.

The niece translated what I had said into Spanish, and Esmeralda nodded.

A family of more than half a dozen filed out of the waiting room, so I suggested we go inside. Once seated, I introduced myself to the niece who sat next to me. Esmeralda was on the other side of her, and the aunt was one seat farther away. I didn't get the aunt's name, but the young lady was Lena, Josie's cousin and "best friend." I sat back and tried to recall where I had seen Lena before, and it occurred to me that she was the girl in the photograph with Josie, the two of them at the beach. When I first saw the picture, I had wondered if she was a friend, or something more. I now felt ashamed of myself for wondering that.

I asked if they had heard from a doctor yet, and she told me they hadn't heard anything recently. Josie was still in recovery the last time Lena had checked with the nurse at the desk.

Esmeralda put a frail hand on Lena's arm and said something to her in Spanish. Lena gave a brief reply, and then turned to me.

"She wants to know what happened to her."

I considered the question for a brief moment before answering. "She was in a traffic accident. Josie and I had been assigned a case that is up in the mountains, and she had gone back up on Saturday and somehow went off the road on her way back down that evening. With her injuries, she was unable to get out on her own. There was no cell signal up there, so she couldn't call for help."

Lena told her aunt what I had said, presumably. I waited for questions, and I was not surprised that several were asked.

"She wants to know how you found her and why it took you so long."

I explained that where she had gone off the road, her car had plunged deep into a gulch and it wasn't visible from the road. She crawled away with her broken leg, and at some point, before passing out, she must have sent me the text. I then explained that the text was brief, just stating that she had been in an accident on the mountain, and that I hadn't even received the text until late Tuesday night. I told her it must have been a fluke that her phone found a signal—if only for a second—and relayed the message that had likely been sent three days before. I didn't mention anything about her being held against her will.

After Lena finished explaining all of that to Esmeralda, she listened as her aunt had but one other question. Lena paused for a long moment before relaying it to me, and I wondered if she was searching for the right words. Sometimes there was just no way to translate some things.

Finally, Lena said, "She wants to know why you weren't with her, if she's your partner."

I knew then that Lena had been reluctant to ask a question that seemed accusatory, if only in some slight fashion. I pondered it for a short time before answering.

"Tell her I said that's a damn good question, and all I can say is that I'm sorry. I'm very, very sorry."

Esmeralda didn't respond after Lena translated my statement to her. She looked at me, and then she looked away, decisively. Lena looked down at the floor for a minute, and then she pulled a romance novel out of her large purse and began reading.

The idle chat was clearly over, so I pushed out of my chair. "I'm going to see if I can find anything out," I said.

The nurse at the desk reviewed something on her computer when I showed her my badge and asked if she could tell me the status of Josefina Sanchez. A moment later, she picked up a phone on the desk and pushed three buttons on the keypad. She asked someone on the other end of the line if there was any additional update on the patient, Josefina Sanchez. After listening for a moment, she thanked the person and hung up.

"They don't expect her to be out of recovery for several more hours. It will be quite a while before anyone will be able to see her, and that's if all goes well."

"Were there complications?"

"That I couldn't tell you, sir."

I nodded, thanked her, and stepped away from the counter. As I paced the hallway, avoiding the waiting room, the comments by Farris played over and over in my head. What bothered me most—yet it hadn't sunk in when he had said it—was that Spencer had suggested during his interview with Farris and Marchesano that the Watkins kid had probably been good for the William Brown murder, the rapist who had been backed against a tree and executed. That was a leap to take, especially for someone who knew so little about our case.

It occurred to me that I needed to get back to that case sooner rather than later. The captain and his week off would have to take a deferment. I had no time for time off.

I needed to interview the victim's family members, and I also needed to talk to the girl our victim had been convicted of raping, as well as her family members. If Watkins was good for Brown's murder, great. A solve is a solve, and the ones that didn't require trials were the best of all the solves.

But if Watkins wasn't good for that murder, I needed to find out why

Jacob Spencer had suggested that he was. Maybe it was as simple as his having hero syndrome. He rescued a deputy sheriff and solved a murder, all while killing a bad guy. That's what he'd tell his friends over beers.

Or maybe there was more to it.

Spencer had told me and Floyd about his long history with the people on the mountain, and it seemed he knew them as well as anyone—maybe better. It could be his familiarity with the Watkins clan that had caused him to assume it was one of them who killed the man at the tree, and then when he found that it was Junior who had taken Josie, it was that much easier to make that leap.

As that last thought hung in my mind, it occurred to me I should be calling Kennedy or Kramer to find out what they thought of Spencer. Surely they knew him well, working around him in the same jurisdiction. The one thing I had learned was that in the remote outpost known as Gorman, all of the various agencies had good working relationships. Their lives could depend on it.

I glanced at my watch. Several more hours in recovery, at least, the nurse had said. I turned on my heel and headed for the exit.

Before leaving the hospital parking lot, I fished the William Brown case file out of the trunk of my car and put it on the front seat next to me. I started the car and turned the air conditioning up high. It had warmed up through the afternoon on a sunny Southern California day. I thought about how cold we had been on the mountain all night and through this morning. The warmth felt good, but the cool air felt good too. I pulled my notebook out of the case file and flipped it over to where I kept contact phone numbers for each case handy, printed on the inside flap of that case's notebook. Kennedy and Kramer were both listed, just below Santa Clarita and Gorman substation. I knew the numbers I had for the K twins were cell phone numbers, and the odds of them having a signal at any given time up there were far less than even. I tried each number, and both went straight to voicemail.

I pulled out of the lot and punched in the number for Santa Clarita. I spoke to the watch deputy and asked if he showed the Gorman deputies still on duty.

"They're always on duty," he joked. "Hell, they live at their station."

I asked if he could reach them by radio or send a smoke signal and let them know I was headed toward Gorman Station and that I needed to talk to one or both of them. I added that it was important.

As I finished that call, I was coming up to the freeway, and it occurred to me I hadn't eaten all day. I had been going hard on adrenaline and coffee. I pulled through a fast-food drive-thru and grabbed a cheeseburger and a large coffee to go.

When I got onto the northbound I-5, I settled back in my seat and began eating my burger while looking ahead at the mountains that awaited me. The late afternoon sun threatened to disappear in the not-too-distant future, and I hoped that I'd be done with my work up there by then. I cringed at the thought of being in the mountains a second night in a row. Bad things seemed to happen up there after dark.

Forty minutes later I pulled into Gorman Station and saw Kennedy spraying off his department-issued four-wheeler with a pressure washer. Kramer had ropes and gear laid out on the gravel parking area and he appeared to be reorganizing his equipment. It occurred to me again what a unique assignment these guys had up here. Both stopped their work to watch me drive up and park.

"Where's the line for the carwash?" I joked.

Kennedy, still armed with his pressure washer, said, "I'd be happy to wash your car, detective. Especially after we were told that Homicide was paying overtime for this gig."

I smiled. "As well they should. How'd it go with the warrant up at the compound?"

"Everybody went to jail," Kramer said. "That's the good news. The bad news is, I don't think they came up with any evidence that ties anyone to your partner's kidnapping, or to that murder you're working on, the Brown case."

I nodded. "What'd everyone go to jail for?"

"Manufacturing. There were two active labs in trailers back beyond that tree line to the south. Oh, and Old Man Watkins got knocked on his ass by one of the SWAT guys."

I smiled, picturing it. The three of us had gathered together not far from where I parked. "Doesn't surprise me. Listen, if you boys have a few minutes, I'd like to talk to you about some of the players up here, get your unadulterated opinions. Straight talk, from two guys I know I can trust."

Kennedy turned and indicated for me to follow. I did, and Kramer brought up the rear. He looked back at me as we approached the office. "I get the feeling we're going to need a cup of coffee for this conversation."

Kramer said, "Or something."

Inside, Kennedy readied the coffee maker while Kramer and I took our places around a small oval dining table that was cluttered with reports and files, two laptop computers, and a printer. Kramer said, "You'll have to excuse the mess. As you can see, this is our briefing room, report writing room, and break room. It's an all-in-one deal." He smiled widely after he said it, and then began shuffling most of it toward one side so that we had uncluttered places to sit.

Kennedy took a seat while the coffee brewed a few feet from us. "So, what do you want to know about this place? We're not giving up our good hunting spots and fishing holes, if that's what you're after."

"Actually, I was wondering about that," I said, smiling.

"You'd be surprised how often it happens," he continued. "Guys will pull in and you know before they're out of their rigs that they're off-duty deputies. Usually the younger ones, guys still working the jails. They'll tell you where they work and then say they're up for the weekend—a lot of times it'll be the day before opening day of deer season—and they were just curious if we could point them to a good place to find a deer."

The coffee maker hissed as the last of the coffee drained into the carafe. Kennedy went back into the kitchen and began pouring three cups while he continued the story. "Depends on my feel for the guy, what I'll tell 'em. You know how it is, you can tell if a guy's a good dude or not pretty quick once you get to talking to him. Well, if I like him, I'll send 'im to my third- or fourth-best areas for deer. I never give up my best spot or my backup spot."

"What if you don't like the guy?" I asked.

"Oh, I'll usually just tell 'im the deer hunting's no good up here, it's not like it used to be. Maybe give him some general guidelines—'I'd try up Frazier Mountain,' or 'Stay west of the interstate'—that type of deal. If I really don't like him, I'll just say, 'That's why they call it hunting, pal. Good luck.'"

He brought two cups over and put one in front of me and the other in front of Kramer, then stepped back over for his own. When he sat down, I got right to it.

"Well, speaking of knowing if you like a guy or you don't—*right off the bat*—I need to find out if I'm off-base on somebody you boys know. But it has to stay right here, between us. I know I can trust you two."

Neither spoke. Kennedy nodded to spur me on.

"What do you guys think of Jacob Spencer?"

They exchanged glances.

"Let me throw a few things out there for you before you begin," I said. "When I met him, I had a good feeling for him, thought he was a squared-away guy. At least, that's how he seemed to me. I'm usually pretty good with that too, but I've also been wrong on an occasion. Well, as you know, he dumped the Watkins kid when he caught him at the shed with Josie. In doing so, he probably saved my partner's life, and I'm grateful to him for it."

Both of them waited, neither in a hurry to chime in.

"They sent him down to Santa Clarita to be interviewed by Homicide, common practice for cops who've been in a shooting—as both of you know—and Rich Farris and his partner, Lizzy Marchesano, interviewed him. Do you guys know either of them?"

Kramer was shaking his head as Kennedy said, "I don't think so."

"Farris is a black guy, average build, short-cropped hair that's starting to gray a little on the sides, I just noticed today. He's got bright white teeth and you see them a lot because he's always smiling and joking around. Great guy."

Kennedy looked over at his partner. "I think he handled a suicide up here a few years back."

Kramer nodded.

"His partner, Elizabeth Marchesano, is also black. Straight hair, nice figure, real pretty. She's married to an LAPD SWAT guy. The point is, both of them are good people, good cops with plenty of experience. Lizzy is newer to the bureau, but Farris has been there since Christ was a corporal."

"And?" Kramer asked.

I paused. "They didn't have a good feel for Spencer. Something about him bothered both of them. Farris has great instinct, so it's hard to discount anything he has to say about a case, witness or suspect."

"A suspect?" Kennedy said.

"I'm just saying, he has a good read on people he interviews, and he was bothered by a few things Spencer said, and by his demeanor I guess, or maybe his disposition would be a better way to put it."

Both of them seemed to consider the information for a moment before Kennedy finally spoke. "Are you worried that it didn't go down the way he said it did?"

"I really don't know. I'm not even sure I care, if you know what I mean. But I really want to know what you two think of him."

Kramer blew out a breath. "Personally, I don't like him. Never have."

3 8

K ennedy had little to say about the game warden, Jacob Spencer, other than that he was always on the mountain doing his job, aggressively seeking poachers. That was his thing, Kennedy said, poachers. It's what drove him to spend all of his time creeping through the woods in his pickup, on his four-wheeler, and by foot. Kennedy had likened him to many of the young cops on patrol who would aggressively prowl the streets and alleys every minute of their shifts in order to catch bad guys and make great arrests. Some were after dope dealers, some were passionate about burglars, others focused on gang suppression and were hard on their foe. "I just think he's young and aggressive. Nothing wrong with that."

I said, "Yeah, and sometimes, when we're young and overly enthusiastic, there can be a little street justice exacted at times."

Both of them watched me for a moment before Kennedy asked, "That what you think, he blew away the Watkins kid because he's a poacher?"

I shrugged. "I don't know. I guess it's not fair of me to think anything until we get Josie's statement—and that's if she even saw what happened. I mean, there was a knife near the body, and Spencer says he shot in self-defense. Who are we to question that, absent compelling evidence to the contrary? But what bothers me is that Watkins had a pistol on his hip.

Why would he go at an armed game warden with a knife, if he has a pistol?"

Kennedy nodded. "Yeah, that is interesting."

Kramer said, "The dude has always given me the creeps. There's something about him, you know?"

"Like what?"

"I don't know. I guess for one, the dude's a loner. He avoids close relationships with his fellow cops in the area, which is different from the rest of us up here. He never joins us for lunches or dinners, and he's never attended any of our barbecues or other social gatherings. I mean, we have get-togethers with everyone around here, chippies, Kern County deputies, forestry agents—even firemen. But Spencer never participates."

Kennedy shrugged as if to dismiss his partner's concerns. "So, he's a loner."

Kramer argued there was more to it. "I checked up on him with a friend of mine who's with Fish and Game, a guy who used to work this area before Spencer. He knew him, and he agreed the guy was a strange duck, but didn't really think much more of it. So I had him do a little background on the guy. He—my buddy with Fish and Game—works admin now and has access to all of the personnel records. He found a couple of interesting things out."

"Jesus Christ, Charlie," Kennedy said, "you're running backgrounds on other cops now?"

Kramer ignored the comment. "He was disqualified from LAPD back in the nineties during the background phase. A few years later, he got hired by the county police, you know, the guys who work security at the hospitals and other county buildings. Apparently, the standards to be hired by them are lower, so a lot of the guys who can't get hired or who have been fired by legit agencies, go there. Once they get a couple of years under their belts, they lateral over to smaller agencies. The small agencies save money by picking up trained and certified cops, so they overlook the fact that in years past other agencies have disqualified them for whatever reasons. So if a guy follows that route and does well, he can eventually move to a larger agency."

"Like Fish and Game," I said.

Kramer nodded. "Like Fish and Game."

"And we have no idea what DQ'd him from LAPD?" I asked.

Kramer stood and went to the coffee pot. Before topping his mug, he held the pot toward Kennedy and me at the table, a gesture to ask if we needed refills. Both of us shook our heads. He watched the coffee fill his mug as he answered. "That's as much detail as they will provide anyone, absent a court order. He must've had good references from that point forward though, because nobody seemed to care about his history with the LAPD."

"Nobody at Fish and Game, you mean."

Kramer nodded. "Yeah, Department of Fish and *Wildlife*."

"Whatever," I said. It would never be anything other than Fish and Game to me, and most others. The name had been changed in the interest of political correctness. I didn't do political correctness. They had changed the name of the Department of Corrections to something about hugs and rehabilitation. I still called it the Department of Corrections.

"I've always thought he was an okay guy," Kennedy chimed in. "Why are we jumping on him after he dumped the guy who took your partner?"

I drained the rest of my cup and set it down on the cluttered table in front of me. "I don't think anyone's jumping on him. Farris thought he was odd during his statement, and I think he has a problem with the fact that Watkins had the pistol. Truthfully, it makes me wonder too."

"If he pulled the trigger too fast on the Watkins kid," Kennedy said, "I doubt we'll ever know. But he likely did us all a favor. And at least she won't have to relive the whole ordeal in court."

He was right, but I didn't want to admit that part of it. Jacob Spencer might have done us all a big favor, but that didn't mean he hadn't also crossed a line that cops should never cross. I was beginning to wish Farris had never mentioned his concerns about the guy. Now I would be the one who carried the burden. I would be the one to take Josie back through it in order to make sure it was all right. And then I would have to decide what to do with it, if anything. Or I would have to live with it, should I choose to move past it and never question it again. That was a difficult thing to do for a man wired the way I was wired.

I stood up from my seat and looked from one mountain cop to the other, thanking each for their time. As I moved toward the front door, I stopped and turned back to face them at the table. Both were watching me. "Let's keep this between us three for now."

They both nodded in agreement. I thanked them for the coffee and closed the door behind me.

I drove to the nearby McDonald's where I got a cup of coffee at the drive-thru window and parked away from all others at the back of the lot. I set my coffee on the dash and left the car running while I went through the Brown file.

The rape report of Joanna Harding was the focus of my attention now. William Lance Brown was named in the report as the suspect, and the one who would later be convicted and sent to prison. I hadn't yet had a chance to read the entire report, so I went through it from front to back once before going through it again and making some notes. My impression of the matter is it was a weak case, questionable as many of these types of cases can be, and likely why a plea deal had been offered and accepted.

In my Brown case notebook, I wrote down and highlighted Joanna's name and address for easy reference. Then I programmed the address into my phone's navigation application. If nothing had changed, she lived just a few miles north of where I sat, off of Frazier Mountain Road.

I put the report back in the file but kept my notebook out. The coffee on my dash had steamed the windshield, so I switched the fan to the defrost mode, grabbed the cup, and started north on the interstate.

AFTER INTERVIEWING JOANNA HARDING AND HER FATHER, I LEFT THE mountain and headed back to the city with more questions than answers. When my phone showed a solid signal, I called Floyd to run it by him.

"The father's in a wheelchair and his brother died last year from cirrhosis."

"The girl's father? The rape victim?"

"Uh-huh."

"I'll be damned. I guess that clears them for your mountain murder, huh? What's the girl's relationship with the Watkins kid?"

"She doesn't know him."

There was a pause, and I pulled the phone from my ear to make sure I hadn't lost the call.

Floyd said, "Then why would the game warden be so certain that the kid was also responsible for your rapist murder?"

"That's the question. I've been trying to reason through it, and all I can come up with is that he made the leap after finding Watkins with Josie. I mean, it's not that far of a stretch. How many maniacs could be running around on one mountain?"

"Maybe it was the old man who killed the rapist. He had a rifle on his four-wheeler."

"Maybe. You want to go visit him again?"

"Hell yes, I do," Floyd said.

I chuckled. "Might not be the best idea right now."

"Yeah, whatever. Listen, I have to go. We're walking out the door to go to dinner, and I probably shouldn't screw this up." He lowered his voice to a whisper. "Cindy's about had it with you, pal."

"With me!"

"Yeah, you're the one who keeps getting me into all this shit, screwing up my vacations and days off. Getting me into fights."

"Whatever, man. Go have dinner. I hope it sucks."

He clicked off and I secured my phone back into its dash-mounted cradle. I had another half hour to Santa Clarita, so I left the radio off to avoid any distraction while I recalled the conversations I had had with the K twins, Rich Farris, and now Joanna Harding and her father. Something was amiss. But what?

I arrived at the hospital as the sun was setting in my rearview mirror and the temperature beginning to drop, a welcome sign that fall was near. Soon the days would be shorter, the nights longer and cooler, and baseball would be heating up in the final stretch just as football was getting started. I loved everything about the fall, other than the fact it was a prelude to the holidays. The only thing I liked about the holidays was that the increased death toll kept me from realizing I was as miserable as half the sons-of-bitches who hung themselves or sent bullets through their power plants or drank themselves to death amid the holiday joy, their way of stating their final grievances.

At the hospital the waiting room was empty. I asked the nurse and she directed me to Josie's room, but warned, "She's only allowed one visitor at a time."

When I peeked inside, I saw the mother, the aunt, and the cousin, Lena, huddled around her bed. Josie was sleeping. Lena got up and nodded for me to follow her outside.

"Can you stay? I think I should take them home and let them get some rest, come back tomorrow. But I don't want to leave her unattended. I can drop my mom and aunt off and come back to spend the night with Josie."

"I can stay, Lena. I'm used to staying up all night. This will be a piece of cake for me. I'm good at dozing in chairs."

"Are you sure?"

I smiled. "Sure, I'm sure. That's my partner in there."

The ladies each kissed Josie's forehead and told her goodbye. Lena hugged me and told me goodbye, but Esmeralda just turned and walked away. When they left, I rearranged the furniture to have the comfy chair closest to her bed, with a view of the muted TV and Josie all at once.

It didn't take long before my eyes grew heavy and I began nodding off. Soon, I too was asleep. But I didn't rest peacefully. I dreamt of the night on the mountain, seeing the events unfolding in different ways. I saw Spencer smile widely and pull the trigger, blasting the Watkins kid away. I saw the kid pleading for his life, backing away from Spencer, but taking a slug through the heart nonetheless. I saw William Lance Brown backing against a tree, and I saw Spencer smiling at him too, and squeezing off the fatal shot. I saw the scenario unfold when I approached Spencer at the shed, only this time, he turned and smiled at me, and raised his pistol toward me. There was a flash of light and I jolted awake with a shout.

Josie's tired eyes were set upon me.

"Are you okay?" she asked.

"You're awake." It was all I could think to say to avoid discussing the dream I had had that was fresh in my mind and had felt real to me.

"Someone around here needs to be," she said, and tried to smile.

I sat up and wiped my mouth with the back of my hand, and then rubbed at the sleep in my eyes. I looked around the room to buy time as much as to refresh my memory of how I came to be in this place—how we both came to be in this place. If only it were all a bad dream.

Josie asked for water. As I poured her a cup, she used the remote to raise the bed to more of a seated position. I placed a straw in the cup of water and handed it to her. She took a sip and paused, and then sipped it some more before handing it back.

"Thirsty, huh?"

She nodded and then laid her head back into her pillows.

"You feel like you can talk about it?" I asked.

She shook her head and closed her eyes, and soon she was back asleep.

39

The next afternoon I woke after a nap on my couch and wondered if I had dreamt again about Spencer on the mountain, the smiling, murdering Spencer. I couldn't remember. Which is akin to not knowing that people are suffering and dying at every moment; the lack of knowledge doesn't lessen the damage, it only makes it more bearable to not know. *Ignorance is bliss.*

I went to the fridge for water and almost grabbed a beer instead. But I fought off the urge and decided a run was what I needed. My body had been neglected in every manner possible for nearly a week: lack of sleep, a terrible diet, and no exercise. I wasn't going to be in great shape after plodding across two or three miles of Burbank concrete and asphalt, but I'd feel better for the effort and I'd have less guilt about the beers I knew I would consume later this evening.

During my run, I couldn't shake the idea that Game Warden Jacob Spencer had deliberately, unjustly—and *with malice aforethought*—shot and killed both William Lance Brown and Johnny Watkins, Jr. I thought about my conversations with Farris, the information from the K twins, and the vision that had come to me the day before when I had fallen asleep at Josie's bedside. It wouldn't be the first time I had conjured up a theory in my sleep that helped solve a case. Not that I have some magical power, but sometimes it takes powering off all other parts of one's mind to truly find the focus that is needed to piece difficult puzzles together. It was similar to the use of hypnosis, where recollections of events are made clearer as peripheral awareness is reduced through deep relaxation and mental focus.

If it was the case that Spencer had gunned down Watkins without justification, it would be difficult to prove unless Josie had seen it clearly and could articulate some indisputable fact that contradicted Spencer's statement.

I knew I had passed the halfway mark for a three-mile run, and I was glad of it. Though being lost in thought made the run less painful, I was out of shape, tired, and now hot and sweaty under the afternoon sun. I looked forward to cooling off with a cold beer. I glanced at my watch and did the math: my current pace was embarrassingly nearly twelve minutes per mile. I picked up the pace for the home stretch.

But what about Billy Brown? There would never be anything other than circumstantial evidence to put Spencer at the tree of death when the rapist was shot through the heart. Unless the bullet that had been recovered could be matched to a gun, and that gun could be linked to Spencer. Those were a lot of ifs. A confession would be in order. I pictured myself and Farris going at Spencer together, working the kid over until he folded like a lawn chair.

A horn blast from behind startled me, and I realized that I had drifted into traffic as my mind was anywhere but on the run. I scooted over and waved as if to say sorry, and as the car passed by, I mumbled, "Asshole."

But maybe I was way off and not giving the young warden the benefit of the doubt where I had no reason not to. Maybe my imagination was getting the best of me.

I turned onto my street and checked my watch. Much better pace, and only a half-mile left. I picked up my speed and focused on staying loose as I opened up my stride.

It was crazy to think a game warden would gun down a man in cold blood. Maybe he hadn't actually needed to shoot Watkins, but then again, all shooting situations are subjective. State of mind was everything, and it could very well be that his state of mind was purely driven by a sincere fear for his life or personal safety. So be it.

I sprinted the last eighth of a mile, feeling better now that I had burned some calories and worked up a sweat, and reconciled the Jacob Spencer deal in my mind. Unless Josie could tell me something in contrast to his statement, it was a done deal. Put it to rest, Dickie, before you drive yourself insane.

I came across the property line of my apartment complex with my chest out and head up as if I was in it for the gold. In my mind, I had bounded through the streets like a gazelle. In reality, I knew I must have looked like I would die with each step, like I hated every second of what I was doing, like I'd never run a mile before in my life. I paced the front of my building with my hands on my hips, victoriously, triumphantly, an athlete recovering from an epic event. An athlete desperately in need of oxygen. Jesus, I needed a beer.

"Hello, Detective."

I turned to see my neighbor walking across the front of the building. She was headed from the parking lot toward her apartment. She wore gray slacks and a matching blazer over a white top, and in her arms she cradled a stack of files that would stand a foot tall when placed on a desktop or table.

"Hey there," I said, still huffing.

"Out for a run, I see."

I glanced at my watch. "Yeah, trying to get back at it. It's been a busy week. And when it gets busy, exercise is always the second thing to go."

She had stopped to face me as I stepped toward her. The sun glistened off of her oversized, aviator Ray-Bans. Under the bright sunlight, I could see the fairness of her freckled skin.

She smiled. "What's the first?"

I tilted my head, pondering the question.

"You said it's the second thing to go, exercise."

"Oh, yeah . . . sleep. First the sleep goes. It's the easiest to forego when you're busy. But next is your workout. No way you can take time to exercise if you don't even have time to sleep. Then—to make matters worse—you start eating like shit because you're on the go."

"A triple whammy," she said, and smiled again.

It occurred to me that I was smiling broadly as well.

After an awkward moment, she turned. "Well, it was nice seeing you again."

I followed as she started toward our apartments. "Hey, I didn't get a chance to properly introduce myself."

She stopped and turned to face me. I lifted the sweaty cap off of my head with my left hand while extending my right. "Richard Jones. My friends call me Di—Richard."

She shook my hand. "Emily Bruce. Glad to meet you, Richard."

"Is that Irish, by chance?"

"Scottish, mah lad," she said.

"Ah. I would have guessed that second. The red hair and all."

"You appear to perhaps have a bit of Irish or Scot in you as well."

"I'm a mutt. My dad liked to say we were German and Scots-Irish. I'm not even sure what that means. I do know I prefer scotch when it comes to whiskey, though I'll drink the Irish too."

She still held a smile. "You and I will get along just fine, Richard."

"I happen to have a few to choose from, if you wanted to maybe have a taste or two tonight."

We had both turned and started for our apartments again, moving slowly, neither in a hurry, but my invitation had stopped us both again. She was looking at me while apparently thinking it over, or just playing it out.

"I don't know," she said, "I really need to study these files tonight." She lifted them an inch or two as if I hadn't seen them.

I reached out. "Can I carry them for you? How rude of me not to have offered."

"It's okay, but I've got them."

I waited.

"Maybe one drink wouldn't hurt."

I smiled. "Let me shower and get cleaned up. I was going to pick up barbecue tonight—I'm really craving a good meal—so if you're hungry—"

She was shaking her head, but only slightly. "Oh, I don't know—"

"You have to eat, and I'm going out to get something either way. What do you say?" I glanced at my watch. It was barely past noon. "Are you home for the day, or only for lunch?"

"I'm in trial, and the court has recessed until tomorrow at nine. So it was try to study in the office, or do so in my quiet little apartment."

"Yeah, I love it here," I said, glancing around the property. "Nice and quiet."

"Nice and quiet," she agreed.

In the moment that passed, I decided to be more assertive. "Okay, so here's the deal. You come over at seven and I'll have dinner and a drink ready for you. You can even bring your files and study, if you'd like. Maybe I could help you, depending on what you're working on."

"You don't even know what I do."

"You're a cop," I said, confident in the information I had received.

She laughed. "Where did you get that?"

"I have my sources."

Emily shook her head, smiled, and said, "You need better sources, Detective."

"Oh Jesus, you're an attorney, aren't you?"

"Federal prosecutor."

I hadn't seen that coming, and it gave me considerable pause. My experiences with federal prosecutors hadn't been great. But, to be honest, I hadn't dealt with them often, only when they were going after cops on civil rights violations. They were, of course, part of the federal law enforcement system, and that system is one of which most "local" cops— meaning cops who work for county, city, and state governments—are not fond.

"Let me guess," she continued, "you hate the feds."

I chuckled. "It's not that I *hate* the feds, but . . ."

She turned and started toward our apartments again, the two entry doors side-by-side at the end of the building. I walked alongside her.

"It sounds like one of those topics that would be best avoided," she said.

"Or at least discussed over a drink," I said.

"Or not at all."

"Yeah, probably best. Though before I agree to father your children, I'll need to make sure you haven't sent any of my friends to prison."

I could see her green eyes pop wide open behind her glasses, shocked, but a smile crept onto her face and her eyes relaxed. "Definitely a discussion to be had over cocktails," she said.

"So it's a date?"

We had arrived at her door and stopped. Her keys were in her hand, as they had been since I first saw her walking from the parking area. I now noticed a Monadnock attached to the ring, a six-inch baton that, over the years, many women had begun carrying on their keychains. Some were trained to use them for self-defense. Many of the women who carried them were the wives, mothers, and daughters of cops. I checked her ring finger closely, not to see if she wore a wedding band, but to see how recently she had. It was difficult to tell because of her fair skin.

She keyed her door open and stood facing me in the threshold. With her free hand, she pushed her sunglasses up into her hair that appeared more auburn than red in the shade of the building. "I'll tell you what, Detective Jones, I'll agree to dinner and *one* drink. As neighbors, soon to be friends. I'm not looking to complicate my life."

I felt sweat dripping down my back and wondered if I emitted the odor of a men's locker room at the moment. She had caught me at my worst and agreed to dinner; it could only get better from here.

"Great," I said. "I'll pick you up on my way back to my apartment with the food. I'll even walk you home at the end of the evening."

"Sounds good, Detective. I'll see you then."

She closed the door behind her, and a smile bloomed across my face. I stepped over to my door just feet away and paused as I reached for the handle. It was open.

40

When I worked in South Los Angeles, I would often stay at the station bunkhouse. I worked nights and often had court during the day. When time permitted, I would workout in the station gym and jog in the same neighborhood I patrolled, packing a Smith & Wesson .38 Special concealed in a sock. You can pull the trigger and shoot through a sock without ever removing the gun from its hide, and most people had no idea what I was carrying as I jogged along Compton or Florence Avenues, or across Firestone Boulevard, or down Central Avenue, or through the gang-infested neighborhoods within those boundaries. The gangsters likely knew, but they also knew I was a cop, and would probably assume I'd be armed. No white boy other than a Firestone deputy would be jogging through those neighborhoods.

But this was Burbank and I didn't carry a gun when I jogged. It was so safe, in fact, that I didn't lock my apartment and burden myself with carrying my keys during a run. But I had closed the door behind me—of that I was certain—and now it stood ajar. I couldn't hear any movement inside, and it wasn't open enough for me to see. I pictured my gun and keys on the kitchen table next to my cell phone, and I thought about rushing in and going straight for the piece. But what if it was no longer there?

I took three steps back and lightly tapped on Emily's door. I could feel her open it and was aware of her presence, but my eyes were glued on my apartment door. She had started to speak but my hand stopped her. Without turning my head, I whispered. "Do you have a gun?"

"Yes," she whispered, urgently.

I didn't have to ask her for it. I saw in my peripheral vision that she had disappeared into her apartment. Moments later she touched my arm lightly and presented a pistol to me. It was a Glock Model 43, the frame a stylish Tiffany blue beneath a stainless-steel slide.

I took the gun and said, "Go back inside, lock your door, and lay on the ground until I come back."

I stepped forward quietly and heard her door click closed behind me. I waited and listened again for a long moment before slowly pushing my door open and scanning the interior over the barrel of the Tiffany blue Glock. A thought crossed my mind that I would be a legend in the department if I dumped a burglar with such a fashionable weapon, though I'd never live it down.

The living room was clear and appeared undisturbed. The kitchen and dining room were around a corner, beyond my view. I took and held a breath before proceeding. Tiffany led the way as I moved out into the living room, which allowed me see into first the kitchen and then to see the dining room, one slice of the pie at a time. There was no reason to stay close to a wall as you see in the movies; bullets easily tear through the false security of walls.

The kitchen and dining room were clear. Only the one bedroom and bathroom remained to be searched. Using the same approach, I cleared both. Nobody was there. I lowered the gun and walked back into the living room where I stood in silence for a long moment, studying the contents of my small apartment. Being a bit OCD, I know when things are out of place. When investigating crime scenes, I always imagined what might be missing. It was easy to see what was in front of your face, but recognizing that something was missing from a place you had never before visited could be a challenge, and the practice of it had expanded my mind, or at least my imagination.

As I looked around the room, I replayed my exit and knew for sure that I had closed the door tightly behind me. Someone had been in my apartment, but nothing was disturbed, and it didn't appear that anything was missing.

Emily Bruce appeared in the doorway. My first thought was to say that I had told her to stay in her apartment, but I refrained from doing so.

"What happened?"

There was no reason to alarm her. "My door was open. I must have not closed it tight. Nothing's disturbed."

I walked over and handed her the pistol. "Very pretty. Thank you for letting me use it."

She smiled. "Well, I'm glad you didn't actually have to. Anyway, it's cute, but it's also deadly."

"I'm sure," I said, thinking the statement could apply to both the Tiffany blue pistol and the redhead who owned it. "Okay, thanks again. I have to jump in the shower and get some things done. I'll see you at seven?"

"See you then, Richard."

I closed the door behind her, and my smile disappeared. As I looked around the room, my mind raced to make sense of an intruder who took nothing.

So if he took nothing, why was he here? Had he left something behind? That was the question. I thought about bugs and hidden cameras, and those thoughts naturally flowed to the FBI. And federal prosecutors.

I thought back to the timing of Emily's appearance. Not just today, but also the timing of her arriving at the apartment shortly after I moved in.

But why would the feds be interested in me? I had used deadly force in a couple of situations over the past several years, but each instance was fully justified. The latest case had involved a hitman—

The wheels stopped spinning at that thought. The last man I had shot and killed had been a hitman for the mafia. He had been contracted through the Mexican mafia to take me out as retaliation for a previous shooting where I had killed an associate of theirs.

Anything was possible, I guessed. But what would the mob be doing in my apartment? That part didn't make sense.

Feds. That's what made the most sense.

I thought about confronting Emily, but quickly talked myself out of it. If I was wrong, there would be no more neighborly chats, let alone dinner and drinks. Even if I was right, both would be out the window; there would be no socializing after that. No, I needed to play it smart. From this point forward, I would presume that all conversations in my apartment and on my cell phone were being monitored and recorded. And until I figured this out, I'd play it cool with Emily, my new, sexy Scottish neighbor, who happens to be a fed. Red the Fed. She'd probably kill me if I called her that to her face. But Floyd, he and I would no doubt call her that when we spoke of her privately.

I plopped onto my couch with my gun and cell phone. I put the gun on the arm while I checked my phone for messages. There were several, but none of any great importance. I visually examined the phone, but there was nothing notable about it. I knew that software could be quickly installed with no trace left behind. There was software that could track my every move, record all of my calls and texts, and record conversations in the room, even when the phone sat idly.

None of this made sense.

I grabbed a beer out of the fridge, locked the doors and windows, and went in for a shower.

4 1

The next morning I found Josie sitting up in her bed, picking at a tray of hospital food that had been called breakfast and resembled prison chow. I set a vase of wild flowers on the table near her bed and handed her a Danish I had picked up along the way.

She smiled and pushed a lock of hair behind her ear. "Thank you. That was very thoughtful."

"The flowers, or the Danish?"

"Yes."

I moved a newspaper from the chair next to her bed and sat down in it. "How are you feeling, partner?"

She dropped her fork onto the tray of food and rolled her eyes. "Like shit. And this morning the doctor came in and said they have to do another surgery, but they're going to send me to a specialist at USC. Hip replacement, I guess. Like an old lady."

I smiled. "Well, I told you this job would age you."

"You weren't kidding."

"I'm only thirty."

She rolled her eyes. "You wish."

After a moment, I said, "When do you go? And will you stay at USC?"

She shrugged, and then adjusted her gown at the shoulders and pulled the neckline higher. "They don't know. But I want out. Can you get me out?"

"I wish."

She picked up the Danish and began unwrapping it. "Not working today, I take it."

She must have guessed by my jeans and polo shirt wardrobe. I shook my head. "I'm off for a few days now. I think I might take a week off. You wore me out this week, kid."

"Yeah, well, it was like a vacation for me, partner. You know, all I did was lie around."

I waited a moment, contemplating whether or not I should ask again. I decided that I should, because it needed to be discussed. We were both seasoned cops who had seen the worst that mankind had to offer. There shouldn't be anything we couldn't talk about. Besides, she was now alert, and in relatively good spirits.

"Can we talk about that week, Josie?"

"Sure. What would you like to know? I didn't do much, didn't get out to see a lot."

Her candor surprised me, but her humor at a time like this did not. "All of it. Tell me everything."

She took a bite of her Danish and then set it on the table that had been wheeled over her bed. It was cluttered with the food tray, a collection of plastic cups, a box of tissues, and various packages of plastic silverware and napkins. She pushed the tray away and leaned back into a pile of pillows behind her.

"Where do I start? . . . I don't remember anything after the crash until the boy started visiting me. I just woke up in that shack, tied up on the floor. It was awful, Dickie."

She wiped at her eyes with the backs of her hands. I waited, silently.

"Tom—you know about Tom now, right?"

"Yes. I'm very sorry, Josie."

She nodded. "We went up there just so I could show him where our latest murder was. He's interested in all of that, and we didn't have anything else to do. It seemed like it would be a nice drive. We don't really go out much—neither of us likes crowds. *Liked*."

She paused again.

"We picked up some food to go, some beer, and drove up. For some reason—and I have no idea why—when we were coming back down the mountain, not far from the murder scene, a truck came out of nowhere and ran me off the road. That's it."

I watched her as she closed her eyes, and I waited to see if she had more to say. A moment later she opened them, and we stared at each other without blinking.

"What can you tell me about that week, after you were tied up in the shed? What did he do to you?"

"They didn't do anything to me, thank God. I kept waiting, and wondering, but I swear they never laid a hand on me. The kid was really nice to me, most of the time. He'd come by and feed me. I think he rode a motorcycle."

"You said 'they.' Was there someone other than the kid? And by kid, do you mean the one who was there that night, the one who was shot?"

She nodded. "I don't know why I said that. It was only him, the kid. I think."

"Could there ever have been anyone else?"

Her eyes drifted away from mine and seemed to fix on something distant, a place far away and a time in her past that she probably hoped to forget. When her gaze drifted back, her eyes were dark, uncertainty showing in her expression.

"I don't think so," she said slowly, her eyes still searching for recollection.

"You have no memory of how you got from the car to the shed?"

Again, she shook her head. "I crawled for a while, looking for him—Tom. But that's all I remember. I kept calling out to him, but there was nothing. No response."

"Could there have been two people?"

She shrugged. "Only the kid came to me."

I nodded but said nothing.

A moment later, she said, "Wait—"

"What?"

She had showed a glimmer of excitement, but it quickly went away, and her shoulders sagged in defeat.

"Never mind."

"What is it, Josie? Everything is important."

"It's just—there was this one time when a different motorcycle came. I assume it was a motorcycle, or a four-wheeler, or something. But it sounded different than the kid's bike. His sounded like one of those dirt bikes that make a high-pitched sound. This one was different. Mellow, like something you putted around on, not something you hauled ass with. Maybe it was a four-wheeler."

"Did someone visit you on that occasion?"

"No, that's what was weird. See, I assumed it was the kid—who else would it be? But now I just don't know. Why did he not come in? I remember waiting, and wondering about that after it went away. I could hear it leaving."

"What day was that? Do you remember?"

She chuckled. "Are you kidding me? I don't know what fucking month it is."

I nodded again. "Okay, what about the time of day? Early or later?"

"It was after dark. Shortly after the sun went down. Just like the night it all happened."

I thought about that for a moment. "When did the kid usually come?"

"Mostly in the daytime, I think. Yeah, daytime. He would untie my hands and—well, you don't want to hear all of this—but he'd give me a bucket and go outside, and I'd take care of stuff. But the last night—the night it ended—it was dark, and I told him he needed to stay and shine the light." She sat up and looked at me with a hard expression. "I was going to kill him and escape. I had a plan for that night, and then—"

I waited but she didn't finish. She collapsed back into her pillows and pulled the blankets up around her neck.

"Then what, Josie?"

She spoke at the ceiling above her. "Then, the game cop came."

I waited again, but soon I realized she wasn't going to go on without being prompted to do so. Maybe not even then. I gave her plenty of time before doing so.

"Had you ever seen him before?"

"The cop?"

I nodded.

She shook her head. "I don't think so." Josie then turned her head to face me, and she frowned. "Why did you ask me that?"

"It's nothing. Just—"

"Don't hold back on me, Richard."

"Look, there's just some things that need to be tied up. I won't hold anything back. I promise."

She squinted at me, and I wondered if it was because she didn't believe me, or if she was angry with me. Maybe both. She had never called me "Richard" before, not even when she first arrived at Homicide.

"Okay, last question, and I'll let you get some rest."

"You have a hot date or something? I mean, I've got nothing to do. Quite frankly, I'm bored to death. You don't have to leave."

"No, but when we finish this, I'll tell you about the hot date I had last night. That will give us plenty to talk about. Weird shit."

She smiled. "I literally cannot wait. Okay, shoot. Last question."

"Did you see the shooting? I mean, the moments leading up to it? Did you see what happened in there?"

"That's about three questions rolled into one. No, is the answer. The kid had untied my hands. The man appeared outside. There was a light, and the kid turned to face it. I had no idea who was out there, but I saw the moment as my one opportunity to get free. I had started untying the ropes around my ankles when I heard the cop say 'Freeze,' or something like that. 'Drop it.' Whatever. There was a gunshot, and it was over. The kid almost fell on top of me."

"Think it was clean?"

She frowned again. "I think he saved me from who knows what. Why would you ask that? He—the warden—told the kid to hold it, or something, and then he shot him. The kid had a knife in his hand."

"You saw it?"

"What, the knife?"

I nodded.

"He used it to cut my ropes, which is also interesting. It occurred to me later that he normally untied me, so I think he was planning to kill me that night. But yeah, he had the knife, the warden showed up, told him to drop it, and shot him. I saw the knife on the ground after."

"You think he was going to kill you? The kid."

"Why else would he cut the ropes? He said he was trying to help me, that he was going to get me out of there, but that was obviously a lie."

I nodded and looked away.

After a moment, Josie said, "Hey, partner, let's hear about this hot chick. Is she Latina at least? You know, nobody makes better wives and mothers than us Latinas, and I won't even torment you with what great lovers we are."

I smiled. "No, she's not Latina. It's all wrong, and now that I think about it, I probably ought to quit before someone gets hurt. She's a redhead. She's Scottish, and she's also a federal prosecutor."

"Damn, partner. What are you thinking?"

I shook my head. "Who knows. But you want to hear something crazy? Something way out there? I mean, you know me and my luck, not to mention my imagination."

"Shoot."

I told Josie about coming back from my run and finding my apartment door open, but how nothing had been taken. I told her my concerns about my phone being tampered with or my apartment being bugged. She asked why anyone would do such a thing and I shrugged and told her you never know with the feds.

"That's it, you think the feds are on to you? Wait, you think she's part of it, don't you?"

I shrugged again.

"Mother Mary and Joseph, Dickie, what is your problem? Have you thought that through? I mean, seriously, dude, that's just insanity. It was probably the wind, or you just screwed up and left it open. That, or like your other partner says, you're already trying to screw up another relation-ship. You need to see somebody about that."

"Like who, a shrink? I tried that once and it made everything worse."

Josie flipped her covers off, revealing her gown-covered glory, one leg wrapped and restrained from the ankle to the hip. "I'm dying in here."

"So you think I'm off on that deal, the fed connection?"

"Dickie, I think you're off your rocker. But I love you anyway. You better still be my partner when I come back. You think you've got trouble with women now, you just try to trade me off for a new partner."

"Okay, deal."

I stood up from my chair and paused at the side of her bed, gently massaging her arm. "I'll come back and see you tomorrow."

"You better check, make sure I'm still here."

"Will do," I said, and started for the door.

"And I want the details about you and the fed."

I stopped, looked back, and smiled. "Red the Fed."

Josie smiled.

I pulled the curtain across the door and headed for the exit.

J acob Spencer sat low in his pickup, his head barely higher than the driver's side window. He had chosen this spot behind a delivery van because it allowed him to keep an eye on the Crown Vic without being seen by its driver, who he was sure would turn out to be the homicide cop from the mountain. *Jones*, he thought, irritated. No doubt he was there at the hospital to see his partner. Spencer knew he couldn't afford to be seen by anyone, just in case this didn't go well. In the event she remembered that first night, specifically. He would know by how she received his visit, and then he would decide what to do with her.

Spencer reflected on the night it had happened. He had seen them at the murder scene and panicked, not knowing that the body of the poacher had already been found. Having *no* idea that the two in the car were cops. Jesus. Now he might have to finish this, which he found regrettable. Because it was one thing to kill a poacher, quite another to kill a woman cop.

He watched Dickie leave, but still waited thirty minutes before starting through the parking lot on foot. His head swiveled left and right as he walked toward the emergency room doors, checking the parking lot for any additional sheriff vehicles. He didn't see any. The glass doors slid open and Spencer walked through a room with plastic chairs and benches scattered about on a tile floor, about half of them occupied by sour-faced civilians who all seemed to be exasperated by the length of time they had been waiting. Spencer nodded and gave a half wave to the lady behind the desk, strutting past her with confidence and purpose. Attitude and a uniform opened doors for you.

The watch deputy at Santa Clarita Sheriff's Station had told him over the phone that Josie was in 314, so he went directly to the elevator and pushed the three with his knuckle, careful not to leave a print. He didn't know how this might end.

He had thanked the watch deputy after obtaining the room number, and told him he planned to visit tomorrow, covering his bases on the recorded line. He even thought to mention that today, he was headed back up to the mountain, and would be out of range. He then turned his cell phone off before driving into town.

When Spencer walked into the private room, he found Josie sleeping peacefully. He closed the door behind him, glanced through its window, and saw that the nurses' station buzzed with activity. He walked to the foot of the bed and looked at the pillows stacked around her body, and then looked at the monitor over her shoulder, wondering if there was an alarm on it. He couldn't tell from where he stood, so he slipped down the side of the bed and moved the monitor slightly to check the back and sides.

"Hey there."

Startled, he stepped back from the mobile rack of machines, medicine bags, and monitors, and stuffed his hands into his front pockets. He smiled widely. "Hi there. How are you feeling?"

Her smile was strained, and he wondered how much pain she might be in. But he found her demeanor encouraging, thus far.

"I'm sore, but I'm grateful to be here, and to be alive. Thank you for what you did."

He looked down at the floor. *The bashful boy. Coy.* Playing it up, he gently swiped at the tile floor with the toe of one boot. When he looked up, he gave her his best puppy dog eyes and held her gaze for a moment before speaking. "I'm sorry it had to happen. To you, to him, to me. I'm conflicted over the whole thing. It all feels very surreal."

JOSIE LOOKED AROUND THE ROOM, WISHING DICKIE WAS STILL THERE. SHE hoped he would come back for some reason, maybe to ask a question, or to tell her something he had forgotten to mention. Anything. When she looked back at Spencer, his eyes appeared intent, thoughtful. They softened quickly, and she wondered if this guy was a good actor. She would see. From what Dickie had told her about Farris's concerns with the game warden, and by the questions Dickie asked her, Josie realized that there might have been more to his sudden appearance at the shed when he killed the boy. Was he a hero? Or was he part of all of it? How might it have played out had her partner not shown up at that exact moment?

Why was he here to visit her? Just for conversation, or was it something else? His gaze now seemed predatory as he stood next to her bed, revealing his smile for the disguise that it was.

Josie was in pain, uncomfortable, and embarrassed about the ordeal she had been through. She was ashamed to think of herself as a victim, a pitiful woman who had been held against her will in the woods. She decided now was the time to find her strength, to turn the tables on this man. Put him in the hot seat as if they were in an interrogation room and she was the one in charge. She needed to see his responses to a few tough questions so she could know if there was more to this warden who had been credited with saving her.

"So, was that your first?"

The corners of his mouth turned down as he tipped his head to the side, considering his answer perhaps. She had asked many cops that question before, and on two occasions, detectives had asked it of her. It was a common question in the course of officer-involved shooting interviews, and one that required no thought before answering.

She studied him, carefully analyzing his physiological reactions. She would weigh them against whatever answer was to come. "Officer Spencer, was that the first time you killed a man?"

Spencer's gaze darted away, his eyes losing their softness for the moment. Then his mouth turned up into a smile—a creepy one that reminded Josie of a movie that had frightened her as a child, one where an otherwise expressionless chauffeur smiled wickedly while the son of dead parents was ushered into the back seat of a black car. The smile faded on Spencer's face and his eyes became soft again.

"Yes, it was," he said, his head nodding almost imperceptibly. "I hope it was the last."

She saw his Adam's apple, pronounced against his thin neck, fluctuating rapidly beneath the tight skin of his throat as if a golf ball were trapped in his esophagus, blocking his windpipe. His mouth seemed dry and his skin suddenly pale. He fidgeted, rocking slightly on his heels.

Josie took his hand, and it seemed to unnerve him. "It never gets easier," she said, softly.

He slowly withdrew his hand and stepped back, putting distance between them. "Listen, I should go."

Josie nodded, and continued watching.

"I've got to get back up to the mountain."

"I appreciate you visiting."

He paused, then turned to look back at her. "Feel better. I'm really glad everything turned out okay."

Josie nodded, and he was gone. She grimaced as she wiped his sweat from the palm of her hand. It had been exactly what she expected to find when she placed her hand in his. She had seen the signs of deceit: the dry mouth, a rapid heartbeat pulsating through the veins in his neck, his attempt to wipe the sticky perspiration against his pants legs while he stammered and stumbled with his answer—the assertion that the Watkins boy had been the first.

She opened the drawer next to her, pulled out her new county cell phone that Lopes had brought her earlier that day, and she sent a text to Dickie:

You and Farris might be onto something. He came to visit, and he's creepy. Plus, he's a liar. That kid isn't the first person he killed. I'm certain of it now.

She hit send and put her phone away. Dickie wouldn't read her message until he was home, and he might not see it until tomorrow if his hot redhead was there when he arrived. Josie settled back against her pillows and closed her eyes.

As she drifted into a slumber, she saw Spencer's face as it had been today in her room, the deceitful smile of a chauffeur, a man with dark secrets behind steely eyes. And in her dream, the image of the warden's face dissolved and was replaced by that of the looming mountain, ominous in the darkness. Josie's eyes popped open. The night she was dragged to the shed . . . could it have been?

Her heart raced and her temperature rose, and she felt moisture gathering on her forehead and beading across her cheeks and nose. She threw her blankets off to cool herself, and retrieved her phone. Dickie hadn't replied to her earlier message. She began frantically typing with two thumbs:

Don't close the William Brown case. He did it. I'm convinced. I think he took me to the shed. When I return, we're going after him. You and I, partner, we're going to get him. Love, Josie

She started to put it away but decided to add one more line.

And Jones, bring me another Danish tomorrow.

I love staying connected with my readers through social media and email. If you would like to connect, find me on BookBub, Amazon, Goodreads, Facebook, Instagram, and Twitter. You can also sign up for my newsletter and receive bonus material, such as the action-packed short story, Harder Times.

As a newsletter subscriber, you will receive special offers, updates, book releases, and blog posts. I promise to never sell or spam your email.

Danny R. Smith

Dickie Floyd Novels

Independent authors count on word-of-mouth and paid advertising to find new readers and sell more books. Reviews can help shoppers decide about taking a chance on authors who are new to them.

I would be grateful if you took a moment to write a review on Amazon.

Thank you!

Danny R. Smith

The Following is a preview of Book 5 in the Dickie Floyd Detective series.

AVENGED

(A Working Title)

It was our turn in the barrel.

The lights were dimmed now that the phones had stopped ringing, and the vast office—home to eighty-some homicide detectives—had emptied of its few final night owls. Josie and I, however, were there manning the phones on the graveyard shift.

I had just finished updating the on-call schedule on the grease board that hung on the wall above my head. I sat reclined as much as I could be in an office chair, my feet propped on the desk. Josie's heels clicked across the tile floor. I looked up to meet her gaze as she stopped at the counter between us, a cup of coffee in her hand.

"How is it we get early mornings in the barrel *and* we're first up for murders at six?"

She was looking past me toward the board where I had just changed Josie's and my position in the rotation for murders.

"Apparently Martinez and Castro have a meeting with the sheriff at nine, so your lieutenant said to pull them out of the rotation until it's finished. He doesn't want them getting hung up on anything and not making it downtown."

"A meeting with the sheriff?"

I nodded. "And his entourage. They should be done by noon and we'll be back to sitting third in the rotation."

"If we haven't caught," she said, offering a slight smile to let me know she wasn't complaining.

"We'll be good."

She pushed a lock of hair behind her ear and lightly blew on her steaming coffee.

"I look forward to a new case," she said, "but I hope we can get a few hours of sleep before it comes in. I'm ready to get back into the swing of things around here. You know?"

Detective Josefina Sanchez had been off for six months recovering from a broken leg and fractured hip, and dealing with some psychological issues that remained after being held captive for nearly a week. Cops were the world's worst victims of violent crime; we were wired to overcome and conquer. When that didn't happen, the scars ran deep. I knew.

"I'm glad you're back, Josie. It's been a long six months running solo around here, getting paired with different partners every rotation."

"Anything good?" she asked.

I watched her sip her coffee as I told her about a case Rich Farris and I had picked up together in her absence.

The victim, Jackie Melvin Lowe, was a Blood gang member and up-and-coming rapper. In the neighborhood he was known as "J-Lowe." When he first broke into the music industry, he had taken the name "D.J. Low Boy." He didn't want to use "J-Lowe" and be compared to Jennifer Lopez. But "D.J." sounded like the titles of *players* and *hustlers*, not gangsters whose lyrics were harsh and dark and told the stories of life in the ghettos and prisons of the white man's America. So when he cut his first album—*Riding Low with Killer B's*—he dropped the "D.J." and had quickly gained fame as "Low Boy," a hardcore gangster rap artist.

But fame had its drawbacks. When *the hood* was the most important part of one's life—which was the case with hardcore gangsters—homies came first, family second, and "bitches" were way down the list. The homeboys demanded that it remain so, that they rode together no matter where "the car" went: music videos, award ceremonies, road trips to Vegas and New York. They expected to be rolling together, high and hard, each getting a piece of the action. And Low Boy and his entourage did roll hard, but only for a year.

The night Low Boy was killed, the entourage was curiously nowhere to be found, and he didn't die in the glow of his name in lights. No, Low Boy had been gunned down in the darkness of a perilous street in the city of Compton, in his own neighborhood, unceremoniously.

The murder had originally appeared to be a random gang killing—something that is all too common on the streets of Compton and South Los Angeles—but the victim's status had given me and Rich Farris pause. We had wondered if the murder was an "in-house" hit, a case of his being killed by fellow gang members. If not that, maybe it was related to the rap industry, of which the dynamics were similar to traditional organized crime syndicates; players were being whacked by people they had known their whole lives and with whom they may have just shared a meal or a drink. But in the rap industry, there were no warehouses or garages where the dead would fall neatly onto plastic and be disposed of in the harbor or woods. Rappers were gangsters, and when they killed, they killed gangster style. Our victim had been sitting in a Cadillac in front of his homeboy's house, smoking a blunt, when someone had walked up and filled his red-clad, gold-laden, obese body full of lead.

I finished telling Josie about the gangster rap case as she drained the remainder of her coffee and then stared at the cup as if contemplating a refill.

It was almost three now and we were both tired, having come in for barrel duty on the early morning shift after being in court all day yesterday. Neither of us had been able to get more than a short nap before relieving the PM desk crew. Now we only had a couple of hours left until we'd both be able to go to our homes and get some much-needed sleep—unless and until we got called out.

"You can relax," I assured her. "It's a cold and rainy Wednesday morning. Nobody's going to die before noon."

She regarded the board once more and then looked over her shoulder at the muted TV that hung on the wall and showed a local news station covering the weather. Her soft, brown eyes came back to me.

"What's the meeting about?"

"Martinez and Castro?"

She nodded.

"One of those dog and pony shows for the executives, briefing them on their case and answering their stupid questions."

"What'd they have that's got the old man interested?"

By "old man" I knew she meant Sheriff Rolando Guzman, though he was far from being a senior citizen. In fact, I had more time on the job than he had and was probably older too. But he had been elected sheriff of Los Angeles County and now sat behind a big desk with fancy furnishings and a view of the city that I still tromped through night and day with scuffed wingtips and worn-out fedoras.

"The woman that went off the balcony in West Hollywood," I said.

"That wasn't a suicide? I saw it on the news. A couple weeks ago, right?"

"Just before you came back," I said. "And whether or not it was a suicide remains to be seen. Martinez and Castro don't think so, and neither does the family, apparently. But the reason the sheriff has his eye on this one is there are political overtones. Apparently, the victim had attended a conference and was seen with a city councilman in the hotel bar afterward."

Josie shook her head and rolled her eyes, showing her disgust. I wondered if it was directed toward the councilman or the dead woman who had apparently entered the danger zone with a married councilman, even if unwittingly. Josie picked up her mug and turned back toward the kitchen. "Want a cup?"

"Not for me, partner. I'm going to try to get some sleep while it's quiet. No reason not to; you never know when the big one will come in and we'll be back to running full speed ahead."

"It's Wednesday; remember?"

I smiled. "Touché."

"I'll be at my desk if you need anything," Josie said, turning from the front counter. "I can work on some old cases while the phones are quiet."

What she would actually be doing was stalking a game warden named Jacob Spencer. He was the man who had been credited with saving her when she had been taken, but a shroud of doubt hung over the case. Josie and I—particularly—were skeptical about what had really happened on the mountain, and we were determined to discover the truth. Josie had somehow—*magically*—managed to procure background investigation reports from several law enforcement agencies to which Spencer had applied. She had obtained personnel records from his current employer, the Department of Fish and Wildlife, and reports from every arrest he had ever made and every citation he had ever written. How she had gotten it all, I had no idea. Whenever she had time, she sifted through these files, and she scoured social media where Spencer had established a presence but not much more. Josefina Sanchez was on the bite.

"Suit yourself," I said.

I picked my fedora up off of my lap and covered my face. In my mind I could match her gait with the clicking of her heels, seeing the slight limp she had been left with from her ordeal. The footfalls faded and I knew she had entered the carpeted squad room. I pictured her approaching her desk in her gray and white checked slacks, her shapely, athletic figure something that couldn't be ignored in a testosterone-driven environment like law enforcement—limp or no limp. Though much had changed over the decades and generations, there were no policies ever written that could change what a man naturally saw and thought about. Most of us had learned to keep our mouths shut and our flies zipped to avoid being caught up in the workplace harassment drama, but that didn't mean that nature had somehow been neutralized in the office.

The desk line rang for the first time in hours and it jolted me upright in my chair. I punched the blinking light and glanced at the clock on the wall. It was almost five in the morning, nearly time for our relief to arrive and about time for Josie and me to be up in the rotation for murders. I lifted the phone to my ear and tried to sound as if I hadn't been sleeping.

"Sheriff's Homicide, Jones."

Josie rounded the corner and our eyes met while a female on the phone began telling me she was a deputy sheriff and they had a death to report in Palos Verdes. I frowned at the phone. I frowned at Josie. I frowned at the muted TV that now showed an infomercial about some type of diet or nutrition scam.

Palos Verdes was within the Lomita sheriff's station jurisdiction, and it was not the type of place we often went to investigate murder cases. There were accidental deaths, recreational deaths—boating or diving accidents— and the occasional suicide, someone jumping from one of the high cliffs into the Pacific Ocean. But seldom a murder. Nonetheless, it was more than likely that one of us—me or Josie—was going to have to drive from Monterey Park to Palos Verdes to have a look.

"I'm sorry," I said, now fully awake, "I missed your name."

"Jessica Lambert, Lomita Station."

"Okay, Jessica, what do you have?"

Josie passed behind me and sat down in the adjacent chair, pulling a Dead Sheet from the file tray. One would be required no matter the type of death being reported. She readied a pencil over the sheet and watched me, waiting. Probably, like me, hoping it would be a natural death and that the deputy had already located a treating physician who would agree to sign the death certificate. That would allow Josie and me to drive to our homes and crawl into our beds rather than fight traffic to the coast.

Deputy Jessica Lambert said, "We have a murder to report, sir."

I cupped one hand over the mouthpiece and reached toward Josie with the other, indicating the Dead Sheet. "She's calling in a murder."

Josie handed it to me and glanced at the grease board, then checked her watch. As my eyes moved to the paperwork before me, I was left with the image of Josie smiling widely as she settled back into her seat.

The Dead Sheet is a living document that would be updated periodically throughout the beginning stages of the investigation as facts and details developed. For now, I wrote down the date, the time of notification, the person making the notification, her employee number and assignment, and then I hovered my pencil over the empty line where the victim's name would be memorialized once it was known for certain. Sometimes that day never came, and John or Jane Doe would be assigned a file number along with a coroner's case number. Other times, the person is known, but maybe not yet positively identified; there was a reason these forms were completed in pencil and not pen.

"Do we have a name yet, Jessica?"

"Yes sir. Edward Robert Benton, Junior."

"Jesus Christ, not—"

"Yes," Deputy Lambert interrupted, "it's the mayor's kid."

Dickie Floyd Detective Novels

- A Good Bunch of Men
- Door to a Dark Room
- Echo Killers
- The Color Dead

SHORT STORIES

- In the City of Crosses - A Dickie Floyd Detective Short Story
- Exhuming Her Honor - A Dickie Floyd Detective Short Story
- Harder Times: A Cop Goes to Prison - Not a Dickie Floyd Story - Free to Newsletter Subscribers, visit dickiefloydnovels.com

ABOUT THE AUTHOR

Danny R. Smith spent 21 years with the Los Angeles County Sheriff's Department, the last seven as a homicide detective. He now lives in Idaho where he works as a private investigator and consultant. He is blessed with a beautiful wife and two wonderful daughters. He is passionate about his dogs and horses, whom he counts among his friends.

Danny is the author of the *Dickie Floyd Detective Novel* series, and he has written articles for various trade publications. He publishes a weekly blog called The Murder Memo, which can be found at dickiefloydnovels.com.

He is a member of the Idaho Writers Guild and the Public Safety Writers Association.

Made in the USA
Columbia, SC
27 April 2019